POINT DECEPTION

SHARON McCONE MYSTERIES BY MARCIA MULLER

POINT DECEPTION

MARCIA MULLER

WARNER BOOKS

An AOL Time Warner Company

WARNER BOOKS EDITION

Cover design and art by Jerry Pfiefer

Warner Books, Inc.
1271 Avenue of the Americas
New York, NY 10020

Visit our Web site at
www.twbookmark.com

An AOL Time Warner Company

Printed in the United States of America

Originally published in hardcover by The Mysterious Press
First Paperback Printing: May 2002

10 9 8 7 6 5 4 3 2 1

For Bill Pronzini,
who aids and abets me every page of the way.

A number of persons, knowingly or otherwise, have provided inspiration for or assistance with this novel. I'd like to thank:

Sharon DeLano, for not allowing my imagination get the best of me while we were stranded by the side of California Highway 1.

Bette and Jim Lamb and Peggy and Charlie Lucke, for setting the scary ideas to brewing on our first trip to "Cascada Canyon."

Robin Reese, for Chrystal.

Detective Lieutenant Bruce Rochester of the Sonoma County, California, Sheriff's Department, for technical assistance.

Melissa Ward, again, for her research talents.

Soledad County, California, is a fictional creation, sandwiched between Mendocino and Humboldt Counties. I apologize to my neighbors on the coast for so drastically altering its configuration. Sometimes we writers can't resist playing God.

POINT DECEPTION

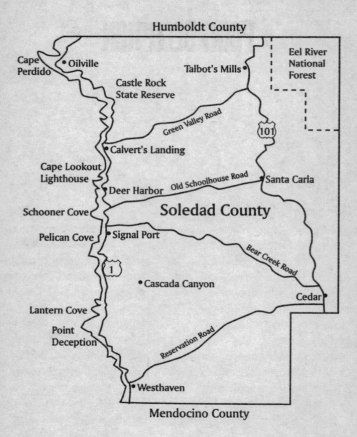

Chrystal

Friday, October 6
4:00 P.M.

T hings look different when you're scared. And I'm scared now. Little Chryssie's scareder than she's been her whole life. Jude told me I'd never get away with it, but I thought I had, and then somebody saw me up there in all those trees, and now this damn Mercedes is dead on the coast highway where my cell phone won't work. God, I'm in trouble. Making Jude right. Again. Always.

Yeah, things look different. On the drive up from where I stayed outside San Francisco last night—not a lot of miles, but over four hours on these twisty roads—the sea was pretty, sparkly, deep blue. Made me feel good. Still is pretty, but now I don't want to look at it. All I can think is that people drown in there. And the pines in the canyon—walking through them, I felt like a little girl in church. Then the memories came back, and I felt like a little girl, all right. But not in church. No way.

Jesus, this is an awful place to break down. Turnout, but it's on a blind curve, and I could just barely get the car off the road before it conked out for good. Middle of nowhere, nothing on the bluff but pampas grass and burned trees from when they must've had a forest fire. Nothing but more trees on the other side of the highway. Dead-looking truck over by the fence.

Lots of traffic, but nobody'll stop to help me. Hood's up, they can see I'm broke down, but does anybody give a shit? No. They just keep zooming by in their sports cars and campers and SUVs, having a good time. Acting like I don't exist.

4:35 P.M.

Sheriff's car. Woman driving. For sure she'll stop.

Nope. She's around the curve already. Gone. Our tax dollars at work, like Leo used to say. Well, not *my* tax bucks. Little Chryssie don't pay no taxes in California.

So what do I do now? I'm a great big target sitting here by the highway. Whoever saw me in the canyon knows what I look like, maybe what the car looks like, but I didn't see them. They could drive right up and I wouldn't know who they were or what hit me. I could be dead before—

Damn this car! Damn it!

Okay, come on, calm down, think now. You're not playing this smart.

Maybe they didn't see me clear up there. Or see what I was doing. And even if they did, it might not've meant anything to them. Just because somebody hollers at you . . .

Two choices. Stay by the car and take my chances. Walk away and maybe take a bigger chance. Two choices, but either way the first thing to do is lose the evidence. Lose it *good* like it was before.

4:49 P.M.

So what've we got here? Pampas grass, big clump of it. Stuff just takes over, specially along this part of the coast. What did Jude always say about that? Something to do with the plants being scouts for an alien life-form, staking out the edge of the continent for the arrival of the mother ship. God, she could be weird sometimes! She said she did it on purpose to drive us crazy, but I think it might've been the dope talking.

Well, aliens got no use for what I'm gonna hide here. This pampas grass is fine for what I got in mind.

4:55 P.M.

Somebody coming! Cover it fast. There, that's good, real good.

Where the hell are they? Oh, over there by the cliff. Oriental guy and a white girl, climbing up the slope with a big cooler between them. They're fighting. Wind's blowing this way, I can hear every word. She says he's paranoid about Fish and Game. He tells her to shut up. She says she used to think things weren't working out between them because of their cultural differences, but now she knows it's because he's an asshole. Jesus, they sound like Jude and Leo.

I could hide here till they're gone, but maybe they'll call a tow truck for me. Leave a message for Jude that I got in and out okay, too. That way I wouldn't have to take my chances hitching on the highway.

If they ask, I'll tell them I came down here to take a pee.

5:43 P.M.

It's getting cold, even inside the car with the windows rolled up. Better dig that sweater outta the trunk. Jesus, I wish the tow truck would come.

Keep on wishin'. Pretty woman with the weird Oriental guy said it might take two hours. Don't they have Triple A garages up here in the boonies? Don't their cars ever break down? That old pickup of theirs looked like it was ready to.

Oriental guy sure acted spooky. Wonder if he saw what I was *really* doing in that clump of pampas grass. Nah, they were too far away, dragging that big cooler. Bet they had something illegal in there. Drugs off some boat outta Mexico? Nah, nobody'd make a drop while it's still light. Didn't the girl say something about Fish and Game? I read someplace there's a lot of abalone poaching going on up here. Bet that's what they were doing. Take more than the limit, sell it to some restaurant, make big bucks.

That's okay, though. None of my business. What matters is they said they'd make my calls. Meantime the evidence is gone till I can come back for it. And little Chryssie's just a dumb tourist with car trouble.

Dumb, anyway. *Real* dumb.

5:47 P.M.

A pickup, and it's slowing down. Old man driving. Slowing down some more . . . yeah, to stare at my ass while I'm leaning into the trunk. I don't believe it! See anything you like, buddy? Now he's speeding up. Old fool doesn't know I'd be happy to give him a piece if he'd help me.

Wish I'd packed warmer clothes, but how could I know it'd be so fuckin' cold on the coast? Was even warm in San Francisco. Lucky I dragged this old sweater of Leo's along.

There, that's better. I love this sweater. Hangs all the way down to my knees. I'll crawl in the car, lock the door, wait.

6:29 P.M.

Weird how the fog blows south, curls around the point, heads back north at me. Ugly, dirty-looking stuff. Makes me feel lonesome.

Well, what's new about that, Chryssie? When *haven't* you felt lonesome?

At least I'm warm now, even though I'm scareder than ever. It's the dark coming on that's spooking me. The dark and the fog and every set of headlights that flashes round the bend. There's no radio reception and I forgot to bring any tapes along and I sure as hell don't want to think about the stuff I remembered in the canyon.

An unexamined life is not worth living, Chrystal.

Jude's voice. It's like she came along inside my head. She was always nagging at me with lines like that, but I never noticed her doing any deep thinking of her own. And besides the canyon, what *is* there to think about? Leo, long dead and all

I've got of him is this ratty sweater? Jude, sick and needing me like I never needed her? Dave, who's into bondage, or John, who talks about killing his parents, or Timothy, who always cries? Sean, who seriously likes to hurt women? The other pathetic middle-of-the-night voices?

No, thanks. I'd rather count cars on the highway.

Camper, going north. SUV tailgating it. Sports car hugging the southbound curve and disappearing in the fog. Big white pickup, jacked up on oversized tires, a bar of lights on top of the cab. Got a lotta those here in redneck country. I've seen at least ten just like it. Another camper. Another. Got a lotta them too. . . .

6:59 P.M.

Fifty cars later, and I can't keep from thinking. About that last night in the canyon. About Jude and Leo, too. Him I miss in a weird way, but her—God, she's been a pain in the ass. Some people die graceful, but not Jude, oh no. Bitch, whine, erase the few good memories I had of her.

And that canyon . . . What was it Jude said? Oh yeah: "We all have a place that our minds return to long after it's been altered by time and its inhabitants are gone. The canyon is mine."

I oughta remember, she said it three times Saturday night. Real proud of herself for thinking of it, even if she was in a bad way. Still claims she's a poet. Poet, my ass!

It's been almost two hours now, and no tow truck. He's gotta be coming soon. I can't stay in the car much longer. I'm so scared my skin feels tight, and it's hard to breathe. I'll stand outside for a while, duck down if anybody but the tow truck stops.

Funny, now I'm more scared of what's *inside* of me than what might be outside in the dark.

7:10 P.M.

Pickup, turn signal on, slowing down. Help, or—?

No help. No nothing. It's speeding up and the signal's off. Man and a woman inside, heading south. They saw me, I didn't duck in time.

Jesus, do I look that scary? I mean, I'd never pass for no Girl Scout, but I don't look like an escaped con either. And this Mercedes sports car is about as respectable as cars get.

I'm starting to hate this place. Really hate it. What's *wrong* with the people here?

7:45 P.M.

God, it's dark, except when a car comes along. I hate the dark, always sleep with a light on—

Something coming. Get ready to duck. But wait a minute—

It's the tow truck! About time, dammit.

Lights shining in my eyes. Come to Chryssie. And don't make no excuses about how long it took. Just get me outta this miserable hole.

He's climbing down, walking over here. Big and slow and probably stupid. He's not saying anything and he's not looking under the hood. He's—

Oh no! *No!*

Oh my God not *this*!

SOLEDAD COUNTY SHERIFF'S DEPARTMENT
CENTRAL DISPATCH

Date: October 6, 2000   Shift: 3   Beat: 2
Deputy: Swift, R.A.
Car: 450
Time out: 16:00   Time in: 24:17
Mi out: 54,021   Mi in: 54,179
Condition out: good   Condition in: slow leak, right front tire
Shotgun out: 4 rounds   Shotgun in: 4 rounds

Time	Description/ Location of Observation/Dispatch	Activity
16:03	Disp: 911 disconnect, 1371 Ridge Rd., County	Misdial
16:36	Disp: shots fired, vicinity Mar Vista & Sheep Ranch Rd., County	Adolescents, transferred to parents' custody
17:55	Obs: traffic accident, Hwy 1, SP	Transferred to CHP
18:22	Disp: trespassing, 4221 Hwy 1, DH	Subject had left the area
19:49	Disp: unwanted individual, CL Pier	Subject believed he was Jesus. Transferred by ambulance to County Hospital.
20:59	Disp: disturbing the peace, 120 Lafferty Rd., DH	Partygoers warned

23:17	Disp: citizen report of DUI, Hwy 1, DH	BOLO issued
23:28	Obs: disturbing the peace, SP Hotel parking lot	Subjects warned to disperse
23:47	Obs: abandoned vehicle, Point Deception Turnout	Tagged

Saturday, October 7

Well, aren't you a lovely sight."

Sheriff's Deputy Rhoda Swift leaned closer to her bathroom mirror, not liking what she saw. Puffy skin, reddened eyes, dark circles—the evidence was all there.

"Tied one on, didn't you, lady?"

Seven years ago after Zach finally moved out, she'd been shocked when she realized she'd started talking to herself. Now she accepted these conversations as routine, even enjoyed them. But not on mornings like this.

Granted, her bad mornings were seldom due to excessive drinking. Zach's leaving had forced her to take a good hard look at her use of both booze and pills, and for two years after that she'd touched neither. She still shunned the pills, and her alcohol intake was normally limited to the occasional glass of beer or wine, but certain events on last night's patrol had tipped her carefully balanced scales, and this morning she'd have to confront an empty bottle beside the kitchen sink.

Worse than the evidence of her self-indulgent behavior was the image that had filled her dreams: that of a slender young woman in cutoff jeans and a blue tube top standing beside a disabled sports car, her long blonde hair blowing in the breeze.

Rho had spotted the car at the Point Deception turnout at 4:35 P.M. yesterday while returning north along Highway 1 from a routine call. Old black Mercedes, two-seater, vintage early eighties, body in good condition, but problems under the raised hood. Driver, she thought, must be off getting a tow truck. She'd note it in her log so the morning shift officer would know to tag it if it hadn't been removed by then.

She'd driven past, looking for the mileage marker, when she saw the woman leaning against the Mercedes' rear bumper, arms folded against the chill on the air, dressed all wrong for this changeable climate. Probably had more money than good sense. Bought a nice classic car, then didn't maintain it. Even if she had a cell phone, it wouldn't work on this remote stretch, so now she was stranded, undoubtedly without food or water, and too lazy to hike to one of the houses scattered over this sparsely populated area. Rich people!

Rho noted the marker's number and pulled over on the shoulder to let a logging truck pass before making a U-turn toward the disabled vehicle, but the radio interrupted her.

"Unit four-five-zero."

She keyed the mike. "Four-five-zero."

"What's your location?"

"One-half mile north of Point Deception turnout."

"Proceed to intersection of Mar Vista and Sheep Ranch Road. Ten-five-seven, Code Two."

Ten-five-seven: firearms discharged. Code Two: urgent.

The twisting in her stomach was no longer knife sharp, as it had been for years after she responded to her first call of that type. But the tingle in her throat and quick choking sensation—she shouldn't have that reaction.

After all, a tragedy like that couldn't happen again.

And of course it couldn't, she thought now in morning's sensible light. Last night's 10-57 had borne no resemblance to the one which triggered the six-year binge of drinking and pill taking that culminated in her losing her husband. Just a couple of teenagers taking out mailboxes with their father's Model 12. She'd lectured them and hauled them home for another lecture that began before she was out the door. Still, she'd allowed her preoccupation with that call and the others that followed to prevent her from checking on the woman at Point Deception until her shift was nearly over, and when she'd arrived there the Mercedes was still in the turnout, its hood raised, but its driver was gone.

A routine stop, nothing irregular about the situation, so why had she yielded to the compulsion to drink when she got home? And why had the woman's image been superimposed upon the landscape of her already troubled dreams?

Of course Rho knew the answer: It was the time of year when, for her, everything took on a disturbing and distorted shape. Five days from now—October 12—marked the thirteenth anniversary of that first 10-57, and the mass murder in Cascada Canyon.

* * *

Guy Newberry leaned toward the motel room mirror to inspect the nick he'd just made on his chin and realized his hands were shaking. He hadn't slept well the night before, owing to the strange bed, the unaccustomed sound of the sea, and too much fried food and beer for dinner. And each time he'd awakened, it was with the nagging sense of something left undone, with potential serious consequences.

He gave up on a smooth shave, pressed a wad of toilet paper to his chin, and went to stand on the room's small balcony. Nine thirty in the morning, and the fog was lifting. It looked as though it would be another beautiful day. So why the unsettled feeling—?

That was it: the girl with the broken-down car he'd spotted by the roadside some fifteen miles south of town.

It had been around four forty-five when he saw her leaning against her black Mercedes. He eased up on the accelerator of his rental car and assessed the situation as he cruised past—a game he had often played on long driving trips, and one that kept his journalistic skills honed to their customary fine edge.

The subject: Young, probably in her early twenties; pretty in a hard, streetwise way. Argumentative set of jaw, defiant tilt of head, posture sullen yet potentially seductive. In short, trouble.

The setting: A turnout on the ocean side of the highway; asphalt pitted and broken, littered with cans, bottles, and other debris. Tumbledown split-rail fence barely blocking access to a long sloping plain dotted with burned-out trees and strange plants whose fluffy beige fronds swayed in the offshore wind. Sunbrowned grass crisscrossed by deer tracks and footpaths. Old Chevy truck with a salt-caked windshield and pitted paint pulled close to the fence.

The problem: The Mercedes had broken down suddenly, so the girl barely had time to nurse it beyond the stripe dividing the turnout from the highway. She'd probably been there a while, and nobody'd stopped to help her. Nobody *would* stop, given her appearance, and certainly not Guy Newberry. He didn't need that kind of trouble. Besides, he had a reservation at the Sea Stacks Motel in Signal Port and was anxious to get registered, settled, and explore this new and potentially fertile territory.

As his view of the girl disappeared from the car's mirror Guy congratulated himself on his still-keen powers of observation. Even a three-year hiatus from the writing business hadn't appreciably impaired them. Perhaps the scene he'd just witnessed would play a small part in his upcoming saga of a town in trouble. A metaphor for—

You know, Guy, you really can be an asshole.

Diana's voice, spoken with humor. Her gentle reminder that he was about to fall victim to his own high opinion of himself.

"Okay," he said, "I'm an asshole. I suppose I should've stopped to help that girl, but she looks like she's got a major attitude problem."

And a major car *problem.*

"Stop nagging me. It's a sign of poor mental health for a man to drive along the highway holding a defensive conversation with a dead woman."

Well, what about that live *woman back there?*

He sighed, pulled onto the shoulder, and made a

U-turn. It was hell, he thought, when the most lasting thing a man's wife had bequeathed him was a conscience.

Now, as the morning sun began to dapple the sea, Diana's voice nudged him again.

Apparently not that much of a conscience.

"I went back, didn't I? Wasn't my fault she was nowhere near the car."

You could've called out, looked for her.

"I could've, but I didn't. Good Samaritanism only goes so far."

Yes, you can be an asshole.

Rhoda Swift put on a pair of sweats, went out on the porch, and whistled for Cody. In good weather she made it a point to walk her property on the ridge above Signal Port—for exercise, but also to bask in the pride of ownership. She'd lived in the brown-shingled cottage on ten acres for two years and still couldn't believe it was hers. The house needed a new roof and cosmetic work, and the cost of a replacement septic tank loomed large in the near future, but there was a big chinaberry tree in the front yard, an apple orchard, woods, a stream, and what local real estate people—laughably, to Rho's way of thinking—called a filtered ocean view. On a clear day like this one, she could probably see the Pacific if she stood on tiptoe on the porch railing.

Cody came loping from a stand of pyracantha bushes, twigs caught in his ears, and fell in at Rho's side. The four-year-old blond Lab loved these walks and made numerous detours to check out sounds in the underbrush, interesting smells, and burrows that he hoped moles might be enticed from. Rho headed for the woods where the old boarded-up outhouse stood, crossed the stream, and wandered through the gnarled apple trees, where the air was pungent with last summer's windfalls. But what was usually a keen pleasure in her surroundings was spoiled by the intrusive image of the young woman at Point Deception. Guilt was what she was feeling, guilt over not helping her.

And guilt, her father—once also a deputy with the department—had often told her, was humanity's most wasteful emotion. "You're feeling guilty about something," he'd say, "take action. If you can't right one wrong, address another." She didn't always agree with Jack Antolini, but in this case he was a hundred percent correct.

"Come on," she said to Cody, "we're going to town."

The shabby red pickup truck almost didn't stop for Guy Newberry. He stepped back to the safety of the motel driveway, and the vehicle came to a screeching halt inches from where he would have been had he proceeded.

"Asshole," he muttered, and was about to give the driver a one-fingered salute when he saw she was very pretty: close-cropped black hair; small, fine-boned face; big momentarily horrified hazel eyes. A yellow Labrador retriever sat on the passenger's side, wearing its seat belt.

"Sorry!" the woman called.

He went over to the window, which was half rolled down, and patted the Lab's protruding snout. "That's okay. I wasn't paying attention either."

"Are you sure you're all right?"

"I'm sure."

She gave him a faint smile and a wave of the hand be-

fore she shifted gears and drove on. Guy watched the
truck until it turned into the parking lot of a small strip
mall, noting the bumper sticker that said SUPPORT YOUR
LOCAL SHERIFF'S DEPARTMENT. Then he angled across the
highway to the Signal Port Hotel.

The two-story weathered frame building with a sagging front porch and balcony was easily the largest and
most prosperous-looking in the half-mile-long business
district. It no longer offered lodging, but its kitchen had
been serving up hearty meals since 1877. That much he'd
learned the previous evening when he'd stopped in for a
few beers, fish-and-chips, and some local color.

He crossed the lobby to the dining room, a high-
ceilinged space with a small gas-log fireplace and
chrome-and-Formica tables and chairs reminiscent of the
1950s. No other customers were there, nor were there
signs any had been. He sat at the table by one of the front
windows, and after several minutes a surly-looking
blonde waitress appeared, looking annoyed at his presence, and took his order. Across the lobby the bar was
open, an optimistic sign advertising Saturday brunch,
Bloody Marys and mimosas included, but from where he
sat he saw no takers.

The scene in there had been pretty much the same the
night before. When he'd expressed surprise to the bartender that business should be so slow on a Friday, the
man said it was status quo after Labor Day. Signal Port
had four bars, fewer than four hundred and fifty residents,
and on weekends what tourists came through blew their
money at Tai Haruru on Calvert's Landing Pier up north
or down at Restless Waters in Westhaven. He, the barkeep, preferred it that way.

Guy then took a corner table and nursed his beer. A stocky gray-haired man whom the bartender had greeted as Will was going over some plans with an urban type in a cashmere sweater. The urbanite's blonde, bored wife played the pinball machine and cast glances at the male patrons. Her eyes rested on Guy for a moment, then dismissed him. Possibly he looked too much her own kind to interest her. A mixed-race couple—the man Asian, the woman Caucasian—were quarreling in low voices, she doing most of the talking. Something about how their luck would run out someday and then he'd damned well wish he'd spread around more good karma. He kept telling her to let it rest, there was no reason he should've done a stranger any favors. A man with an earring—gay, from his mannerisms—was knocking back martinis at the bar. After his third he asked the bartender what the hell was wrong with this town. The barkeep said, "Can't help you there, Kevin," and went back to drying glasses.

Now, with similar friendliness, the waitress brought Guy's austere breakfast of a toasted bagel and tomato juice and slammed it down on the table with a force that would have registered on the Richter scale. He tried to engage her in pleasantries—usually an easy task for him—but met with stony resistance. When he asked for a newspaper, she told him he'd have to buy one at the stands in front of the supermarket. Then she withdrew, leaving him to eat while contemplating the highway, where cars mainly passed through without stopping and beside which few pedestrians walked.

Yes, he told himself, toasting his good fortune with his tomato juice, he'd come to the right place. Signal Port would make excellent fodder for his next "penetrating and seminal"—God, the things reviewers will say!—examination of a town in trouble.

Today he'd start asking the serious questions.

That was a close call with the man on the highway, Rho thought as she turned into the parking lot of the Soledad County Coastal Substation. At least the guy had been nice about it—not common behavior in Signal Port, where locals tended to be prickly about anything to do with traffic. He was a stranger, of course, and not a bad-looking one, with that thick silvery hair and tanned, craggy face. From the city, probably, and trying to fit in on the coast, but his wool shirt was too good quality and his jeans too crisp and new for him to escape notice. Coming from the Sea Stacks and heading for the hotel, an overnighter who would soon be on the road and, hopefully, forget about the woman who had almost run him down on his way to breakfast. Who would never realize said woman was a sheriff's deputy.

The parking lot in front of the rambling prefab building tucked behind the cable TV office and hardware store was crowded this morning. Sheriff's department cruisers, a highway patrol car, and several California Department of Fish and Game vehicles overflowed the marked spaces, and a county minivan was pulled in front of the substation's entrance. DFG officers were herding a line of male prisoners—all of them Asian—onto the van for transport to the jail in Santa Carla.

So this morning's pre-dawn raid on abalone poachers operating down at Pelican Cove had happened as planned. Rho squeezed her truck between the trash Dumpster and a cruiser and got out. "You stay here,

Cody," she said. The Lab whined, but stopped straining at the seat belt. As she took the steps of the substation two at a time, one of the DFG men grinned and flashed her a victory sign.

As usual, Valerie had the heat turned too high, and the interior was stifling. Rho twisted the thermostat's dial, and the clerk looked up from her knitting—another of those strange garments that were too short to be capes and too long to be collars. They seemed to be all Valerie Middleton knew how to knit, and eventually each of her acquaintances would be gifted with one which, after enthusiastic thanks, would be consigned to the back of the closet. Now she set her needles aside and regarded Rho with bright little eyes set deep in her beaky bird's face, the corners of her mouth twitching in disapproval.

She saw, Rho knew, the signs of a hangover. Valerie had worked for the department since Rho's father was a rookie, and was thoroughly familiar with all the deputies' histories. The clerk had been known to come down hard on the men for reasons as trivial as allowing their wastebaskets to overflow or leaving the seat up in the restroom, but other than this facial tic she'd offer no criticism to Rho. Her gruffly maternal attitude toward the substation's only female officer could be a source of embarrassment, but on mornings like these Rho appreciated it.

Valerie said, "It's supposed to be your day off. What're you doing here?"

"Just couldn't tear myself away."

"That's just as well. Wayne was asking after you."

Wayne Gilardi, her counterpart on the morning shift. "Was he in on the bust?"

"Yes. You'll find him in the interrogation room with one of the suspects."

Rho set her bag under the desk she and Wayne shared and went down the hall to the room that did double duty for departmental meetings and interviews with witnesses and suspects. When she stuck her head through the door she found the big, gray-haired officer seated at the table across from a slender Asian in baggy work clothes. Wayne got up and joined her in the hall, shutting the door behind him.

"So what's happening?" Rho said.

"For openers, we collared a dozen poachers. All Vietnamese. We suspect they're affiliated with that ring operating out of Oakland."

Poaching of the endangered abalone had become a huge industry along the coast, involving not only divers, but wholesalers, buyers, and deliverymen. Both in season—which ran from April 1 to June 30, and again from August 1 to November 30—and out of season, individual divers would harvest more than the legal daily limit of four shellfish and pass them off to middlemen who then sold them to restaurants, mainly in the San Francisco Bay Area. Six months ago a group of property owners near Deer Harbor had gotten together to patrol their coves in the early hours of the morning when poachers typically slipped in by boats laden with their scuba diving gear. Acting on their tips, Fish and Game had arrested six Vietnamese men whose statements hinted at a much larger operation. An investigation, called Haliotis IV, after the abalone's scientific name, had been ongoing since then, and hopefully this morning's arrests would lead to the ringleaders.

"So what's with the guy in there?" Rho nodded at the interrogation room. "It looks as if you've already processed the others."

"Right. DFG's waiting on a second minivan to take the last six to County, but this one—a diver called Zhi Phung—might have something for us. As soon as I read him his rights he tried to make a deal, swap information. And not about their operation."

Of course not, Rho thought. That information was DFG's concern. Besides, the poachers were known as a tight-knit group, bound by their culture and, in many cases, family ties; so far those who had been arrested had adamantly refused to inform on their fellow members.

"What kind of information?" she asked.

"About a crime he witnessed—a kidnapping."

"That's major. What did he give you?"

"Zilch. While we had him in the holding cell he changed his mind. Probably was persuaded by the others not to cooperate. Now he's claiming I misunderstood him because he doesn't speak much English, but his was as good as mine when I arrested him. Even the threat of an obstruction charge didn't sway him."

"You want me to talk to him?"

"Yeah. You're better with these ethnic types."

Better than you, anyway. Rho entertained few prejudices, while Wayne was notorious for his distrust and dislike of minorities. "Okay, I'll see what I can do."

Zhi Phung was still seated at the table when Rho entered the room, his eyes focused on the beige wall across from him. They moved slowly to her, but otherwise he didn't acknowledge her presence.

She introduced herself, added, "I hear Deputy Gilardi's been giving you a hard time."

The man's expression remained blank, as if he didn't understand her, but she saw intelligence and comprehension in his dark eyes.

"Deputy Gilardi becomes impatient when someone makes him an offer of information and then withdraws it," she added, "but I am a very patient person." To emphasize her point, she sat down across from him.

Zhi shrugged and looked away.

"I understand you've witnessed a kidnapping," Rho said. "That's a very serious crime. For information about it, I think my department would be inclined to persuade Fish and Game to do some very serious dealing."

"I do not have much English," Zhi said.

"You have enough to answer yes or no to my questions. Did this kidnapping occur here in Soledad County?"

No response, but why would he offer to make a deal with Wayne if it hadn't?

"Did it happen this morning?"

Nothing.

"Last night?"

Zhi's eyes moved toward hers, and she saw a nervous flicker.

"Was the victim a man?"

Nothing.

"A woman?"

Another flicker.

"Was the kidnapper—"

"I do not understand."

"Mr. Zhi, was the kidnapper—"

"I want my lawyer."

No fool, Mr. Zhi. He'd said the words that by law would force her to put an immediate end to the interrogation. Rho stood, leaned across the table till she loomed over him. "I suggest you tell your attorney what you know. He'll be able to work out a deal that's in your best interests."

A kidnapping, she thought as she left the room. Here in the county. Last night. A woman. Witnessed by an abalone poacher who would've had to drive north on Highway 1 to one of the abandoned piers where the divers typically launched their boats. Who would've had to drive past Point Deception and a woman left vulnerable because of a broken-down car.

Guy stepped onto the porch of the hotel, bracing himself against the strong offshore wind. Behind him the waitress affixed to the glass door one of those signs that said "Open Again At" above a clockface with movable plastic hands, and pulled the shade behind it. Saturday brunch had not met with success, and the staff was forgoing lunch in favor of the cocktail hour.

Unpleasant woman, he thought, and the folks at the Sea Stacks were her equals. Come to think of it, most of the people he'd encountered during his brief stay were a shade off-putting, except for the pretty woman in the red pickup, and *she'd* tried to kill him before he'd even had his breakfast.

Town in trouble.

He remained on the porch for a few minutes, surveying the businesses strung out along the highway. Chevron station, unprosperous-looking real estate brokerage, supermarket, drugstore, cable TV office, hardware store, nursery, thrift shop, coin-operated laundry, propane firm. A couple of bar-and-grills that looked as if they catered strictly to locals. Post office was the busiest establishment at this time of day, but the people who greeted each other coming and going didn't linger to talk.

The Sea Stacks was the only motel, and not a very good one. There were no real restaurants except the one in the hotel, no shops catering to tourists. Side roads lined with frame houses on small lots led up into the hills, where a TV satellite dish and a church spire rose above the pines. A mobile home park advertised gracious seaside living, but most of its spaces were empty.

There was evidence that the town had once seen, or been poised on the brink of, better days: A pier extended into the sea across from the hotel, its charter-fishing business boarded up; a weathered sign pointed the way to a yacht harbor. When he'd driven in the previous afternoon, Guy had noted a subdivision on the ocean side of the highway, streets with names such as Cormorant Way and Osprey Lane neatly laid out. Only three houses had been built there, and weeds grew through cracks in the pavement. Across from the subdivision the Pelican Cove Bed & Breakfast, a gabled, gingerbread-laden structure, looked to be in poor repair, and only two cars sat in its lot.

Town in trouble, and Guy was going to lay bare the reasons.

Two months ago, had anyone told him he'd now be standing on a hotel porch in a small coastal California town, shivering in the strong early October wind, he'd have thought them insane. His life was settled, and if he wasn't happy with it, he wasn't unhappy either. But then, at a dinner party at his literary agent's home in SoHo, he'd been seated next to a man named Dunbar Harrison, and the whole thing was set in motion. Orchestrated, he thought, by his agent, Marta Backus, who was sick and tired of waiting for Guy to write another book.

It was ten years since his first portrait of a troubled town, set in an Alabama hamlet torn apart by a series of racially motivated killings, had made the best-seller lists. Six years since his much-praised study of a small midwestern town rocked by scandal and corruption capitalized on that first success. Four years since he stopped contributing articles to newspapers and magazines. Three years since he shelved his major work on an entire country in trouble. Three years since Diana died and everything solid and good went out of his life.

Three years, and Marta Backus apparently had decided it was time for him to get back to work.

Dunbar Harrison was a man Guy knew casually. His family had made their money generations ago in New England manufacturing, and Dun had attended all the right schools, excelling at nothing. For years he'd drifted on the fringes of New York's theatrical world, contributing the occasional review to unimportant publications and backing off-Broadway plays that invariably did poorly. A pleasant enough man in his late forties, but he didn't relate well to others, and his demeanor was curiously dispassionate. At least that was how most people saw him. To Guy, he seemed haunted.

Given his take on Harrison, he'd been surprised at Marta's dinner party to hear Dun energetically lobby him to make Signal Port, California, the subject of his next book. It was his kind of material, he insisted. In what way? Guy asked. A mass murder had occurred there thirteen years ago, and had virtually destroyed the town. Hadn't Guy heard about it?

He thought back to where he'd been then. In Asia, working on a major series of articles on the emerging Pacific Rim economy for the *Times*. As was typical, he'd buried himself in his project and paid little attention to what went on at home, certainly none to a crime in a California town he'd never heard of.

"No," he said to Dun, "I haven't. But don't tell me any more. I'm not planning to write another book."

"Once you know the story, I'm sure you'll want to pursue it."

"Sorry, Dun, I'm retired."

"Please hear me out."

Dun's intensity intrigued him. A slight prickle traveled up his spine, the beginning of the old excitement when an idea was presented to him. He tried to suppress it. "Did Marta put you up to this?"

"Actually, I came to her with the concept. But she thinks it's a surefire winner. Just listen—"

"No." This time his refusal was less a rejection of the idea itself than an instinctive safeguard against it becoming contaminated. When he began entertaining the possibility of a story, he didn't want to hear too much detail, particularly if it was biased, inaccurate, or incomplete. And given Dun's excitement, his account was likely to be all three. Instead, Guy preferred to learn only the bare bones—who, what, when, where—then assign his research assistant to gather complete information. But before he tackled the volumes of material, he'd travel to the place armed with only a brief summary, and immerse himself in its culture. What he uncovered by spending time in the community and getting to know its people breathed life into his story and revealed facets of it that no amount of professional research could unearth.

Dun had no way of knowing that, however, and he flinched at Guy's abruptness, looking away. When he turned back, Guy was shocked by the expression on his face. The intensity was gone, but instead of disappointment, it had been replaced by anguish.

"All right," Guy said, "we'll talk about this in the morning."

Dun's twisted face sagged with relief. "You're going to do it."

"I'm going to *think* about doing it." But the prickle was back, stronger than before, and this time he did nothing to suppress it. How could he resist a story that had such power over a man like Dunbar Harrison?

He spoke with Marta before he left her party. Eight weeks later, more intrigued than ever, a contract signed with his publisher, he was on his way to Soledad County.

Rho propped her hip on the corner of Valerie's desk and picked up the clipboard that held this morning's faxes from Santa Carla—notices and memos that rolled off the machine in a steady stream from the Soledad County seat. As she paged through them she asked the clerk, "You know where Wayne went?" He'd left the substation after the last of the poachers were loaded onto the second van.

"On a four-five-nine up at Deer Harbor. Second home. Valuable jewelry and antiques taken." Valerie smirked and picked up her knitting. "Now, I ask you, what kind of people leave valuables in a vacation home where they don't even have an alarm system or a private patrol?"

"People who hope to defraud their insurance companies."

"I tell you, you work in a place long enough, you see it all."

"Yeah, you do." Rho sighed, skimming a memo that said the department's request for funds to hire two more patrol officers and a detective for the coastal substation had been turned down by the county board of supervisors.

The trouble with policing Soledad County, she thought, was that it was too damn big and diverse. You had national forest to the east; Santa Carla, Talbot's Mills, and Cedar along the Highway 101 corridor; the coastal ridge; and the coast itself. The coastal area extended from Westhaven at the south to Oilville—whose now dry wells were among the first to be drilled in California—at the north. In between lay small towns, state reserves, large ranches, and wilderness.

This single substation served the nearly one-hundred-mile coastal stretch. Rho, nine other deputies, and Station Commander Iverson worked the facility, their territories overlapping with those of the inland cities. None of the coastal towns had its own police department, and even with the cooperation of the California Highway Patrol, the job was overwhelming.

It didn't help that the department's Investigations Bureau was located at the county seat. Should a serious crime occur on the coast, detectives were dispatched from Santa Carla, but more often than not they relied on patrol officers such as herself to do the real legwork. As a result, she and her fellow deputies were more skilled at investigation than their colleagues inland and their work was more interesting, but they performed detectives' duties for patrol officers' pay. Many of the deputies complained about that, but Rho didn't care. Often, like today, she worked during her time off.

She set the clipboard on the desk and stood. "If you talk to Wayne," she said to Valerie, "tell him I'm heading down to Point Deception to check on an abandoned vehicle."

Valerie took her eyes off her knitting and regarded Rho with a keen, birdy gaze. It said that she pitied her for many reasons: for having no husband, no children, no life outside her job; for throwing herself into her work in an attempt to atone for mistakes that under normal circumstances rookies were expected to make; for having thirteen years ago stumbled into abnormal circumstances that continued to haunt her.

Or maybe Valerie didn't feel that way at all. Maybe Rho simply pitied herself.

When Guy returned to his motel room at a few minutes after three, the door stood open. Late for the maid to be making it up, especially when it appeared that only two other units were occupied. He approached warily, ready for unpleasantness at the end of a frustrating and unpleasant day.

A woman with enormous buttocks—what one of his British friends called "posterial exuberance"—was bending over to put the final touches to making his bed. As he stepped through the door she straightened and whirled, one hand going to her throat as her face went pale. Then she flushed, muttered something about having to take her son to the dentist—presumably the reason she'd been late to work—and fled, leaving a caddy of cleaning supplies on the small table next to his laptop and file boxes.

The maid, Guy thought, was clearly as strange and unfriendly as all the other citizens of Signal Port whom he'd encountered that day. At the supermarket, the hardware store, the pharmacy, the small public library. Even the folks at the realty office, usually a place where newcomers were eagerly welcomed, had been distant and discouraging. In two bars where he'd stopped for a beer, he'd been on the receiving end of vaguely hostile glances. At the beach, the people he'd complimented on their dogs shied away from him.

An unfriendly town, yes, but there was more. Guy caught the scent of xenophobia.

He went to the table and picked up the caddy, intending to set it outside the door, and his gaze rested on the file boxes. The lid of one was askew. Setting the caddy down, he raised the lid. His files had been disturbed, no question about that.

By whom? Given her reaction to his arrival, the maid was the likely culprit. But there was also the unfriendly motel proprietor and his sour-faced wife. Or some unknown other party. Were strangers' possessions routinely intruded upon in this town?

Or was the reason for the intrusion something unique to him? Unique because he intended to turn the spotlight on the thirteen-year-old unsolved murders in Cascada Canyon?

*   *   *

The black Mercedes was still parked at the turnout, its sheen dulled by saltcake, its windows misted. Rho pulled her truck over by the fence; as she started to get out, Cody yelped. She fixed him with a stern look and said, "Later." The dog was well trained, but people drove fast on this stretch, and she didn't want to take any chances with him, particularly on a blind curve.

Three other vehicles were parked in the turnout, two pickups and an old sedan. Fishermen, who went through the gap in the fence and across the grassy slope to clamber down the cliff to the cove. The land was owned by an old man who used to run sheep there—Gregory Cordova, the descendant of Basques who had migrated to the coastal region generations ago. He lived all alone in a ramshackle farmhouse at the south end of the property and didn't care if people crossed for fishing access so long as they didn't bother him or camp there. His hand-painted sign of a tent with a line through it was overgrown by gorse, but by and large his wishes were known and respected.

Rho approached the Mercedes cautiously, conscious that she was off duty, without the uniform and badge that gave her authority. Last night she'd thought it odd that the woman had gone off without lowering the hood, and she'd shone her flashlight through the windows to make sure she wasn't asleep inside. Now she looked into the engine compartment to see if she could pinpoint the source of the trouble, but apparently it was beyond her expertise. She circled the car once, then tried the driver's side door. Unlocked, and a cursory search of the interior turned up nothing but a couple of marijuana roaches in the ashtray; the glovebox held no registration, insurance card, or other identifying papers.

She backed out of the car and went to the trunk. Inside was a first-aid kit that looked to be standard equipment and a duffel bag whose contents had been dumped out and scattered across the compartment. Pair of jeans, a couple of T-shirts, blow dryer, a few changes of women's underwear, toiletries kit. The kit contained the usual items, but no prescription medicines that would show its owner's name.

Ransacked, or had the woman been looking for something in a hurry? Either way, she'd packed for only a short trip.

Rho shut the trunk and went back to the driver's side door, where she located the metal plate showing the vehicle identification number. She'd run it and the license plate through the DMV's central files, get a name and address. The car would be towed and impounded if it wasn't removed within forty-eight hours.

For a few minutes she stood beside the Mercedes, putting herself in the young woman's place. Traffic whizzed by on the highway—heavy because it was Saturday—but no one stopped and what few people who glanced her way averted their eyes quickly. No one cared about a woman who appeared to be stranded with a disabled vehicle in this isolated place. They were too caught up in their travel plans or their errands or their pursuit of a good time to give a damn.

Too caught up to give a damn—as she herself had been yesterday afternoon. Except it was her *job* to give a damn, her responsibility to offer assistance and guarantee safety.

* * *

Guy lowered himself onto a stool at the hotel bar and ordered a Beck's. The bartender said, "So you're back."

"Yeah, I am." When the man returned with the beer, he added, "Not much here for a tourist to do, is there?"

"Don't get many tourists." The bartender looked pointedly at Guy's new L.L. Bean shirt that still showed creases from packing. "Not the kind that stay more than one night, anyway."

"I thought this part of the coast was a vacationer's dream." It had been described as such in a giveaway paper he'd earlier picked up at the supermarket. The paper made scant mention of Signal Port, however.

The barkeep shrugged. "Parts of it, yes. Parts of it, no. A town like this, it's ordinary. Just a place where people live out their lives, working and raising families."

"Former doghole port, isn't it? Logging town?"

"Right."

"Rumrunning port during Prohibition?"

"That too."

"Colorful history. Seems your chamber of commerce could exploit it."

"If we wanted them to. Which we don't." The bartender moved along to another customer.

Five o'clock now, and the bar was filling up. Maybe Saturday nights at the hotel were more lively. Guy studied the other patrons in the mirror of the backbar: men and women who looked as if they spent most of their time outdoors. He tuned out extraneous noise, listened to their conversations. Identified several distinct groups: commercial fishermen discussing the week's catch, which had been disappointing; loggers complaining of the new forestry rules that had been adopted at the first of the year; ranchers and hands talking about their stock and the possibility of a wet winter. An extended family, all dressed up for a special occasion, occupied a round table toward the rear. From the wrapping on the presents piled there, Guy assumed they were celebrating the older couple's wedding anniversary. A much younger pair at a small table leaned toward each other over their drinks, heads close. At the start of a similar life's journey, and Guy envied them.

After a while he began to recognize some of the people who came in. The racially mixed couple who had been quarreling in here last night took a table near the windows and drank, not speaking. Will, the man who had gone over the blueprints with the urbanite, was at the bar with a redheaded woman who would have been stunning were it not for fifty extra pounds and tense lines around her mouth and eyes. Guy's gaze lingered on her as he tried to identify what her problem might be. It wasn't Will; he touched her hand often, called her "Virge-honey," and occasionally brought a faint smile to her lips.

In one corner a couple was half hidden by the jukebox. The man was youngish, in his twenties, with spiky hair and cheap but trendy clothing. The woman was blonde, and when she turned to look for the waitress, Guy realized she was the urbanite's wife. The two were holding hands, but the man kept looking at his watch. Whenever he did, she pouted and shook her head. Once she said loudly, "Please don't go, darling!"

Interesting.

The crowd ebbed and flowed. The extended family were called to the dining room and a rowdy group of drinkers claimed their table. The straying wife and her friend finally left, and another pair who had just entered took their place. The man was big and graying, with a gut that hung over his belt buckle. The woman was the black-haired motorist who had almost run Guy over. Unaccountably he felt a stir of disappointment. Such a pretty woman, and seemingly the most pleasant person in town. Was that her husband?

He continued to watch them as they ordered drinks, and finally he saw that while the man wore a wedding ring, the woman did not. They were discussing something seriously, she ticking off items on her fingers, but their body language was wrong for intimacy. Perhaps they were just friends or business associates.

Whatever, she was certainly one pretty woman.

"So what're you saying, kiddo?" Deputy Wayne Gilardi asked Rho. "That the woman with the Mercedes was the victim of the kidnapping that poacher claimed he witnessed?"

"It's possible. The situation's irregular, anyway. The Mercedes' VIN doesn't match with the license plate. Plates were reported stolen six months ago in Ventura County. My check on the VIN shows the car's registered to a Richard Bartlow, address is in Corona del Mar, Orange County. But there's no phone number for him, listed or unlisted."

"So he moved, forgot to send the DMV a change of address."

"And the stolen plates?"

"Maybe he can afford a Mercedes because he knocks over liquor stores for a living."

She tapped her fingers on the table, irritated. "It's irregular, I tell you."

"No, what's irregular is you going to the trouble to check out ownership of an abandoned vehicle on your day off. I say the girl knew the plates were hot and walked away from a potentially bad situation. Or she'll be back tomorrow with her boyfriend, who thinks he's a great auto mechanic."

She shook her head, sipped wine, looked around. The bar was filling up and— Oh, hell!

"What?" Wayne asked. He could read her only too well.

"Nothing."

He turned, scanned the room. His eyes came to rest on Alex Ngo, who slouched alone at a table near the windows. "Fuckin' gook," he said. "At least Lily's not with him for a change."

Rho didn't point out that the jacket slung over the back of the chair opposite Alex looked like one Wayne's younger sister often wore.

Wayne turned back to the table, downed half his beer. "God, I'd like to get something on that little bastard!"

"Such as?"

"Come on, kiddo, you've heard the rumors."

"You mean about the abalone poaching."

"Yeah. One of the Fish and Game guys who went out on the raid this morning said they're ninety-nine percent sure that Ngo is hooked in with that ring of poachers."

"What do they have on him so far, other than the fact that he's Vietnamese and a diver?"

"One of their surveillance photos shows him with a

fellow called Phuc Ky Phan of Oakland. Phuc's one of the middlemen the divers pass the abalone off to."

"And Alex was photographed in the act?"

"No." Wayne scowled. "He was photographed drinking beer with Phuc on Calvert's Landing Pier."

"And that makes them ninety-nine percent certain he's hooked in? What if Phuc's a relative? Or a friend? Their knowing each other doesn't prove a thing."

"Why're you defending the bastard, Rho? You know how he treats Lily. You've seen the bruises on her face. You remember when I had to drive her to the clinic because two of her ribs were busted in a so-called fall. I swear, if he's involved her in this poaching business—"

"Wayne, stop. I'm not defending him." Lily had just come out of the restroom and was walking toward Alex. "All I'm saying is that DFG has no proof. They'd better get more than that before they arrest Ngo."

Wayne followed the direction of her gaze and turned. His face reddened and then he was off his chair, fists clenched at his sides.

Christ, Rho thought, not another scene like last week!

Quickly she stood and followed, but by the time she caught up with Wayne, he was looming over Alex, in his face and shouting.

"I told you what'd happen if I saw you with her again, you fuckin' gook!"

Rho grabbed Wayne's arm, tried to pull him back. He shook her off and she stumbled against the next table. The bar grew quiet.

Alex sat with his arms folded, acting as if Wayne wasn't there, but Lily half rose. "Stop it, damn you!"

Wayne grasped his sister's arm and dragged her all the

way to her feet. "Go outside and wait for me in my truck."

"I'm not— Ow! That hurts, you bastard!"

Someone stepped between Rho and Wayne now, a tall man who moved swiftly and confidently. He got Wayne in a restraint hold, breaking his grasp on Lily. Said to the couple, "Get out of here. Now!"

They went, while Wayne struggled against his captor. Rho stepped forward to intervene and recognized the man. The tourist she'd almost run down that morning.

"Let him go," she told him. "I'll handle this."

The black-haired woman took over, and Guy released his hold on her friend. She grasped him by the arms and spoke forcefully, her delicate face close to his.

"You can't keep doing this, Wayne. You're only driving her away from you."

"Fuckin' gook's wrecking her life—"

"No, *Lily's* wrecking her life, and till she realizes that and decides to do something about it, nothing you say or do is going to change things."

"Guess you're the expert on that, Rho."

The woman recoiled, taking her hands off him. "What the hell's that supposed to mean?"

He shook his head and turned on Guy, giving him a shove that knocked him against the jukebox. "You don't know who you're dealing with, buddy. Keep your goddamn hands to yourself!" Then he started for the door in a tight, angry stride.

Guy pushed away from the jukebox and rubbed his shoulder, where Wayne's hand had caught him. The woman came over to him and said, "Thanks. I owe you. Where'd you learn that hold?"

"In the navy, shore patrol. May I buy you a drink?"

"Let me buy you one." She headed back to her table and Guy followed, taking the chair Wayne had vacated. The noise level in the bar was returning to normal. Probably altercations were a normal component of Signal Port's Saturday-night festivities.

"Your friend doesn't like Asians much," he commented.

"My colleague at the sheriff's department, Deputy Wayne Gilardi, doesn't like that particular Asian—and for good reason."

Guy remembered the SUPPORT YOUR LOCAL SHERIFF'S DEPARTMENT bumper sticker on her truck, and winced. She was a cop. And so was Wayne. Jesus . . . !

"I'd've never grabbed him like that if I'd known—"

"No way you could have. He's off duty."

"Still, you don't go around assaulting the local law."

"You're perfectly justified when the local law's making an ass of himself. Besides, his fellow deputy nearly assaulted *you* this morning. Recovered from that scare yet?"

"Fully. My name's Guy Newberry, by the way." He waited to see if she might recognize it, but if she did, she gave no sign. Writers, he thought wryly, labored in obscurity. Even best-sellers like himself failed to achieve notice unless they were celebrities in some other field or at events where the attendees expected to see them. On the one hand, anonymity made his type of work easier, but on the other it could be deflating.

"Rhoda Swift." She offered her hand, and he clasped it. Her grip was strong and straightforward.

As she signaled to the waitress he said, "So you're with the sheriff's department."

"Thirteen-year veteran, work out of the substation here in town. And you're a stranger to the coast."

"It shows that much? Well, yes, I'm from New York City. But I'm thinking of relocating. What's it like to live in Signal Port?"

She frowned—more puzzled by the question than displeased, he thought. "Like living in any small town, I guess. Everybody knows you, your life history, your business. And they're pleased to hash it over with anybody else who'll listen. Fortunately, you also know about them, so in the end everybody's even."

"You've lived here your whole life?"

"Except for college in another small town."

"Ever had the urge to get out, try a big city?"

"Not particularly. I'd still be carrying the small-town girl around inside me. Now you, Mr. Newberry—"

"Guy."

"Guy. And please call me Rhoda. What is it you do that allows you to consider relocating to someplace this remote?"

Rhoda Swift, he thought, might be more friendly than her fellow townspeople, but just as adept at fielding questions. And he sensed that, as a member of the sheriff's department, she'd close off completely if he revealed the reason he was here. So he opted for a half-truth.

"Freelance writing," he said. And with the intention of making her thoroughly bored with his profession, he launched into a monologue about the new laptop he'd bought for the trip.

The evening proceeded pleasantly, if not very profitably, through drinks and dinner, but ended abruptly when Rhoda's pager went off and she returned the call from the phone in the lobby. She came back to the table tight-lipped and obviously upset, but would offer only the terse explanation that a potential witness to a serious crime had been killed in his cell in the county jail in Santa Carla.

Chrystal: Before

Friday, October 6
10:32 A.M.

Jesus, this road! I thought a couple of those stretches back in Mendocino County were white-knucklers, but this one's got them beat to hell. Take a curve too fast and you'd be screaming all the way down the cliff. And it's a long way down.

How the hell do people up here survive, driving this thing every day? Guess they get used to it. Must get used to being so far away from everything, too. Haven't seen a house in miles, just cows on the hillsides. I remember what Jude used to say about the cows: that they were specially bred with their legs shorter on one side so they could stand up on those steep slopes. Thought she was a riot, but it drove Leo nuts every time she said it.

Mileage sign. Signal Port's thirty miles north. Less to where I'm going. But miles seem longer up here than on regular roads. Lots longer.

Jesus, Chryssie, watch your driving! You come too far now

to screw up and take a nosedive off the cliff. You're nervous, is all. All those instructions and warnings Jude gave you— they're fuckin' with your head.

Why'd she send me up here if she thought I couldn't get away with it? Desperate, I guess. Greedy, too. Well, why not? Me and her, we never had nothing. And why shouldn't she believe I can't pull it off? All my life she's been telling me I'm a loser.

Well, not this time. This time Jude's gonna be wrong.

Sunday, October 8

She was kneeling in the fog-damp pine needles, the boy's body so slight that she easily cradled him in her arms. Blood bubbled at his lips as he gasped for breath, his eyelids fluttering. She thrust frantic fingers into his mouth, trying to clear his airway.

Sirens in the distance. The backup vehicles.

"Come on, come *on*!"

The boy's body convulsed, and blood gushed from his mouth, soaking her uniform shirt. She was losing him.

"No please God no!"

Headlights washing up the drive. Pulsars turning the pines grotesque. Red and blue flashing over the suddenly still face of the child she hadn't been able to save. A young blonde woman stood over her, long hair blowing in the wind, eyes asking why—

Rho jerked upright in bed, shuddering. For a moment she was still at the crime scene in Cascada Canyon, but then familiar things—the glow of the digital clock, the outline of the window, Cody's soft wheezing—began to lead her back to the present. She hunched over, elbows on knees, hands pressed to her wet eyes.

As always during the transition from nightmare to reality, she faced a bitter truth: When little Heath Wynne died in her arms that night, a part of her had also died. Her dreams of a family, her marriage, any semblance of a normal life—all were doomed. The family because she couldn't bear to bring a child into a world where he might become a bullet-riddled corpse. The marriage because her husband badly wanted the children she refused to give him. The normal life because, once she stopped the drinking and pill taking, she needed to maintain rigid control in order to function, and that kind of control precluded love and intimacy. Like the children, those feelings were best not conceived.

Most of the time she managed, even managed well. She was good at her work, good to her friends. She had her new home, was planning improvements and a garden. And the nightmare, thank God, came less frequently.

But now, four days before the anniversary of the murders, it had returned two nights running in a subtly altered version, the presence of the young blonde woman forcing her to confront both the distant and recent past. Why—?

The phone rang. She squinted at the clock, saw it was quarter to seven. After fumbling with the receiver, she gave an interrogatory grunt.

Wayne Gilardi's voice. Something about it made adrenaline course through her like a fast-acting virus.

"Say again, Wayne."

"A floater. Woman. Point Deception. Couple of surf fishermen spotted her in Lantern Cove. I could use your help, kiddo." Wayne betrayed no anger over last night's scene in the bar. No contrition, either. And now, after the way he'd spoken to her, he—a mediocre investigator at best—had caught an important call and had the nerve to ask a favor.

"What's your location?" she asked.

"I can be at your place in five minutes."

"Give me ten."

Guy stood on the deserted pier, watching the fog move. A dirty-gray billowing mass that made it seem more like night than early morning. He'd been unable to sleep and had come down here for a breath of fresh air and some fresh thinking.

Hours in the company of Deputy Rhoda Swift the night before had convinced him he might have to change his approach with the citizens of Signal Port. In spite of drinks and food and flattering attention, she'd remained remote. A polite remote, but unyielding. And she'd volleyed most of his questions back at him as if he were hurling them at a rubber wall.

The only things he'd learned from her could be summarized briefly: Signal Port had been a wonderful place to grow up. She'd wanted to live there her whole life. She'd attended college at Chico State—wherever that was—with the intention of returning home and teaching on the elementary level, but positions were unavailable in the unified school district, and eventually, on the advice of her sheriff's deputy father, she'd applied to the department. She'd been married once, to a contractor who left her and the town seven years ago. They'd had no children. The Lab's name was Cody. She'd gotten him from the pound two years ago when she bought a house on ten acres on the ridge. Her .357 Smith & Wesson revolver was better protection than the dog, who was determined to be everyone's best friend.

Surface details, the kind people exchange on a first date. And yet there was a current beneath them, something that frequently darkened Rhoda Swift's hazel eyes and made her look away from him. In her story there was a structured quality to time, as well as one of those major breaks that people refer to as "before" and "after."

Before I was born; after. Before Kennedy was shot; after. Before I became a writer; before I made the bestseller lists; before Diana died. . . .

After.

There were many other breaking points in Guy's life, but the significant one was the loss of Diana. It was as if she, a professional photographer who shot the pictorial sections of his books, had reversed one of her negatives, turning black to white, white to black. The underpinnings of his life were suddenly gone, and he began to doubt his most basic assumptions.

Not so, however, with Rhoda's loss of Zach, the contractor husband. Her significant break had occurred long before that, thirteen years ago, soon after she joined the sheriff's department. She probably didn't recognize it as such, didn't even realize how frequently she'd alluded to it, but it had formed a subtext to their conversation.

Thirteen years: The timing was right. If she could be persuaded to open up, Rhoda Swift would become a valuable asset to his project.

Guy shivered and zipped up his parka. For a while he'd been dimly aware of a change in the traffic pattern on the highway behind him. Now he turned and saw a sheriff's department cruiser speed past, heading south. A volunteer fire department rescue truck followed, and a helicopter flapped by offshore.

Something major happening.

Perhaps another "before." Another "after."

"It *could* be the woman from the Mercedes," Rho said, studying the sodden body on the stretcher. "She had blonde hair and was wearing a blue tube top. But I only caught a glimpse of her."

"Why didn't you stop?" Ned Grossman, a detective who had flown in by helicopter from Santa Carla, asked. There was a faint accusatory note in his voice that she chose not to react to.

"I had to respond to a Code Two, and after that things got busy. When I checked back there before my shift ended, the woman was gone."

Grossman, tall and lean with iron-gray hair and thin-rimmed glasses, nodded, apparently satisfied. "You catch the call?"

"Wayne Gilardi did. He picked me up on his way here."

The detective looked displeased at the mention of Wayne's name. He and his colleagues at the Investigations Bureau, Rho knew, were aware of the individual levels of skills among the coastal area deputies. "Okay," he said, "Gilardi'll have to assist on this, since he caught, but I want you as well."

"Yes, sir."

Grossman turned away to talk with his short, balding partner, whom he'd introduced as Denny Shepherd. Rho walked to the edge of the cliff above the cove from which the emergency technicians had recovered the partially clad body. Lantern Cove—so called because during Prohibition rumrunners had set kerosene lamps down there to distract federal agents from their clandestine activities at Signal Port.

In the normal course of her work Rho often had occasion to view dead bodies—those of people who had died of natural causes, the victims of traffic accidents and drownings, the wife or husband or friend who had been shot or stabbed or bludgeoned by someone near and dear. But this instance was different. If the victim was the stranded motorist—and Rho was inclined to believe so— she'd not only seen her in life but also been visited by her in her dreams. And she could have prevented her death.

The tall grass behind her rustled. Wayne's voice said, "Grossman just told me he wants both of us on this."

"Yeah, he said the same to me." She pointed to the detective and his partner as they descended to the cove with a pair of her colleagues.

Wayne asked, "What do they think they're gonna find down there? Won't be any evidence. She didn't go into the water here."

"No." Rho consulted her knowledge of the currents, pictured this week's tide table. "It would have to be someplace north, no farther than Deer Harbor and no earlier than last night. She isn't bloated or banged up enough to have been in the water any longer."

"Yeah. You know, I liked this better when I thought it was a simple case of a stranded tourist wandering out here in the dark and falling off the cliff."

"But the fact that all she's wearing is that tube top,

plus those bruises on her wrists, throat, and thighs—we're looking at murder here. Probably rape-and-murder. Kidnapping too."

"So you think she was the woman that gook poacher saw getting snatched?"

"It'd be a big coincidence if she wasn't."

"And her murder was connected with the poaching?"

"Maybe. Did you hear that Zhi Phung was strangled by one of his cellmates last night?"

Wayne frowned. "No. Why wasn't I told?"

"Central reported the death to DFG, who tried to reach you. When you weren't available, they called me."

His eyes flicked away from hers and scanned the horizon. Rho knew him well enough to guess that he'd been unavailable because he'd hit the bars after the scene in the hotel.

She went on, "Zhi may have been killed because someone from the poaching ring abducted the woman. Or his murder may have been simple retaliation for breaking their code of honor. I doubt we'll find out soon, if ever, because none of the cellmates is talking."

Wayne compressed his lips and shook his head. "Jesus, something like this couldn't've happened at a worse time. With the anniversary coming up, it'll revive all the old fears and suspicions."

The anniversary of the canyon murders. The fears and suspicions that a monster still lived among them.

"Don't get ahead of yourself," she said. "Grossman's a good detective, and discreet. He'll keep a lid on this. Nobody's going to know much of anything till Santa Carla releases the autopsy results. In the meantime, I've already gotten started on the Mercedes angle. Once I locate its owner, I can get an ID on our victim."

"A little while ago you said it *might* be her."

"I know, I was being cautious. But what're the chances it's not?"

"Slim."

"Okay, we'll talk with Grossman once he gets back up here and get rolling. I'll handle the ID. You start asking around for anybody who might've seen her, see if you can get a handle on the chain of events, establish a time line. An appeal on the public-access TV station could help."

The big deputy didn't respond. Rho looked at him, saw his conflicted expression.

"What?" she asked.

He shook his head.

Earlier he'd mentioned the old fears and suspicions. Now they were working on her. "Wayne, how'd you know she was still at the turnout after nightfall?"

"What?"

"You said you liked it better when you thought it was a case of a stranded motorist wandering out here *in the dark.*"

"You would catch that." His mouth twisted wryly. "Okay, Friday night I was . . . seeing somebody down in Westhaven. On my way back I spotted the woman in my truck's headlights. She was wearing a long sweater, down to her knees, but her legs were bare, and she must've been cold. Normally I would've stopped, but I was late getting home and worried about catching hell from Janie. So I didn't."

He paused, shaking his head. "Dammit, Rho, it's my

job to look out for people, but I just left her standing
there. What the hell does that make me?"

Guy crept along in the line of rubberneckers past the
turnout where he'd seen the girl on Friday afternoon. Her
black Mercedes was still there, but now it was being
winched up onto a flatbed tow truck, and the turnout was
clogged with emergency vehicles and sheriff's department cruisers. The helicopter he'd seen earlier had put
down beyond the fence. Yellow crime-scene tape cor-
doned off the area, and highway patrol officers waved the
traffic on.

He pictured the girl, her long blonde hair stirring in the
sea breeze. How long had it taken before Diana's con-
science-prodding voice forced him to U-turn? Five minutes, max. A brief interval, but enough time for
something to have happened to the girl. If this commotion had anything to do with her. They might simply be
towing the abandoned car to make room for the other vehicles.

Still, he felt a twinge, as well as a certain curiosity,
mainly because he suspected that Rhoda Swift might be
one of the officers on the scene. But there was no escap-
ing this endless line of traffic—

He spotted a dirt track to his right, house numbers
hanging crooked on a fencepost. When he braked and
turned in there the driver of the car behind him leaned on
his horn. The rutted track wound through a thick stand of
pines and terminated at a clearing where a weather-
beaten two-story farmhouse slumped. A barn and some
outbuildings lay in a state of disrepair to the south, and an
old pickup was pulled into a makeshift shed. Guy stopped

his car and got out, eyeing the house warily. No smoke came from its brick chimney, no dogs barked, no one appeared at the door or windows.

He remained by the car for a moment, getting his bearings, then began walking through the pines toward the sea. On their far side a barren bluff stretched toward cliffs that fell away to whitewater. Guy angled north, past burned trees and huge clumps of those strange plants with fluffy beige plumes that he'd observed on Friday. At the cliff's edge he braced himself against the wind and looked down.

It was low tide, and the rocks on the floor of the cove lay exposed, slick and slimy-looking in the gray light. Larger birdlimed formations rose above the placid offshore water, thick layers of black kelp swaying around them like submerged shag carpeting. Guy could smell the kelp: pungent, herbaceous, briny. Then the wind shifted, and he heard sounds that drew his attention to the downslope.

Sheriff's deputies, two of them, and a pair of men in plainclothes were descending to the cove, probably to search for evidence of whatever mishap had occurred there. Guy had a familiarity with crime scenes, as he'd once covered the police beat for a now defunct New York State daily, and the sight stirred memories. Many of them bittersweet, because it was at one of those scenes that he'd met Diana, then a television camerawoman. He quickly filed them away so he could concentrate on the present.

"You're trespassing, young man."

The voice, cracked with age, came from behind him. He turned slowly, saw a man whose eroded face matched the voice, standing some five feet away with a shotgun cradled in his arms. In his seventies, perhaps his eighties, with wispy gray hair and a gap-toothed mouth, dressed in plaid wool and denim.

Guy said, "I thought this was public land."

"Bullshit," the man replied, not unpleasantly. "You had to come up my driveway to get here."

"How much acreage do you own?"

"One hundred ninety-seven on this side of the highway, and a small parcel on the other, where my wellhouse is. Was my grandfather's, my father's, mine. When I'm gone it'll be the bank's, and good riddance."

"Why good riddance?"

"Place is cursed, God's truth."

"How?"

"Ask a lot of questions, don't you? What's your name?"

"Guy Newberry."

"I'm Gregory Cordova. Now, Mr. Newberry, why'd you come out here?"

"I was curious about the commotion up at the turnout. Thought this would be a good vantage point." He motioned at the cove. "What happened, anyway?"

"Floater. They brought her up a while ago. You went to a lot of trouble to satisfy your curiosity. Not from around here, are you?"

"No."

Gregory Cordova studied Guy, his dark eyes squinting. "You wouldn't be a tourist. Don't have the look. Businessman, passing through? Nope, somebody on a schedule doesn't take the time to come out here just 'cause there's a little commotion. Not a rancher or fisherman, either. That tan's the kind comes from one of them salons they got now, and you don't work with those hands."

The old man was a good observer, even if he'd gotten the part about the tan wrong, and since he appeared to enjoy his guessing game, Guy remained silent.

"That accent—it tells me you come from back east someplace. New York?"

"Right."

"So what's a New Yorker doing here? A nosy New Yorker, no less. You a reporter?"

"Something like that."

Gregory Cordova's weathered face grew still, his eyes watchful. "What's 'something like that' mean?"

"I'm a writer. Nonfiction books and articles." Even now it felt strange to make the claim, having spent the past three years denying it. Turning his back on the work he loved because it gave him pleasure, and he hadn't wanted any good feelings to intrude upon his grief. Hadn't wanted them to dilute the guilt he felt over the way Diana died.

The old man was silent for a moment. Then he nodded, as if Guy had confirmed something he'd known all along. "You're here to write about those young folks up the canyon," he said.

Finally someone here had given voice to the tragedy. "Yes."

"Folks've always been afraid that'd happen."

"Why?"

"Why not? None of them want it stirred up. It'd raise all the old questions, make them look funny at their friends and neighbors again. Hell, they've used up so much energy trying to pretend it never happened, they're plain worn out."

"What about you, sir? Have you tried to pretend?"

"Not me. I feel for the folks involved, but it didn't have anything to do with my life."

"You sound as if you know a good deal about what happened."

"Couldn't help but know. Everybody does, on this stretch of the coast. And that canyon's not all that far from here, entrance is up at the north end of my property. Nowadays I pretty much hole up here to home, but not back then. I had to pass by there all the time. Know as much as anybody does. More, maybe."

Guy's interest in what was happening in the cove faded for now. He asked, "Would you be willing to talk with me? Give me your impressions?"

The old man considered, long and hard. "I'm willing, Mr. Newberry. Sooner or later somebody's got to take the skeletons out of the closet, dust them off. That somebody might as well be me."

Rho was coming to a dead end on the Mercedes. She hunched in front of the computer, irritated with its slowness, and when it froze up and crashed—as it was increasingly prone to do—she let forth a howl of frustration.

Valerie's hand touched her shoulder, and she started. She hadn't heard her get up from her desk. "You need a break," the clerk said. "Something to eat, too."

"Don't you go getting all maternal on me!" she snapped.

"Then do it for my sake. I'm tired of listening to you curse and moan."

"I've been that bad, huh?"

"I've seen you worse. You're still trying to locate the owner of that car, right?"

"Right."

"Well, I may be able to help you there. My nephew Ron, the one with the twins? He used to be a service manager for Euro Motors in Santa Carla."

"And?"

"Mercedes is a very thorough company. What do you expect—Germans. Anyway, they keep detailed maintenance records on every car, track when they're serviced, that sort of thing. If the owner took it to the dealership to be worked on, they'll have his name and address in their nationwide data bank."

"And of course it's Sunday, when the service departments're closed."

"Yes, but there's another way of getting the information. They also have a twenty-four-hour emergency road service. They can tap into the dealership records for you."

"I mean it when I say this land's cursed."

Guy relaxed in the platform rocker next to the old man's woodstove, coffee mug in hand. Gregory Cordova was having difficulty getting around to the subject of the murders, and Guy was content to let him ramble. Context, after all, was important.

"My grandparents had eight children. Four of them died in an influenza epidemic. My father had run-ins with the rumrunners who trespassed on the land during Prohibition. They poisoned his well and shot his sheep. My two boys didn't want anything to do with the place. They bought a fishing boat and were drowned in a storm. My wife went crazy and killed herself. The daughters-in-law took my grandchildren and moved away. Now they're scattered all over the map, my great-grandchildren too. Three years ago a trespasser who was camping up by the turnout didn't put out his fire. Those burned-out trees you see are the result of it. If the Department of Forestry fire brigade hadn't responded fast, the flames would've jumped the highway and spread all the way up to the ridge."

"You and your family have had a long run of bad luck."

"Don't take me wrong. I don't feel sorry for myself. Never did. You take what you're handed and make do."

"That may be your philosophy, but from what you told me, the people around here didn't make do after the murders."

"No, sir, they did not. There was a lot of hysteria at first, but then they put a lid on it, screwed it down tight. Initial reaction was shock. So many dead, and there had to have been more than one killer. Folks wanted to blame the victims. Said they brought it on themselves. After all, they were outsiders, rich outsiders by our standards, and there was evidence one of them had been manufacturing drugs. A logical assumption, given the circumstances. But even so, laying blame was hard to do, given that two of them were little children. And when you saw pictures of Oriana Wynne, the six-year-old that survived . . . well, you couldn't help but feel."

"The little girl was hiding, never saw the killers?"

"Right. She said her mother heard shots down the

canyon and sent her and her brother away from the house. He wasn't so lucky. Anyway, everybody figured some drug-dealing strangers would be arrested soon, but when a month went by and nothing happened, folks started to look at each other and wonder. Tempers got short, words got exchanged in public and private, people started arming themselves against their neighbors. That winter was bad. Always are—cabin fever—but it was about the worst. When spring came, they were all ready to forget the murders ever happened. Only forgetting a thing like that takes a hell of a lot of work."

"Any idea why the case was never solved?"

Gregory Cordova shrugged. "Was a big case, got nationwide publicity. Everybody wanted a piece of the pie—sheriff's department, highway patrol, the feds. One hand didn't know what the other was doing. Evidence got tampered with or lost. A lot of the blame got unfairly heaped on the officer who answered the radio call and found the first bodies."

Guy felt the familiar excited prickle travel up his spine. "Who was that?"

"Sheriff's deputy. Woman. Name of Rhoda Swift."

Thirteen years ago. Before.

Thirteen years ago. After.

"You say 'unfairly.' Why?"

"Rho Swift is a fine woman. She's turned into a good officer. But back then she was new to the department, had only been working there three weeks. Then she walked into an ungodly mess. One of the little boys, Heath Wynne, died in her arms. It's no wonder she made mistakes."

"You said there was a radio call?"

"Yes. Neighbor woman reported hearing shots fired. That's not unusual here. But the woman heard what sounded like semiautomatic weapons and people screaming."

"This neighbor—who was that?"

"Virge Scurlock. She and her husband, Will, own the adjoining acreage. Big tract, and the house is a long ways from the canyon. Sounds up there get muted or distorted. That's why Virge didn't call it in until it was too late."

Guy pictured the couple in the bar: the tense-faced redhead and her solicitous husband. "This Will Scurlock, what does he do for a living?"

"Contractor. Decks, woodworking, that sort of thing."

"Does his wife have red hair?"

"So you've seen them. Virge used to be a beauty, but in past years she's taken up eating in a real serious way. Not that you can blame her, having to live next to that canyon. It's been left exactly like it was the night of the murders, and now it's falling to ruins."

"The property hasn't been sold in all these years?"

"Who'd want it? Besides, Susan Wynne's family back east—people name of Harrison, who took her little girl to raise—don't want to sell."

Harrison, Guy thought. Maybe those years off from writing had taken their toll after all. He hadn't made the connection between Susan Wynne's birth name and that of the man who had interested him in this project. Susan was probably Dunbar Harrison's younger sister. And, come to think of it, hadn't someone mentioned an orphaned niece going to live with Dun after old Mrs. Harrison died? Now Guy better understood the haunted quality he'd sensed in the man, as well as his anguish when he thought Guy was turning down his idea.

He asked, "Why don't the Harrisons want to sell?"

"What I heard was that Susan Wynne's mother wanted the property left just like it was as a monument. As a kind of reproach to the folks that live here, too. Don't know what comfort that could've given her, but people take their solace in strange ways. Anyway, until she died last year it just sat there with a local security patrol guarding it. After her death, whoever inherited stopped paying on the contract, didn't respond to the company's inquiries."

"But the taxes are current?"

"Maybe. Or maybe they've decided to let it go to the county. I hear the family's rich. Rich people can afford to toss away what makes them uncomfortable."

Or to send an unsuspecting journalist to rip open the town's old wounds, find answers for them. But had Dun been so foolish as to think he wouldn't find out his motives? Or had he assumed that by then Guy would be so fascinated with the story that he'd fail to take offense?

If so, he'd been right on the second point.

"This deputy," he said, "Rhoda Swift. How'd she cope with being blamed?"

"Bad, at first. She was born and raised in Signal Port, daughter of a deputy herself. Being blamed showed her how a town can turn on its own. She got drunk and stayed drunk for a few years. Would've lost her job, but the station commander cut her a lot of slack. He was there that night too. Her husband left her, but maybe that was good, 'cause afterwards she shaped up. Didn't try to run away, either, just settled down to being the best deputy we got. I'll tell you, Rho Swift's a tough one. Good one, too."

Yes, Guy thought, his instincts told him the same.

"One more thing, Mr. Cordova," he said. "Will you direct me to Cascada Canyon?"

Rho sat with her feet propped on the desk, leafing through an old issue of *Field & Stream* without really seeing it. An hour had passed, and Mercedes' emergency operator had yet to get back to her with information on the abandoned car. The door opened, slammed shut. She looked up. Wayne, red-faced and scowling.

"Dammit, Rho," he said, "Grossman may have tried to put a lid on the murder, but word's all over town. The EMTs stopped in for coffee at the Oceanside earlier, and after they got through talking, we might as well've posted it on the Internet."

She dropped the magazine, lowered her feet to the floor. Now they had a potentially bad situation on their hands. Besides igniting the town's collective paranoia, the nature of the crime might make people who had seen the woman on Friday reluctant to come forward. "What's the reaction so far?"

"About what you'd expect. Folks're grim, and a lot of the women're scared. I've canvassed half the town and only found two witnesses who'll admit to seeing our victim at the turnout."

"There must be dozens."

"I know that, and I'll keep canvassing till they own up." Wayne paused, frowning. "People're acting strange, and here's one example: When I stopped in at the hotel, Virge Scurlock was in the bar watching the 'Niners game."

"What's strange about that?"

"She's not a sports fan. Will usually comes down by himself to catch the games on the big screen, but today he had an appointment with a client up at Deer Harbor. Virge told the waitress—that Becca Campos—that he'd dropped her at the supermarket, but she decided to stop in for a drink before she did her shopping."

"So?"

"She isn't much of a drinker, but today she was getting shitfaced on stingers."

"When was this?"

"Around one thirty, and she was well on her way. Becca said she came in about noon."

"You're right—it is strange. You talk with her?"

"Yeah, and she wasn't making much sense, but I did find out that she'd already heard about the murder." Wayne paused, thoughtful. "You know, a couple of years ago Will and I got drunk together. Right after Janie threw me out for those three months. He was supposed to be consoling me, but I ended up consoling him. He told me that every year since the canyon murders, Virge has gotten more and more squirrelly."

"I've heard the same."

"Well, she's squirrelly as hell today, and I think maybe we should—"

The phone rang. Rho said to Valerie, "I'll get it."

Mercedes, with the current address and phone number of the car's owner, one Richard Bartlow.

"I've turned up something out here that's raised an interesting issue," Guy said over the phone to his research assistant, Aaron Silber, "and I need to check a fact with you. It's probably in the material you gave me, but I don't have time to plow through it right now. Who's paying the taxes on the Cascada Canyon property?"

Silence, except for the clicking of Aaron's keyboard. Guy pictured him: wiry-haired, lean-faced, hungry eyes staring at the screen through tinted glasses, a smile on his thin lips. Nothing had pleased Aaron more than Guy's call saying he was about to begin another book. He'd willingly set aside two potential clients—"Political analysis, advertising demographics. Who needs that?"—in order to return to Guy's employ.

"Damn!"

Guy held the receiver away from his ear. "What?"

"I didn't run a check on ownership. Major oversight. Sorry, Guy."

"No harm done. But do it now. My source here thinks Dunbar Harrison's family may still own it."

"Harrison? Fellow who talked you into the project?"

"One and the same. I think his sister was one of the victims, and he wants me to play detective."

"Kind of bogus of him not to tell you."

"Well, it's a complicated situation."

"You don't have to tell me that. I put together those files." More silence except for the keys tapping. "Son of a bitch! The database I use doesn't cover that area!"

Again Guy distanced the receiver from his ear as he looked at his watch. After two. He'd stopped for an early lunch at the bar-and-grill called Oceanside on his way back to the motel, and the conversations he'd overheard had prompted him to eavesdrop in a number of other establishments. The atmosphere in town was edgy and could verge on the dangerous after nightfall. If he was to visit Cascada Canyon and still be back to observe the public reaction to what was widely rumored to be a rape-and-murder, he'd better be going.

"Listen," he said to Aaron, "can you get me the information by tonight?"

"Of course I can." His assistant sounded a shade prickly. He didn't like Guy to imply that anything was beyond his capabilities, and his professional pride had been hurt by his glaring oversight.

"Then do that, and I'll call you later."

"I can leave a message on your voice mail—"

"The Sea Stacks isn't the Hyatt Regency, Aaron. They don't *have* voice mail, and I don't want the clerk taking that kind of message. Besides, I may have questions. I'll call you."

"I don't own the Mercedes anymore," Richard Bartlow of Santa Barbara said. "I gave it to my son when he went off to graduate school in Nevada."

Now we're getting someplace, Rho thought. It had taken her over an hour to reach the car's registered owner. "When was this, sir?"

"Last summer, shortly before he enrolled at UNLV."

"That's Las Vegas?"

"Yes."

"May I have your son's address and phone number?"

"Don't tell me he forgot to register it in his own name! He was supposed to take care of that immediately."

"Apparently he neglected to do so. If you would—"

"That's Sean. You give a kid a beautiful classic car, you'd think he could at least—"

Rho noted the name. "Sean's phone number, sir?"

"What's this about, anyway?"

She stifled an impatient sigh. "The car was abandoned on Highway One outside of Signal Port and has been impounded."

"That can't be. I spoke with Sean on Friday, and he said he had no weekend plans other than studying for an exam."

"Perhaps he loaned the car to a friend."

"He knows better than to do that. But when did any of my children ever follow their better instincts?" Bartlow gave her a number in the 702 area code and added, "When you speak with Sean, please tell him he owes his father an explanation."

Guy made a U-turn and pulled the car onto the shoulder some two hundred yards south of the dirt road leading into Cascada Canyon. This was a lonely stretch of highway above the turnout at what Gregory Cordova had told him was called Point Deception, near the upper boundary of the old man's property. The land was thickly forested to either side of the pavement, and although the sky had cleared that morning, it now was overcast. When he got out of the car he felt the full blast of a chill offshore wind and turned up the collar of his down jacket before he began walking along the shoulder. Cars and trucks sped past, their occupants paying him little attention.

The road into the canyon was more of a dirt track like Gregory Cordova's driveway, weeds and thistle plants growing so high on the center hump that Guy could tell no vehicle had passed over it in years. Massive wooden pillars carved like totem poles stood to either side of the entrance, but the gates had fallen off and lay rotting on the ground. A NO TRESPASSING sign on one of the pillars was pitted with rust.

He paused for a moment till he heard no traffic approaching from either direction, then stepped onto the property. Beyond the fence lay a gently sloping meadow covered by pines and high grass. It was even chillier under the trees and the wind came gusting from behind him, whistling as it penetrated the canyon ahead. He walked slowly to one side of the driveway, to avoid the prickly thistles. After about twenty yards the land rose steeply on his right, overgrown and topped by what he thought was a redwood grove. To his left he saw an old car tucked under an overhanging pine tree. A white Buick sedan blanketed in at least a foot of needles. He went over, squatted, and cleared the license plate. The last, barely readable registration sticker was for 1987.

He straightened and circled the car, checking out the rotted interior through the broken side window and trying the trunk, which opened with a creak. Its only contents were some rags and a spare tire. Guy shut the lid and took out a point-and-shoot camera loaded with extra-fast film, then moved around the car, snapping various shots. On this second pass his foot banged against something, hard enough to smart. He looked down and saw a manhole cover, scanned the surrounding ground and located the hole, deep in the needles. A metal drum half full of liquid was buried there. Motor oil or other hazardous waste which a do-it-yourself mechanic had disposed of. Guy replaced the lid and photographed it.

The driveway continued to curve uphill, more steeply under tall trees. A blue jay set up a racket in one of them, and he looked up. A cable was tangled in the branches and hung down. Utility line, its end raggedly broken or cut. Beyond the tree the line was still strung parallel to the driveway. Guy recorded it on film.

Now he could make out a dark, boxy shape through the vegetation, and as he moved closer he saw it was a house. A plain, shingled rectangle with a shadowy front porch crowded with indistinguishable objects. He veered off the drive, pushed through waist-high grass, and stopped at the bottom of its steps. Wicker outdoor furniture, grayed and tattered by the elements. Wooden flower boxes, also gray, containing dead weeds. After taking several more photographs, he went up on the porch, rubbed grime from a window, and tried to peer inside. All he saw was the yellowed back of a shade. The screen door had been ripped from it hinges and leaned against the wall. Guy turned the inner knob and let the door swing open into shadow. Odors rushed out at him: musty, stale. This, he knew from Aaron's summary, was the house where the first of the victims, the Blakeley family, had been found.

He took a small, nearly flat square of plastic from his pocket and pressed its center. It emitted a bright, laser-like beam, the latest in featherweight but powerful flashlights. Moving it around, he saw cobwebs and spiders' nests, great clouds that shifted in the sudden draft and let drop husks of dead insects. Dark curtains, in tatters where rats had gotten at them. The hulking outline of a woodstove. He stepped inside, snapped the window shade up, and filtered light rushed into the small room.

It contained a scene of wild disorder: overturned chairs and lamps and end tables; a bookcase lying on its side, volumes spilling off the shelves; a smashed television set. Three fading white outlines were stenciled on the plank floor, one of them pathetically small. He shone his light downward, saw rodent droppings and dark stains that disappeared into the cracks between the boards. Shone the light upward and saw the blood-spatter patterns on the walls.

Jesus, why hadn't someone honored his dead by having this cleaned up? Or, better yet, razed?

He'd moved to the center of the room now, and was taking in small, more ordinary, but no less gut-wrenching details: a vodka bottle and two glasses on the coffee table; a paperback lying facedown and broken-spined on the rat-gnawed couch; knitting needles and a half-finished garment protruding from a basket; two carelessly discarded sandals; a child-size pair of blue tennis shoes.

The crime scene appeared to be exactly as it was thirteen years before, but Guy sensed a more recent presence. He shone the light on the floor again and spotted tracks in the dust that looked as if they'd been made by a pair of athletic shoes. They crisscrossed the room and entered what he now discovered to be two bedrooms, a bath, and a kitchen.

A curiosity seeker? Someone with a taste for the macabre? Probably. When? Not recently, but perhaps within the past year.

He went back to the main room and stood in its center. Soon he felt a sensation of the blood running slower in his veins. Time both shrank and telescoped: He was here at this very minute; he was here on the night of the murders; he was caught in between, as the years went by and nothing changed. Never had he felt so affected and vulnerable at a crime scene, and while it unnerved him, he decided to go wherever his emotions would take him.

He closed his eyes to the terrible sights and opened his other senses.

Hear: silence. Feel: cold. Smell: dry rot and the taint of old fires. Taste: dust.

Try again.

Hear: wind whistling. Feel: draft through leaky window frame. Smell: ashes stirred by downdraft in woodstove. Taste: ashes and dust.

Go deeper.

Hear: cries, faint. Feel: fear. Smell: fear. Taste: fear.

Now you're getting it. Once again.

Hear: echoes of gunshots.

Feel: panic.

Smell: blood.

Taste: my own blood where I've bitten my lip.

He opened his eyes, moved swiftly toward the door, and stepped out on the porch, where he sucked in deep breaths of clean air. He'd been in the house longer than he realized, and dusk had fallen. Nothing moved there in the shadows, nothing made a sound except the wind whistling deep into the canyon. He wanted to follow it, visit the other scenes, but that was impractical and, besides, he'd always had the sense to know his own limits. Tomorrow he'd return, but for now he'd gotten far more than he came for.

The fog ushered in the night, wiped out all traces of the fine weather. Rho switched on the cruiser's headlights, and their beams hit a solid wall of white boiling up from Schooner Cove. Then, as the road curved inland, the fog was gone and every striation in the bark of the tree trunks stood out in sharp relief. She'd lived on this north coast her entire life, yet the patterns of the fog still fascinated her. Why, for instance, should Schooner Cove draw it in so heavily, while Pelican Cove did not? Why, even when the rest of the shoreline was socked in, were the coves north of Deer Harbor clear, almost tropical? She knew the scientific answers, of course, but she liked to think there were less understandable forces at work as well.

Why did a young woman have to die?

The question came from nowhere, so strident that she felt as if someone else had asked it out loud. She wanted to ignore it, concentrate on the mundane aspects of her patrol. But there was no ignoring it on what promised to be a dark, uneasy night.

The radio calls she'd been listening to described the local population's state of mind: nervous reports of prowlers and the discharge of firearms; two domestic disturbances; a 911 disconnect; two D&Ds; one DUI. A heavy volume of calls for any given time period, and particularly for Sunday. The citizens of Signal Port and environs were acting out their paranoia.

Rho turned up the volume on her radio. She licked dry lips, wished she'd remembered to fill her water bottle. Then she thought, Stop kidding yourself. What you really want is a drink.

She wouldn't dream of drinking while on duty, of course. Even in her worst days she'd managed to abstain long enough to work her shift sober. Now when the craving came over her, she could usually ignore it and satisfy it later with a glass of wine or beer in good company. But tonight it demanded full attention, and she knew if she later gave in to it, she wouldn't stop with one drink, and she'd take that one and the others that followed while alone.

She tried to concentrate on how she would handle Sean Bartlow, the current owner of the Mercedes, when she reached him at his number in Las Vegas. She tried to think of ways the department could calm and reassure the area's troubled populace. But the craving swelled, the prospect of a drink floating in her consciousness like a cloud that she could use to blot out everything, past and present.

When he reached the tree where the downed utility wire was tangled, Guy stopped and listened. For half a minute he'd been aware of sounds coming from the slope that led up to the redwood grove. Now he heard nothing but the wind. He went on toward the highway, hands deep in his jacket pockets.

More sounds: crackling in the underbrush, then footsteps on the driveway behind him. He glanced back, but could see no one in the gloom. He rounded the curve where the old sedan crouched under its shroud of needles and moved to one side. The footsteps came on, and a tall figure appeared. Six foot four, maybe five, and slender. A man wearing a peaked cap.

Guy waited till the man was abreast of him, then stepped forward and shone his flashlight on his face. "Hold it right there." The air of authority in his voice— he might've hated shore patrol duty, but he'd acquired certain assets during his tour—brought his pursuer up short.

"Jesus, man, you scared me!" the stranger exclaimed.

Guy relaxed and took inventory of him: hiker's clothing, complete with small backpack and knobby walking stick; neatly trimmed beard, dark brown shot with gray; small nose, slightly skewed as if it had been broken and not set properly; dark deepset eyes; old scar over right brow; peaked wool cap covering the hair; startled look turning to a scowl.

"You're trespassing, man," his pursuer added.

Guy was prepared for such a challenge. "No, *you're* trespassing."

"Huh?"

"That's right."

The scowl melted into bewilderment. "Who the hell're you?"

"Name's Guy Newberry. I was sent out from New York by the owners to check on the property." And in a way, he had been.

"What owners?"

"People name of Harrison. Now, who are you?"

"Clay Lawrence. I live on the other side of the hill." He motioned toward the grove.

"I thought people name of Scurlock own that land."

"They do. I'm their tenant, rent a little cabin from them."

"And what're you doing over here?"

Clay Lawrence shrugged. "I like to watch night come on from the redwoods. Technically that grove's part of this property, but there's nobody here to care. I saw you walking along the drive and . . . Well, you must know what happened here."

"That was thirteen years ago."

"Yeah, but in this canyon it feels like it was yesterday. Have you looked around?"

"Some."

"Weird, isn't it? Creepy. Nobody ever comes here, not even kids looking for a place to drink or screw."

Guy thought of the footprints in the dust at the Blakeley house. "You sure of that?"

"Reasonably. Folks in town call it an evil place, when they mention it at all."

"What about you?"

"Do I think it's evil? As much as a place can be, I guess."

"No, I mean, do you come here often? Have you looked around?"

"I did when I first moved into the cabin, back before I knew about those murders. But never again. No way."

"You go inside any of the buildings?"

"Uh-uh. That's criminal trespass."

"But you're trespassing on the land now."

Lawrence shifted from foot to foot. "It doesn't seem like it. I mean, land's land. Houses, that's personal."

"So why'd you follow me?"

"I don't know, I just did. After what happened today . . . You know we had another murder?"

"The girl they fished out of Lantern Cove? Yes. Don't tell me you thought I was the killer, hiding out where nobody ever goes?"

"Look, man, I didn't think. It just seemed like the thing to do. And if you find *my* behavior weird, you oughta take a look at what's going on in town."

"What's happening there?"

"According to my girlfriend, Signal Port's about to go nuts. She's a waitress at the hotel, so she sees it all."

"Civil unrest?"

"Could happen. This is a hard-drinking community, Mr. Newberry. A lot of the people're hot-tempered because the local economy sucks. They use their fists to settle arguments, usually in the parking lots of the bars. And a lot of the pickups in those lots have gun racks. Draw your own conclusions."

"I'd say the town's in for a rough night."

"Yeah, and I'll tell you what—this canyon's creepy, but at least it's not dangerous. No matter *what* walks here at night, it's a lot more benign than the folks in town."

"Yeah, that's my car," Sean Bartlow said. "Where'd you say it is?"

Rho felt her heartbeat accelerate. She warned herself against becoming impatient with him. "Soledad County. It was abandoned on Highway One south of Signal Port."

"The bitch! I told her to take good care of it."

"Who, Mr. Bartlow?"

". . . Friend of mine. I loaned it to her."

"And her name is?"

"Why d'you need to know?"

"We're trying to locate the driver on an unrelated matter."

"What matter? What'd she do?"

"Please, Mr. Bartlow, her name?"

". . . Chrys."

"The full name, please."

"I don't know her last name. She's just somebody I met at one of the clubs on the Strip."

You're lying, Rho thought. "You loaned your car to someone whose full name you don't know?"

"Right."

"Did she tell you where she was going?"

"Only that she . . . had to visit her sick mother."

Lie number two. "I see. Is this your license-plate number?" She gave that of the stolen tags on the Mercedes.

"No." He rattled off the number of the plates that belonged on the car. "You've got the wrong person. That's not my car after all."

"It's yours. The VIN matches. But someone's switched the plates for stolen ones—"

"Oh my God!"

"Mr. Bartlow, we need your friend's full name. If you don't cooperate you could be charged with obstruction, maybe even as an accessory to a felony."

"Felony! Yeah, okay then. Her last name's Ackerman. Chrystal Ackerman. C-h-r-y-s-t-a-l."

"And you know her from where?"

"Is this gonna get back to my father? I mean, technically he still owns the car."

"There'll be no need for that, providing you cooperate fully."

Silence, except for Sean Bartlow's harsh breathing. "Okay," he said, "I didn't meet her at a club. Chrys is a sex worker. Phone sex. I've been calling her for about a year, and a few months ago I talked her into coming to my place. She's been coming ever since, and last weekend she asked to borrow the car because hers isn't reliable enough for a long trip."

"A trip to northern California?"

"Yeah."

"But not to visit her sick mother."

". . . No. She said she had a business deal going, had to meet somebody up there to finalize it. She told me she'd cut me in if I let her use the Mercedes. I need the money. My father's a tightwad."

"All right, Mr. Bartlow, do you have an address and phone number for Ms. Ackerman?"

"I don't know where she lives, but I have the number of her private phone." He recited it.

"Thank you. Only a few more questions. Will you describe her, please?"

"She's about five-five, long straight blonde hair, gray eyes, great body, butterfly tattoo over her right nipple."

"Her age?"

"She said nineteen."

"Anything else about her that you recall?"

"We talked fantasy, not reality."

"Think, Mr. Bartlow."

"Good Christ, what am I supposed to remember? She's nothing but a whore!"

Nothing but a whore. Nothing but a woman with a broken-down car. Nothing but a floater.

But now Ms. Nothing had a name: Chrystal Ackerman.

Chrystal: Before

Friday, October 6
11:19 A.M.

There it is, the place Jude calls my legacy.

Looks awful run-down, with those gates laying on the ground and monster weeds growing in the driveway. Funny, we must've driven through them dozens of times, but none of it looks familiar.

Go north, Jude said, park at the wide place by the speed-limit sign. Follow the little stream uphill to the wellhouse. Cross the footbridge, and you're there. Get in and out quick.

But Jesus, what if the stream's dried up or the wellhouse and the footbridge aren't there anymore? I don't remember them either.

Big blank, that whole year, even if I was six years old. Like a hole in my memory. Good thing too. What Jude told me is too awful, too depressing. I got enough bad memories without carrying that one around with me.

There's the wide place. Pull in, get out, lock the car. Stream's supposed to flow under the highway through a culvert. Yeah, I see it. Running downhill fast—clear, clean. There's nothing like that in the desert. Or trees like these. And the air here—it almost hurts to breathe it.

Okay, I'm following the stream, but I don't see no wellhouse. Maybe— Wait, there it is. Ancient shed with a big wooden tank that looks like a grungy hot tub. Newer cinderblock tank next to it, covered with moss. Me and Eric and Heath and Oriana, we—

Oh!

We used to play in the wellhouse. Climbed into that slimy tub and pretended we were at some Hollywood party. Eric's idea. His dad was gonna be a hotshit screenwriter as soon as he got something written. Everybody's folks were gonna do something important, get famous. Even Jude and Leo. Well, we know how that turned out.

Eric, Heath, Oriana. I remember them now. They've been dead longer than they were alive.

No, not Oriana. She survived. She was the lucky one. Well, maybe not so lucky. She was the *only* one. . . .

Sunday, October 8
Evening

You want to tell me what happened here, Mr. Jacoby?"

Rho sat facing one of the proprietors of the Pelican Cove Bed & Breakfast in the inn's high-ceilinged parlor. Kevin Jacoby was a slender, handsome man in his thirties, but at the moment his features were twisted in shame. Around them lay a scene of wreckage, and Jacoby's partner, Brandon Fuller, was in the kitchen being treated by EMTs from the Life Support District for a broken arm and other less serious injuries.

Jacoby glanced toward the hallway. "Is he going to be . . . ?"

"All right? Yes. And he doesn't want to press charges against you, but I still need to hear in your own words what happened."

Jacoby expelled his breath noisily. "God, I've never

done anything like that in my life. I just snapped. I feel terrible about it."

"I'm sure you do. What precipitated the snapping?"

"Well, we'd been drinking." He motioned at a silver cocktail shaker that lay on the oriental carpet, leaking liquid and ice. "But that wasn't really the cause of it."

"What was?"

"The guests leaving. They were the last guests we had booked through the end of the year, and they were supposed to stay till Wednesday. I could tell they didn't really like it here, and this morning they went to the hotel for brunch and heard about that murder. Came back, packed, and left. Afterwards Brandon got quiet and moody. Tonight when I finally pressed him, he said he didn't think we were going to make it with the inn."

That didn't surprise Rho, but she asked, "You're not doing well?"

"Not at all. The place has great potential, and people stop here, but they don't stay long, and they don't come back. Tonight I told Brandon it's this town. There's not much to do here, and it's kind of . . . demoralized. That was when he let me in on the secret."

"What secret?" As if I don't know.

"About those murders years ago in Cascada Canyon. Apparently he's known about them for quite some time, but didn't bother to enlighten me."

"And his withholding knowledge was why you snapped?"

"Not exactly. I mean, I hated his keeping a secret from me, but I realized he did it so I wouldn't worry about the inn any more than I usually do. No, what made me explode was that he didn't find out about the murders before we sank our last dime into this place. You see, Brandon was responsible for the property search. He was supposed to check into anything that might have a negative impact on our investment. But he fell in love with the inn and went blindly ahead. Tonight he admitted it. And I just . . ." He motioned at the disorder around them.

Rho studied Kevin Jacoby. In the year and a half he'd lived in Signal Port she'd never seen him display anything but courteous and mild-mannered behavior. "Well, Mr. Jacoby," she said, "you and your partner are going to have to do some serious talking. Maybe make some hard decisions."

He nodded. "I feel awful about everything, including taking up your time when the sheriff's department should be doing everything they can to find out who murdered that poor woman."

If only we had adequate staff for an all-out effort, Rho thought. "We're working on it. We've put out an appeal, both by word of mouth and on the public-access station, for anyone who saw her yesterday afternoon at Point Deception turnout to contact us."

Jacoby's face grew thoughtful. "Point Deception. This woman, what did she look like?"

Rho described Chrystal Ackerman, and the Mercedes.

"Oh my God! Brandon and I saw her twice. First at a little before three when we were going down to the lumber yard in Westhaven, and again on the way back at quarter to five."

"You're sure of those times?"

"Reasonably. We left here about two thirty, and I looked at my watch on the drive home." A stricken expression spread over Jacoby's face. "Oh God, what did I do? Brandon wanted to stop to help her, but I said we didn't have time, we had to get back to pay Becca, the woman who cleans for us, before she left for her waitressing shift at the hotel. If I'd been less concerned with the damned inn and more concerned with helping somebody in trouble, that woman would be alive tonight!"

How many times, Rho wondered, would she hear the same regret from others?

As Guy shut the door of his motel room and started across the parking lot, a bottle smashed on the nearby pavement and a car loaded with teenagers sped south on the highway, burning rubber. A dozen beer-swilling young people sat on the tailgates of their pickups under the lighted sign of the supermarket. Rap and rock competed from two of the trucks' radios. The kids yelled at friends in passing vehicles, made rude comments to shoppers pushing their carts. One old woman gave them a wide berth, the neon glare highlighting her apprehensive face.

Small-town kids, Guy thought. Keyed up by the edgy atmosphere but too young to fully understand what had triggered it. For them the mass murder in the canyon was simply part of the local folklore, and this new murder an excuse to engage in antisocial behavior. They were just getting off on the breakdown of order, like teenagers in any town where there were few amusements.

"Assholes," a man's voice said.

Guy turned to face Hugh Dawson, proprietor of the Sea Stacks. "Those kids?"

"Who the hell else. They're laughing now, but they won't be in a few minutes. I just called the sheriff."

Dawson was a balding, pinch-faced man who wore a perpetually sour expression. Probably had never done anything wild in his life, or if he had, he was determined no one else should share the experience. Guy said, "I think the sheriff's department has more important things on its hands than a bunch of rowdy kids."

"Mister, they're underage and drinking in public."

"But not really harming anyone."

Dawson's narrowed eyes sized Guy up, and then he nodded wisely. "Of course, you're from New York City. What goes on there, those kids must look like model citizens to you."

"Hardly. But—" A cruiser was pulling into the parking lot. It stopped near the kids, and Deputy Wayne Gilardi got out.

Guy watched with interest as he motioned to one of the boys, clamped a hand on his shoulder as he spoke to him. The kid said something smart, judging from the look on his face, and Gilardi shook him, raising his voice. The other teens had tensed at the arrival of the law. Now they were scrambling for their vehicles and starting engines. As Gilardi slammed the boy against his cruiser and wrenched back his arms to cuff him, the others pulled onto the highway in a spray of gravel.

"Damn," Dawson said, watching Gilardi force the boy into the backseat of his cruiser, "he only arrested one of them. Scared the shit outta the rest, though. Wayne's tough, and they know it."

"In what ways is he tough?"

Dawson frowned. "Mister, you sure do ask a lot of questions about things that don't really concern you."

And you, like your fellow townspeople, sure don't answer them. "The reason I ask about Deputy Gilardi is that I had a run-in with him in the hotel bar last night."

"Yeah, I heard about that. Over his slut sister and her slope boyfriend. And then you had drinks and dinner with the lovely Rhoda Swift. How'd you manage that?"

"I asked her."

"And she accepted. Amazing. There're any number of men in this town who'd like to get next to that nice ass of hers, but she keeps them at arm's length. How'd you rate?"

"Maybe because I'm interested in more than her ass."

"Guess so. She know what you want is the inside dope on the Cascada Canyon murders?"

Guy raised an eyebrow.

"Oh yeah," the motel owner said. "I know why you're here. Maid got curious about your files when she did up the room this afternoon, took a good look at them. Then I took a look. We don't much care for nosy reporters here. You better have yourself packed by checkout time tomorrow."

"I've reserved the room for two weeks—"

"Sorry about that. Plumbing's about to go on the fritz. And we're full up."

Guy motioned at the lighted Vacancy sign.

"So I forgot to turn on the No."

"Uh-huh." He nodded, scanning the parking lot, empty except for two cars, including his own rental, and a press van from a Santa Carla TV station.

Dawson grinned, enjoying himself. "Checkout's at eleven. I'll have your bill ready." He turned and walked back toward the office.

Guy watched the traffic move by, hands deep in his

pockets. Being evicted from his motel room was an inconvenience, but there was always Pelican Cove Bed & Breakfast. And if its owner was equally inhospitable, he'd make do somehow. He'd worked before under far worse conditions and come out intact.

Yes, he thought bitterly, guilt and loss wrenching in his gut, he'd come out intact. And right there lay his problem.

He'd come out intact, but Diana hadn't.

The haze of light from Deer Harbor vanished in the rearview mirror as Rho entered the hairpin turn by the campground north of the village. The inside of the cruiser was fogged, so she lowered her side window; the bark of seals on the offshore rocks mingled with the familiar mutter of the radio. Lots of calls during the past hour, and all time off for deputies had been canceled. Word of the rape-and-murder had spread up and down the Soledad Coast; a visible sheriff's department presence was the first step in reassuring the uneasy populace.

Her headlights moved over tree trunks, over the gated fences of the expensive properties that lined this dark stretch of highway. Most were second homes of affluent people from the San Francisco Bay Area and beyond— used only a few times a year by their owners and frequently rented out by various local realties. Rho couldn't imagine allowing strangers to occupy her precious space, use her things, and sleep in her bed, but she supposed if she were carrying a huge mortgage on pricey oceanfront property she wouldn't be so fastidious. As it was, her little house on the ridge ate up a disproportionate chunk of her paycheck.

After she'd driven for a few minutes it grew cold in the cruiser and she raised the window. The radio continued its drone, and the white lines of the highway threatened to hypnotize her. California Highway 1, which ran unbroken from the state's northernmost town, Crescent City, to the Mexican border.

The citizens of Soledad County had a peculiar relationship to Highway 1, she reflected, and in a way it was justified. The two-lane strip of pavement was dangerous: Vehicles spun out of control on its curves and crashed over the cliffs; pedestrians who crossed on the wrong stretch were frequently picked off by speeders and logging trucks; rock- and mudslides, thick fog, blinding rain—all did great damage. But the highway was also the artery that connected them and allowed the county's lifeblood to flow from isolated ranch to small town, from primitive forest to tiny hamlet. In that way it also nurtured. When a mother warned her child, "Don't you dare cross that highway," or a seasoned trucker announced, "No way I'm driving that highway in this weather," their voices held a curious combination of awe and affection.

The radio nudged her consciousness with her car number, and she keyed the mike.

"What's your location?" the dispatcher asked.

"North of Deer Harbor, passing Mulzini Acre."

"Proceed to the Lindsay house and see the man about a ten-six-five."

Missing person. "Ten-four."

Interesting. The Lindsays were second-home people. Alan was a powerful sports attorney in San Francisco, and his wife, Samantha, had a successful jewelry-designing firm. The local grapevine said that Samantha made frequent trips to the oceanfront estate without her husband, during which she picked up men at bars from Calvert's Landing to Westhaven, and apparently she wasn't above such behavior when Alan was in residence. Will Scurlock, who was designing an elaborate system of decking on the Lindsay property, had told Rho that things seemed a bit strained there recently. And she herself had seen Samantha leaving the hotel bar last night with a guitarist and singer who had a long-running gig at Tai Haruru. If Samantha was missing, Rho would have to exercise extreme tact in interviewing her husband.

The gates to the estate appeared on the left: large and ostentatious, set into a high stone wall. Rho turned in, spoke into the intercom; a man's voice answered and after she identified herself, the gates swung open. She drove across a flat, unlandscaped bluff toward a sprawling cedar-shingled house where lights shone in every window. All that space for two people who didn't even live there full-time.

The front door opened as she parked, and a man came out, shielding his eyes against the headlights' glare. Rho recognized Alan Lindsay's wavy dark brown hair and cleft chin. He wore jeans and an Irish-knit sweater; his body was in as fit a condition as most of the athletes he represented. As she walked toward him she saw that his chiseled features were warped by anxiety.

"Thank you for getting here so quickly," he said. Without giving her the chance to reply, he ushered her into a foyer that was more expensively furnished than her own living room. "This way," he added, moving along a hall. It ended in a greatroom that was larger than her entire house, with a massive stone fireplace and a wall of glass facing the sea. At Lindsay's urging she took a white leather chair, perching on its edge.

Before she could speak, Lindsay said, "My wife, Samantha, is missing. She's been gone since around four this afternoon."

Rho noted the time: nine forty.

Lindsay added, "I know it doesn't seem long enough to be concerned, but given this rape-and-murder—"

"You're right to be concerned. Your wife left here at four?"

"Yes. She was going to the organic market in Westhaven. I called there and one of the checkers confirmed she'd been in and done her shopping."

"Perhaps she had other errands? Or ran into a friend? Stopped for a drink?"

Something flickered in Lindsay's eyes, vanished as quickly as it had appeared. "Samantha told me she was coming straight home. She doesn't have any friends up here, and I've already called . . . her usual haunts. No one's seen her."

"These usual haunts—what are they?"

Lindsay had been pacing in front of the glass wall. Now he glanced at his reflected image, looked away as if he didn't like what he saw, and sat down on the sofa. "Restaurants, shops—you know."

"Can you provide me a list of where you called?"

"Try the phone book," he snapped. Then he blinked, hearing what he'd said. "Ah, hell. What's the use? I'm sure you know about Samantha, Deputy Swift. The entire Soledad Coast knows about her. She's beautiful, rich, talented, and a mistress of indiscretion."

"Meaning?"

"Do I need to spell it out for you? The usual haunts I called were bars and the homes of men she's slept with—those I know about, that is."

Rho looked away from his pained face and studied the notebook she had balanced on her knee. "I understand, but I'll still need that list. Tell me: When the two of you are staying here together, does she customarily go off by herself?"

"Not frequently, but she's been known to."

"Yet you've never reported her missing before?"

"No."

When Rho looked up at Lindsay he'd composed himself. In fact, his face was masklike. She asked, "Is there something different about tonight—besides the murder—that leads you to believe your wife might be in danger?"

"Yes." He licked dry lips, hesitated. "God, I hate going into private things like this."

"If at all possible, we'll keep what you say confidential. And remember, anything you tell me may help us locate Mrs. Lindsay."

He sighed, big shoulders rising and falling. "All right, then. I know what Samantha is, but I still love her. And in her way, she loves me. If she's not coming home, she always calls. Always. But tonight she hasn't. If she were off with . . . someone else of her own free will, she would've let me know by now. That's the way it works with us, especially at a time like this."

Guy sat at the hotel bar, his beer untouched, brooding over the events that had changed the course of his life. Guilt, strong and bitter tonight, assailed him.

Diana, he thought. If only I hadn't taken on that particular project. If only I hadn't persuaded you to help me. If only I'd used better judgment—

"Mr. Newberry?"

He started, swiveled toward the source of the voice. Lily Gilardi, dressed in black jeans and a heavy turtleneck sweater, her dark hair caught up in a ponytail. She registered surprise at the intensity of his look and took a step backward.

"I . . . um, I wanted to thank you," she said. "You prevented a real bad scene last night."

"Don't mention it. I gather your brother doesn't much care for your boyfriend."

"Wayne *hates* him. By the way, have you seen Alex? I was supposed to meet him, and he's nearly an hour late."

Guy shook his head and motioned at the empty stool beside him. "Let me buy you a drink while you wait."

"Why not?" She slipped onto the stool, caught the bartender's eye. He poured a glass of wine and set it in front of her. "Town's kind of crazy tonight," she commented. "Big fight going down in the parking lot at the Oceanside when I drove by. Sheriff's department's called in the CHP to help out."

"People are having a pretty extreme reaction to a stranger's murder."

"You wouldn't think it was if you lived here."

"No? Why not?"

She shrugged, making wet circles with her glass on the lacquered surface of the bar.

"What *is* it like to live here?"

"Terrible. You've got all these great towns on the coast—nice restaurants, shops, things to do, tourist bucks pouring in—and then there's Signal Port. Even quiet places like Oilville and Deer Harbor have *something* going for them. At least folks there aren't scared to death of their own neighbors."

"And here they are? Why?"

She flashed him a scornful look. "Come on, Mr. Newberry. Hugh Dawson over at the Sea Stacks has been telling anybody who'll listen about you being a reporter who's writing a book on the Cascada Canyon murders. If you want to know anything, ask me. But I'm warning you—I was just a kid when they happened, so you probably know more about them than I do. If those files Hugh claims you've got are as thick as he says."

So his cover was completely blown. Well, it had to happen sooner or later. And while it could cause problems, ultimately it would work to his advantage if he could develop contacts like Lily. Of course, he was going to be in big trouble with Rhoda Swift. . . .

"Mr. Newberry," Lily said, "if you knew something about a crime, something that might help the cops, would you go to them and tell them, even if it meant getting you and somebody you cared about in a lot of trouble?"

He studied her. She was looking down into her glass, a thick lock of hair that had escaped the ponytail screening her face. "That would depend on the crime. And the trouble."

"Like I said, a lot of trouble."

"I take it we're talking about the murder of that woman."

She nodded. "Normally I'd stay out of it, but she seemed like an okay person."

"You talked with her?"

"Me and Alex. At Point Deception. She asked us to call a couple of numbers for her, but Alex wouldn't let me. I feel really, really bad about that. And there's something else—"

"Hey, babe, what's this?"

Lily swiveled, her knees bumping Guy's stool. "Honey!"

Alex wore a beige down jacket with smears of mud across its front, and there was a dirty smudge on his high cheekbone. His gaze grazed Guy's face, suspicious, bordering on the hostile, and then shifted to Lily's. "I asked you, what's going on?"

"Mr. Newberry just bought me a drink, that's all. What happened to you?" She motioned at his jacket.

"Skidded off the road. Truck got stuck in the ditch, I had to push it out."

"Oh, poor baby!"

"So what were you and Mr. Newberry talking about?"

She flashed a warning look at Guy. "What it's like to live here."

"And you told him like paradise."

"Yeah, right."

Guy said, "May I buy you a drink, Mr. Ngo?" He pronounced the name as a Vietnamese would.

Alex's eyes flickered in surprise, but all he said was, "Thanks, but Lily and I've got things to do."

"But, honey, I thought we were having dinner—"

"Plans've changed. We'll take a rain check, Mr. Newberry." He pulled Lily off the stool and propelled her toward the door, a hand on either of her shoulders.

Guy watched them go, thinking that Lily was destined to make bad choices and be pushed around by the men in her life, even the ones who were concerned for her welfare. And Alex Ngo was the kind who could swiftly scent that quality in a woman and use it to his advantage.

Too bad Alex had shown up. Guy would have liked to know the "something else" that Lily had alluded to.

Rho pulled her cruiser next to Wayne's at the foot of the Calvert's Landing Pier. The deputy leaned against the car, one foot propped on its bumper, arms folded across his chest. The parking lot was jammed with vehicles, and on the second floor of the small shopping arcade the lights of Tai Haruru restaurant glowed warmly; on the bluff above, the floodlit facade of the Tides Inn seemed stark in comparison.

"Hey, Wayne," she called as she got out of the cruiser. "The dispatcher passed along your message. What's happening?"

"Let's take a walk, huh?" He motioned toward the pier.

Rho nodded and fell into step beside him. "Everything seems under control here."

"Now it is. I broke up a fight earlier—couple of guys who'd had too much navy grog. Had to beat the shit outta them. One came at me with a tire iron, the other wanted to help. They're on their way to the lockup at County, along with a kid who just couldn't keep from talking trash at me."

Rho was silent. She doubted the tire iron story, and busting a kid for talking back was excessive force. When they reached the end of the pier, she asked, "So why'd you want me to meet you?"

"We got a problem." The big deputy leaned with his

back against the rail, facing her. Waves lapped against the pilings, and the scent of brine, creosote, and kelp was strong. Rho thrust her hands in the pockets of her uniform jacket and waited.

Wayne said, "It's about that writer fellow you had dinner with last night. Guy Newberry."

She listened with mounting unease as he related the story that was making the rounds of the shops and taverns. When he finished she said, "I had no idea why he was here. He told me he was a freelance writer and thinking of relocating, but he seemed more interested in talking about his new laptop than his work."

"And now we know why. Did he ask you about the murders?"

"No. Mainly we traded life histories." Although, come to think of it, Newberry hadn't volunteered much of his own.

"You say anything about the murders?"

"God, no!"

"I don't have to tell you how bad it could get if he opens up that can of worms."

"Yeah."

"What kind of fellow is he?"

She considered. "Well, up to now I'd've said a little full of himself but basically decent. But—"

"The folks at the hotel said he seemed very interested in you. So here's what I'm thinking: Maybe if you talked to him, explained what a book on that crime would do to us, he'd give it up."

"I doubt that. To him, it's probably just business. If I said something, it might make him even more interested in writing it."

"Yeah, maybe, but you never know."

Rho moved to the railing and leaned against it, head down, taking measured breaths. This can't be happening, she thought.

"Thing that worries me," Wayne said, "is that he might try to link this new murder with the old ones."

"How? I don't see any connection."

"Doesn't have to be. He can manufacture one. Writers make up stuff all the time. When I heard about Newberry, I called a buddy of mine on the NYPD. Turns out he's done books like this before, best-sellers. And he used to write for the *Times,* lots of magazines. With his contacts he could get national publicity on what's happening here."

"Like the Wynne woman's family did back when."

"Right."

"Oh, Jesus."

Wayne glanced at his watch, straightened. "I better get going. You heading down to Signal Port?"

"All the way to Westhaven, to look for Samantha Lindsay's car."

"Odds're ten to one she's shacked up with somebody."

"I don't know, Wayne. Apparently it's a deviation from a long-established pattern."

"Well, good luck, kiddo. And think about what I suggested. A personal appeal from you to Newberry wouldn't hurt."

Rho didn't reply. She remained where she was, listening to his footsteps slap along the pier. There was a burst of music and laughter as the door of the restaurant opened and shut, the clatter of feet on the stairs, the echo of voices in the parking lot. Engines started up, gravel crunched under tires, and then the sounds faded as the vehicles drove away. Then the night grew quiet, except for the lap of waves and the faint percussive beat of the band playing inside Tai Haruru.

A personal appeal. Wayne was being naive if he thought that would work with a man like Guy Newberry. Now that she knew his real purpose in striking up an acquaintance, she recognized his type: insensitive, egotistical, determined to get what he wanted, no matter what the cost to others. He'd push ahead with his book, and the town would suffer. Her own fragile emotional balance would be thrown off, maybe never recover. Already she was dreaming of that night in the canyon in full horrifying detail. How long before she began dwelling on it during her waking hours?

You already are.

She pressed her fingertips to her temples, shook her head. The gesture did nothing to stem the flow of memories that picked up where her dream had left off.

She'd given Heath Wynne's body over to the medics and was standing paralyzed in her bloody shirt when Wayne drew her aside. "Don't fall apart now, kiddo," he had said. "Get moving and don't fuck up the scene. We've got to find out how many more people are here—dead or alive."

She took a deep breath, nodded, and followed him up the embankment to the driveway. Other deputies were entering the small shingled house where earlier she had come upon three bodies—Claudia, Mitch, and Eric Blakeley, she would later learn. Still others were moving toward a geodesic dome set some distance away in the trees. Wayne turned on a flashlight, told her, "Cover me." She took her .357 from its holster and they continued along the rutted dirt track.

About fifty yards deeper into the canyon they came upon a rough board shack with what looked to be a couple of sheds behind it. Wayne held up his hand for her to stop and moved slowly toward the shack's door. She readied her weapon as he flattened against the wall, reached for the knob, flung the door inward. After he shone the flash around the interior he said, "Nobody."

She let her breath out slowly, motioned at the sheds. He nodded and started toward them. She followed, hands slick with sweat on the grip of her gun. Abruptly Wayne stopped, hearing the same sound she did.

It was only a whimper, but so laden with terror that it might as well have been a scream. It came from the far shed, and Rho hurried toward it, ignoring Wayne's grunt of protest. He caught up with her, and had his flashlight ready when she opened the door.

The shed was actually a sleeping place, with two child-size bunks on the wall across from the small high window. The bottom bunk was bare except for a thin mattress. Rho went over and peered into the top bunk. A sleeping bag was bunched there, and it shook as the whimpers intensified.

She motioned Wayne back, put her hand on the bag. The shape inside it stiffened. "It's okay," she said. "You're safe now."

No response, not even a breath.

"Don't be afraid. We're here to help you."

A small sob.

"I want to take you out of here. Is that okay?"

Louder sobs now.

"Will you sit up for me? So I can help you?"

It was at least fifteen seconds before the bag moved and the child sat up. A girl, maybe five or six years old. Matted brown hair, big eyes made dark by terror and swollen by crying. Bloody scratches and tears on her cheeks. Mouth working, ready to cry out.

Rho reached for her, lifted her from the bunk. Wayne held out his arms, but before she could hand her over, the little girl burrowed against her, locking her arms around her neck and her legs around her waist in an unbreakable hold. She remained that way as Rho carried her down the canyon to safety. . . .

Chrystal: Before

Friday, October 6
11:57 A.M.

What're those things? Oh my God—Bernhard's shack and the kid boxes. It's all coming back now.

Bernhard built them for when the grown-ups partied, so us kids could sleep there and not get in the way. Tiny bunkhouses, one pink and one blue. Gray now.

The grown-ups partied a lot—and hard. They had white Christmas lights strung in the trees and stereo speakers mounted on poles. Nobody from outside got invited, except for Jude and Leo, and that was on account of Leo and Bernhard being tight from way back. Come to think of it, nobody but us ever came to the canyon.

Loud music. Weird food experiments. Running around in the woods after dark. The smell of weed. Ghost stories in the kid boxes. And Bernhard.

We called him "uncle." He paid us more attention than any of our folks did. He was supposed to be some kind of inventor, had his lab hidden way back in the canyon where it gets real narrow. But he wasn't no inventor, that was just a story the grown-ups made up for us. What he was doing back there was cooking meth.

Jude told me the papers said Bernhard was who the killers were after, the others were just innocent victims of a drug deal gone bad. But the papers got it wrong. Leo and her were in on the dealing, and the Wynnes were bankrolling Bernhard. The stuff in the papers, that was a whitewash on account of the others came from good families.

What's a good family, anyway? People with money and college educations, like them? People who stick together through all kinds of shit, like me and Leo and Jude? People who have a good time together, like us kids and Bernhard?

The cops found Bernhard dead in his lab. Prefab shed like you buy at a lumberyard. He wouldn't let nobody go near it, had barbed wire strung so thick across the path, you wondered how *he* got in and out.

There's the path. I could—

Don't do it, Chryssie. Fast in, fast out.

But it's so quiet here. There's nobody around. Nobody's been here since it happened.

Dammit, the time I spent on this place is the only time I remember being a kid—and I didn't remember it at all till I came back here. Bernhard was a big part of that. I got a right to see where he died.

Monday, October 9
Early Morning

When Rho entered the substation at ten minutes after midnight, Valerie—who had stayed late to field any phone calls concerning Chrystal Ackerman—handed her two message slips and began to explain what they were about before Rho could read them.

"Detective Grossman said to tell you he and his partner are at the Sea Stacks if you need him. They contacted the Clark County, Nevada, department about Ackerman, and they're cooperating. They've already located her apartment from the personal phone number the Mercedes' owner gave you. Took a run by there and spoke with the manager, who said when Ackerman moved in two years ago her mother was living with her. The mother was sick, and the manager hasn't seen her in months, assumes she died. Ackerman lived quietly, and the manager and other tenants didn't really know her. Your contact at the department down there is Detective Ronald Stevens."

Rho glanced at the slips, saw they contained an abbreviated version of what Valerie had just told her.

Valerie was scowling now. "Can you imagine it? Having phone sex in an apartment you shared with your *mother*?"

"It's a living." Rho couldn't imagine doing anything in proximity to her mother, who had abandoned the family when she was only eight. "Any further responses to our requests for sightings of Ackerman?"

"Finally, yes. Everybody who called saw her at Point Deception. All of them drove past. All of them feel guilty about not stopping to help her. Have you located Samantha Lindsay?"

"No. There's a be-on-lookout on her."

"She's probably just up to her usual tricks."

"You don't know that."

Valerie shrugged, her expression indicating that it would take a great deal to convince her of a different scenario. "By the way, your father called earlier this evening. He wants you to stop by."

"Why?"

"Just to talk."

Which meant he was sitting around with too much time on his hands and drinking. Jack Antolini was long retired from the department on disability. He missed the job and had too few interests to keep himself occupied, so he drank, quizzed Rho about every aspect of her work, and generally was critical of her performance. By now he'd heard she was assisting on the Ackerman case, and must be chomping at the bit to hear every detail.

"If he calls again," she told Valerie, "tell him I'm very busy, but I'll try to stop by this week."

"He's your father and a lonely man, Rhoda. How much trouble would it be?"

"I said I'd try, didn't I?" She set the message slips in the box she shared with Wayne, and when she turned saw Valerie watching her with an analytical expression. "What?" she snapped.

"Well, don't bite my head off!"

"Sorry. It's late and I'm tired."

"I guess you are. How're you holding up otherwise?"

"Fine. I've been taking my vitamins like a good girl."

"I don't mean physically."

"How, then?"

"Well, this is the first murder of a non-domestic type you've had to handle since. It must raise some painful memories."

Since. Spoken as if the word were capitalized, no further explanation needed. Valerie, like the rest of them, couldn't put a name to what had happened thirteen years ago. Rho felt a sudden emotional shift. No, something more akin to an emotional earthquake. She was sick of the euphemisms and evasions. Possibly had been sick of them for a long time.

"Why don't you just come out and say it?" she asked.

"Say what?"

"Since eight people were slaughtered in Cascada Canyon."

The harshness of the words echoed off the institutional green walls. Valerie put a hand to her lips. When the phone rang, she stared distractedly at it before picking up.

"Yes, Will," she said. ". . . Oh no! . . . Deputy Swift's here. I'll send her . . . Yes, I'll be glad to." She replaced the receiver and spoke to Rho without meeting her eyes. "That was Will Scurlock. Virge is missing too."

The knot of anxiety that had been present in Rho's stomach since early morning gave a painful tug. "Since when?"

"He's not sure. He fetched her from the hotel around two. She'd been drinking heavily, so he took her home, poured her into bed. Checked on her at four, and she was asleep. Then he worked on some plans, had supper, watched a couple of movies on TV, and fell asleep in his chair. When he went to the bedroom a few minutes ago she was gone, and one of her jackets was missing from the coatrack. Poor man's beside himself."

"I'm on my way."

Guy set his file box on the motel room bed and pulled out the one labeled "Victims." Then he sat down with it at the table in front of the glass door leading to the small balcony. Although it was well past midnight, he wasn't tired. An earlier conversation with Aaron Silber had, in fact, invigorated him. Aaron confirmed that Susan Harrison Wynne's mother had been paying the taxes on the Cascada Canyon property until her death late the previous year, when her son, Dunbar, took them over. That issue—and Dun's motives—clarified, Guy decided it was time that he became better acquainted with those who had died there.

He paged through Aaron's summary of the bare facts. The two couples who lived in the canyon had become friends while students at the University of California at Santa Cruz, an innovative campus employing such practices as giving written evaluations, rather than grades, for course work. Members of a clique who all had artistic aspirations, they thrived in the sheltered atmosphere of the wooded hills above the midstate coastal town, but not in the real world they faced after graduation. Their chosen fields were tough to break into and highly competitive; graduate schools looked askance at transcripts that could not be boiled down to a standard grade point average. Even mundane jobs were hard to find, and, having been raised in well-to-do households where their every need was catered to, they lacked the drive to pursue them.

Several years after graduation Susan and Forrest Wynne got together with their best friends, Claudia and Mitch Blakeley. The purpose of their reunion was serious: They'd all concluded they were dissatisfied with how their lives had turned out. Susan and Forrest were struggling to no avail at their professions. For Claudia and Mitch, real estate and banking had grown tedious, as had juggling their employers' demands with raising their young child. But now Susan Wynne had a solution to these problems.

Susan was about to come into control of a substantial trust fund established for her by her paternal grandfather. She proposed that the four of them find a large tract of country property, which she would buy as a retreat where they could live and pursue their artistic endeavors. She would pay for putting in a septic system, well, and whatever other utilities were necessary, and they would help each other build their homes. The Blakeleys would only be required to contribute their labor and the materials for their house.

Claudia and Mitch loved the plan. They'd been saving toward a home of their own, but real estate prices were rising faster than the amount in their passbook. Materials for a small house were within range, however, and the idea of forming an artists' colony with their best friends intrigued them. Of course, the land would have to be in an area where both property prices and the cost of living were low, and even then money would be tight, as the terms of the trust stipulated Susan could only withdraw so much cash per year. But the two couples—who held an exalted opinion of their own talent—assured one another that once they got on with their real work, fame and fortune would not be far off.

Claudia, a real estate agent, was put in charge of a statewide property search, and three months later she reported that she'd found the perfect place, a secluded tract in Soledad County called Cascada Canyon.

Will Scurlock had always impressed Rho as a man who preferred to think before he spoke and consider the consequences before he acted. But tonight—or this morning, as it was now nearing one o'clock—he was anything but self-contained. As she examined the bedroom from which his wife had vanished an indeterminate amount of time before, Will babbled and ranted and occasionally smacked his big fists against the wall.

Virge, he claimed, had been forcibly taken from their bed.

Then why, Rho countered, was her down jacket missing from its peg on the hall coatrack?

Well, maybe it wasn't missing. Maybe it was in one of the trucks or at the dry cleaner.

But hadn't Will said earlier that Virge had been wearing it when he brought her home from the hotel? And that he'd hung it up himself?

Okay, maybe whoever took her had sneaked into the hall for the jacket. He'd been watching TV, napping. He wouldn't've noticed. Besides, Virge would never have gone out at night by herself—not with a killer on the loose. Someone had taken her, and he—

"Will," Rho said, "get a grip."

As she'd hoped, the words snapped him out of it. He sank onto the bed and put his hands to his eyes. "Jesus!"

"Will," she said after a moment, "Virge isn't the first woman to disappear tonight."

"No? Who else?"

"Samantha Lindsay. Isn't her husband a client of yours?"

"Yeah."

"Does Virge know her?"

"Why, you think there's some connection?"

"It had entered my mind."

"Well, as far as I know they've never met. Or if they did, it was only in passing. Samantha's . . . well, she and Virge don't have much in common."

Rho crossed to a door with old-fashioned glass panes; when she flicked the light switch beside it she looked out onto a patio. The door was latched but not locked. On the far side of the patio a flagstone path led away through a screen of rhododendrons.

"Where does that path go?" she asked.

"The greenhouse. Virge is . . . used to be quite a gardener."

"Is it possible she went there?"

"No. She hasn't bothered with it for years. Besides, there's only one key, and it's on the hook in the kitchen."

"Anyplace else on the property she might've gone?"

"Well, the tenant's cabin. Clay Lawrence. Sometimes she visits him, takes him baked goods and plays gin rummy. But only when I'm not home and she needs company."

Rho knew Clay Lawrence by sight: a rustic type in his early forties who was often seen around town with Becca Campos, a waitress at the hotel and part-time housecleaner. "You call him?"

"I tried, but his line was busy, and I didn't want to leave the house in case Virge came back."

"I'll stop by there later. How do I get to the cabin?"

"Just follow the driveway. It ends there."

Rho sat down beside Will. "Virge's drinking today—what brought that on?"

"I'm not sure. I asked her, but she wasn't making any sense. Kept saying she was the one deserved an explanation."

"Of what?"

"Damned if I know."

"You two have a fight beforehand?"

"No. We never fight. I can't risk upsetting her."

"Anything else you know of that could've set her off?"

"That murder, I guess. We saw the woman at Point Deception around six Friday night, but didn't stop. Afterwards Virge felt bad about that, but even so, I don't understand why she felt the need to drink. She isn't much of a drinker. And why did she do it in public? We've got plenty of booze here in the house."

"Maybe she didn't want to drink alone."

"Maybe."

Rho hesitated, framing her next words carefully. "I've heard that Virge has become a little unstable."

"A little?" Will laughed bitterly. "Try a lot. She's afraid of everything. A windstorm, an animal prowling in the shrubbery, a car backfiring down on the highway—anything'll set her off. She's dropped all her interests except for food. Gardening, needlepoint, volunteer work. And in the food department she goes overboard. It's like she's eating to sedate herself."

"How long has this been going on?"

He shrugged. "Years. A condition like hers progresses very slowly. At first you don't notice it, then you normalize it, but finally one day you wake up and say, 'Wait a minute, something's not right here.'"

"Has she seen anyone about it?"

"No. She doesn't think anything's wrong with her. Claims she's just being cautious. And as for the food, she says cooking's her new hobby. I tell you, Rho, she's running scared."

"It's hard to believe. She's always been so strong. After the . . ." She hesitated, then strengthened her new resolve and gave voice to it. "After the canyon murders, she was a rock."

Will raised his eyebrows. "Well, so you're finally talking about them. You're right, she *was* strong. And you, of all people, ought to know that."

"I do. She held me together that night, and for days after. If it wasn't for Virge, I'd've embarrassed myself in front of the department, the reporters, the TV people. She made me strong."

"Yeah, she did. And what did you do to repay her?

Crawled into the bottle, left the case to people like Wayne Gilardi, who couldn't find their asses with both hands. Some thanks that was."

Rho winced at the sudden attack—more so because what he said held some truth.

"There wasn't anybody at the scene that night as smart as you," Will added. "Nobody from here, none of the detectives they sent out from Santa Carla, either. If you'd tended to business, maybe my wife wouldn't be the way she is today."

Now he'd gone too far. In the years since the murders, many people had accused both her and the department of ineptitude, but never Will or Virge. It hurt and angered her to find he'd concealed his true feelings.

"Look, Will," she said, "I screwed up, but you can't blame one person for those murders going unsolved. And Virge is responsible for her condition—with a whole lot of enabling from you."

"Where do you get off—"

She stood. "It isn't helping your wife for us to sit here airing old grievances. I'll be in touch when I know something."

Guy turned to the first of the victim profiles: Claudia Robinson Blakeley.

She was thirty when she died. The daughter of a San Diego stockbroker, she'd displayed a talent for photography at an early age and later became interested in filmmaking. UC Santa Cruz was her second choice; she originally wanted to enter the prestigious filmmaking program at UCLA, but didn't have the grades.

The accompanying photograph showed a young

woman with a halo of frizzy blonde hair and a wide smile. Her eyes were her best feature, large and long-lashed. The photo had probably been taken in the canyon, judging from the pines in the background.

Claudia married Mitch Blakeley during her senior year in college, and their son, Eric, was born seven months later. At first the young family remained in Santa Cruz, but after two years they went to San Diego, where Claudia's father arranged a job for Mitch in the trust department of a bank and Claudia took a sales position with a large real estate firm. In spite of two incomes, money was always tight, and several times Claudia's father had to bail them out of debt. Two months before they had their reunion with the Wynnes, he told the couple that they could expect no further financial support from him.

Family and friends described Claudia as extroverted and fun-loving, but self-centered and unfocused. She was a natural at selling homes, but lacked attention to detail and often lost out on closing sales by failing to keep appointments. She banked part of her commissions, hoping to buy a house someday, but ran up large credit card balances that forced her to dip into her savings. Her marriage by and large seemed a happy one, but her parenting skills were below average and several times her mother spoke to her about neglecting Eric emotionally. Workers at the daycare center Eric attended noted that the grandmother was a more significant presence in the boy's life than the mother.

Guy turned the page, removed the photo clipped to Eric's profile. Taken the year he died, it showed an eight-year-old with a chipped front tooth, curly reddish-blond hair, and a scattering of freckles across his snub nose. He looked at the camera in a tentative way, as if unsure of his place in the world or his ability to fill it.

The little boy's expression plucked at Guy's emotions, set off chords of pity, because in it he recognized himself. His parents had been remote, wrapped up in one another to the exclusion of their only child, and he'd struggled to measure up to friends who were secure of their parents' love. In his self-aware moments he realized that the arrogance he'd developed once he discovered the thing he could do and do well stemmed from that early deprivation. In his less aware moments he simply felt sad.

Guy wondered what Eric might have been like had he reached his own age. A fiercely driven overachiever like himself? A total loser? Mr. Average? No use in speculating. The boy who was described as an avid reader and clever storyteller had died along with his parents in the living room of the small canyon house Guy had visited that afternoon. A bullet from a semiautomatic weapon seemed a brutal fate for an eight-year-old whose worst crime had probably been to sneak a puff off one of his parents' marijuana cigarettes when no one was looking.

And then there was his father, Mitch Blakeley. The face in the photograph Guy next looked at showed a thirty-year-old man with rough-hewn features, unkempt dark hair and beard, and small eyes whose faraway gaze said his thoughts were elsewhere. According to those who knew him during his childhood in the Central Valley town of Fresno, Mitch had always been a dreamer. He read voraciously: during and after school; in the library and at the dinner table; through television shows and family gatherings. His mother despaired because he "always had his nose in a dirty old dust-catcher," but Mitch ignored her. When he wasn't reading, he enlisted his few friends in acting out parts in dramas he created: Amazon boatmen battling piranhas; rebel soldiers in the hills of Cuba; crew members of a spaceship under attack in a far-away galaxy.

Eventually Mitch raised his nose from the "dust-catchers" long enough to discover the movies, and from then on his spare time and allowance were consumed by trips to the theaters. He began his first screenplay when he was fourteen, learning the format from a library book, and had completed over a dozen by the time he graduated high school. His English teacher deemed them "technically competent."

UC Santa Cruz offered Mitch a scholarship, but once there he became more interested in drugs and women than in studying. After two years he dropped out and moved to an apartment near the waterfront, supporting himself by dealing marijuana and working part-time delivering pizzas. But he returned frequently to the campus in the hills, because he'd become intrigued by a young woman named Claudia Robinson.

For two years after his marriage to Claudia and the birth of their son, Mitch worked full-time as an assistant manager at the pizza restaurant and wrote like a demon in his spare time, but his screenplays were ignored or rejected. When the pizza franchise folded and Claudia's father offered to set him up in a career in banking, he reluctantly packed up his typewriter and moved the family to San Diego. The life of a struggling artist, he told friends, was not his thing.

Neither was banking. According to colleagues in the trust department, Mitch hated his job. He put in the bare minimum of hours and often left early, asking others to cover for him. His salary was good, but he spent all of it, and whenever he managed to get ahead he'd make a trip to Las Vegas and blow the money at the blackjack tables. The trips, he told one of his coworkers, were the only way he could cope with the mediocrity of his existence.

Apparently the mediocrity had persisted until his death, Guy thought. Investigators had found no completed screenplays in the canyon house, only a fifty-page fragment that had been penciled over and over until it was barely readable.

As she left the Scurlock house Rho noted that both vehicles—Will's big white superaccessorized Dodge Ram, and Virge's little blue Toyota pickup—were in the driveway. If Virge had left voluntarily, she'd gone on foot or caught a ride with a friend. But what friend? As Will had indicated, his wife had gradually closed off to others during recent years. Rho could remember a time when Virge's friendly smile would welcome you to the hospice thrift shop and the volunteer fire department spaghetti feeds, but the memory was dim at best.

She started the cruiser and continued up the driveway. It was paved only to the house, then turned into your standard dirt ranch road. To either side lay softly sculpted meadows where Will's father used to run dairy cattle. Will, however, had no love of ranching and sold the herd after he inherited the property.

Up here on the ridge the fog had receded. Cold moonrays highlighted details: a eucalyptus tree split by lightning many years before; a downed rail fence; a rocky outcropping from which Will's dad used to fly the flag for the family's Fourth of July barbecues. Rho and her father had attended all of those gatherings, and if Jack Antolini drank more than most others, his daughter understood. Her mother's leaving had been a bitter blow to them both.

Dad, Rho thought, assailed by guilt as she remembered his earlier phone call to the substation. It wasn't that she didn't love her father or want to see him, but she would've liked to see him under normal circumstances, and those didn't prevail anymore. Jack had been forcibly retired after being badly injured in a high-speed chase near Calvert's Landing only two months before the canyon murders. He'd chafed at his inability to take part in the investigation, tried to orchestrate Rho's every move, and ultimately became her harshest critic. If she thought Will had been rough on her tonight, she had only to remember the things her own father said.

The cabin came into view, and now Rho recognized it as the place teens would sneak off to during the parties: brown-shingled, with small, high windows and a flat roof topped by a rusted stovepipe. To one side was a ramshackle shed and a big stump with an axe stuck into it; a neat stack of firewood leaned against the cabin wall, tarped against the coming winter rains. An old pickup near the woodpile was jacked up as if Lawrence had been working under it. Light glowed from behind the cabin's drawn curtains, and as she approached the door, it opened and a tall, thin man peered out at her.

"Mr. Lawrence?"

"Yes?"

"I'm Deputy Rhoda Swift—"

"Ah, yes, I've seen you in town. You belong to the handsome Lab, Cody."

"How d'you know his name?"

"I made his acquaintance outside the post office one day. I was admiring him and a passing gentleman introduced us."

Rho was standing on the doorstep now, a round of tree trunk embedded in the earth and slick with moss. Clay Lawrence towered over her, his head nearly touching the doorframe. His lips, in a nest of gray-brown beard, were smiling, and laugh lines crinkled at the corners of his deepset eyes. In spite of the lateness of the hour, he looked fully awake.

She said, "You must be a dog person, if you know I belong to Cody and not the other way round."

"Actually I'm an animal person. I like all kinds." He motioned for her to come inside.

The cabin was tiny, with a galley kitchen on one wall and a woodstove in the corner. Single bed with a shelf above it holding dozens of paperbacks. Broken-down easy chair upholstered in lurid purple flowers that matched the fabric of the curtains—Virge's taste. Nothing else, but where would he put it? Rho couldn't imagine living in such a small space.

As if he knew what she was thinking, Clay Lawrence said, "The rent is very cheap," and motioned for her to take the chair.

She sat, unable to avoid a mental comparison between it and the white leather chair at the Lindsay house. Lawrence added, "I'd offer you something, but I'm short on supplies."

"That's quite all right," she said. "I only want to ask you a few questions. When was the last time you saw Virge Scurlock?"

He sat on the bed, eyebrows knitting as he thought. "Friday morning, before I made my monthly trip into Santa Carla. I dropped off my rent money and we talked. What's this about?"

Rho ignored the question. "You're sure you didn't see her on Saturday or Sunday?"

"No. I stayed over in Santa Carla. What's going on?"

Rho explained about his landlady being missing. "Will said she often visits you. Did she ever mention someone named Samantha Lindsay?"

"No. Who's she?"

"Another missing woman. I thought there might be a connection."

"You mean, they might've gone off together?"

"It's not probable, but I'd like that better than Virge going off by herself."

"Yeah. I can't imagine her doing that."

"I gather you know her fairly well."

His lips tightened. "As well as I want to."

"What does that mean?"

"Virge can be . . . difficult. When I first moved in I thought she was charming in a ditzy sort of way. She'd show up here with cookies or brownies, and I'd invite her in and make tea. Sometimes we'd play cards. But then she started showing up every day. And she got demanding."

"How so?"

"She wanted me to be here whenever Will was away at night. Wanted me to drive into town with her. Ordered me to come over and fix stuff at the house. I tried to put some distance between us but it didn't work, and she's gotten clingy and kind of obsessive. To tell the truth, she's turned into a pain in the ass. I'll be glad when my lease is up."

"When's that?"

"Three weeks, and I'll be going home."

"Where's home?"

"Seattle. I was born and raised there."

"What made you leave?"

"Is this an official inquiry, Deputy Swift? Or are you just being neighborly?"

"It's Rhoda. And I'm being neighborly." Truth, mostly. She found herself liking Clay Lawrence and wishing she'd gotten to know him earlier in his stay.

"Okay, I left because my marriage busted up. My wife was involved with one of my coworkers, and I needed to get away. So I got in my car and drove south till it broke down in some godforsaken town. From there I hitched."

"How come you stopped hitching here?"

"My last ride dropped me off in front of the hotel, and I was hungry. A pretty woman waited on me, and we hit it off, so I decided to stay a while."

"Becca Campos."

"Right. She does housecleaning for Virge and knew about this cabin. Aside from Virge, the place has been good to me. I'll miss it."

"So why go home?"

"It's time."

"Becca going with you?"

"No. From the first we've known our relationship was no-strings. I'm not ready for another commitment. Maybe I never will be. Becca understands that."

Rho wondered. She'd seen the way Becca linked arms

with Clay as they walked through town, noted her smiles and body language. But that was none of her business.

"Clay," she said, "can you think of any place Virge might've gone tonight?"

He considered, shook his head.

"Would she hitchhike on the highway?"

"God, no! Woman's afraid of her own shadow." He thought some more, eyes moving quickly, and then they grew still. "There's the canyon," he said.

"Cascada Canyon?"

He nodded.

"She wouldn't go there."

"Well, you probably know her better than I do, but for the past six months or so she's been talking a lot about those murders. Asked me a couple of weeks ago if I'd go there with her and help her confront her fears. Of course, I said no. I was afraid of what it might do to her." He paused. "You know, yesterday evening . . . There's this grove of redwoods to the far side of this property."

"And?"

"I was up there around dusk watching the fog. I go there late almost every day. It's kind of like meditation for me. Anyway, I noticed this guy down in the canyon, following the driveway toward the highway. First person I'd ever seen there, so I followed him and we talked. He claimed he was sent out from New York by the owners to check up on the property, but his story didn't ring true to me."

"Describe him, please."

The description matched Guy Newberry. He'd certainly been busy since he arrived in town.

* * *

Guy stood on his balcony, listening to the wash of surf on the rocky beach before tackling the remaining profiles of the victims. Claudia and Mitch Blakeley, he thought, were examples of a type he'd encountered all too often: indulged as children; blessed with small talents and large aspirations; cursed with an unwillingness to work long and hard at anything. In short, dabblers.

And no doubt envious of those who had succeeded. They didn't recognize the toil and sacrifice that success demands. They didn't acknowledge the years of paying dues to a club in which the payee was denied full membership. What had one of the New York dabblers said to him several years ago? Oh yes: "Talentwise, there's not much difference between the best and the worst of us, but some are chosen and some aren't. It's as if somebody's sprinkling gold dust around. One person it sticks to, another it doesn't."

He couldn't debate the first assumption; with a few notable exceptions, talent fell into a fairly narrow range. And luck certainly played a strong role in any individual's career. But if there were some latter-day Tinkerbell flitting about, what made her dust stick to one person and not the other was a coating of good, honest sweat.

In accordance with that thought, he went back inside to the profiles.

Susan Harrison Wynne, murder victim, thirty-one years of age. The wealth that flowed from Harrison Industries had cushioned her from birth: nannies; private schools and lessons; the brownstone in the East Seventies; summers at the family estate in Bar Harbor. But the cushion was not without its protruding springs. Her father divorced her mother for a younger woman when she was thirteen. Her only sibling, Dunbar, was usually away at school—no source of comfort. Her mother took to traveling and bringing home lovers who never lasted out the year.

Great sums of money and a difficult family life usually bring isolation and loneliness, but not so with Susan. She went out of her way to make friends, and they helped her keep intact her natural warmth, intelligence, and humor. Classmates and teachers from her boarding school days described her as an instigator of hilarious pranks and harmless disruptions for which even an ogre of a headmistress found it hard to punish her. Adventurousness and intellectual curiosity became her hallmark.

When the time came for filling out college applications, Susan tore up those from the eastern schools her adviser recommended and instead applied only to the "alternative" campus at Santa Cruz. There she became intrigued with organic gardening and worked tirelessly in the campus plots. Horticulture led naturally to the culinary arts, and soon she was taking lessons from a chef at an innovative California-style restaurant downtown. The owner had brought in a fine arts major from the campus to create a sculpture for his courtyard dining area, and Susan, who had seen the young man around but never spoken to him, soon fell in love with Forrest Wynne. Before long they took an apartment together, and when Susan, on the recommendation of her mentor, was accepted at the Academy of Culinary Arts in San Francisco, Forrest transferred to the College of Arts and Crafts in nearby Oakland. Before they moved north, they married and soon conceived their first child, Heath.

There were two photographs of Susan Wynne clipped

to the profile. Guy removed them and studied the one
dated shortly after Heath's birth. A heart-shaped face
framed by straight light brown hair; faint smile revealing
dazzlingly white teeth. Nothing exceptional about the
features until you looked into her eyes.

They glowed with warmth, intelligence, and kindness.
Even in a photograph they appeared to look beyond the
surface of what they saw. This was a woman who was
sure of who she was and could accept others on whatever
terms they presented themselves. She would have been a
good listener and willing to aid friends with her considerable insight. And she wouldn't have been afraid to tell
you when you were being an asshole.

Susan Wynne had had eyes like Diana's. How could
someone look into such eyes with hatred and cruelty?
And yet they had died in much the same manner.

Shaken by the thought, Guy set the photo down and
picked up the second one, dated the year Susan died. In
it, her hair was short and uneven, as if she'd lopped it off
herself. Her skin was roughened and blotchy, her lips
cracked and unsmiling. But her eyes were the worst evidence of change: dark pools in which nothing lived. Cold
pools that offered nothing to anyone.

Drugs, Guy thought. Disappointment, too. And the
daily grind of a primitive life in a damp canyon where
everybody's dreams had died.

Quickly he turned the photo over and went back to the
profile.

Susan had difficulty finding suitable work after gradu-
ating from the culinary academy. The restaurant business
was demanding for the mother of—now—two small children, and even though she could afford help, she missed

spending time with Heath and Oriana. For a while she considered opening her own restaurant, but felt she lacked the necessary experience. Besides, Forrest's once-promising career had foundered, and he needed her attention. Instead of a restaurant she decided to invest a portion of her trust fund in a property where she and he and their best friends could pursue their work in peaceful surroundings. Her old mentor in Santa Cruz had urged her to write a cookbook, and promised to recommend it to his publisher.

At this point the material in the profile grew thin, because of the isolated lifestyle the residents of the canyon adopted. Susan worked on the cookbook, as evidenced by stacks of files filled with recipes, text, and notes. She and Forrest also home-schooled the three children; investigators found workbooks and teaching aids in the geodesic dome. Layers of primitive, blood-spattered drawings were tacked to their refrigerator door by magnets.

The man with whom Susan had chosen to spend her life had little by way of appearance to recommend himself. The photograph attached to Forrest Wynne's profile showed him to be tall and thin, with a concave chest and a small round head covered with hair that stood up in wispy tufts. As he posed on a downed tree trunk in the woods, he looked ill at ease and humorless.

The son of a Marin County attorney and his artist wife, Forrest sculpted from early childhood in sand, mud, modeling clay, and any other material that could be molded to the highly original and sometimes unrecognizable forms that peopled his imagination. Although his father disapproved of his plans to study art, his mother—a painter—encouraged him.

In Santa Cruz, Forrest blossomed. He'd been the odd duck in the elitist confines of Marin, but at college he found acceptance. And he found success in the form of a showing at a local gallery and the commission of the courtyard sculpture for the restaurant where he met his wife. He told friends that in Susan he'd found a soul mate: a woman who understood his work, overlooked his flaws, and would always be there for him. At first the years the Wynnes spent in San Francisco were good ones; he began to gain recognition and to land commissions. But then disaster struck.

One of his sculptures was accepted by the city arts commission for the lobby of the Moscone Convention Center—an interlocking series of arcs rising high, which he titled *Hope*. Unfortunately, an art critic for the *Chronicle* and not a few outraged citizens noticed its uncanny resemblance to an upended eggbeater, and the subsequent outcry over the squandering of public funds on something that looked better suited to the kitchen than to the convention center forced the commission to reverse their decision. It didn't help when the newspaper revealed that Forrest's wife had trained as a chef.

Devastated by the ridicule, Forrest sank into depression. Toward Christmas of that year he made a suicide attempt—half-hearted, but Susan knew that any attempt should be taken seriously. It was time, she told him, that they leave the city. He agreed; he had frightened himself and didn't want to further hurt his wife and children.

The profiles contained very little information on those children. Because they were home-schooled they had no classmates or teachers to provide detail, and no one from the immediate area really knew them. Susan's mother had only met her grandchildren once, at a stopover at San Francisco Airport. Dun Harrison never laid eyes on his nephew, and Oriana was a stranger to him when she came to New York after her parents' death. Forrest's father died long before either child was born, and his mother moved to an artists' colony in Vermont. Friends and neighbors of the family in San Francisco described Heath as "serious" and Oriana as "sweet."

Heath's photograph confirmed the description. Facially he resembled his mother, but in expression he took after his father. He posed in front of the family's geodesic dome, thin arms folded across the chest of his striped T-shirt, fine brown hair dusting his forehead, mouth set in a grim, straight line. The picture was dated only a few days before he died at age nine, and the boy looked as if he already knew the world to be dangerous and cruel.

There was a wire service photograph of Oriana. An older woman in a fur coat—presumably her grandmother—was ushering her toward a jetway at San Francisco International. The six-year-old had turned her head and was staring behind her, big anguished eyes peering from under their uneven thatch of bangs as life as she'd known it receded. It was the last photograph taken of Oriana Wynne; once she arrived in New York, she legally became Oriana Harrison, and the doors of wealth and privilege closed against the curious.

There was one other victim at the geodesic dome that night, Forrest's younger sister, Devon. Twenty-five years of age, and described by friends as being addicted to abusive relationships, she'd been drifting around the country since she left college at nineteen. Her last trek had taken her across the country from Vermont, where she'd paid a visit to her mother. Devon—whose photograph showed a thin young woman with lank blonde hair and an old bruise below her left eye—would have done well to stay in the Northeast.

Rho had just radioed in a be-on-lookout on Virge Scurlock when Central Dispatch announced, "All units, vicinity Highway One and Point Deception, ten-five-zero-Frank. Repeat, all units—"

The Scurlock property was only a few miles from the scene of the fatal traffic accident, so she put on her pulsars and headed north. Virge, she thought. No, not Virge. Couldn't be. Both trucks were still at the house.

The fog was thick by the sea, and it diffused the lights from the vehicles pulled onto the western shoulder, about half a mile south of the point. A pickup, two cars, a cruiser, no ambulance yet. Neither the pickup nor the cars looked as if they had been involved in the accident. She parked, got out, and hurried toward the cruiser. Wayne had been first on the scene. Like herself, he was giving his all to the job tonight, working—by now—a triple shift. The cruiser's headlights revealed his sagging facial skin and reddened eyes. He hadn't much more to give.

Wayne was talking with a man who leaned against the back of the pickup, ashen-faced and looking sick. Rho put her hand on the deputy's arm. "What've we got here?"

"You still working, kiddo? Well, what we got is Samantha Lindsay. Her car skidded across the centerline, went into the ditch. It's not a bad drop, but she rolled, and the convertible top was crushed. She probably died instantly. Tow truck and ambulance're on the way."

Rho nodded, noting the gouges the tires had cut into the damp earth beyond the shoulder. Her mind superimposed on them the image of Samantha's perfect face. One careless moment at the wheel . . .

Wayne said, "This is Mr. James Hutton. He found the car. Mr. Hutton, Deputy Rhoda Swift. Why don't you fill her in on what happened."

Wayne's tone alerted her that something was irregular about the situation. He wanted the man to repeat his story so he could check for inconsistencies.

Hutton ran his hand through his thinning hair. "Well, the way it happened, I was driving down from Eureka to Mendocino. And I had to take a leak—excuse me, ma'am, relieve myself. So I pulled over here and went into those bushes. I probably wouldn't've noticed the car, but one of my headlights is cocked from an accident I had last week, and it picked up the metal of the front bumper. So I climbed down there, and—" His voice broke and he swallowed before continuing. "Car's upside down, roof's flattened, and she's in there. I checked for a pulse, but there wasn't one, and she's real cold."

"What did you do then?" Rho asked.

"Ran up here and started flagging down cars." He motioned to a Volkswagen Jetta. "That guy stopped first, and then the fellow in the Mustang came along. He drove to a house, used the phone to report it." He paused, running his fingers through his hair again. "Jesus, she was a mess, all twisted and cut up from the broken windshield. Door was sprung open, she could've got out, but maybe she was gone before that happened."

Rho glanced at Wayne, who nodded. "Thank you, Mr. Hutton," she said and followed her colleague to the rear of his cruiser. "So what is it with his story that bothers you?"

"Nothing now. I believe him. But there's a second set of footprints leading down to the wreck, and mud on the inside of the sprung door. And Samantha was robbed."

"Robbed."

"Yeah. Wallet's empty of cash and credit cards. It and her purse were dumped next to the car. Diamond ring's missing, as well as a Rolex watch that she never took off, even in—"

Rho regarded him steadily as she waited out his sudden silence.

He shrugged and looked away from her.

"You never cease to amaze me, Gilardi," she finally said.

"Yeah, well, it wasn't like I was a member of an exclusive club."

"When did this happen?"

"Come on, Rho, you don't need details."

"We've got a dead woman down there—"

"An accident victim. Doesn't give you the right to pry into private affairs—hers or mine."

He was correct, of course. Samantha Lindsay had been doing exactly what she'd told her husband she would: driving straight home after shopping in Westhaven. For one reason or another she'd skidded off the road and died, and out of respect for the dead, private matters should remain private.

"So what d'you make of the robbery?" she asked.

Wayne shrugged. "Somebody saw the car go off the road and decided to take advantage of a bad situation."

"Plenty of bad situations tonight. You catch the squawk on Virge Scurlock?"

"Uh-huh. What's that all about?"

She explained about her conversations with Will and Clay Lawrence.

"You know, kiddo," he said, "something's bothering me. For years we had a pretty peaceable community here. Drinking, drugs, petty theft, domestic problems, yes. But that kind of stuff happens all the time in an area like this. So now in the space of three days we got a rape-and-murder, civil unrest, a disappearance, and a sort of ghoulish robbery. All that since one event: the arrival of this Guy Newberry. Is it possible he's doing these things to stir up trouble, get publicity for this book he's writing?"

"I sincerely doubt it. Even mystery writers only kill on paper."

"Yeah, I'm clutching at straws, looking for somebody to blame things on. And since I don't like the man . . ."

"Look, Wayne, if it would make you feel better, I'll talk with him, try to find out what his plans are. In the meantime—"

"I know. I caught the call, I get the job of telling Alan Lindsay his wife is dead." Wayne's mouth was set in a grim line. Notifying the families of victims was a thousand times worse than dealing with the scene of a tragedy.

Guy took a sip of Jolt Cola—more potent than coffee and twice as tasty—and picked up the photograph of the last victim, Bernhard Ulrick. Pale, thin face, cleft chin, tight wiry blond curls. Gold-rimmed glasses made him look studious. It was his high school graduation picture, the only one Aaron had been able to dig up. At age thirty-two he'd died of multiple bullet wounds, his face a bloody hole, his body shattered. The vicious nature of the slaying and the fact he was killed in a prefab building tucked deep into the canyon, surrounded by chemicals and paraphernalia for manufacturing methamphetamine, had naturally led the authorities to label him as the primary target.

Ulrick was one of Mitch Blakeley's friends from his days of drug dealing in Santa Cruz. Born into a large and insular German community in Chicago, he drifted west after high school, eventually ending up in the seaside college town. At the time of his murder, his family were all dead, but others in the midwestern working-class neighborhood remembered him as a youth of large dreams, all of them involving amassing great sums of money. The method of doing so mattered little to Ulrick; wealth seemed an end in itself. He was well versed in many scams—fencing stolen goods, running cons on the naive and elderly, selling drugs and firearms—but he was never once arrested. He had a sixth sense for when the law was about to close in, and would shut down his operations and run.

Ulrick was long gone from the central coast when the Blakeleys and Wynnes left Santa Cruz. Material on his next few years was sketchy, but he'd surfaced in such diverse places as Anchorage, New Orleans, Atlantic City, and Honolulu—always scamming and using whatever connections he possessed. When he turned up at Cascada Canyon some eleven months before the murders, his appearance probably didn't surprise the residents. Ulrick was known as a man who had a way of finding people.

And also, Guy thought, of finding their weaknesses.

So what do I have here? he wondered, rubbing his eyes and taking another shot of cola. A toxic situation, for sure. Two naive families living an isolated existence. A predator with a plan for them.

Several substantial withdrawals from Susan Wynne's trust fund contradicted the assumption that the families hadn't known about Ulrick's meth lab. Guy suspected that the money had gone for setting up the lab, and that the Wynnes and Blakeleys were living on the proceeds of drug sales. After the initial outlay for land and building supplies, the families had invested very little money in the canyon, and their living expenses could not possibly have been high enough to justify the withdrawals.

He scanned the summary of the sheriff's department investigation, noting that deputies had acted upon rumors that another couple was involved with the canyon residents—streetwise people who were said to have the nerve and connections to distribute the meth. A cabin on the ridge was raided the day after the murders, but by then the occupants—who had been squatting there—had fled, leaving behind most of their household possessions but nothing to identify them.

To Guy the rumors seemed too vague to have justified the issuance of a search warrant. A man and woman with a young daughter were occasionally seen driving through the gates to the canyon in their shabby orange VW bus. People in town who claimed to have had dealings with them described them as poorly dressed and standoffish, paying for all their supplies in cash. But, Guy knew, rumors have a way of becoming everyone's fact after a tragedy. The strongest connection that he could see between the squatters on the ridge and the canyon people was a deer track that led down from the cabin past a pond where the families had posted a sign that read "Ye Olde Swimming Hole." The authorities had been unable to tell whether the track was also used by humans.

Rumors, Guy thought, rubbing his eyes again.

What had Gregory Cordova said to him that morning? *I know as much as anybody does. More, maybe.* The old man struck him as a deliberate sort. If he'd been talking about mere rumors, he'd've said "I've *heard*."

Tomorrow he'd find out what Cordova meant by "more."

Chrystal: Before

Friday, October 6
12:02 P.M.

here's Bernhard's lab. Door's open and the whole thing's leaning funny. Jesus, these rocks're wet and slippery. Why's there so much water . . . ?

Oh yeah, stream's changed course, flooded out this end of the canyon. I don't want to wade through it. What did I expect to see, anyway? Bloodstains, bullet holes, chalk marks like on TV shows? Nah, I hate that shit. I guess I was just curious because I never came here before.

Never?

Of course not. Bernhard wouldn't let nobody—

Oh God! Once . . .

I remember it all so clear now. Me and Heath daring each other to sneak up the canyon. Then going together 'cause neither of us had the guts to go alone. Was September, hot. I could smell dry grass and pine needles. The air was dusty. We were sweaty.

The lab's door was open, like now. There was a bunch of

stuff on a table, I don't know what, but I suppose it looked like the kind of stuff an inventor would have. Me and Heath, we squatted down behind the bushes. We could hear Bernhard talking inside, and that was funny because he must've been talking to himself. We couldn't tell what he was saying, and after a few minutes Heath gave me a come-on sign and we snuck around to the side where there was a little window. The grass rustled and I started to sneeze. Pinched my nose hard. After a few seconds the sneeze went away.

Bernhard's voice, real clear now: "You know where it is, honey. Tell me."

Somebody said something, real low.

"Oh, sure you do. Tell Uncle Bernhard."

Uncle? Heath looked at me and I looked at him. None of us kids were allowed here, so who was Bernhard talking to?

"Please, honey. If you can't tell me, show me."

Bernhard's voice was funny. I'd heard Leo talk to Jude like that late at night when they thought I was asleep in my curtained-off corner of the cabin. I didn't know what it meant exactly, but now I didn't like it. I tugged on Heath's arm, wanting to run away from there. He snuck closer to the window.

I went after him, tugged again. He was going to look inside and I knew if he did, things would change in some awful way.

Heath slapped at my hand and went up on his tiptoes. Looked through the window.

Bernhard said, "Please, honey. Show me. Uncle Bernhard'll be real good to you if you do."

Heath dropped down on all fours. His face was scrunched and red, and he looked so silly that for a second I almost forgot I was scared and started laughing. But then he grabbed my hand and we ran, not even caring if we made noise, all the way down to Bernhard's shack and past the kid boxes and through the woods to the wellhouse.

We flopped on the ground, leaning against the holding tank and panting. I asked, "What did you see?"

"Uncle Bernhard and Oriana."

"What were they doing?"

He didn't answer.

"Heath!"

"Look, Chryssie, we can't ever tell anybody what we did today."

"Uncle Bernhard and Oriana know. We made a lot of noise getting outta there."

"They won't tell."

"Why not? He's gonna be mad at us—"

"Chryssie, shut up and listen to me!"

Heath was older—nine. I did what he said.

"They won't tell, and nobody'll know if we don't. But from now on you've gotta stay away from Uncle Bernhard. You understand?"

"No."

"Okay, you're too young to understand. Please just do what I tell you."

"Why?"

"Chryssie, please! Promise!"

Of course I didn't understand any of what was going on then—or maybe I did, sort of like animals do—but the way Heath yelled at me, I promised. And after I promised, he did too.

I've kept that promise to this day. Yeah, and so has Heath. That was in September, and two weeks later he was dead.

Monday, October 9
Morning—Afternoon

Rho wasn't scheduled to work Monday morning, but she didn't intend to run her usual errands or clean house. Things went on hold when she assisted on an investigation. She put in a quick call to Detective Grossman to inform him of what she would be doing, then phoned the Clark County detective who had visited Chrystal Ackerman's apartment building. He confirmed the facts in his message and added that he was waiting on a court order that would allow him to enter the apartment and search for information on the victim's next of kin.

Rho said, "If you run across anything linking her with anyone in my jurisdiction, will you let me know?"

"Sure thing. By the way, this morning I spoke with the woman who owns the service Ackerman worked for. She called in on the weekend, said she was taking a few days off. Woman thinks the mother may be in a nursing home, but she doesn't know where."

"Ackerman operated out of a service?"

"Yeah, Dial-a-Pal."

"How does that work, exactly?"

"Service has a nine-hundred phone number, and calls're switched to individual lines in the employees' homes. Charges—two-fifty to three bucks a minute—go on the customers' phone bills. Service collects from the phone company, then pays the worker her cut, which isn't much more than minimum wage. The idea is for the worker to keep the client on the line as long as possible; they say an average hold time of eleven minutes makes it profitable."

"This stuff must be regulated. Are there restrictions as to what the workers can say or do?"

Stevens laughed. "I hear they use a lot of euphemisms. Things like 'melons' for 'breasts,' 'globes' for 'buttocks.' You ask me, there's not much difference."

"What about soliciting?"

"Service prohibits it, but that doesn't stop them. There's nothing to keep a worker from giving her private number to a client, like Ackerman did to Sean Bartlow."

"You have any idea what kind of women do this work?"

"They seem to be all across the board. A lot of housewives stuck at home with small kids. People with few skills. Anybody who has a good telephone voice and isn't squeamish. It's a good deal for people like that—as bona fide employers, the services're required to pay into Social Security, issue IRS forms. Some of the better ones even offer benefits."

You learn something every day, Rho thought. "Did the owner of Ackerman's service tell you anything about her?"

"Yeah, and it's kind of interesting. Ackerman was an artist, drew while she talked on the phone."

"While she was having sex?"

"For these workers, it's not sex. Most of them have been at it so long that the fantasies're scripted, they can just reel them off the tops of their heads. So Ackerman drew—charcoal sketches. She gave one to the owner of the service, who thinks it's very good."

After Rho ended the call, she sat at her desk for a while, staring into the dregs in her coffee cup and contemplating the contradictions that could exist side by side within an individual. Chrystal, crafting her drawings while titillating men on the phone. Rho, controlling herself rigidly while entertaining her demons. On the surface, their lives would have seemed to be polar opposites, but hadn't they really been sisters under the skin?

Guy set his laptop in the trunk of his rental car under the watchful gaze of Hugh Dawson. He slammed the lid shut and turned to face the motel owner.

Dawson smirked and said, "Guess you'll be heading back to New York now."

"Just because you kicked me out of your motel? Hardly."

"No place else to go. Fags that own the B and B had a big fight, closed it down. Guess they'll be going back to San Francisco where they belong."

"There're other towns and places to stay along the coast," Guy said. "Besides, I like it here." To prove his

point, he took a deep breath of fog-damp air, raised his
eyes to the ridge, where the sky was already turning blue.

Dawson's smirk faded.

Guy asked, "You say the owners of the B and B might
be moving?"

"Probably."

"That means they'll be selling the place. Maybe I'll
buy it." Dawson's face pulled into deep, sour lines. Guy
gave him a jaunty wave as he got into his car.

Sometimes, he told himself, he displayed sheer genius
when thinking on his feet.

Rho was on her way out the door when Cody barked
and met her gaze with soulful, pleading eyes. "Okay,
come on," she said, "but expect to spend a lot of time in
the truck today." The Lab shot through the door ahead of
her and was already waiting at the carport when she got
there.

Maybe, she thought as she belted him into the passenger's seat, it wasn't fair to keep such a big, active dog
when she was gone so much. If she wanted companion-
ship, perhaps a cat would be better. She'd had several and
knew they didn't suffer as much as dogs from their owners' absence. But when she'd bought up here on the ridge
it had seemed too isolated and a dog seemed like a good
idea. Now that she was comfortable in her surroundings
she'd become much too attached to Cody to give him up.

"And I never would, I promise," she told him.

Cody cocked his head and regarded her as if he understood.

She'd decided to stop by the substation before she
headed to the Sea Stacks to talk with Guy Newberry.

There she ran into Detective Grossman, who was on his way out to interview a potential witness in the Ackerman case.

"CJIS check came back negative for a record on her," he told Rho. "I expected as much, since she lived out of state. Nothing from NCIC yet. The feds're slow. And no autopsy results, either. By the way," he added, "you and Gilardi're relieved of patrol duty till further notice. Keep on the case, and we'll meet here this evening at nineteen hundred hours."

No one was at any of the desks when Rho entered the building, but as she checked her inbox she heard Valerie coming down the hallway that led past the interrogation room and holding cell to the rest- and supply rooms. "Good morning," Rho said.

"What's good about it? At six o'clock the Santa Carla TV station did a news segment on the murder and public reaction to it. And they rehashed the other. San Francisco and Sacramento papers have already called. Grossman ducked them, had me refer them to our public information officer, who you and I know is an idiot. Other cities and the TV stations are now getting into the act, and fifteen minutes ago Gregory Cordova called to tell us that a film crew from Santa Carla just started setting up at Point Deception turnout."

Valerie's voice sounded strange, congested. Rho looked up, saw she was red-eyed and blotchy-faced. "Hey, you been crying?"

"Oh . . ." Valerie sat down at her desk, sighed heavily. "I can't help it. It's Virge. She's still missing. Will and their tenant, that Clay Lawrence, are organizing a search party. They'll meet at the Scurlock place at one, fan out over the whole area. I wish I could help, but my arthritis won't let me."

Valerie looked so downcast that Rho ran through the schedule she'd planned and readjusted it. Until she heard more from Clark County or saw the autopsy results on Ackerman, there was little to do of urgency. "I'll go in your place," she told the clerk.

"Would you? Thanks." Her eyes filled with tears and she blinked them back. "Poor thing. She must feel so alone and scared."

Unless she had gone off voluntarily or met with foul play, Rho thought, but didn't voice it. "You two are good friends, right?"

"We used to be, before."

There it was, another euphemism. "You mean before the canyon murders."

Valerie stiffened. "Do you have to . . . ?"

"Like I told you last night, it's time we started calling them what they were."

". . . I don't know. Maybe."

Rho sat down on her desk, facing Valerie. "Tell me about your friendship with Virge."

"We were best friends from kindergarten on through high school. She married Will right after graduation, I married my husband a few months later. We stood up for each other. Our babies were born three weeks apart." Valerie smiled at the memory.

"We used to take them to the playground and the beach together. Called ourselves 'blue-jean mommas,' because we didn't think having babies meant you had to get old and dowdy. When my husband left, Virge was there for me. When Will got hurt falling off some scaffolding and couldn't work for six months, I was there for her."

She paused, her gaze somber and distant. "Those babies—her Rick and my Joe—were best friends too. Should've been as many years as we were. But then my Joe was killed by that drunk driver, and Rick drowned in that high surf the next year. Those were things the blue-jean mommas didn't count on. We outlived our own children."

Rho closed her eyes, and the image of Heath Wynne's dying moments appeared as if her lids were a projection screen. Quickly she opened them.

"You know what hurts?" Valerie added. "Those children in the canyon, they shouldn't've died either. But everybody made such a fuss over their deaths. Nobody except for really close friends made much of Joe's or Rick's."

"Valerie, that's not so." Rho could remember the shock waves that had spread through the community after the accidents.

"Oh, people were nice. They brought food and said all the right things and came to the services. But nobody was . . . horrified like they were about those children in the canyon. Virge's and my boys, their deaths were just . . . ordinary."

Rho understood what she meant, felt her pain. No death should be ordinary.

"Rhoda?"

"Yes?"

"Your father called again."

Oh hell. "I'll stop by there before I go up to the Scurlocks'."

"I know he'd appreciate the attention."

She didn't reply.

"Rhoda?"

"Yes?"

"Take it from me: Don't neglect the people you love. Every minute is precious."

The woman who answered Guy's knock at the door of the Pelican Cove Bed & Breakfast was at least six feet tall and wore her dark brown hair in a knot that was secured to her head by what looked to be a pair of chopsticks. She hugged a bundle of flowered sheets to her ample breasts, and her glare bored into him on eye level.

She said, "What's the matter, you can't read the sign? We're closed."

He put on the smile he used with reluctant interviewees, what he called boyish and disarming, and Diana had called an ass-kissing grin. Apparently the woman was on Diana's side; the lines between her eyebrows deepened.

He said, "I was hoping you might take on a guest anyway. It would be long-term, and I don't require frills. I'd be glad to pay your highest rate—"

"I told you—"

"For God's sake, Becca, don't turn away a paying customer at this juncture!" A man's voice spoke behind her.

The woman called Becca half turned and directed her scowl at the speaker. "You said—"

"Never mind what I said. I'll handle this." A slender man with wavy dark hair and finely chiseled features stepped around the woman. In spite of his good looks his skin had an unhealthy pallor and there were pronounced purplish shadows under his eyes. "Go finish the laundry," he added.

"It's finished."

"Then go do . . . whatever it is you do."

Becca made a snorting sound and moved away.

The man said to Guy, "I'm Kevin Jacoby, one of the owners. Did I hear you mention a long-term stay?"

Guy nodded and introduced himself. "I had a room at the Sea Stacks, but the proprietor took a dislike to me."

"Oh, that old fart. He dislikes everybody. I can fix you up with a room, Mr. Newberry. In fact, you can have your pick of all ten."

Guy followed him into a high-ceilinged foyer with a massive oak reception desk, where Jacoby produced a guest register and proposed a surprisingly modest weekly rate. "I can't in good conscience charge you any more," he said. "It's not feasible to provide you with breakfast since we have no other guests, and it won't take Becca long to make up your room. By the way, don't mind her. She's in a bad mood this morning because I told her I'd have to let her go. She'll be bringing you fresh towels by the armful once she realizes you've temporarily saved her job."

The corner room that Jacoby showed him to was spacious, with a fireplace and a turret window overlooking the highway and the sea. The decor was what he'd come to expect from B&Bs, floral prints and dried flowers and bowls of potpourri and an overabundance of throw pillows. But he supposed he could put up with froufrou in exchange for privacy and the absence of old man Dawson. He made two trips to his car, left his things unpacked, and was on his way out when Jacoby stopped him.

"I couldn't help but notice your laptop and file boxes," he said. "Are you some kind of writer?"

"Yes, freelance."

"Well, if it's a quiet place to encourage your muse that you're after, you've found it. The town's half dead. Even my partner's decamped. But that's another story."

Guy waited, but the story didn't materialize. After more small talk, he said good-bye to Jacoby and left the inn.

Becca was leaning against his car, clad in a wind-breaker and smoking a cigarette. As he came toward her she dropped the butt to the ground and toed it out. "I want to apologize for being rude before," she said.

"No apology necessary. I understand you were upset about losing your job."

"Yeah. Thanks for saving it. It's not much, but it fits easy with the rest of my schedule." She sighed. "This is sure one of those Mondays."

"Something else wrong?"

"Besides my boyfriend being about to dump me and a million other things? Nah."

She was so downcast that Guy tried to cheer her. "I can't believe any sane man would dump a pretty woman like you."

"Oh, it's not dumping, not exactly. He's just decided to go back to his old life in Seattle. Which leaves me here, in my old life that wasn't so hot."

"I'm sorry, Becca."

"Thanks, Mr. Newberry." She smiled wanly at him and

walked toward an old Honda that was parked at the side of the building.

Guy had always been the kind of man to whom total strangers would confide their most intimate secrets. It was a gift that sometimes involved him in superficial and inane conversations, but went a long way in developing useful sources.

Guy Newberry had checked out of the Sea Stacks over an hour before.

"Did he say where he was going?" Rho asked Hugh Dawson.

"Mentioned the B and B, but it's closed. Don't think we're gonna get rid of him anytime soon, though."

"If not, why'd he leave here?"

"I threw him out." Dawson nodded proudly, as if he'd performed a patriotic act.

"And why'd you do that?"

"Bastard's gonna write about them murders, stir up a hornet's nest. You ask me, it's better to let sleeping dogs lay."

Rho never would have thought that an allusion to the Cascada Canyon murders could make her smile, but Dawson's mixed metaphor actually caused the corners of her mouth to quirk up.

He noticed and frowned. "What the hell's so funny?"

"Maybe it's time we wake up those dogs, Hugh. Stir up those hornets. Follow them and see where they lead us."

"You gone crazy?"

"No, I think I'm about to go sane."

She left the motelkeeper with his mouth agape and

went out to her truck. When she drove by the B&B she saw only Kevin Jacoby's Ford Escort parked there. Newberry could have gone north to find a room at the Deer Harbor Inn or one of the more luxurious establishments at Calvert's Landing, or south to one of the numerous motels at Westhaven. She called Central Dispatch and put out a BOLO on him. Then she headed for the defunct yacht harbor where her father lived aboard his old cabin cruiser, the *Rhoda A*.

"Suspected you'd be back."

Gregory Cordova motioned at the rocker by his woodstove where Guy had sat the day before and brought him a mug of coffee without asking if he wanted any. As he sat opposite him, the old man added, "I hear from my mailman that things've been lively in town."

"Lively's a good word for it. What did he tell you?"

"Well, folks've been acting up. And Samantha Lindsay was killed in a car wreck last night."

"Who's she?"

"Beautiful blonde-haired woman. Married to a handsome fellow who looks like he plays a lot of golf. Second-home people."

"I think I've seen her a couple of times in the hotel bar."

"Let me guess: At least one of those times she was with somebody besides her husband."

"Correct."

Cordova shook his head. "Sad thing when a woman— or a man—strays like that. Makes you wonder what's lacking there. Me, I always looked but I never touched. Used to tell Felicia—my wife—that the day I stopped looking she might as well plant me six feet under. Hell, the other day I even gave a good once-over to that woman got herself killed."

"You saw her at the turnout?"

"Sure. Cutoff jeans riding up over a nice curve of ass. What the hell else was I supposed to do?"

"But you didn't stop?"

"No. Me and a whole lot of other folks." The old man shook his head regretfully. "The way of the human animal these days, I guess. But these young people, they seem so capable. And I was tired from my shopping and not thinking clear. But you know, while I was carting my groceries into the house, I had a feeling, was like a goose walking across my grave. Her grave, probably. It's not my time yet. Now and then I wish it was. I've outlived my usefulness, would gladly trade places with that girl if I could. And now another woman, Virge Scurlock, has gone missing. Only hope it's not more of the same."

"Since when is she missing?"

"Disappeared from her bed sometime last night. They're putting together a civilian search party, calling for volunteers, but . . ."

"Odd, these things happening immediately before the anniversary of the murders."

"Yes, it is."

Guy hesitated, looking down into the mug he held and swirling the coffee. "Mr. Cordova, before I left here yesterday you said that you know as much as anybody else about the murders. And then you added, 'More, maybe.'"

The old man nodded.

"You also told me that it's time to take the skeletons out of the closet and dust them off."

"I seem to recall saying something of that nature."

"Well, how do you feel about picking up that dust rag and going to work?"

The *Rhoda A* was a forty-year-old CrisCraft that had once been named the *Mary A* for Rho's mother. After Mary left town with an itinerant bartender who had briefly worked at the hotel, Jack Antolini renamed the cruiser and maintained her well till Rho went off to college. Some of Rho's fondest memories were of the time she'd spent aboard her namesake. But when she moved back to Signal Port she discovered that her father had let the craft deteriorate, and since he'd moved onto her after his forced retirement, he'd done little maintenance. Now the *Rhoda A* was shabby and barnacled and rode low in her slip, the only tenant of the abandoned marina.

Jack came up on deck as Rho approached: a big man with several days of gray stubble on his face and broken veins on his broad nose, wearing rumpled work clothes and an Oakland A's cap. When he saw who was coming he broke into a wide grin that revealed tobacco-stained teeth and called, "Permission to come aboard granted, Deputy."

She stepped onto the boat and hugged him. He smelled of Irish whiskey and cheap cigars and probably hadn't bathed in days, but the solidity of his chest and arms called forth memories of the nights when she would wake from dreams of abandonment and chaos, crying for her mother. Jack had always been there to comfort her when he wasn't working, and only a quick radio patch away while on duty.

They went down to the cabin, Jack leaning heavily on

the railing to compensate for the bad leg that had resulted from his car crash. While she seated herself at the small table, he turned down his scanner and poured them both coffee, lacing his liberally with Irish. Rho held back the critical words that automatically came to mind. They would only lead to a quarrel, and besides, she was not one to talk. She may not have satisfied last night's craving for alcohol, but only because it had eventually been overwhelmed by exhaustion following her overlong shift.

"So where's that mutt of yours?" Jack asked. He was Cody's biggest fan.

"I left him at the substation. Valerie's had a gift for him in her desk for days—a new chew bone—and I couldn't tear him away from it."

Jack snorted. "It's a wonder she hasn't knitted him one of those things she makes. Someday you'll leave him there and when you pick him up, he'll be wearing it and looking like an idiot."

"She means well, Dad."

"You think I don't know that? She's a good woman, has had a hard life. Of course, you could say the whole damn town's had a hard life. What's your take on these latest developments?" Jack leaned forward, eyes glittering greedily.

Rho brought up her guard. These work-related discussions always went badly. "Well, we don't have the autopsy results on Chrystal Ackerman yet, but I think we can safely say it was rape-and-murder. Our appeal for people to come forward with information places her at Point Deception somewhere between fifteen hundred fifty and nineteen hundred hours, but nowhere else, and we doubt she was killed there. Clark County, Nevada, is trying to contact next of kin, and if whoever that is can't shed any light on where she was going or why, I guess Ned Grossman or Denny Shepherd'll have to fly down there, go over to her apartment, talk in person with the people who knew her."

"Any chance the Lindsay woman's death is related?"

"There's nothing to indicate that was anything other than an accident."

"There's a circular out on her jewelry and credit cards."

"Someone robbed the body, yes."

"Someone who caused the accident, maybe."

"There was no damage to her car consistent with involvement with another vehicle." She heard her language become stilted, as if she were trying to justify her theories to Station Commander Iverson.

"What about the Scurlock woman?" Jack asked. "Is her disappearance related to the murder?"

"Only in the sense that the murder made a previously unstable woman flip out."

"You taking a good look at Will Scurlock? Cases like that, you always look at the husband or wife."

"There was nothing in his behavior to make me suspect him of any wrongdoing."

"Uh-huh." Jack's tone was skeptical.

"Look, Dad, I was there, and you weren't!"

Hurt flickered in his eyes and he looked away. Rho bit her lip, ashamed both for snapping at him and for reminding him that he hadn't been and never again would be officially present at a crime scene. He drained his mug and went back for more—straight Irish this time.

"Who's this Guy Newberry you've got a BOLO out on?" he asked, his back to her.

"You don't miss a word that comes over that scanner, do you?" She tried to force affection into her tone, lighten the atmosphere.

"I was a deputy for over thirty years, Rhoda. I can hear scanner broadcasts in my sleep."

Rhoda. He really was hurt. He'd always called her "honey" or, since she'd joined the department, "Deputy."

"Well, Guy Newberry is a writer from New York City. He came out here to do a book on the Cascada Canyon murders. At least that's what Wayne heard. I want to talk to him about the project, but I can't locate him since Hugh Dawson kicked him out of the Sea Stacks."

Jack turned and leaned against the counter. "Why'd Dawson do that?"

"Because of the book."

"Well, Hugh's an asshole, but he's got a point."

"Does he? I wonder. Besides, kicking him out of the motel isn't going to stop a man like Newberry. I've met him."

"He's got to be stopped."

"How?"

"You should know, Deputy."

"What does that mean?"

"There's stuff in the property room at headquarters. Plenty of incriminating stuff. Plant it on him, pick him up, give him the option of leaving the county or going to jail."

"Oh, come on, Dad!"

"Goddamn it!" Jack exclaimed. "Where's your backbone? This town has suffered enough. The department's been embarrassed enough. No New York City writer who doesn't give a rat's ass about the problems we've got here should be allowed to ridicule us in print. And he sure as hell shouldn't be allowed to ridicule my daughter!"

Here we go, she thought. He's really into it now. "Why would he ridicule me?"

"Do I have to point out the obvious? I guess I do. One, because you panicked and didn't get a dying statement from a witness. Two, because you disturbed a crime scene. Three, because you took an incomplete statement from another witness, and the omissions weren't caught till the FBI stepped in. Four, because you broke the chain of physical evidence. Are those enough reasons for you?"

Rho gripped the table's edge, fought for control. Her father's anger filled the small cabin.

"We've been over this before," she said. "I'll go over it again, but this is the last time. Ever. I couldn't get a statement from Heath Wynne; he was only a little boy, dying in extreme pain. The shed I took Oriana Wynne out of wasn't technically a crime scene. Yes, I was distracted and unfocused when I took Virge Scurlock's statement, but show me anyone who wouldn't've been after what I'd gone through. And as for breaking the chain of evidence . . ."

"Yes? How're you gonna justify that?"

She voiced it, for the first time ever. "I didn't misplace those blood samples, Dad. Wayne did."

Gregory Cordova remained silent when Guy finished summarizing what he already knew about the Cascada Canyon killings. Finally he said, "You may know a lot about those people, but I know things the sheriff and even the FBI didn't find out."

"Why didn't you share them with the authorities?"

"I had my reasons, but they're not important anymore."

"Then shall we get started?" Guy turned on his tape recorder.

The old man looked askance at it, then shrugged. "Okay, first thing is about that couple who used to visit the canyon with their little girl. Squatters in an abandoned cabin on the ridge. Sometimes I'd see their old bus parked under the pine trees when I passed the canyon on my way to town. But a lot of times they were there without the bus."

"Meaning they knew about the deer track past the pond and used it."

"I'd say they used it most every day. Their little girl was always playing with the canyon kids in that meadow by the highway."

"So they could've had something to do with the murders, come and gone unobserved."

"Except on that night they drove straight through the gate."

"You saw that?"

Cordova nodded. "I was fixing my fence at the far north end of my property. Damn fishermen were always pulling it down till I decided to give them access at the turnout. This was about an hour before dark. Bus was still there when I went back to the house."

Interesting that he hadn't reported their presence. "What d'you recall about the family?"

"They were kinda raggedy. Man was maybe in his mid-thirties, the woman younger. Little girl around five or six. Parents were standoffish, but the little girl was friendly. She'd see me working around my property and wave."

"Can you describe the parents?"

"Woman had beautiful red hair down to her ass. Man played the guitar, sang. Sometimes I'd see him sitting in the van with the side door open, keeping the Wynne fellow company while he worked on his car, and he'd be making music. Wasn't very good, but at least he could carry a tune."

"The newspaper said that Oriana Wynne could only give a first name for the little girl, Chrissy. There was no mention of the parents. You ever hear their names?"

"No."

"Is it possible they could've killed all those people?"

The old man shook his head. "No way. Would've taken more than a man and a woman—and a slothful man and woman at that. No, I think they saw what happened and took off."

"So that's all you know?"

"About them, yes. Now, there was somebody else living in the canyon for a while, a man maybe in his late twenties. Was there for around a month, but two weeks before the murders he was gone."

"Can you describe him?"

"Tall, thin, blond hair. I saw him in the meadow a couple of times, clearing land for a fall vegetable garden. Got it spaded up and had sacks of fertilizer and compost there, but it never got planted."

Guy considered. The man probably didn't have anything to do with the killings, but the timing and abruptness of his departure was interesting.

"There's one other thing," Cordova said. Excitement rippled under the surface of his voice and he leaned forward.

This is it, Guy thought. He's saved the best for last.

"That Blakeley woman, she had an outside interest. Couple of times I saw her leaving the property up north by the speed-limit sign. Came down a path through the bushes near where the stream runs under the highway in a culvert. Would be a car waiting for her. She'd get in and off they'd go. I found that kinda interesting, so I played detective. Waited there to see how long they'd be gone. Two hours at most and he'd drop her off. Big clinch before she got out."

Guy asked, "Did you recognize the man?"

"Yes."

"But you didn't tell the sheriff's department about this, either."

"No. The man was somebody I didn't want to make an enemy of. Had a reputation for violence, even back then."

"Who was he, Mr. Cordova?"

The old man's eyes glittered as he gave up his secret. "Deputy Wayne Gilardi."

"Wayne misplaced those blood samples?" Jack stared at Rho in disbelief.

"You heard me, Dad."

He came back to the table, slumped on the bench seat. "And you covered for him all these years?"

She nodded.

"Why, honey?"

"Because he was my mentor from the day I joined the department. He stood up for me against the guys who didn't want a woman to be a deputy. Besides, Janie was pregnant and he was up for promotion to a higher pay grade. An error like that would've screwed his chances."

"He ask you to take the blame?"

"No."

"He tell you not to?"

"Yes."

"But you did it anyway."

"Right. I didn't have as much to lose."

Jack looked at her with respect. "I'm proud of you, Deputy."

"Well, everybody made mistakes—at the scene and later on. None of us, right on up to Detective Lieutenant Marx, were prepared to handle a crime like that. I didn't see any reason for Wayne to suffer. I was a rookie; it was to be expected of me."

Her father shook his head. "To be expected of you by everybody but your old man. I was tough on you. Too tough, and now I'm sorry."

"Not as tough as some." She thought of Will Scurlock's tirade. "Besides, you're a perfectionist, and you were frustrated because you couldn't help out."

"Still, I should've been more supportive of my girl."

She made a gesture of dismissal. "I could use some support now."

"Name it."

She hesitated, unsure if she could trust the sudden change in Jack's attitude. "I'm worried about Wayne, Dad."

"Why?"

"He's changed. I didn't fully realize how much until I was talking with Will Scurlock about the gradual change in Virge. Wayne was always on the tough side, but he's graduated from knocking around drug dealers to roughing up anybody who crosses him. Last night he was right on the edge—kicked ass before he ran some people in for petty infractions."

"Not good in a sensitive situation like this."

"No, and it's not just his professional life that's messed up. He's got at least three different women on the side, and Janie's threatened to leave him. Her coworkers at the cable TV office tell me she's turned up with bruises on her face and arms more than once. Wayne beat the shit out of Lily's boyfriend last month, and Saturday night he jerked her around in public."

"So what's causing this?"

"I think that Wayne, like the rest of us at the department, feels guilty because we never solved those murders. Guilty and angry, and he's taking it out on everybody else."

Jack was silent for a moment. "Before, you said you didn't think this Newberry fellow could be stopped from writing his book."

"I very much doubt it."

"You also seemed to wonder if trying to suppress it was a good idea."

She nodded. "Maybe it's better if he brings it all out in the open. Maybe then we'd have closure."

Again Jack was silent, and she knew better than to interrupt his thoughts. Before he spoke, the set of his mouth told her he'd reached a hard conclusion.

"If that's what you want, then you know what to do."

"Do I?"

"Yes, you do, Deputy. But since you seem somewhat confused, allow your old dad to spell it out for you."

*   *   *

Guy had been back in his room at the bed-and-breakfast only minutes when someone knocked on the door. He sighed, thinking it was either Kevin Jacoby or Becca Campos. Both were pleasant enough but seemed needy, and at the moment he was in no mood to lend a sympathetic ear. He'd claim to be working, put off whoever it was till later.

When he opened the door, however, Rhoda Swift smiled up at him. She wasn't in uniform, just jeans and a heavy hooded sweater, but the brittle quality of the smile told him this wasn't a social call. Her eyes moved past him to his file boxes and laptop. "I hope I'm not interrupting your work," she said.

"Not at all. I haven't even unpacked yet. So you've heard I've been banished from the Sea Stacks. How'd you find me?"

"I put out a BOLO—be-on-lookout—on you, and one of the other deputies spotted your car. I want to invite you to a search party. Virge Scurlock is missing, and her husband's organizing it. Those of us who have the time are to meet at their place at one. They need everybody they can enlist."

Both her quasi-official manner and the nature of the invitation intrigued him. "I'll be glad to help. Let me get my jacket."

Rhoda insisted on driving, and once he'd belted himself into the passenger's seat of her truck, which was covered in the Lab's hair, he settled back to admire the way she handled the highway's curves. A police-band radio muttered under the dash, and after a minute he asked, "Do they require you to have a radio in your personal vehicle?"

"No, but most of us do. We're understaffed and the

county is hard to police. If there's trouble in the vicinity or someone needs backup, we want to know so we can be there."

After that she spoke little, only to ask if he found his new room comfortable, and resisted his few attempts at conversation. As they drove south he occupied himself by noting the landmarks: the entrance to Cascada Canyon; Point Deception turnout; Gregory Cordova's dirt drive-way. About a mile beyond Cordova's place Rhoda cut sharply to the left and they followed a paved drive that led high onto the ridge. A sprawling yellow house stood in a clearing, its vintage early fifties or perhaps late forties, with a glassed-in porch. An abundance of gnarled rose bushes that still bore papery-looking flowers surrounded it, and a couple of outbuildings with a disused appearance stood nearby.

The driveway ended in a large paved area where over a dozen vehicles were parked, and another dozen spilled over onto the grass beyond. A crowd was gathered in a side yard, and Deputy Wayne Gilardi stood on a platform improvised from cordwood, calling out names. As Guy and Rhoda approached his eyes flickered with surprise and disapproval.

Guy scanned the crowd, noting familiar faces. The bartender from the hotel, a clerk from the supermarket, a waitress from the Oceanside, the maid from the Sea Stacks. Will Scurlock and his tenant, Clay Lawrence, stood next to the platform. Lawrence spotted Guy and nodded.

"Okay," Gilardi said, "take a look at those maps we passed out."

Xeroxed sheets of paper fluttered as people consulted

them. Guy glanced at one the man next to him held. It was a hand-drawn map marked off in grids.

Gilardi went on, "Group One'll cover the area south of here. Your leader's Clay Lawrence. You take your direction from him. Group Two'll move east across the ridge. You follow Will. I'll lead Group Three from here to the highway, then north to the property line. Your leaders have walkie-talkies, so if you find anything, tell them and they'll communicate it to the others. You'll be hearing planes overhead, because Westhaven's pilots' association has volunteered to make an aerial search, but they tell me we've got a better chance of finding Virge than they do. So you're it, folks. Any questions?"

Rhoda called, "Why only north to the property line, Wayne?"

He frowned. "What's that, Swift?"

"Aren't you going to search Cascada Canyon?"

Some people had been talking in low tones while Gilardi gave his instructions, but now silence fell.

The deputy glanced at Will Scurlock, who shook his head. Wayne said, "It's not necessary. Virge would never go there."

"Are you sure of that?"

Again Gilardi glanced at Scurlock, who made an impatient gesture. "Swift," he said, "are you volunteering?"

A ripple of uneasy comment spread through the crowd.

"I'll be team leader for that area, yes."

"Well, Mr. Newberry there'll have to be your team. Everybody else is assigned."

"Fine by me."

"Then let's get started." Gilardi shot Rhoda a hard look before stepping off the cordwood.

Rhoda turned and began walking toward her truck. Guy followed. People gave them a wide berth, several casting puzzled or uneasy glances. When they were driving along a dirt track toward the north end of the property he asked, "Why're you doing this?"

"We're looking for Virge."

"You heard Wayne. She'd never go to the canyon. Her husband looked as though he agreed."

"You know, Guy, my former husband always thought he knew exactly what I would or wouldn't do—and more often than not he was wrong."

A downed tree, many years down, judging from the smooth, silvery sheen of its bark, lay across the track in front of them. Rhoda stopped the truck and said, "From here on we walk."

Guy got out and followed her, noting the stiffness of her spine, the jerkiness of her gait. On edge and under rigid control, he thought. Scared? He wondered if she'd planned beforehand to go to the canyon or if her volunteering was strictly impulsive. Whichever, it must be difficult for her to return there after these many years.

They moved through forestland on ground thick with needles, where pinecones lay in abundance and large bright orange mushrooms grew. A car backfired on the highway, and momentarily Rhoda's steps faltered. A plane's engine droned low overhead. The trees grew taller, denser, and then Guy spotted the first of the giant redwoods. His eyes were drawn upward along their deeply striated trunks to sunlight filtering hazily through their branches. He stopped, but Rhoda walked on, into a clearing. When he caught up with her—

"What in God's name is that?" The arrangement of

rusted, twisted metal rose amidst the trees. It resembled a
half dozen electric drill bits, their shanks embedded in
concrete.

"One of Forrest Wynne's sculptures. There's another in
front of their geodesic dome. He was supposed to be a genius, but . . ." She shrugged.

Guy recalled the eggbeater controversy that prompted
the Wynnes to flee San Francisco. The artist had had an
unfortunate affinity for common household objects. He
walked around the sculpture, trying to make sense of it.

"D'you know what this was called?"

"No."

"Well, I don't suppose it matters now."

Rhoda didn't reply. She was standing with her hands
thrust in the pockets of her sweater, head turned toward
the canyon. Steeling herself, Guy sensed, for a return to
what they both knew to be an evil place.

Rho motioned to Guy and started toward the slope that
led down into the canyon, adrenaline coursing through
her. She didn't really believe Virge Scurlock had gone
there, not to the birthplace of the demons that plagued her.
But Rho's demons had been born there too, and she'd
reached the point where she needed to confront them.
Needed also to show this man the canyon as she knew it.

Damp needles made the downslope slippery, and she
moved with care. Behind her she heard Guy slide and
right himself with a grunt. Ahead she saw the row of
poplars that grew along the stream, their golden leaves
moving fitfully in the breeze. Water splashed over rocks,
glinting in the sunlight, running faster than she remem-

bered. A weathered humpbacked footbridge spanned the stream bed.

The bridge was what Heath Wynne had been running toward when he was shot.

Rho stopped, taking a deep breath. Guy came up beside her.

"This canyon," she said, conscious of a tremor in her voice, "is named for the waterfall near its end, that generates this stream. There's a second stream on the far north side of the property near the wellhouse." Before he could comment she turned and moved across the bridge. Its planks were spongy under her weight.

"We're in the center of the property now," she went on. "Thirty-one acres. This bridge is on a triangle with the Blakeley house and the drug lab. The Wynnes' dome is directly ahead of us through those trees."

"Why are you talking like a tour guide?" Guy asked.

"Am I? I'm sorry. But I want you to understand this place, if you insist on writing about it."

"We're not looking for Virge Scurlock, are we?"

"Not really. That was an excuse to get you here. I knew none of the others would come along."

"You didn't need an excuse. You could've just asked me."

"I suppose so, but I know you've been here before. I was afraid you'd already drawn your own conclusions and wouldn't want my input."

"I don't work that way."

"Good." Now she was aware of a curious detachment, as if someone else had taken over her mind and body. She began walking along the stream bed. Everything was familiar—that rock, that tree, this curve of the bank. Etched into her mind many years before, yet she felt no connection. The graveled path that had led to the bridge had mostly washed away during a dozen rainy seasons, yet . . .

She stopped, faced Guy. "This is the spot where Heath Wynne died. In my arms."

He looked down at the ground, then up into her eyes. Silently. His eyes, she saw, were changed, as if something in her experience had communicated itself to something in his.

"If you're to write this story," she said, "there are things you need to know. You have to get it right. To do justice to the victims, our town, and my department. I can tell and show you those things."

"Do you want me to write it?"

"I think so, but even if I didn't, I know I couldn't stop you."

"Probably not. The Harrisons, Susan Wynne's family, want it told. For, I think, the same reasons you do."

"Closure."

"And answers. There are answers hidden here. And I've a reputation as a man who can get them."

Guy stood with Rhoda next to the eggbeater sculpture in front of the geodesic dome and experienced the night of the murders through her halting words.

"In her nine-one-one call, Virge said the shots she'd heard definitely came from the canyon. I was first on the scene and found the Blakeleys' bodies in their house. I called for backup and an ambulance and was on my way here to check on the others when I heard someone moaning."

"Heath."

She nodded. "He was close to death, and there was nothing I could do except try to comfort him, but I think I talked myself into believing that somehow I could make him hold on. You know how you do that under certain circumstances? Imagine your will is so strong that by force of it you can prevent the inevitable?"

Oh yes, he knew. When Diana was shot he'd thrown his body across hers, imagining he could protect her, even though the bullet had already entered her brain, even though she was already gone.

"What is it?" Rhoda asked.

She'd seen his pain. He turned away from her, stared up at Forrest Wynne's enormous sculpture. He'd never spoken with anyone about that subject except on the most factual and superficial of terms, and he certainly wouldn't go into it with a relative stranger.

He said, "Your experience is becoming very real to me."

"Is it? Ever since we came into the canyon I've felt as though I'm sleepwalking."

"That's natural. You're insulating yourself. How quickly did your backup get here?"

"Very. We've got a good response rate. Wayne was first. He found Heath and me, directed the EMTs to us. Afterwards he and I found the little girl who survived. I'll show you where later."

"That was Heath's sister, Oriana. Where were their parents?"

"In the dome. Dead of multiple gunshot wounds. Because of that, and the fact that each of the Blakeleys was shot only once, we assumed at first that the Wynnes were the shooters' primary targets. But when Wayne and another deputy found Bernhard Ulrick . . ."

"He was in his drug lab?"

"Yes. Wayne saw a light burning up canyon and they went to investigate. I stayed down by the Blakeley house with Oriana. She wouldn't let anybody but me touch her. Anyway, Ulrick had been shot repeatedly with a semiautomatic weapon. His body was literally shredded."

"How did Wayne handle the situation?"

"He was badly shaken. We all were. None of us had ever encountered that kind of crime scene. But you know, he maintained fairly good control until he went into the Blakeley house to see how the evidence collection was going. When he came out he ran through the trees to that old car that's still sitting there and beat on it with his fists."

That could mean Claudia Blakeley had been more than a casual lay to the deputy, Guy thought.

"Why're you asking about Wayne?"

He didn't want to tell her about Gilardi and the Blakeley woman, not yet at least. "I guess because, aside from you, he's the only person I've met who was here that night."

"He's the only person who was here, aside from me, who's still alive or in the area. Station Commander Warren died six, seven years ago. Detective Lieutenant Marx, who headed the investigation, got a job with Yolo County. The others are working in other parts of the state or out of law enforcement entirely. That investigation really cost the department."

"Because the murders were never solved?"

"Yes. And because the FBI made it plain that they considered us both inept and corrupt. And because people didn't want to live in a place where something that horrible had happened. But we weren't inept or corrupt. We were human. We made mistakes."

"Such as?"

"When I interviewed Virge I got the sequence of what she heard screwed up. Wayne misplaced the blood samples from the scene of Ulrick's death. We all overlooked things, didn't secure the scene properly. But even big, experienced law enforcement agencies make those kinds of errors. I've always thought the real fault was in Sheriff Caxton's failure to bring in the FBI right away. He had a big ego, wanted his people to solve a case that made national headlines. It wasn't until the victims' families pressured that he gave in, and then it was too late."

Rhoda looked so pained that Guy shelved his line of questioning and started toward the geodesic dome. Its windows were filthy, and it resembled a deflating balloon, gradually caving in upon itself. When he turned the knob and pushed, the door stuck in its frame, swollen by moisture.

Initially the room beyond was disorienting, its curving walls giving him the impression he'd stepped under an inverted bowl. A kettledrum fireplace with seating around it stood at its center, and beyond that pie-shaped areas devoted to various activities were separated by low partitions. The kitchen was small but well equipped, the play area overflowing with toys. Archways opened to the additions he'd seen from outside. As in the Blakeley house, a thick layer of dust overlay everything, as well as the handiwork of spiders and rats. Two chalked outlines showed faintly on the floor by the fireplace, and—

Guy squatted down and sighted along the linoleum. Old footprints, like those he'd noticed at the Blakeley house the day before. Similar large size, similar tread. A persistent thrill-seeker, or someone with a real purpose?

"What's that you're looking at?" Rhoda asked.

He hadn't heard her come up behind him, and when he started, he realized how badly the scene had him spooked. "Somebody's been here recently. There're footprints in the dust. At the Blakeley house, too."

"How recently?"

"Not in the past twenty-four hours, if that's what you're thinking. But within the past year." He stood. "I see where two people died. Forrest and Susan?"

"Right."

"What about the sister?"

"In the bathroom, hiding in the shower." She motioned at one of the archways.

"You come inside here that night?"

"No, but later I saw the photographs. I had to stay with Oriana till the county social services said they couldn't send anybody out for her. Then I took her to the Scurlocks', where I interviewed Virge and she spent the night."

"So she let Virge comfort her?"

"Oh, yes. Virge has a special way with children and she relates to another person's pain. She and Will lost their only son to a drunk driver when he was fifteen."

Pain. Loss. Death. Jesus, why was he here in this gruesome memorial to wasted and truncated lives? Why, when he had finally begun to heal from his own pain, loss, and death, had he placed himself in a situation where he was forced to confront these things all over again?

"Guy?"

He pivoted, scanning the room with a professional eye. Forced himself to separate his own emotions from those that must be trapped here. At the Blakeley house he'd felt fear and panic, but now . . .

"Guy?"

He shook his head, motioned for her to be quiet.

It felt different here. Fear and panic were present, yes, but there was something else. He pictured Susan Wynne's empty dark eyes as they appeared in the second photograph he had of her. Pictured Forrest, and realized the reason behind his apparent lack of humor. It was present in the musty air, as strong as if they had died only yesterday.

Resignation.

Susan and Forrest had gradually been giving up on life, perhaps since the day they arrived in the canyon. Work had slackened off into idle talk and drug use, and the accompanying death of the spirit. That last night they'd heard the shots at the Blakeley house and realized what was coming. Susan had the presence of mind to send her children away, possibly to tell Forrest's sister, Devon, to conceal herself, but otherwise they'd done nothing.

"Guy?"

He turned. Rhoda was looking at him with the same surprised expression as must be on his own face.

She said, "They just gave up. You feel it too, don't you?"

Chrystal: Before

Friday, October 6
12:11 P.M.

Running down the canyon like a scared little kid. Like me and Heath did that day. Gotta get a grip— *Jesus!* What's that noise?

Oh yeah, one of them hawks. Real screamers. Make awful sounds like they're being tortured. Like the scream I heard when I came down the hill on the deer path that last night. Only it wasn't no hawk.

No, Chryssie, don't go there.

Yeah, like I could stop now.

Jude and Leo left me alone in our cabin that night. They were going down to the canyon but they said I couldn't come along because they had to talk about grown-up things with the others. They were real serious, kinda nervous too.

After a while I got scared. They hardly ever left me alone at night, and it was windy outside. All sorts of sounds, and even though I knew it was just the trees and stuff, I hid under the covers. The cabin really creeped me. It was so old and crummy and smelly, no wonder nobody minded us squatting there. After a while I decided anyplace was better, even outside in the dark, so I got up and put on my jeans and a sweatshirt and headed for the canyon.

The moon was out, so I could see the path where the deer wore down the grass real good, didn't even need a flashlight. When I came up on the pond, I scared off a couple of does that were drinking from it. That was when I started to hear something that sounded like Fourth of July firecrackers. And people yelling.

They were having a party down there, I thought right then, but Jude and Leo hadn't taken me along. Everybody was having a good time but me.

At first I wanted to cry, but then I got mad and started walking faster. It wasn't fair. I hadn't done anything bad. Why was I left out?

After the pond, the path went under some trees. It was awful dark in there, and I kept tripping over roots and stuff. I walked straight into a tree trunk and smacked my forehead. It bled, and then I *did* cry. But not for long because I heard a booming sound, closer by than the others. And I knew it was a shot. I'd heard lots of those. Leo had a gun and he liked to plug beer cans on the stump behind our cabin.

I stopped. Wanting to go down there and see what was happening. Wanting to run back to the cabin and hide in my bed.

Noises in the bushes. Mountain lion! They lived in the hills. One of them snuck down into the canyon and ate Eric's cat.

Run, Chryssie!

He's getting closer!

Then Jude came out of the bushes, nearly on all fours. Her

hair had leaves in it and there was a big scratch on her face and her hands were muddy. She didn't see me, went right by.

I called to her and she stopped. Turned around. She was out of the trees, standing in a patch of moonlight. Her face looked as white as the moon and I'd never seen anybody that scared.

"Chryssie?" she whispered.

And then we heard him. A man yelling, "No no no please no!" And we heard the scream.

It started low and went up and up till every little hair on my arms was standing up straight and my skin got all pimply. I put my hands over my ears but they couldn't block out the shots. *Rat-a- tat,* over and over again like in a war movie.

Jude grabbed me and we ran all the way back to the cabin. Leo was there with the bus. By the cabin door Jude squatted down so she could look me in the eyes and put her hands on my shoulders.

She said, "Something very bad happened tonight, Chrystal. A grown-up thing you don't need to know about. We're never going to talk about it again. You understand that?"

And I said yes, I understood. I didn't dare ask any questions, not when Jude looked at me like that.

Right away we went into the cabin and cleared out all our little stuff and packed it in the bus. Leo said to leave the furniture. And then we split for Oregon. In Portland Leo switched license plates with a car parked in a dark corner of some lot and we left the bus with the keys inside on the street. Then we hitched over to Vancouver, Washington, where he had a buddy who would let us stay with him for a while.

We never did talk about that night again, not till last Saturday when Jude had that real bad seizure and was afraid another one would be the end of her. Yeah, she told me about the murders and the secret she kept all those years. But she sure didn't tell me anything as scary as what I remembered today.

Monday, October 9
Afternoon—Evening

R ho no longer felt as if she were sleepwalking. A moment before she'd connected with the events of that long-ago night on a visceral level. She watched Guy nod in reply to her question and said, "How can we know that the Wynnes just gave up, after all this time?"

He shrugged and motioned for her to precede him outside, where she sucked in fresh air. Everything now looked different, as if she'd removed a pair of dark, distorting glasses.

Guy said, "I've always subscribed to the theory that powerful emotions become trapped in the place where they're experienced. A receptive person can tap into them simply by being in the physical environment. It's similar to the so-called art of psychometry, where the receptor reads something about the owner of an object by handling the object itself."

"You believe that stuff?"

"Yes and no. What I do believe is my experience of it."

"But you said *powerful* emotions. Resignation—that's weak, passive."

"Not always. I'd define it as powerful when it comes to allowing yourself to be killed. And there's another element operating here: The Wynnes may have been creating a diversion so their children could escape. In short, laying down their own lives for Heath's and Oriana's."

Too bad it hadn't worked for Heath. Too bad he hadn't run to the bunkhouse with his sister. "You know," she said, "we always wondered why the Wynne children didn't stay together. I assumed from where I found him that Heath was trying to get to the Scurlocks' for help. But why didn't Oriana go with him?"

"Maybe they didn't start out together."

"No, one of the few things she remembered was that she and her brother were in the dome's play area when they heard the first shots."

"He was older and could run faster, so he was the one who went for help?"

"Probably. But here's another question we had: Given that the bunkhouse is an obvious hiding place, why wasn't she killed?"

"Either the shooters didn't know about her, or they decided to go after their primary target, Ulrick, instead. If they did know about her, they must've counted on her being unable to describe them."

"I guess. It would be interesting to talk with her, see if she's remembered anything more."

"I intend to try. Shall we take a look at the rest of the property?"

Rho stayed outside while Guy examined the bunkhouses and the shack where Bernhard Ulrick had lived. The formerly blue bunkhouse and the shack had not been part of the crime scene, and she didn't need to have another look at the little pink structure where she'd found Oriana. When he came out he was frowning, but shook his head when she asked him why. Holding something back on her, or simply disturbed by the emotions that surely must live there?

Guy looked at his watch. "It's after three. You want to keep going, or call it a day?"

"Let's keep going. I want you to see all of the canyon, but I'm not sure I can make myself come back another time."

They walked uphill on a path made narrow by encroaching pyracantha bushes. The ground was soft and muddy in places from heavy fog and recent rain. Guy didn't speak, and Rho sensed he was working out something, rearranging facts he'd previously known to fit with what he'd learned today. Another plane droned overhead and she looked up in time to see its white tail section glide above the pines.

"Wait a second." Guy put his hand on her arm.

"What is it?"

"Someone's walked along here recently." He pointed down at a series of impressions in the mud. "Two people. From the size of the prints, I'd say a small woman, and either a large woman or a man."

She went over and squatted down to examine them. "They must've been made after it rained last Thursday. The larger ones're superimposed on the smaller. Tread of the larger prints looks like athletic shoes. And look how deep they are—whoever made them was quite heavy. They go right, toward the stream, while the smaller ones go straight."

She stood up and began to follow the larger prints, ducking under thorny pyracantha branches that were heavy with red berries. On the other side of the thicket a ledge of rock extended over the stream bed. The footprints led to it.

Guy was thrashing around in the bushes behind her and now he let out a yelp.

"Be careful in there," she called. "They've got big stickers."

He emerged, sucking his right thumb. "I already found that out."

"City slicker."

"Watch it, woman. You're talking to a man who's hacked his way through jungles."

"Then it's a wonder you survived."

She started across the ledge, conscious of the rush of the stream and splash of the nearby waterfall. When she peered over the edge, she saw the drop was significant, eight or ten feet, and—

"Oh my God!"

"What is it?" Guy asked.

She didn't reply. A figure dressed in jeans and a blue jacket lay prone on the rocks below. Its left arm was outflung, and the sun picked up glints from a diamond wedding band. Rho recognized it and the thick fall of red hair as Virge Scurlock's.

Guy came up beside her and looked down. "Jesus," he said softly, "she *did* come here."

*   *   *

Guy stayed with the body while Rhoda went back to her truck to radio in. She'd been upset, but professionalism quickly took over, and she'd climbed down into the stream bed to make sure the Scurlock woman was dead. Her neck appeared to be broken, she told him when she came back. She'd taken quite a fall and had probably died instantly.

Guy watched her go, wondering if her assumption that Virge's death was an accident had validity. He couldn't get the image of the woman's tense face out of his mind, and if the canyon murders had affected her as strongly as Gregory Cordova claimed, he couldn't imagine her venturing here alone.

Three deaths: A murder. An accident. And now an apparent accident. Coincidence, maybe, but when deaths piled up, particularly in a remote and sparsely populated area like this, there was usually more to it. His journalist's nose for trouble was smelling something unpleasant, but he couldn't identify the odor.

For a moment he toyed with the idea of climbing down to take a closer look at the body, but quickly dismissed the notion. He'd leave the investigation to the professionals. Besides, the tragedies that had occurred in the Signal Port area since his arrival were not the focus of his research. He could incorporate them into the book as dramatic counterpoint, but he should concentrate on the old murders. Plenty to think about there; the sensations he'd both experienced and not experienced on his two trips to the canyon disturbed and puzzled him.

He'd told Rhoda he believed his experience of such phenomena, but that wasn't quite true. They had happened too sporadically over the course of his career to be trusted, unless they could be backed up by hard fact. And he was no natural receptor. If he were, surely he would have been able to tap into the currents of emotion that had moved under the surface of those last days in Asia, before his blind selfishness had caused Diana to lose her life.

No, he didn't believe. Or receive.

The lack of sensation he'd experienced in the little bunkhouse was proof of that. The child who had hidden there had been in extreme terror, yet he'd felt nothing. Perhaps he was only capable of tapping into adult emotions. Or perhaps the ability simply came and went at will.

He considered the events of the fatal night, trying to reconstruct them in a logical fashion. The family who were squatting on the ridge had arrived in their bus before dark. At sometime after dark the killers entered the property, probably from the highway, since they had cut the utility wire. They shot the Blakeleys, then Heath as he fled, then the rest of the Wynne family. And last they shot Bernhard, who was probably hiding in his lab, hoping they wouldn't realize it was tucked back there at the very end of the canyon.

But what about the other family? Had they left before the killers arrived, or seen them and escaped? Chances were they'd seen something, or they wouldn't have abandoned their cabin and most of their possessions.

Damn! Those people were key to what had happened here, but no one alive knew their last name, where they had gone next, or what had become of them.

Rho stood beside the muddy path with Ned Grossman and his partner, Denny Shepherd, while they waited for the photographer to finish with Virge's body. It had taken a long time for everyone to assemble at the scene, and now the light was fading. The wind had risen, blowing chill and steady. Grossman, who possessed not an extra ounce of body fat, shivered and turned up his collar. Rho had just finished explaining Virge's emotional state, and from the expression on the detective's face she gathered that he was entertaining the notion that Virge hadn't come to the canyon alone.

"Where's Gilardi?" he asked, glancing around.

"I don't know, sir. The last I saw him he was headed out with one of the search parties."

"Jesus, why'd he have to be the one who caught the call on Ackerman?" Grossman glared at Rho as if Wayne being the responding officer were her fault. "He wasn't worth squat at that scene, and now when we could use his help, he doesn't show up at all. Maybe it's just as well. This way he can't lose any of the evidence."

She stared at him.

"Oh yeah." He nodded. "When I first joined the department I made it my business to familiarize myself with both personnel and unsolved cases. After I met you and Gilardi it didn't take me long to figure out that he was the type to lose evidence and you were the type to cover for him."

"How many people're aware of that?"

"Not many. But don't take the blame for his mistakes again, particularly on any investigation of mine."

"I won't, sir."

Denny Shepherd had been standing apart while they talked, but now he came over and grinned nastily at Rho. "Swift, I hope you didn't fuck up the scene down there."

She regarded him silently for a moment, deciding she didn't like Shepherd. He was the type of short man who compensated for his lack of stature by acting tough and talking crudely—and impugning others in order to bolster his sagging self-esteem.

"I did not fuck up the scene, Detective Shepherd."

"You said you went down there."

"Only to make sure the victim was dead."

"Hell, after all your years with the department, you can't tell a stiff from, what, twenty feet?"

Grossman said, "Shut up, Denny."

Shepherd shrugged.

Rho looked around for Guy Newberry and spotted him squatting down on the path and examining the footprints in the mud. Most civilians were ill at ease at crime scenes, but Guy conducted himself with assurance. He attracted little attention and was careful not to touch anything or get in anyone's way, but she knew he was cataloging every detail.

Grossman said, "That the guy who was with you when you found the body?"

"Yes." She explained who he was.

"We gonna have trouble with him?"

"You mean is he going to put in a call to people he knows in the media? No. He wants to keep anything he finds out here for himself."

"Good. I want to keep a tight lid on this, so we don't have a repeat of last night. Scene's been secured, and everybody's been warned that they talk to so much as one person, they're looking for a new job. There're some press people from Santa Carla staying at the Sea Stacks, but I'm banking on them heading home when there's nothing further on Ackerman."

The department's part-time photographer, Dave Moretti, struggled through the pyracantha thicket, loaded down with camera gear. He motioned that they were free to go down to the stream, and Grossman and Shepherd started over there. Rho remained where she was. She'd already seen the body, and would leave the evidence collection to the detectives and technicians.

Guy straightened and came toward her. "You okay?" he asked.

"Yeah. What had you so interested over there?"

"The tread on Virge's shoes. It's similar to the tread on the shoes that made the footprints in the dome, and the ones in the Blakeley house. Same shoe size, too."

"But if she made those prints, it would mean this wasn't the first time she came to the canyon."

"Yes, it would."

"Look, Guy, I noticed her shoes when I went down to check for a pulse. They're Reeboks. You can buy them at any department store or factory outlet in the country."

"Well, it was just an observation."

And a good one. She waved to Dave Moretti and called, "You think you can get some shots inside these houses?"

"With a flash, sure. What am I looking for?"

She introduced him to Guy. "He'll show you."

As the two men walked toward the dome, Rho pulled the zipper of her sweater all the way up and stuffed her hands into its pockets. Dusk was falling now, and her flesh rippled as the wind whistled in the far reaches of the canyon. Another person dead in this desolate place, this time a friend, yet she couldn't muster up any feeling. The sensation of sleepwalking had returned shortly after she'd seen Virge's body, coupled with a profound apathy. She was simply going through the motions.

A disturbance by the bridge to the redwood grove drew her attention. Will Scurlock came scrambling up the slope to the driveway, wild-eyed and disheveled. He reached level ground, stumbled, and almost fell. As he righted himself his eyes met hers, pleading with her to tell him that what he'd heard wasn't so. When he saw her expression he seemed to crumble.

Quickly she moved forward, put her arms around him. "I'm so sorry, Will." Inadequate words, but none were adequate at a time like this.

"Oh Jesus," he said, "why Virge? *Why*?" Then his knees buckled.

Rho sank to the ground with him, cradled his grief-torn face against her shoulder, as long ago she'd cradled Heath Wynne's. No more going through the motions. This was as involved as the job—as friendship—got.

Guy came out of the geodesic dome with Dave Moretti and saw Rhoda on the ground with her arms around Will Scurlock. The man was sobbing uncontrollably. Will's fresh grief brought his own, slightly tempered by the passage of time, to the surface. He swallowed, turned away, and motioned Moretti toward the Blakeley house.

"Life sucks," the photographer said.

"Amen to that."

"No question about it. Take Will. He had this great family, then all of a sudden his boy's gone. He and Virge weather the loss because they love each other, but then those murders happen and she starts to lose her mind. Now she's gone, so what's he got left?"

"I don't know. What?"

"Nothing. Well, there's all that land, but what d'you bet he sells it? Big house like that's gonna seem awfully empty without her. There's the business. Will's always been successful along those lines, but work isn't everything. For a while there was somebody on the side, and none of us blamed him, given the situation at home, but Will's too decent a guy to keep something like that going for long, not loving Virge the way he did. So what's left? Nothing."

"Who was the woman?"

"Not your business, mister. She's an okay girl, just kinda mixed up."

Interesting.

They reached the Blakeley house and went up on the porch. Moretti shook his head. "Damned creepy. I'm glad I wasn't working for the department back then."

Guy opened the door, motioned him inside, and with the aid of his small flashlight located the more distinct of the footprints. As Moretti worked, the camera's strobe created a series of flash-frozen images: a black spider in its intricate white web; a Rorschach blot of bloodstains on the wall; frayed threads hanging from the arm of the sofa. And—

"Shoot this, would you?" Guy said.

The man aimed where he indicated, and the strobe brightly illuminated an area behind the open door where the dust was smeared as if something had been dragged across it. A few long blonde hairs were snagged on a splintered floorboard.

When Moretti finished Guy said, "I'll stay here. Would you ask Deputy Swift to come down, please?"

Rho took two aspirin from the container she kept in her slingbag and washed them down with coffee. Her head ached, her eyes burned, and the glare of the interrogation room's fluorescents didn't help any. She, Ned Grossman, Denny Shepherd, Wayne, and Harve Iverson—the substation commander—had assembled there to brainstorm, as Grossman termed it.

The detective finished passing out a sheaf of papers, sat down, and said, "We have three cases of suspicious or unusual deaths, which may or may not be related. I've called this meeting, even though it's much later than we'd planned, in order to get moving on them. Santa Carla's currently experiencing a crime wave of its own, and Investigations can't send anyone else out, so the four of us are it. Commander Iverson will coordinate our investigation with his patrol officers. I've told Swift and Gilardi that they're relieved of patrol duties until further notice so they can concentrate on these cases. I'm aware this will put a strain on the other deputies in the area, but that's how it's got to be."

"I've already asked for assistance from the Talbot's Mills and Cedar patrol commanders," Iverson said. "They'll cooperate."

Rho glanced at Iverson, a big, dark bear of a man, and noted the pronounced puffiness under his eyes. Harve had had a mild heart attack last year, and she hoped the pressures of the current situation wouldn't provoke a second.

Grossman nodded, riffling the pages in front of him.

"Okay, in addition to policing the area adequately, we may have trouble with the press. The Santa Carla TV people were filming here this morning and found out about the Lindsay death and Scurlock disappearance. Calls've come in here, and I've referred them to Santa Carla, but I doubt we can keep a lid on the Scurlock death for long. And given that it happened in that canyon . . . well, you know what that means."

Widespread interest, national publicity, and chaos, Rho thought.

"Let's take each case in order," Grossman said. "First, Ackerman. The autopsy results are in, and you have copies of them, but I'll summarize. Cause of death was manual strangulation. The bruises on her neck indicate a strong person with large hands. Bruises on her thighs are consistent with rape, but there was no semen in her vagina, no proof either way. Time of death isn't easy to pin down, as her stomach was empty, but she'd only been in the water a few hours before she was spotted. As Swift has pointed out to me, the prevailing currents and tides indicate she may have gone in as far north as Deer Harbor, but more likely closer to where she was found."

Rho said, "Her killer may have picked her up at Point Deception and kept her alive for over twenty-four hours, then."

"Right. And that brings us to what your journalist friend found in the Blakeley house. Your turn, Swift."

She explained about Guy's discovery of the hairs. "They're on the way to the lab to be compared with Ackerman's."

"Okay," Grossman went on, "we had a possible witness to her abduction, an abalone poacher who was picked up in that DFG raid. Unfortunately, as you know, he was strangled in jail, and his cellmates aren't cooperating. If it turns out that the hairs found in the canyon house are a match for Ackerman's, I'd be inclined to say that while the witness saw something, his fellow poachers weren't involved. These guys come up here, take the abs, and leave. I doubt any of them even know about the canyon."

"Ackerman was strangled too," Shepherd said. "Isn't that a gook method of killing?"

Grossman gave his partner a withering look. "Take a tour of San Quentin, Denny. In addition to Asians, it's full of Caucasian, black, and Hispanic stranglers."

Shepherd shrugged.

"Now," Grossman said, "Swift and I have been in touch with Clark County, Nevada, where Ackerman lived. They still haven't gotten back to us with the results of their search of her apartment. Maybe they're inefficient, maybe their court order didn't come through. If we get nothing satisfactory from them in, say, twenty-four hours, I want you, Swift, to go down there."

Wayne grunted softly and shifted in his chair, while Shepherd looked annoyed. Grossman was undercutting their seniority.

"I've talked with a dozen people who spotted Ackerman on Friday," he continued, "and we'll be talking with more of them. The Scurlock woman's death—when we release news of it—will prompt a new rash of tips. No matter how far-fetched they may seem, take each seriously. I can't stress that enough. Gilardi, tomorrow I want you to backtrack along the route Ackerman would've taken to get here. Since she's not from the area, she probably didn't take one of the ridge roads, so start with Highway One. Check every restaurant, bar, motel, and shop south of here till you come up with a lead. Pretty girl in an expensive car must've made an impression on someone. Santa Carla will have photographs of her for you by nine hundred hours."

Rho glanced at Wayne. His face had reddened and he pressed his lips together for a moment before he said, "How far south on Highway One? San Francisco? The Mexican border?"

Grossman shook his head as if Wayne were a child who had disappointed him. "Do what you have to, Gilardi."

Wayne flushed more deeply but didn't respond.

"All right," the detective said, "let's go on to Samantha Lindsay. Autopsy showed death was caused by massive internal injuries, all consistent with our reconstruction of the accident. Probably she swerved to avoid an animal on the highway. No evidence any other car was involved, and there were no drugs or alcohol in her system. Case should be closed, but there's still the problem of her being robbed. We've circularized, but so far we've received no reports of credit card use or attempts to dispose of the jewelry. Patrol officers throughout the county will keep on that, and Detective Shepherd will coordinate."

Shepherd didn't look any more pleased with his assignment than Wayne, but he held his tongue.

"Now," Grossman said, "we come to Virginia Scurlock. Last seen by her husband twenty-some hours before Swift found the body. We won't have the autopsy results till tomorrow or possibly the day after, but the preliminary examination indicates death from a broken neck, which may or may not be consistent with the fall she took. There is some question about why she went to the canyon."

Rho said, "I'd like to point out one thing."

"Yes, Swift?"

"Last night when I interviewed the Scurlocks' tenant, Clay Lawrence, he said Virge had once asked him to go with her to the canyon so she could confront her fears. He refused, but she may have decided to go on her own. She'd been drinking heavily, possibly to steel herself to do it."

Grossman considered. "Anybody have any idea what set off this drinking?"

Wayne and Commander Iverson shook their heads.

Rho said, "The Ackerman murder, most likely."

"Then there's something for you to do, Swift: Talk to the bartender at the hotel, the other patrons, anybody who saw or spoke with her on Sunday. Go over every minute of, say, the previous forty-eight hours with her husband." He paused, looking around the table. "Okay, we've all got our assignments. We'll reassemble here at eighteen hundred hours tomorrow."

Rho stood and shrugged into her sweater. When she looked down for her purse she saw a rawhide chew bone lying under the chair. "Oh no!" she exclaimed. "Cody!"

Grossman looked up from gathering his papers. "Who's Cody?"

"My dog. He was—" Then she thought of Valerie, pictured her reddened eyes and trembling lips as she spoke of her old friend Virge being out there somewhere, alone and afraid. By now Valerie knew Virge was dead and had

probably cried herself to sleep, the Lab close by her side.
Rho was thankful that she'd inadvertently provided the
clerk some comfort on what had to be a painful night.

"Dog's missing?" the detective asked, looking concerned.

"No, he's fine. I left him here earlier, and our clerk's
taken him home."

Grossman smiled knowingly. "Sometimes I think people in law enforcement shouldn't be allowed to have pets.
I've got a dog myself—big old mutt named Everett. On
Sunday I rushed out of my place so fast that I forgot to
feed him. Had to call a neighbor, ask him to go over
there, and he, the neighbor, was real apprehensive.
Everett gets rambunctious when he isn't well provi-
sioned."

Rho laughed—not much, but still it felt good. After a
long, draining day filled with loss and grief, it was a relief to talk about something as mundane as a dog who got
testy when denied his rations.

Behind her Wayne said, "That's right, Swift, laugh, why
don't you? Your star's on the rise. Maybe you'll get a promotion."

She swung around, ready to blister him with a reply,
but he slammed out the door.

Guy noticed Lily Gilardi as he was leaving the market,
where he'd gone to buy another disposable point-and-
shoot camera. The young woman was walking north on
the shoulder of the highway, her head bent, long dark hair
blowing in the wind. He hurried to his car, pulled out of
the lot, and drove up beside her. When he opened the passenger-side door and called her name she started.

"Oh, it's you, Mr. Newberry."

"It's me. Need a ride?"

Lily looked longingly at the car, but indecision clouded her eyes. "I don't know—"

"Come on. I'll buy you a drink, something to eat, if you like."

". . . Thanks. I could use a drink. But not at the hotel, okay? Alex hangs there, and I don't want to see him."

"We'll go to the Oceanside, then."

She got in, sweeping her thick dark hair across her left cheek, but not before Guy caught sight of a fresh bruise. He didn't comment, simply pulled away from the shoulder.

Lily said, "I heard about Mrs. Scurlock."

"Oh? How?" Rhoda had told him the sheriff's department was releasing no information tonight, in hope of preventing another out-of-control public reaction.

"Wayne's wife, Janie. I went to see her, and she told me about it. Said you were there when Rhoda Swift discovered the body."

"Yes, I was. Have you told anybody?"

"No. Janie said not to. Was it . . . awful?"

"It wasn't pleasant. Will Scurlock's in bad shape."

"Poor Will. He really loved her, in spite of her problems."

"How'd you know that?"

"You can tell when people're really in love." Lily's face was mournful. Nobody would ever make that claim about Alex and her, and she knew it.

Guy pulled into the lot at the Oceanside and followed Lily through the dining room and into the bar. She chose a booth over which a fishnet loaded with glass bobbers was suspended. A large stuffed fish trophy—some kind of long-nosed shark—glowered down from the wall.

After the waitress had taken their order Lily said, "You still want to ask me questions about those murders? I told you I was just a kid then."

"Did it ever occur to you that I don't want anything? That I might enjoy your company?"

She laughed cynically. "A guy who can take Rhoda Swift to dinner doesn't need to hang with the likes of me."

"And what are those 'likes'?"

"See for yourself." She brushed her hair back, exposing the damaged cheek. "I'm just your basic small-town slut."

"Alex tell you that?"

"Yeah, right before he hit me."

"Just because he likes to hit women doesn't mean it's your fault."

"That's what they tell you, but try believing it." She pushed up the sleeve of her sweater, began fiddling with her watchband, and Guy saw another bruise on her arm. A bruise curiously at odds with the beautiful gold links that fitted loosely around her thin wrist.

"Why do you stay with him, Lily?"

"I'm in too deep not to. Besides, I got no place to go."

"You said you went to see Janie before. Couldn't you stay with her and Wayne?"

"God, no! I went to see Janie because she'd understand what I'm going through. Wayne's always beating on her too."

"Then maybe she needs to get out. You two could go in together on a place—"

"Look, if the price of this drink is listening to you tell me how to run my life, I don't need it!" She started to slide out of the booth.

Guy put his hand on her arm. "I'm trying to be a friend. No more advice unless you ask for it. That's a promise."

"Okay, then."

They drank in silence, and after a while Lily said, "Mrs. Scurlock—was it an accident?"

"Possibly."

Her eyes widened. "You mean it might've been suicide? Or . . . murder?"

"The sheriff's people won't know till they get the autopsy results."

Lily shuddered and finished her drink. "D'you think it had something to do with that other woman who was killed?"

"Possibly," he said again.

"Oh God."

"What, Lily?"

Silence.

"If you know something about that—and you indicated last night that you do—you should tell the sheriff's people."

"I thought you said no advice."

"I'm sorry. But couldn't you at least tell your brother?"

"Tell *Wayne*?"

"A relative—"

"Jesus, you don't understand a thing, do you? Wayne's a maniac. He scares me to death, even worse than Alex.

If I told him what I know, he'd figure out for sure what we're into. And then he'd kill Alex. Maybe both of us."

Rho waved to Ridley Bodine, night-shift bartender at the hotel, and he came down to meet her at the plank. "You working yesterday when Virge Scurlock was in?" she asked.

The heavyset, bearded man nodded. "The other guy and I alternate football Sundays."

"Did Virge say anything to indicate why she was drinking so heavily?"

"She still missing?"

So the department's lid on the news was holding. "Yeah."

"Too bad. Well, let me think. . . . After her third stinger I suggested she might want to go easy. She said she was trying to make a decision and she made decisions better when she'd had a few. When I warned her not to drive in her condition she told me it wasn't a problem, since Will was using her truck and would pick her up later. So I served her a couple more drinks and then he came and fetched her."

"She talk with anybody else while she was here?"

Ridley looked thoughtful, stroking his beard. "Mimi Griggs and her boyfriend from Santa Carla—I can never remember his name—were at the next table, and they may have talked. Otherwise I don't remember. Was too busy serving drinks and watching the 'Niners get the shit kicked outta them."

Mimi. Rho felt a tightening in her gut. "Thanks, Ridley."

She started for the door, but the bartender said, "You

want to talk with Mimi, she's back by the jukebox with her boyfriend from Calvert's Landing."

Ridley was aware of the history between Rho and Mimi and, she suspected, waiting for a reaction. She shrugged and smiled. "Hardly seems fair, does it? She's cornered the market on all the eligible men in the county."

She made her way to the table where Mimi, the town insurance agent, sat with a tanned, blond-haired man who spent most of his time surfing near the Calvert's Landing Pier. Mimi, a willowy brunette whose birthday was only two days before Rho's, looked up in surprise at her approach. She said something to her date, and he got up and carried their empty glasses to the bar.

"So what's happening, Rho?"

"I need to ask you a few questions."

"Of course. Sit down." She motioned at the other chair.

Rho sat, trying to conceal her unease. Nine years ago her former husband, Zach, had numbered among Mimi's conquests, and her old friend's betrayal had carved an unbridgeable chasm between them.

Mimi leaned toward her and said in a low voice, "This about Virge Scurlock?"

"Yes. I—"

"Look, I know she's dead. And I also know you people don't want a repeat of last night, so I haven't told anybody."

"Who told you?"

". . . Well, a lot of people in the county have scanners. Word's getting around."

"Who told you?"

Mimi's lips twitched in irritation. "Will, of course. When a man's wife is insured for a million dollars with a double indemnity clause and she dies accidentally, he's quick on the phone."

"I can't believe Will could be that callous."

"Can't you? I guess not. You've always been on the naive side."

"That's not true. And I know grief when I see it. Will was completely broken up earlier; he didn't just turn around and file a claim."

"Then maybe it was a purely altruistic gesture on his part. He probably figured I'd die of shock if I heard on the local grapevine that my company's going to have to pay out that kind of change on a policy I wrote."

Rho and Mimi had been friends since the third grade; she knew when the woman wasn't telling the truth. It was there in the belligerent tilt of her chin, in the way her fingers played with the edge of the table.

"What's the real reason Will called you?"

Mimi shook her head. "Ask your questions and leave me alone, Rho."

She studied her for a moment. "All right. Ridley said you spoke with Virge when she was in here yesterday."

"Briefly."

"About?"

Mimi's date returned with fresh drinks. She took hers, dismissed him with a flick of her hand. "I expressed concern about her drinking, asked her what was wrong. She said . . . Let me see if I can get this right. She said, 'Don't ever try to do somebody a favor. You might end up owing more than you can handle.' But when I asked her who and what, she told me to forget it."

"And then?"

"And then Will came in and started fussing over her like she'd been soiled by the bad company she was keeping and took her home."

Mimi's bitter tone alerted Rho. It was the same way she'd spoken during their one and only confrontation about Zach, when Rho had gone to her house in a drunken rage and demanded she stop seeing him. Then she'd said, "I'm surprised he'd tell you about us, given the way he tries to protect you from every little thing. God, he even acts like you're being victimized by the booze, instead of doing it to yourself."

"You're seeing Will, aren't you?" Rho asked.

Mimi's eyes widened, but she recovered quickly. " 'Seeing.' What a quaint term."

"Answer the question."

"It's none of your business."

"This is an investigation of a suspicious death. Answer it."

"All right! Keep your voice down. I was seeing him, but only sporadically, and it's been over for more than a year now."

"So why'd he call you after he found out Virge was dead?"

"I told you—"

"The truth this time."

"Jesus! He . . . Oh hell, he was scared. He wanted to warn me not to tell anybody about us."

"Why would he worry about that if it had been over for a year?"

Mimi's fingers tapped on the rim of her glass and she

ran the tip of her tongue over her lips. "All right, but this can't go any further. Promise, Rho."

"You know I can't do that."

"Promise you'll at least try to keep it to yourself."

"I'll try."

"Okay. That policy on Virge, I talked Will into it. She was getting crazier and crazier. She'd had some minor accidents, one with the truck, another by falling from a ladder at home, another while hiking on the ridge. He said it was like she was living so much inside herself that she couldn't look out for the hazards outside. He knew it was only a matter of time till something major happened, so I told him to upgrade their hospitalization insurance and suggested a ten-year term policy with double indemnity."

"And he liked the idea?"

"No. But I convinced him that he deserved to be compensated for what she was putting him through."

Rho thought back to when she and Mimi had first become friends. The Griggses had lived in the big Victorian that now was the Pelican Cove Bed & Breakfast. Mimi's room was the one with the turret that Guy Newberry currently occupied, and she had a canopied bed and a beautiful doll collection and a closet full of clothes. For her tenth birthday her father bought her a horse that was boarded at a stable near the beach, and he'd promised her a sports car when she got her driver's license. Mimi was generous with what she had, but Rho was still wildly envious of her.

But then it came out that Charlie Griggs, a local manager for the state highway department, had been taking kickbacks from their subcontractors, and he'd gone to prison. Mimi's mother was forced to sell off everything to pay the attorneys' fees, and she and Mimi went to live in the trailer park. Suddenly instead of envying her friend, Rho pitied her. Still, they'd remained close till the night Zach confessed to his affair.

All that loss, of course, accounted for Mimi's drive to succeed, and she'd built her insurance agency into the most profitable on the Soledad Coast. But loss had also created a need that she couldn't possibly fill. Rho could imagine her writing the policy on Virge while contemplating a future with Will, high on the ridge with two million dollars as a cushion.

She said, "So you were only concerned for your client's interests when you made those recommendations."

"Of course."

"You gave no thought to how you eventually might benefit?"

"Aside from my commission, no."

"Aren't there regulations against writing a policy on your lover's wife? And on writing that kind of policy on an emotionally disturbed woman? Weren't there things about the situation that you were bound to disclose to your company?"

"So I looked the other way, presented it in a more positive light. It's done all the time."

"Is it?"

"Jesus, Rho, why're you badgering me? Does this have to do with Zach?"

"Zach?"

"We've never talked about him. Not since the night he told you about us."

"There's no need to talk. It was over years ago. For all three of us."

Rho stood and regarded her former friend. Mimi looked tired, too thin, and deeply discontented. The life she was leading was taking its toll; in a few more years she'd be a desperate, worn-out woman, grasping at whatever man came her way. Rho wished it were otherwise, but there was nothing she could say or do to help her.

"I'll try to keep what you've told me to myself," she said. "But if I ever hear that you're looking the other way and bending the rules for one of your clients again, you're busted."

"Come on, Lily," Guy said. "You and Alex can't have done anything so bad that Wayne would *kill* you."

"You don't know him."

"True." He signaled for another round of drinks.

"Well, I do, and he scares me."

"You weren't too scared to go over to his house tonight."

"I only go there when I know he isn't home."

"In what way does he scare you?"

"He gets really violent. You think Alex is bad, you oughta see what Wayne does to Janie. Used to do to me when I lived with them."

"He always been that way?"

"No. When I was a kid he was real gentle and protective of me. The same with Janie when they first got married. She says something went wrong in him around the time of the Cascada Canyon murders, and he's never been himself since."

"It all keeps coming back to those murders, doesn't it?"

"I guess so."

Guy waited while the waitress placed their fresh drinks on the table and departed. "Wayne's violent streak aside, if you know something about that woman who was murdered, you really ought to tell the sheriff's department."

She shook her head. "They already suspect what me and Alex are doing. If I told them about the woman, they'd never leave us alone. We can't stand them looking too close at us, especially now that he's gone and done something really stupid that—" She bit her lip.

"What's he done?"

"I can't tell you."

"I won't repeat it."

"Oh, sure. You won't repeat it, but you'll put it in your book. No way I'm telling you. I got this philosophy of life: Don't trust cops, don't trust politicians, and don't trust reporters."

"What if you went to Rhoda Swift with the information? She's a good cop. Look at the way she took up for you and Alex the other night when Wayne went after you."

"So she's an okay person. But she's still a cop."

"Cops have been known to make deals if they want information badly enough."

Lily seemed to think about that, staring into her drink.

Guy added, "What if I talked to her, paved the way?"

For a moment she looked hopeful; then she shook her head again. "Rho's only a deputy. She'd have to convince that Detective Grossman to deal, and he's one hard-nosed son of a bitch. I can't risk it, Mr. Newberry."

"Sounds as if what you and Alex are into is serious."

"Maybe not serious where you come from, but around here it's pretty bad."

"Drugs?"

She laughed mirthlessly. "Don't I wish? That's just business as usual here. Half the places up on the ridge got nice-looking marijuana gardens, and you can hear the meth cooking on a quiet night. The sheriff and ATF make busts, but nobody, including them, gets very upset about what goes on."

"And they would get upset about this thing with you and Alex?"

"More like totally pissed. It'd go bad enough on Alex, but he's kind of an outsider, has only lived here a couple of years. Me, though, I'm an insider. I'm supposed to know better. And now this other thing he's gone and done, that's just as bad in its own way. No, Mr. Newberry, I can't risk it."

Rho sat behind the wheel of her truck in the hotel parking lot, experiencing a strange kind of elation. It was all out in the open between Mimi and her now. No more need to ignore one another in public, cross the street if one saw the other coming. And no warm-and-fuzzy reconciliation, either. Mimi had done the unforgivable, and Rho had no intention of forgetting that. But the sense of betrayal on her part and the gloating triumph on Mimi's were over.

It's as if I'm coming alive again, she thought. As if facing the reality of what those murders did to me has set me free in all areas. I don't even want a drink tonight, because I'm no longer afraid to look inside myself and make peace with what I see.

So now what? Ned Grossman had told her to talk with Will Scurlock, but it was far too late for that. As of the time she left the substation there had been no word from Nevada on Chrystal Ackerman, and there wouldn't be till tomorrow. She knew she should go home to rest, but she felt edgy, unable to contemplate sleep.

Chrystal Ackerman: Why had she driven all the way from Las Vegas to Soledad County? Even in the brief glimpse Rho had caught of her, she hadn't looked like the kind of woman who would visit this wild north coast without a good reason. Yet she'd died here, and while logic didn't necessarily dictate it, Rho had a strong feeling that her death was not random, had to do with her purpose in coming.

But what purpose? Where had she been? Those were the critical questions.

Long blonde hairs caught between the floorboards at the Blakeley house. Coincidental?

I don't think so.

Two sets of footprints going up canyon, one made by Virge and superimposed on the others. Virge's prints veering toward the stream. The others going toward the waterfall.

Rho started the truck and pulled onto the highway, heading south.

Guy dropped Lily at the small house she shared with Alex on one of the northern side streets, accepting with a philosophical shrug her assurances that she'd be all right there. The young woman had asked that he not offer advice, and besides, as Rhoda Swift had told Wayne, Lily wouldn't turn her life around until she was good and ready to. He'd keep the lines of communication open, be available to help should she make a decision.

The latter thought surprised him and he smiled wryly. In times past he'd have squeezed Lily for every drop of information about the Cascada Canyon murders, paid scant attention to her problems, and turned away without a qualm. He wrote about towns in trouble, but that didn't mean he needed to get involved with *people* in trouble. But something about this particular place and its inhabitants, both living and deceased, had made him care.

"I'm changing," he said aloud.

You're becoming a mensch, Diana's voice said.

"Why now, though?" he asked her.

Keep it up and find out.

He reached the highway and turned south. As he neared the hotel he saw Rhoda Swift's pickup exit the parking lot and head south too. Odd. She'd described where she lived the night they had dinner; her turnoff was even farther north than where he'd dropped Lily. Out of more than idle curiosity he followed her.

She passed the closed-up business establishments and the sheriff's substation; the yacht harbor where she'd mentioned her father lived, and the unfinished subdivision. When she also passed the B&B he felt an unaccountable twinge. Wherever she was going, it wasn't to see him. Soon her taillights were moving through the heavily forested area outside the town limits, where fog boiled up from the coves.

After fifteen or sixteen miles her brake lights flashed

and the truck veered across the centerline. In the wash of her headlights Guy recognized the collapsed gates leading into Cascada Canyon. That afternoon she'd told him she wasn't certain she could bring herself to go there again, yet here she was.

He continued along the highway, U-turned, and parked where he had the first time he visited the canyon. Then he got out and walked back to the entrance. The truck was pulled inside the gates, where a plastic crime-scene tape stretched. Rhoda had driven in, and, judging from the way she'd positioned the truck, it wouldn't be visible to drivers traveling either north or south. A secret visit, then, that she didn't want the public, the press, or members of her own department to know about.

Guy stepped over the tape and took out his flashlight. Aiming it at the ground, he started up the driveway. Without the light pollution he was used to in the city, the night sky was brilliant with stars. A car sped by on the highway behind him, its tires thumping as it crossed the centerline on a curve. Wherever Rhoda was, her footsteps weren't audible. He kept following the dirt track, past the Blakeley house, past the Wynne dome, toward Bernhard Ulrick's shack and the bunkhouses.

Rho passed the bunkhouses without a glance, her battery-powered torch trained on the ground. Don't look, she thought. Don't remember. Concentrate on why you're here.

She could hear the rush of the stream now, could smell pungent pine and tangy eucalyptus. The torch illuminated Virge Scurlock's large footprints superimposed on the smaller ones. Instead of veering off as she had earlier, she continued up canyon, sweeping the ground with the light. The smaller footprints went straight ahead, but now she saw—

"Hoo, hoo-hoo!"

She started before she recognized the low, sonorous cry of a great horned owl that must be nesting nearby. Remembered how the birds' hooting had frightened her as a child, realized it frightened her even now. An owl, symbol of death, in this place of death . . .

Concentrate!

To the right of the path was a second set of footprints. The same size and tread as the others, but going down canyon. They cut deeper into the earth than the others and were erratically angled. As if the person had been running from something.

When Guy passed the bunkhouses he saw a glow through the trees. Soon after, the path turned and Rhoda came into view. She was squatting down, studying something intently. After a moment she stood and moved along a few yards. Stopped and squatted again, shining her light around. Repeated the procedure twice.

Then the light stopped moving. She set it down and fumbled in her pocket. Pulled something out, a sack of some kind, and plunged her hand into it. Plucked at a bush whose branches hung low over the path.

Evidence bag. She was now inverting it and holding it up to the torchlight. Guy moved forward eagerly and—

Fell on his ass in the mud.

A thump and a yowl of pain made Rho drop the evidence bag. She twisted, still squatting, and clawed at her slingbag for her revolver. Fear shot through her as she thought of what Wayne had impressed upon her from day one: "An officer who goes into a potentially dangerous situation without backup is just plain stupid and can wind up just plain dead."

Gun out and ready, she shone her torch on the target.

What she saw made her fear evaporate and a mixture of anger and mirth replace it. Guy Newberry, her favorite city slicker, lay in a sinkhole next to the path, thrashing about and smearing himself with mud. He struggled to a sitting position, shielded his eyes from her light, and laid a track of Soledad County's rich soil across his forehead.

"Jesus Christ, Rhoda, turn that thing away!"

"I will if you stop shouting. What the hell're you doing here?"

"Following you." He reached out a hand for her help, and she pulled him to his feet, but not before she retrieved the evidence bag.

He said, "I thought you had a problem with coming back here, but now I find you traipsing around in the middle of the night."

"I *do* have a problem." She scowled at him as she replaced her .357 in her bag. "I was so spooked by your graceful arrival that I nearly shot you. Don't you know better than to follow somebody in a place like this?"

"Okay, I'm sorry. Why'd you come?"

"An idea I had. And you know, on the way down here I realized something: After thirteen years with the department, the solution to a case is more important than my own emotional baggage."

"You've solved the case?"

"Not hardly. But I'm on my way." She held up the bag and shook it at him.

Guy moved closer and squinted at the contents of the bag. "I can't see."

Rhoda positioned it against the palm of her hand and shone the light closer. The object inside was a slender curl of gold chain, broken near its clasp, the two halves linked by filigreed letters that spelled out the name CHRYSTAL.

"A bracelet?" he guessed.

"More likely an ankle chain. The branch where it was caught is low enough."

"Who's Chrystal?"

"The murder victim from Point Deception."

"I thought she hadn't been identified."

"No, we're withholding her name till we can locate next of kin. Look here, Guy—this is really interesting."

Guy studied the two sets of footprints she indicated with her torch. "She went up the canyon walking normally, but came back running."

"Right."

"Why didn't anybody notice that this afternoon?"

"Because the Soledad County Sheriff's Department screwed up once again on evidence collection in this canyon!"

Rhoda's tone was raw and bitter. Quickly Guy said, "Not for long they didn't."

". . . No."

He was silent, thinking about the hairs he'd found in the Blakeley house. They must have been left there after Ackerman was dead, but . . .

"So she was here in the canyon before she was grabbed at the turnout?" he asked.

"Either that or the person who grabbed her brought her here and she escaped."

"But only briefly."

"Yes."

Their eyes met and after a moment he realized they were thinking the same thing.

"You never did show me the rest of the canyon," he said.

The only times Rho had ventured into the far end of the canyon were during daylight, in the company of her fellow deputies as they searched for evidence they might have overlooked on the night of the murders. Then she'd gone with a horror of viewing the abattoir where Bernhard Ulrick had died, and an equal horror of appearing weak in front of her colleagues. Now she moved steadfastly along the path, strengthened both by her resolve to find out what had happened to Chrystal Ackerman and by the presence of Guy Newberry, who seemed a stranger to fear.

The sound of the waterfall guided her, and she kept her light trained on the two sets of footprints. Shortly after they passed the fall, the path narrowed and the prints stopped. She paused, shone her light ahead at a wide pool of water.

Behind her Guy said, "What?"

"This is as far as the prints go. The end of the canyon's flooded." She raised the torch and aimed it at where the drug lab should be. The shed had listed to the left. If the rains were heavy this year and the stream rose, the shed would collapse, and at least one of the monuments to the crimes perpetrated here would vanish.

"She could've waded over there," Guy said.

"Maybe. But why? There's nothing inside but some broken-down furniture."

"She had no way of knowing that."

"True."

"Something happened here, though. Something that made her run."

Rho sighed and stepped into the pool. It was about six inches deep with a mucky bottom. Cold water rushed into her athletic shoes. After she sloshed forward a few steps she said to Guy, "You coming?"

"I'll hold down the fort here."

Naturally.

As she got closer she saw that the shed had badly deteriorated. She shone her light through the door, noted that part of the roof had fallen in. Water covered the floor and mildew obscured the blood-spatter patterns on the walls. She hoped never again to witness such a scene: so much blood, bone, flesh, and brain matter. . . .

She shook her head, forced the image away. Tried to step up into the structure. The weight of one foot made it pitch violently. When she withdrew, the shed settled at a more acute angle.

"I don't think she came this far," she said to Guy.

"Then come on back before you get so soaked you catch pneumonia."

She waded toward him. "So what happened here?" she asked. "Why'd she run?"

"Someone was chasing her?"

"There's only one set of prints."

"Maybe it wasn't a person."

"An animal?"

"No."

"What, then?" She took the hand he offered and stepped up onto the bank.

He said, "A memory. I've been talking with the old man down at Point Deception. Gregory Cordova. He claims that the family who were squatting in that cabin on the ridge that your department raided were here on the night of the murders."

A chill that had nothing to do with her wet feet stole over Rho. "Why didn't he tell us that?"

"I suppose because they were already gone, and he didn't want to get involved. Anyway, he doesn't know the parents' names, but he remembers that the little girl was called Chrissy."

Chrissy. Chrystal. Of course, she knew that. Oriana Wynne had given them the name; it was in the casefile. "Ackerman was the right age," she said.

"So why'd she come back here after all these years?"

She studied Guy. He was arrogant and could often be irritating, but there was something likable about him as well. And he was very good at what he did. She could use his powers of observation and keen logic.

"My friend," she said, "that is exactly what you and I are going to find out."

Chrystal: Before

Friday, October 6
12:21 P.M.

God, this place is spooky. And quiet. So quiet I can hear every car on the highway, the way they take the curve too fast, bump over the centerline. *Ka-thump, ka-thump, ka-thump.*

Okay, Jude's instructions. Follow the driveway past the little shingled house, and—

There it is. Eric's house. Only he didn't spend much time there those last few months. His folks were always fighting, and Eric was always crying in the kid boxes. Lots of fighting going on back then. Devon Wynne and her boyfriend till he beat her up so bad and they threw him out and he went to live at Westhaven. And then Forrest beat up Bernhard before they threw him out. I remember crying that night because even though I was just a little kid I knew the good times were over and bad stuff was gonna happen. Sorta the way I've felt all the way up here, only there haven't been any good times and the bad stuff that happened here was years and years ago.

Wish I hadn't come, though. Wish I hadn't got pissed off by Jude's "you'll never get away with it" talk and decided to show her.

So show her, Chryssie. Get a move on—

Oh my God! I don't believe this.

One of them hawks sitting real still on the power line and the tree branches meeting over the driveway. I've drawn that! Over and over, with different angles and light, while I sat on the phone letting men fill my ears with garbage. Drawn it without knowing it was a real place.

Was I trying to remember?

Tuesday, October 10

The clatter of the small apartment's air-conditioning unit competed with a siren on the street. Rho ignored both, transfixed by the wall of charcoal drawings in Chrystal Ackerman's living room. They were all landscapes: some of the desert, others of the mountains, but the best were reminiscent of Soledad County. The one she focused on was of Cascada Canyon. She recognized the utility line where a long-tailed hawk perched and the avenue of trees that arched over the curving dirt track.

Behind her, Guy Newberry said, "What a waste."

"She had talent, didn't she?"

"With training and effort she might've been really good."

Rho indicated the canyon scene. "Recognize this?"

"Of course."

There had been a message at the substation that morning from Ronald Stevens, the Clark County detective, saying his court order had come through and he was free to enter Ackerman's apartment. Did Rho want to be on hand for the search? She immediately asked Ned Grossman for permission to fly to Las Vegas, then called Guy and told him he'd be welcome to join her on the trip. It was irregular, she knew, to allow a civilian—let alone a journalist—to come along, but she suspected that Grossman would understand should he find out. Besides, Guy had offered to save the department money by paying for a rental car.

From the moment she spotted Las Vegas from the air, the visit had taken on a surreal quality for Rho. Mostly low and flat, it sprawled in the middle of the desert, golf courses and parks contrasting with the surrounding barren terrain. But what caught her attention were the buildings that reared up near its center like an overblown Disneyland: the fabled Strip, spiritual home to America's dreams of instant wealth and all the things that luck would shower upon those it favored.

In the airport the electronic tones of slot machines were disorienting. At one of them a man pleaded with his wife to stop playing, as their plane had already boarded. "But I'm *winning*!" she protested. After he dragged her away Guy went over and dropped a coin into the machine, which refused to give up its bounty. He grinned at Rho and shrugged, clearly stimulated by the charged atmosphere.

It was early afternoon and the outside temperature was in the eighties. Rho's sweater felt prickly against her skin. The air was clear, the sunlight pale, as if both had been refined for the pleasure of visitors. Even the rental car was faintly perfumed—a scent that made Rho roll down her window, even though Guy had put on the air conditioner.

Ackerman's street, Paradise Road, extended north from the airport, past the University of Nevada Las Vegas campus. Her building resembled an old motel and stood defiantly between two more imposing and luxurious structures. Stevens, a tall black man with horn-rimmed glasses and an obvious toupee, was already there with a locksmith. Within minutes they were inside. The apartment was a basic furnished unit with beige walls, worn dark brown carpeting, and cheap appointments. Its postage-stamp balcony faced a parking lot and the next building. Its only distinction was the wall of artwork.

Now Rho heard Stevens rummaging in the drawer of a small table next to the sofa. "No cards, no letters, no address book," he said. "Your victim must've been one lonely lady."

She turned away from the wall and went to the kitchen. The cabinets contained cheap glassware and dishes; there were few utensils, fewer pots and pans. Bags and boxes from fast-food outlets were crammed into a trash can under the sink, and the fridge held nothing but jug wine, a tub of margarine, two containers of yogurt, and three apples. A loaf of bread in a basket on the counter had grown mold.

There were two bedrooms, one of them empty, the other in chaos. Unmade queen-size bed, clothing heaped on the floor and hanging over a chair, empty wineglass and coffee cup on one nightstand. The closet was full of clothing ranging from basic jeans and tees to skimpy sundresses.

As Rho was checking the bathroom Guy came in, holding an ashtray. "Marijuana roaches," he said.

"Doesn't surprise me. There were roaches in the Mercedes too." She closed the door of the medicine chest, lifted the lid of the toilet tank and saw nothing concealed there. "All in all I'd say Ackerman led a pretty solitary life. She mainly ate takeout, drank cheap wine, and smoked dope. Judging from her clothing, I doubt she got dressed up and went out on the town. She slept alone, at least at home—no condoms here and that other night-stand's got enough dust on it to prove nobody's set any-thing there in months."

"So she just sat in this apartment and took phone calls and drew pictures."

"Except for when she was turning tricks for clients like Sean Bartlow." She went back to the living room to look for the phone. Stevens indicated two instruments, one white and one beige, at either end of the sofa. The white phone had an answering machine hooked up to it.

"Must be her personal line," he said. "She's got nine messages."

Rho went over and hit the play button.

"Chrys," a voice that she recognized as Sean Bart-low's said, "some cop in Soledad County, California, just called me. She said you abandoned my car on the coast highway. What the hell happened? Call me."

"Chrys." Bartlow again. "Come on. I know you al-ways check for messages. I need to talk with you."

"Ms. Ackerman, this is Cerini Jewelers. Your watch is ready."

A dial tone.

"Chrys, this isn't funny! I've got to do something about my car, but that cop knows the plates I put on it are stolen, and she said something about a felony. I'm afraid to call her back till I talk with you."

"This is Hillcrest Dental, calling for Chrystal. You're due for a cleaning. Please call to schedule."

A receiver being slammed down emphatically.

Another hangup.

"Ms. Ackerman, this is Alfred Parkins at Better Care Nursing Home. We regret to inform you that your mother passed away this morning. Please contact us regarding arrangements."

That message had come in today, at ten twenty-five.

Guy hated nursing homes, and he particularly hated Better Care. On Cheyenne west of North Las Vegas Air Terminal, it was a low-slung concrete-block structure with a flat roof upon which perched dozens of noisy swamp coolers. Not so much as a flower or shrub relieved its grim high-windowed facade. Inside was worse: corridors full of vacant-eyed people being warehoused in wheelchairs; cramped rooms devoid of comforting personal touches; medicinal smells overlying the stench of filth; officious personnel who treated their charges as if they were retarded children. Maybe his next book should be about a *system* in trouble: a healthcare system that abused and humiliated the infirm and elderly. Get in his licks and expose the shame before he became one of its victims—

Self-interest again, darlin'.

"Be quiet."

"What?" Rhoda asked.

He hadn't realized he'd spoken aloud. "I didn't say anything."

"Oh, I thought you had."

Thank God this awful place had her sufficiently distracted to accept his denial. He didn't want this competent and rational woman to realize the man she'd allowed to participate in her investigation frequently carried on lively conversations with his dead wife!

Mr. Alfred Parkins, director of the home and most officious of all, led them into a room containing three beds, two of them occupied by motionless shapes that huddled beneath their covers, silent and seeming not to breathe. The space Judith Ackerman had occupied was tiny: narrow hospital bed; small locker and nightstand; TV mounted high on the wall. But next to the bed was a framed charcoal drawing, a sketch of Cascada Canyon similar to the one in Chrystal's living room. The choice of medium was appropriate, the charcoal creating a brooding aura.

They'd already spoken with Parkins in his office and learned that Judith had died of a stroke, brought on by complications of multiple sclerosis. When he asked who would be handling the funeral arrangements since "that daughter" was also deceased, Rhoda told him he would have to search for other relatives. Her reply displeased Parkins. He steepled his fingers and put on a lugubrious face. A search would take time, he said, and time was money. Couldn't she—

No, Rhoda told him, although her department would share any information they uncovered in the course of their investigation.

Now Guy watched as she opened the locker and sorted through Judith's scant possessions. There was a gentleness in her touch, a respectfulness that pleased him. She seemed to care about this woman whom she had never met, in much the same way she cared about the daughter she'd only once seen alive.

"What kind of a person was Mrs. Ackerman?" she asked Parkins, fingering a fringed scarf in brilliant colors shot with gold thread.

"I'm sorry?"

"What was she like?"

"She was . . . a patient. I didn't have much contact with her."

"Who did?"

"The orderlies. The nurses."

"Her doctor?"

"She wasn't assigned to any particular physician. They rotate."

Guy saw Rhoda's fingers tighten on the scarf. Angry, he thought, in the same way he was.

"She wasn't being cared for by a specialist?" Now her voice carried a critical edge.

Parkins flushed. "This isn't a medical center, Deputy Swift. Our resources are limited, the patients' even more so. Besides, her condition was terminal."

Rhoda flashed Guy a stormy look. She removed the scarf from the locker and placed it on the stripped mattress, then turned her attention to the nightstand. Guy watched her sift through its contents. Eyeglasses, paperback romance novel, lurid-covered true-crime magazine, small photograph album, loose-leaf binder. She glanced through the latter items and said to Parkins, "I'll have to take these, as well as the drawing on the wall, as evidence. Of course, I'll give you a receipt."

She had, Guy knew, no jurisdiction in Las Vegas and couldn't legally take the items; she was probably claiming them as much out of anger as need. But Parkins either didn't know that or wasn't concerned.

The director moved his hand in dismissal. "No receipt will be necessary. Even if we locate a relative, I doubt they'd care about them."

Rhoda's expression said she doubted the word "care" was used with any frequency within the walls of this institution.

Rho moved quickly across the parking lot of the nursing home, glad to be out of the wretched place. Las Vegas was making her edgy—the heat, the traffic, the flatness, the often shabby neighborhoods. Guy, who had been cut off at the door by an aggressive orderly with a wheelchair, caught up with her at the car.

"Why'd you take those things?" he asked. "You know it's not legal."

"I know, but I didn't want to have to wait around for Stevens, and besides, Parkins made me so mad."

"That's why you took the scarf too."

"I guess." She waited impatiently for him to unlock the door, slipped onto the hot passenger's seat. It burned clear through her trousers. "I knew Parkins was right: Nobody'll care about Jude's things. She must've valued the scarf highly to bring it along to the home, where she had no use for it. I couldn't see leaving it to be thrown out or stolen by one of the staff. Somebody ought to have it to remember her by—if only me."

As she finished speaking she realized how foolish she must sound, but Guy glanced at her with eyes full of understanding. "It was a lovely thing to do. What was in the album and the binder?"

"Handwritten poetry and pictures taken with the other families in Cascada Canyon. They prove the Ackermans were the family who were squatting in the cabin on the ridge."

"May I see them?"

"Later. I want to get to that diner Parkins mentioned and interview Sandy Viera before she finishes her dinner break and goes back to work." Viera was the nurse who had known Judith Ackerman the best.

The diner was only a few blocks away: a desert-motif operation decked out in fake saguaro cacti and cattle skulls displayed in wall niches. A bank of slot machines, two of them in use, stood to the right of the door, and at the lunch counter a man in cowboy boots and Levi's hunched over a beer, figuring what looked to be odds in a well-thumbed notebook. A blast of chill air penetrated Rho's clothing. Another thing that bothered her about Las Vegas was the constant abrupt transition from heat to cold, cold to heat.

She scanned the room for a black-haired woman in a nurse's uniform and spotted her alone in a booth by the windows. When she and Guy approached, the woman's eyes grew wary, but after Rho explained why they wanted to talk with her, she nodded sadly and asked them to join her.

Sandy Viera looked to be in her mid-fifties, a plump woman with a round, relatively unlined face and dangly purple earrings that looked out of place with her crisp white uniform. Her mouth drooped as Rho told her about Chrystal.

"So Chrys is gone too," she said. "Damn! This life, you know, it really stinks sometimes."

Rho nodded. "What can you tell me about the Ackermans? Start with Judith."

Sandy Viera set her fork down and pushed her half-eaten salad away. "Jude, she liked to be called. From the way she talked, I could tell that she used to think she was pretty hot stuff. Wild, a poet. But the disease caught her in her mid-thirties and progressed fast. When she came to Better Care she was worn out and bitter. Angry, too, but that's natural. And she lied a lot."

"About what?"

"Well, for one thing, she said her husband was a big-deal musician before he died, but I knew about Leo Ackerman on account of my brother working the Strip. Leo was a fourth-rate guitar player who got canned by every crummy room in town and finally OD'd on bad smack. Jude also said she'd published her poems in fancy magazines and had a book of them coming out, but Chrys told me her only poems were in the binder she kept in her nightstand. Sometimes I'd see Jude reading them, but she wouldn't show them to anybody. There were other lies, lots of them, all told to impress people, but we saw right through them."

"Okay, what about Chrystal? What kind of relationship did she have with her mother?"

"Love-hate, like it is with mothers and daughters sometimes. They argued a lot. Jude didn't like Chrys's line of work, and Chrys would tell her to quit ragging on her because it was her earnings supplementing Jude's Medicare. Jude would lay into her for being an ungrateful kid and complain that she always cared more for Leo—he was only a stepfather—than for her. Jude . . . Well, the complaints were endless."

"She must've been difficult to deal with."

Sandy Viera smiled wearily. "My job, everything's difficult to deal with. Anyway, don't get me wrong. Jude and Chrys didn't argue all the time. Sometimes they'd be kinda nice to each other. Chrys'd get out this pretty silk scarf she bought her mother—must of cost a couple hundred bucks—and tie it around her neck. And then she'd brush her hair. Jude had long red hair, and even though it'd turned brittle and thin and washed out, she wouldn't let us cut it. Chrys gave her one of her drawings, too—hung it on the wall by her bed. Jude loved it, was always staring at it, and Chrys kept asking her why. She said it wasn't her best, so why did her mom want it?"

"Why did she?"

Sandy Viera shrugged. "She never would say. Just smiled kinda sad-like and said Chrys had great talent if only she'd develop it."

"When was the last time Chrystal visited her mother?"

The nurse considered. "I'd say last Monday. The Saturday before Jude had a bad seizure. Came out of it really weakened and asked for Chrys. That night they talked for a long time with the curtain pulled around the bed. When Chrys left she was kinda dazed, like Jude'd given her some bad news. But when she came back that last time, she was different. Kinda hyped, if you know what I mean. She shut the curtains again and stayed till the end of visiting hours. Walked out of there without saying a word to any of us. Never visited her mother again."

"The Bartlow kid was lying about at least two things," Guy said.

He and Rhoda were seated at a window table in a bar

atop the Hotel Franconia, a small, elegant establishment a few blocks off the Strip, where he'd stayed on previous visits to the city. On the way back from Sean Bartlow's expensive apartment on the northwest side—not all that far from Better Care, but light-years in terms of luxury—he'd attempted to amuse her by driving her past some of the more outrageous casinos. Dusk was falling, and the neon glitter was coming into its own: The Eiffel Tower at Paris Las Vegas seemed nearly the genuine article; the Statue of Liberty at New York–New York—which, as a native of that city, he found hilarious—stood in gauche relief against the signature skyscrapers and red, looping roller coaster. But the spectacle had had an adverse effect on Rhoda's mood, and finally he'd brought her to this oasis of civility.

The dazzle of the Strip was still with them, however, and all around the city the desert lay dark and implacable. A silent warning that this land had once been barren and could be rendered so again. Surely would be, Guy thought, if it continued to grow at the current rate of nearly four thousand people per month. Water supplies were not limitless, air quality could not last. Another L.A. in the making? Or would it simply implode someday in one frightening flare of light that left the survivors scrambling back to wherever they'd come from?

Rhoda hadn't responded to his statement about Bartlow. She slumped in her chair, staring out the window. There were weary lines at the corners of her mouth and her lips drooped. When the waiter set their drinks on the table, she straightened and sighed.

"Guess I'm just a country girl at heart," she said.

"Nothing wrong with that."

"Isn't there? All this"—she motioned at the window—"makes me feel insignificant. I don't understand it. I don't like it. Yet somehow I feel I should."

No way to talk her out of her depression, so he wouldn't try. Instead he repeated his comment about Bartlow, adding, "His first lie was about not knowing what business Chrystal had in Soledad County. She told him at least part of it, and he was interested enough to loan her his car in exchange for being cut in on the deal, but apprehensive enough to switch the plates and remove the registration papers."

"He said he didn't know where the plates came from."

"His second lie. Bartlow probably has a collection of plates, because he's dealing drugs in an amateurish fashion."

"How do you conclude that?"

"He claims his father keeps him on a tight financial leash, but that apartment and its furnishings are expensive, as are calls to Dial-a-Pal and services such as Chrystal provided him. He answered the phone five times in the forty minutes we were there, rather than let the machine pick up. Each conversation had a surreptitious tone, ending with a promise to let the caller know later where he'd meet him. And after each call he acted nervous."

"Okay on the dealing, but where do you get the amateurish fashion?"

"Because, until he loaned it to Chrystal, he made his deliveries in a classic car, thinking that switching its plates would conceal his identity in case someone was running a surveillance. Mr. Bartlow's not too bright, and I hope he doesn't tangle with the real pros, or someday he'll be nothing but picked bones in the desert."

Rhoda shook her head. "You got all that from sitting in on my interview with him? I ought to study your methods. I learned nothing useful."

Guy started to preen, but anticipated Diana's reproving voice. "Well, I've had a lot of practice," he said, and thought he heard the faint words *False modesty*. "So what do you make of Jude Ackerman's photo album?"

Rhoda picked it up and paged through it, then handed it to him. "Those first pictures of the three of them were taken at the cabin on the ridge. The rest are with the families in the canyon. Given the number of photos, I'd say they were close friends. I recognize everybody in them except for this man." Her finger tapped a tall, lanky man who posed with Devon Wynne, his arm around her shoulders.

"Devon's boyfriend." He explained what Gregory Cordova had told him about the man who had left the canyon two weeks before the killings.

"Odd," she said. "We had no idea he'd ever been there. And another thing that's odd is that all the pictures in this album were taken during the time the Ackermans spent in Soledad County. Didn't Jude have other photographs?"

"Maybe that time was special to her, and that's why she brought this particular album to the nursing home."

"Maybe." Rhoda picked up the loose-leaf binder and paged through it. "Each of these poems is dated. The first was written in December the year before the murders, the last in January three years after."

Guy checked his watch. "We'd better get over to the airport. We'll read the collected works of Jude Ackerman on the plane."

*   *   *

"Interesting."

Rho looked up from the sheaf of scribbled pages. "What?"

"There're plenty more blank pages in this binder. Did she just quit writing?"

"Probably. And from what I've read so far, it's a good thing. She had no sense of what a poem really is."

"I didn't know you were a literary critic."

"And I suppose you are?"

"No. I don't know the slightest thing about poetry. But I do know emotion when I see it. If it's part of the poetic process, Jude should at least get an A for attempt."

She looked down at the page she'd been reading, ashamed of her hasty judgment. She'd allowed the barely readable scrawl and awkward phrasing to obscure what he'd seen.

Guy added, "It's the emotion that makes me wonder why she stopped writing. People who're passionate about a pursuit don't usually abandon it, even if they're not very good."

"Unless something happened to take away the passion. Like Virge Scurlock when she gave up on all her interests."

"Could have." He looked down at the portion of the pages she'd given him. "Since each poem's dated, I think we can construct a psychological history of Jude during the time she was writing. Perhaps a factual history as well. That might tell us why her daughter went to the canyon a few days after they had two long private chats."

Rho nodded. She'd been wise to bring Guy along, wise to involve him in the investigation. Since he was relatively new to the subject of the murders, his viewpoint was fresher and he discerned things that she had allowed the passage of time to obscure.

"Listen to this poem," she said. "It's dated five months before the murders. 'I walk beside the pond where the deer lay still . . . Going to the place that is my spiritual home . . . Going to the people who are my spiritual family . . . Who love my child as much as their own.'"

Guy shuffled pages. "It's similar to the very last poem. 'I walk through the canyon under the pines . . . The sea breeze stirs their boughs . . . There are no screams or shots, not now . . . I nod to the ghosts of well remembered family as they pass, at peace.'"

"So maybe the reason she quit writing is that she came to terms with what happened. Maybe she was using the poetry to work out her feelings about the killings. Some of the ones she wrote shortly after the murders are quite violent." She selected a page and handed it to him.

He skimmed it, frowning. "Six months after. 'Blood streams down the face of betrayal and blinds its lying eyes . . . The knife strips away the flesh to expose the false heart . . . Screams rise to the trees where the hawks live . . . The hawks who wait for fresh prey . . . The hawks will feast on the torn bodies of the people I love.' I think she confused hawks with vultures. And what's this about a knife? Nobody was knifed."

"Have you ever heard of poetic license?"

"Of course I've heard of it! And some of them shouldn't *be* licensed."

Rho smiled. Guy obviously disliked having his creative powers challenged, and her catching him being literal-minded had stung.

"Go ahead," he said, "make fun of me. I suppose now

you're going to tell me you studied poetry writing in college."

"English lit, with a dual major in early childhood education. And I did write poetry. Even won a couple of prizes. Sometimes when I get bored on patrol I make up poems in my head, but I forget them before I can write them down."

"What kind of poems?"

Rho looked away, sorry she'd mentioned them.

"Rhoda?"

". . . Actually, some of them were pretty violent. Others were sad. I guess I've been working something out, like Jude Ackerman."

"And have you? Worked it out?"

"Close to."

"Then you ought to be able to reconstruct what was going on with Jude." He exchanged the pages he held for hers. "Read on, and then let's see what we can come up with."

Guy tried to concentrate on the scrawled poetry, but he found himself repeatedly stealing glances at Rhoda. She read with intensity, her lower lip caught between her teeth. Occasionally she'd make a note on a folded piece of paper.

The day before, she'd taken him to the canyon out of what he sensed was a need to make him understand the murders and what she'd been through. He didn't flatter himself that her doing so or asking him along on this trip was for personal reasons; she'd been attempting to influence his treatment of the crime in his book, and today he was here to act as a sensor when her powers of observation failed. But moments ago she'd opened up to him and for the first time allowed him into her emotional space. He wasn't at all sure how he felt about that.

Since Diana died there had been women—not many and all on a short-term basis—but none had touched him where he lived. Rhoda Swift was different, however. From the night he'd met her he'd sensed pain, and now he knew it was as great in its way as any he'd experienced. They'd both seen their lives changed by violence, and such commonality often drew unlikely people together. But Guy had learned not to trust the viability of such entanglements, and now he warned himself against becoming closer to this woman. She was as different from him as possible.

East Coast, West Coast. Big city, small town.

Both truth-seekers by profession, though.

No. He: interpreter of hard facts. She: poet, even though she only wrote in her mind.

He: sophisticate, world traveler. She: impressionable, had seldom left her native state.

A loner, not family oriented. A woman with strong community ties and a love of children.

A man who shunned pets. A dog lover.

No way. Absolutely not.

He turned his attention back to Jude Ackerman's poetry. Its initial charm now eluded him. Rhoda's criticism was right on the nose, he decided. Jude hadn't known a poem from a posthole digger.

"So what do you think?" Rhoda asked.

"I think I can't take much more of this stuff."

"Well, I've read it all, and here's my conclusion: In the beginning Jude was in love with the canyon. She'd found a beautiful place and people who accepted and cared for her and her family. I don't think many people had cared for Jude till then. But three-quarters through the year something changed. The poems start to talk about betrayal and lies. After the murders they grow violent, then depressed. It took almost three years for those feelings to turn into peace and acceptance."

He nodded. "There's one upbeat note throughout the time the Ackermans spent in the canyon, though. She apparently formed a close friendship with Susan Wynne." He shuffled through the pages he'd read and selected one. " 'My friend Susan offers coffee and her most precious secret . . . She shares, but I've got nothing to give in return . . . She says it doesn't matter, friendship is everything . . . She wants me to know where her treasure is in case I need it.' "

Rhoda snatched the page from his hand and examined it, her lips moving, face suddenly animated.

"What is it?" he asked.

"The reason Chrystal went to the canyon. It's right here, and I nearly missed it."

Guy's expression was almost comical, Rho thought. She could practically see his overlarge ego deflating like a pinpricked balloon. "You couldn't have known this," she reassured him. "I'm basing it on something we never revealed to the public."

"And that is?"

"Five weeks before the murders Susan Wynne made a substantial cash withdrawal from her trust fund—a quarter of a million dollars. The trust officer at the bank in San Francisco thought it was unusual at first, until Susan explained that they were planning to make some major improvements on the property, and that most people up there like to deal in cash if at all possible."

"Hide their income from the IRS, you mean."

Rho shrugged. "Most of them are barely getting by as is, without turning a chunk of it over to a government that does very little to provide relief to poor people. Anyway, no improvements were ever made in Cascada Canyon, and the money was never recovered. We were afraid that if the information was made public we'd have an invasion of treasure-hunters on the property."

"So the money might've been hidden there in a place that Susan told Jude about."

"Right."

"Then why didn't Jude claim it long ago? And why wait till she was dying to tell her daughter?"

"Well, at first she and Leo were scared—terrified, actually. They ran the night of the murders and probably kept running for a long time. If they ever did try to go back for the money, they'd've found the place guarded. But I'll bet they never went near the canyon again. That kind of latter-day hippie doesn't really care about money, not if putting their hands on it involves a serious risk."

Guy frowned. "Then why did Jude start caring after all these years?"

"She wanted it for Chrystal? Or maybe she wanted out of the home."

"Anyone would. But still, how did she know the situation with the guards had changed?"

Rho couldn't help allowing herself the luxury of a triumphant smile. "There was a reporter in town some months back. From one of those sleazy true-crime magazines. The angle of his story was that it would soon be thirteen years—bad luck, you know—since the killings. He was very interested that the property was unguarded but still nobody ever went there. That magazine we saw in the drawer of Jude's nightstand was the publication he was writing for, and I'll bet it's the issue with his article."

One look at Guy's face told her she'd finally succeeded in impressing him. She tilted her seat back, stretched out her legs, and basked in the glow.

Chrystal: Before

Friday, October 6
12:29 P.M.

Jesus, that creeps me! This place was stuck in the back of my mind even though I didn't remember it. Didn't remember, and all the time I'm drawing it in charcoal.

Of course the canyon's kind of had hold of my life since the night of the murders. Up till then there was still a chance me and Jude and Leo could be a family. She was nice to me, and even though he didn't like kids, he gave me his name and didn't abuse me none like a lot of stepfathers do. But afterwards she was so into herself that she didn't hardly notice me except to criticize. And him, well, forget it.

Yeah, the ones who got killed weren't the only victims that night.

Enough with this standing around feeling sorry for yourself. Get that money, and all your problems'll be over.

So why do I have this feeling that nothing's gonna turn out

right? Why's my skin all crawly, like somebody's watching me, knows what I'm up to? Why—

Stop it, Chryssie!

But Jude said Susan knew something bad was gonna happen to her and her family. That's why she told where she hid the money, so it wouldn't go to waste when the bad thing came down. And it *did* come down.

No, I don't believe in that premonition shit. No way.

Or do I?

Wednesday, October 11

Rho felt a hand gently shaking her. "You're home," Guy's voice said.

She struggled upright from where she was slumped against the car's door, looked around. They were stopped in front of her house and light glowed from behind its closed curtains. Inside, Cody was barking. How—?

Of course. Valerie knew where half the spare keys in the county were hidden. She must've delivered him and left the lights on for her.

"What time is it?" she asked.

"Twelve thirty."

A lifetime since they'd left Las Vegas. "How'd you find my house?"

"You may think you're a hotshot detective, lady, but you've got nothing on me." While she collected her bag and undid the seat belt, he came around and opened the door. "Actually," he added, "I stopped in at the substation and the fellow on duty drew me a map. I took a wrong turn only twice."

"And I slept through it all."

"Yeah, you did. Once I checked to see if you were still breathing."

She fumbled for her keys as she went up onto the porch. Cody stopped barking, recognizing her step.

"Nice-looking house," Guy said. "Kind of isolated, though."

"You get used to it." She slipped her key into the lock, turned to face him. In the glow from the windows and the shadows thrown by the eaves, his profile was lean and chiseled. "I appreciate your coming with me today. You've been a big help." She felt strangely edgy now, wishing he would go.

"I'd say we make a good team." He put his hand to her cheek. Surprisingly, his fingers were rough, their tips calloused. As he leaned toward her she breathed in his scent, that combination of natural odors that is as individuated as a person's fingerprint. His reminded her of autumn.

"Guy . . ."

His lips touched hers, silencing her protest. They were soft, undemanding. They lingered briefly and then, before she realized what was happening, he pulled away, turned, and hurried to the car, raising a hand in farewell.

She watched the taillights disappear down her drive, then simply stood there. On the other side of the door Cody whined. She put her fingertips to her lips. They felt strange, as if the kiss—and admittedly not much of one at that—had changed her physically.

Now what had made him do that? The only interest he'd previously displayed in her was as a conduit for information. And he'd certainly backed off and fled in a hurry. Afraid, maybe, that she'd whack him with her bag?

No, afraid because he'd closed the physical and emotional distance between them, and Guy, she sensed, was not comfortable with closeness.

Well, neither was she. Since Zach left she'd been with a few men, but the affairs were short-lived and she'd been relieved when each lover grew tired of trying to breach the wall she sooner or later put up between them.

With Guy Newberry it wasn't even going to get to that stage. An involvement with him was something she couldn't begin to imagine.

"Now why the bloody hell did I do that? To prove I could?"

Maybe you just like the woman, darlin'.

"There's no future in it."

Since when do you have to entertain expectations of a lifelong commitment to suck face?

"I do not *suck face!*"

In his agitated state, Guy managed to make four wrong turns before he found his way back to the highway, thus adding a profound sense of foolishness to his present emotional baggage. The road was deserted, and he tromped on the accelerator, arriving in Signal Port in record time. A drink, he thought, something civilized that would remind him of home and the life he'd led until that damned dinner party when he'd allowed Dun Harrison to seduce him into this lunacy. He remembered seeing a dust-covered bottle of Speyburn on the hotel's backbar. Probably it had never been opened; nobody in this benighted burg would know single-malt scotch from malt liquor. Which was fine by him because he intended to partake generously of that bottle.

He was settled on a barstool, drink in hand, before he noticed Lily Gilardi at a window table, weeping into her wine. We've got to stop meeting like this, he thought, jerking his chin at her and raising a questioning eyebrow at the bartender, who shrugged.

"Put the whole bottle on my tab," Guy said, holding out his hand.

The barkeep shrugged again and passed it over to him.

Guy left his stool and went to Lily's table. "More Alex trouble?" he asked as he pulled out the other chair and sat.

Lily looked up in surprise. She really was a good-looking woman, he thought, even with a bruised face and snot dripping from her nose. He reached into his pocket and offered her his fresh handkerchief. She looked at it as if she'd never seen such an accessory before, then look it and blew loudly.

"Big Alex trouble," she said. "He's in county jail in Santa Carla."

"Why?"

"Because this afternoon Mr. Smart Guy tried to hock the diamond ring he got off Samantha Lindsay, and the pawnbroker recognized it from the sheriff's department circular and called the cops. Alex told them he gave me Samantha's watch, so Detective Shepherd hauled my ass into the substation and told me they'd maybe cut a deal if I'd testify against Alex. So now I've gotta put him away, and they're starting to ask about the other stuff, and Wayne's gonna kill me."

Guy shook his head, trying to make sense of her

breathless account. "So you're saying it was Alex who robbed the Lindsay woman's body?"

"Yeah. He saw her car go off the road. She was dead when he got to her. It's a bad thing, really bad. He didn't even report the accident."

"And what's this 'other stuff'?"

"Oh, shit, Mr. Newberry, the abalone poaching! Alex is hooked up with these guys outta Oakland, and what we don't sell to them we sell to Tai Haruru, that restaurant at Calvert's Landing Pier, and a couple of other places. Fish and Game and the sheriff's department suspect what we're doing, but so far they haven't been able to prove anything. But now that Detective Shepherd's got me on receiving stolen property, he'll keep the pressure on till I spill my guts. And then I'm looking at jail time, plus a fine I can't pay. All because that asshole Alex couldn't wait to hock the ring outside the county!"

Lily's voice had risen and was attracting attention of the bar's other patrons. Guy covered her hand with his and said, "If you cooperate, it won't go so hard on you."

"Yeah, right. Are you *crazy*? Wayne'll be there in the middle of things, making sure we're both behind bars."

"According to what Rhoda Swift told me today, Wayne's not held in high regard by the department. In fact, Detective Grossman's trying to keep him on the periphery of the cases he's working."

Lily thought about that, alternately mopping her eyes and nose and sipping wine. "Mr. Newberry? What you said last night about Rhoda Swift—d'you think she'd listen to me? Maybe convince them to make a deal?"

"I know she'd listen."

"Then let's go see her. Right now."

The thought of returning to Rhoda's house, where he'd just made a monumental fool of himself, made his blood run cold. "Lily, it's late, and Rhoda's had a long day—"

"Please! She might be my only chance!"

Last night he'd felt himself changing when he'd resolved to keep open the lines of communication with Lily and help her if he could. But then he'd gone and kissed a woman who was not the sort one kissed casually. Who was probably right now lying awake and contemplating cutting off his nuts. It was insanity to return to Rhoda Swift's home tonight bearing the dubious gift of Lily Gilardi.

Insanity, but that was exactly what he was going to do.

Cody's barking woke Rho from a restless sleep. She sat up in bed, saw the wash of headlights across the window. Shrugging into her long wool robe, she hurried across the room and peered out. Her breath caught when she saw a car that looked like Guy Newberry's rental.

"Now what?" she muttered, and headed for the door.

When she switched on the porch light it illuminated two people: Guy and Lily Gilardi. Guy looked uneasy but in charge. Lily had been crying and seemed frightened.

"My God," she said, opening the door, "is it Wayne . . . ?"

Guy shook his head. "So far as we know, big brother's tucked in for the night. But Lily has something to discuss with you. May we come in?"

"Of course." She opened the door wider and they stepped into the front room. Immediately it began to feel too small, and when she glanced around its contents seemed drab and shabby. She saw Guy looking around too, his eyes cataloging and assessing.

The hell with what he thought. It wasn't a New York penthouse, but it was hers and she liked it.

"Sit down, please," she said and excused herself so she could pull on jeans and a sweater. When she came back she found them side by side on the sofa, Cody sniffing around their shoes. She told the dog to lie down, then looked with concern at Lily's bruised and mascara-streaked face. "Are you okay?"

"Yes. No. No, I'm not."

"Can I get you something? Coffee? Tea?"

"Could I have a drink? Some wine, maybe?"

"Certainly. You, Guy?"

He pulled a bottle from his pocket and held it up. Single-malt scotch.

"Trust you to travel prepared," she said as she took it from him.

In the kitchen she poured their drinks and contemplated the coffeemaker where the dregs of yesterday morning's brew remained. Then she poured a scotch for herself. •

When she was settled opposite the sofa, she asked Lily, "What is it you need to discuss?"

Lily glanced at Guy and, when she saw no help coming from that quarter, said, "It's about that murdered woman, the one they found off of Point Deception."

"What about her?"

Another glance at Guy. He said, "Lily wants to help with your investigation, but what she has to tell you may incriminate her. She's hoping you can guarantee her immunity from prosecution."

"It's not in my power to do that. Any deal has to be arranged with my superiors and the county DA's office."

Lily half rose from the sofa. Guy grabbed her arm and jerked her back down. He looked both annoyed and protective of her, and the latter surprised Rho.

He said, "If you were to go to bat for her, I'm sure you could persuade them to deal."

"I don't have that kind of influence, Guy."

"I think you do. Detective Grossman's given you major responsibility for this investigation."

"Still, I can't guarantee anything." She had to stress that, even if it caused Lily to withhold her information.

Guy started to speak, but Lily's voice overrode his. "The hell with it. They already got me on receiving stolen property. They already got Alex in jail for stealing Samantha Lindsay's credit cards and jewelry. No way I can lie about that, so why lie about the other stuff? That's what it was all about with me and Alex—a great big lie. You try to get me some kind of deal, Deputy Swift, but if you don't . . . Well, I got myself into this mess, and now I want out."

Rho nodded approval. "May I tape-record our conversation?"

Lily looked to Guy, who was regarding her like a parent whose wayward child had turned a corner. "It's okay," he told her. While Rho searched her desk for her cassettes and recorder, he took Lily's glass to the kitchen for a refill, patted her shoulder when he returned.

He cares, Rho thought. And not just because he wants to know her secrets. I've misjudged him.

"Tell it however you want to, Lily," she said as she turned on the recorder.

Lily took a big sip of wine. "Okay. I guess you suspect about me and Alex and the poaching. DFG's onto us. It was just a matter of time."

Rho nodded.

"Okay," Lily said, "mostly we passed the abs off to these guys from Oakland, but then things started getting too weird with them. Like they didn't want me to be involved because I wasn't Vietnamese and when Alex said he wouldn't cut me out, they threatened him. So he went around to some of the restaurants here and made his own deal. Anyway, last Friday afternoon around five o'clock we were coming up from Lantern Cove with the day's harvest, and that's when we ran into her. The murdered woman."

"Wait a minute," Rho said. "Five in the afternoon is too late for abaloneing." The divers usually went out at first light.

"Yeah, it is. What happened was we filled our cooler that morning and were starting to leave when Alex spotted these guys he thought were DFG. They weren't, I knew that, but Alex is sorta—no, he's completely—paranoid. So he insisted on hiding the cooler in one of the caves off the cove and coming back for it later."

"All right, you were there around five and . . . ?"

"And that murdered woman . . . What's her name?"

"Chrystal Ackerman."

"Yeah, now I remember. She called herself Chrys. Anyway, she just popped outta this clump of pampas grass where she'd gone to take a pee. Was acting kind a freaky, like we'd caught her doing something she shouldn't, but she seemed nice enough. Told us her car was broke down and her cell phone wouldn't work, asked us to call Triple A for her, plus some number in Las Vegas. I said we would, and she wrote down the Triple A card number and the message to leave at the other number and gave me a twenty-dollar bill to cover the long-distance charge. When I told her it was too much she said we should use what was left to buy a drink on her."

"What was the message for the person in Las Vegas?"

"Number was for some kind of hospital. I was supposed to ask whoever answered to tell Judith Ackerman that Chrys got in and out okay."

Rho glanced at Guy, who nodded.

Got in and out of Cascada Canyon with a quarter of a million dollars.

"And did you make the calls?" she asked.

Lily looked down into her drink. "No," she said in a small voice. "I wanted to stop in Signal Port and use a pay phone, but Alex said we were going straight to Tai Haruru, they were waiting on the abalone. He said we'd have our drink on Chrys in the bar there. And then the bastard took the paper she'd written the numbers on and tossed it out the window." She paused, shaking her head. "I think that was when I started to hate him."

Rho waited. When Lily didn't go on, she said, "I gather this isn't everything you have to tell me."

"Not by half. There's the Samantha Lindsay thing. But they've already got Alex on that, and I said I'd testify if they don't charge me with receiving. At first I felt bad about it, but you know what? It's starting to feel like the right thing."

"Which detective made the deal with you?"

"The little guy. Shepherd."

Rho suppressed a smile, imagining what Denny's reaction to "the little guy" reference would have been. "Okay, what else?"

A sly look crept across Lily's face. She, Rho sensed, was about to play her ace in the hole.

"This could really help your case."

"Then tell me."

Lily took her time, holding out her glass to Guy for a refill. This was her moment in the spotlight, Rho thought, and she was determined to enjoy it. When Guy returned with the wine, she sipped, set the glass down, and sat up straighter.

"Me and Alex, we know where the killer put Chrys's body into the water."

Guy had been annoyed at being relegated to the role of waiter, but Lily's revelation made him forget that. He watched Rhoda conceal her surprise as she asked, "Where's that?"

Lily seemed deflated by the cool response. She folded her arms and pouted.

"Lily?" Rhoda said. "Cooperation is key to making a deal."

"Okay. You know where Quinley's used to be?"

Rhoda nodded. To Guy she said, "In the fifties and early sixties it was a gas station, the only one on this stretch of coast. When the big oil companies came in, it sat empty for about fifteen years. A man named Quinley bought it in the eighties, turned it into a little burger stand, but there was concern about toxic contamination from leaking underground storage tanks, and he was forced to shut down. The building partly burned a few years later—probably Quinley was trying to collect on his insurance—and the land has been for sale ever since."

"I think I've seen the place. All overgrown, with a chain-link fence around it, on the west side of the highway a few miles north of Point Deception?"

"Right."

"Well," Lily said, "what most people don't know is that the cove behind it has some of the best abalone beds in the county, and the gate in that fence is never locked. Me and Alex, we'd pull in there and climb down the cliff, collect enough abs to fill our cooler in record time."

Rhoda looked shocked. "Lily, the runoff from the contaminated soil could be affecting the shellfish. That's why nobody ever harvests there. You and Alex may have been poisoning people!"

She shrugged. "That's not the point. We were down there at dawn on Sunday, and that's when we found it."

"Found what?" Guy heard a note of impatience in Rhoda's voice now.

"Chrys's purse and sweater. I guess the guy who killed her tossed them off the cliff after her body and didn't notice them get hung up on a bush. Everything was still inside the purse: money, credit cards, cell phone. When I saw it I knew something had happened to her, and I wanted to turn it in to the substation, but Alex . . ." She bit her lip.

Guy said, "Alex wanted to keep it."

"Yeah. We left the sweater."

Rhoda flashed him a warning look: *This is my interrogation.* He moved his hand in an apologetic gesture.

She asked, "How much money was in the purse?"

"Sixty-seven dollars and eighty-one cents. She

wouldn't've gotten far on that. And her credit cards . . . the one for Chevron worked, but when I tried the Visa it was turned down for being maxed out."

"*You* tried to use it?"

"Alex made me."

Guy watched Rhoda's lips tighten. She was getting as tired as he of the Alex-made-me routine. Alex may have been the abuser, but basically he and Lily were both predators, feeding off others' misfortunes.

"What else was in the purse?" Rhoda asked.

"The usual crap we drag around with us. One thing was weird, though: Her Triple A card was in some guy's name."

"Sean Bartlow?"

"Sounds right. Oh, and there were these handwritten notes, looked like directions. Go north so many miles from Westhaven, park here, go there."

"D'you still have them?"

"No. Alex tossed everything we couldn't use into a Dumpster up in Calvert's Landing where they're building the new community center. The cell phone, too. Turned out her service provider doesn't have sites up here, so it wouldn't work."

Rhoda made a note on a pad. She asked, "You see any evidence that somebody had been at the Quinley property before you?"

"Well, the gate wasn't latched like it usually is."

"Anything else?"

Lily thought and shook her head. Rhoda sighed and turned the recorder off. She said, "I'm going to have to place you in custody, Lily."

Panic flooded the young woman's features. She

turned, open-mouthed, to Guy. He said, "It's for the best."

"But what about my deal?"

Rhoda said, "I'll try to work that out for you, but till I can, I want you to be safe."

"Safe?" Her voice rose an octave. "Safe from who?"

"Alex, if he makes bail. His poacher buddies from Oakland. Wayne."

At the mention of her brother's name, Lily's face twisted. She leaned forward, breathing hard and clutching at her stomach. Guy squeezed her shoulder, trying to comfort her, but she didn't seem to feel his touch.

He looked grimly at Rhoda and she nodded. For now, both predators would be caged.

First light, and the fog drifted up from the cove behind the ruins of Quinley's. Ned Grossman's car was pulled nose-in to the chain-link fence near the rusted realty sign. Rho parked her truck next to it and got out, shivering in the damp, chill air.

Instead of getting out of his vehicle, Grossman swung open its passenger-side door and motioned her inside. He handed her a white foam cup and said, "Let's give ourselves a chance to wake up while we wait for the others."

She accepted the container gratefully, prying off the plastic lid and miraculously managing not to spill any coffee. Processing Lily Gilardi and finding someone to transport her to jail in Santa Carla, plus briefing Grossman on recent developments, had taken most of the night, and she'd had only a few hours' sleep on top of a grueling day.

She sipped the coffee, willing it to take effect, and

stared at the charred ruins behind the fence. They were overgrown by vegetation that twined up the supports of the gas-station canopy and crawled across the peaked roofline. She pictured the place as it must have appeared in the fifties: a welcome oasis beside a much narrower strip of highway. Its proprietor would have dispensed snacks and soda, beer and bait, and warnings about the hazards of traveling this remote stretch of coastline. The hotel in Signal Port had still functioned then, but there were no other lodging places except small auto courts at Westhaven and Calvert's Landing. Sheriff's patrols were infrequent and emergency care nonexistent. The scattered homes between the towns relied on kerosene lamps and propane, unless their owners had installed costly electric generators; handpumps on sinks and outhouses in the woods were common. People lived and died here without ever traveling farther than Santa Carla, and that journey was time-consuming and difficult.

"What're you thinking?" Grossman asked.

"About how it must've been here back before I was born. My dad's told me stories."

"It was pretty primitive. My grandparents had a cabin near Deer Harbor that they built in the forties. Even when the utility lines were extended north from Signal Port in the early sixties, they never took advantage of the service. Said it didn't matter, and they were right. We had woods full of deer and owls and woodpeckers. A sand beach. A great view of Goat Rock. Some of my happiest times were spent there."

"What d'you remember best?"

"The day the bear stole a blueberry pie my grandmother had cooling on the windowsill. Peach ice cream made in a hand-cranked machine. Corn popped over the fire and soaked in butter. Freshly caught fish frying in the pan, with onions." He paused, the corner of his mouth quirking up. "I guess I don't have to tell you what I focused on during childhood."

"Not a bad focus." She sipped coffee, feeling strangely at ease with her superior officer. "How's Everett doing?"

"What made you think of him? Of course—food. Well, the neighbor who's taking care of him says he and the dog're getting on famously. Trouble is, old Ev's developed a fondness for hamburger—cooked hamburger. Kind of pricey on a cop's salary."

Rho grinned. "To say nothing of an extra cooking chore—" She broke off as a cruiser pulled up beside her truck. "Wayne's here."

"Wayne? Dammit!" Grossman tossed his empty coffee cup into the backseat. "He's supposed to be establishing the route Ackerman took to get here. What the hell's he doing? He shouldn't be on the scene anyway, since his sister's a material witness. God*damn* it!" He threw open his door and got out of the car. Rho followed at a cautious distance.

Grossman walked toward Wayne in the gait of a big cat stalking its prey. Although the deputy had two inches and more than fifty pounds on him, his was the more imposing presence. He said, "Did I request you to be on the scene, Gilardi?"

"No, sir, you didn't, but I thought you could use some help. Besides, I've got a vested interest—"

"Which is precisely why I don't want you here. I have technicians coming from Santa Carla, and when they arrive Deputy Swift will show me where your sister described finding the victim's personal effects, and they'll comb the area. I don't want anyone with a vested interest involved in that process."

Wayne flushed.

Grossman added, "Have you submitted your report on Ackerman's route north yet?"

"I traced her as far south as Sonoma County, to the Ocean Cove store—"

"Put it in writing, Gilardi."

Rho saw Wayne's hands fist at his sides and his shoulders bunch as he prepared to take a swing at Grossman.

Don't, for God's sake, Wayne!

Grossman saw it too. "I wouldn't, if I were you," he warned. "Go back to the substation and write your report. Then take the day off. You need it."

Wayne regarded the detective with a flat, hot stare. Then he pivoted and went to his cruiser. As he turned onto the highway he sprayed Rho's truck with loose gravel.

"Thanks, Gilardi," she muttered.

Grossman was watching the departing car with narrowed eyes. "Our boy's got a temper."

"Yes."

"He always been that way?"

"No."

"What changed him?"

She compressed her lips. Guy had told her about Wayne's affair with Claudia Blakely before he left her house in the early hours of the morning. She was duty bound to report the information, yet she'd withheld it in her earlier briefing of Grossman. To tell him seemed a betrayal of the man who had mentored her.

"What is it, Swift?"

". . . The change in Wayne has to do with the Cascada Canyon murders. They changed us all."

Grossman waited.

She moved to the fence, her back to him, fingering a late-blooming rose that felt like tissue paper. "Wayne's got a reputation as a . . . I guess you could say a ladies' man."

"The reputation consistent with fact?"

"Yes."

"And?"

God, she wished Guy had never shared what he knew! She could single-handedly be responsible for destroying Wayne's career. "At the time of the murders he was involved with one of the victims, Claudia Blakeley."

"You mean romantically involved?"

"Yes."

"You know about it at the time?"

"No. I only found out early this morning."

"Can you substantiate it?"

"There's an eyewitness to Wayne picking Blakeley up on the highway, necking with her in his car—his patrol car, I guess."

"Get a statement."

"Yes, sir. I'll get right on it after I leave here. But do you really think it's evidence of official misconduct on Wayne's part?"

Grossman seemed to weigh his response carefully. "Necking in your patrol car isn't acceptable behavior, but I'd be willing to overlook that. What bothers me is we're talking about an officer who misplaced evidence in the case. And let you take the blame."

"I don't see what misplacing those blood samples has to do with—"

"Don't you?"

"You're saying that he might've deliberately misplaced them? Or tampered with other evidence?"

"I'm saying that he may have been involved in the murders."

When Guy stepped out of his room at the bed-and-breakfast at nine that morning, he came face-to-face with Becca Campos. She clutched an armload of sheets and towels to her breasts as if for comfort, and her eyes were red from crying.

"Becca," he said, "what's wrong?"

"Virge Scurlock's dead. They found her day before yesterday, and the sheriff's department tried to keep it quiet, but everybody was talking about it to those rotten reporters, and now it's on the news and in all the papers."

"Did you just find out about it?"

"No, my boyfriend told me right after, but I just can't stop crying. I loved Virge, she was the nicest person I ever worked for." Her tears spilled over and Becca dropped the linens and buried her face against Guy's shoulder.

What was it with him and the weeping women of Signal Port!

He patted her, murmuring hollow phrases—the sort of meaningless drivel that was one of the reasons he'd distanced himself from his friends after Diana died. Apparently Becca recognized it for what it was. She pushed away from him, fixing him with a cynical look, and stooped to pick up the linens. "Sorry," she said as she brushed past him into his room.

Guy hesitated, then shrugged and went out to see how the other citizens were taking the news.

"That's where it happened." Gregory Cordova pointed down into Lantern Cove. "That Japanese freighter back in thirty-seven. High surf just picked it up and smashed it on the rocks."

Rho didn't try to steer the old man back to the business at hand. Like many of the descendants of Basques who had settled this part of the coast, he had a roundabout way of approaching a difficult subject.

"All those dead men," he went on. "Some of them were no more than boys. I was practically a boy myself, and I learned a hard lesson from the shipwreck. We carried the bodies up and laid them out on this bluff. That was when I realized how unforgiving the sea is. How unforgiving death is. Of course, a few years later those dead boys would've been fighting against us. Strange to think how a person you feel no ill will toward can become an enemy in a very short time."

As Wayne will become my enemy after today.

"Follow me." Cordova set off at a surprisingly brisk pace across the bluff.

The fog was thick this morning, muffling the sound of the sea and cloaking the burned trees so they seemed gaunt figures holding a silent vigil for the sailors who had died on the rocks over sixty years before. Cordova set a course through them to the northeast. When he finally stopped they were at the upper corner of his property where it met the highway.

"Over there is where they'd meet," he said. "The woman would come along the path by the stream, and the man would be waiting in his official car."

"By the woman, you mean Claudia Blakeley?"

"I learned later that was her name, yes. And the man, of course, was your Deputy Gilardi."

"And you observed this how many times?"

"Four, all told, over a period of a month before the killings. Maybe it had been going on for a long time before, I don't know. But once I saw what was happening, I made it my business." His dark eyes peered at Rho from their deep sockets. "Yes, I'm a nosy man. Always have been. I make up for what my own life hasn't offered me by observing the lives of others."

"Are you willing to give us an official statement about this?"

"Is your department going to do something about that man?"

"If we find he's guilty of misconduct."

"He's guilty of being a menace to society and himself. I know. I've made a study of Wayne Gilardi in the years since those killings. Take your statement, but there's something more I have to tell you. Something I didn't tell that writer fellow, 'cause I was hoping he'd come back for the rest of the story. I enjoy his company."

"And what is that, Mr. Cordova?"

"I know where Deputy Gilardi took the Blakeley woman."

A prickling began at the base of Rho's spine, radiated upward and outward to her limbs. Instinctively she knew the old man was about to reveal something she didn't want to hear.

"Where?" she asked.

"Well, the last time they met before the woman was killed, I followed them. To the old filling station up the highway. I guess someone of your age would know it as Quinley's. Most of it had burned down, but a good part was still standing. Gilardi and the Blakeley woman drove through the gate, parked behind, didn't come out for nearly two hours. After they left I investigated. He had a nice little love nest fixed up in there."

Cordova's voice droned on, saying something about a mattress and empty wine bottles, but Rho barely heard it. Her ears were filled with the rush of her own blood, the accelerated beating of her heart.

The old man had told her something far worse than she'd feared.

The town seemed strangely quiet to Guy, with the exception of the sheriff's substation, where a press conference was apparently being held. People drove along the highway, went in and out of the shops, conducting their daily business. But they didn't speak more than was necessary and they avoided eye contact with him and each other. Instead of the rumor-mongering and possible unrest the sheriff's department had feared, a near paralysis had set in with the news of a third death. To Guy it seemed more ominous than the violent acting out on Sunday night, an affliction from which Signal Port might never recover.

He went into the Oceanside and took a window table. He was the only customer. The waitress automatically brought coffee and took his order for tomato juice and a toasted bagel, but departed without her usual smile. Behind the pass-through window the cook's off-key singing was silenced; when he finished preparing Guy's food he didn't give his customary shout for the waitress to hustle. She brought the order and placed the check beside his plate without looking at him.

After he'd eaten he walked up the highway to the supermarket and checked the headlines of the newspapers racked there. Speculation about the three deaths had made the papers as far away as San Jose and Sacramento. Although the Lindsay and Scurlock deaths were described as accidental, the stories hinted at some ominous, although obscure, link to Ackerman's murder.

During the next half hour he dropped into several business establishments and observed the same dynamic: people avoiding each other and shying away from him as if they suspected he was one of the media people. Many seemed withdrawn and depressed. Even those who knew him casually wouldn't take him up on his innocuous conversational gambits or even meet his gaze, and he sensed it had little to do with him and everything to do with their desire to avoid any human connection whatsoever.

Town in trouble. More trouble than it had seen in the worst days after the Cascada Canyon murders.

Rho tried to call Ned Grossman from Gregory Cordova's house, but Valerie told her the detective had flown to Santa Carla on the department's helicopter and hadn't said when he'd return.

"A break in one of the cases?" she asked.

"I'd've picked up on something like that. They did recover Ackerman's purse from that Dumpster up at

Calvert's Landing, and he took it along for Lily to identify."

"Well, if he calls in, tell him I need to talk with him."

On the way back to town she stopped to interview two people who had reported seeing Chrystal Ackerman at the turnout. Both said the woman was alone, both expressed regret at not going to her aid. Nothing new there. It was well past one o'clock when she reached the substation, and she felt a strong urge to keep driving when she spotted Wayne's truck in the lot. But Valerie had also said the reports on the hair samples and Virge's autopsy were in; she wasn't going to allow Wayne's presence to prevent her from going over them.

The big deputy was at the desk they shared, tapping furiously on the keyboard. He didn't look up when Rho came in, but the stiffening of his spine when she took the reports from the inbox told her he was deliberately ignoring her. She looked around at the other unoccupied desks, then went down the hallway to the storeroom at the rear of the building. Surrounded by office and restroom supplies, ammo and extra weapons, she sat down on a stepstool and began reading.

The hairs were a match with Ackerman's. She—or her body—had been in the Blakeley house at some point. Virge's autopsy was inconclusive. She could have died in an accidental fall, or been pushed or thrown off the ledge, or been killed elsewhere and transported there. Photographs appended to the report showed that footprints in the mud matched the tread of Virge's shoes, but not the prints inside the two houses.

The door opened and Valerie stuck her head in. "What are you doing here, pray tell?"

"Enjoying some privacy."

The clerk bristled. "Well excuse me."

"It's not you I'm trying to avoid."

"Oh. He *is* acting bearish today."

Rho nodded, not trusting herself to say anything more about Wayne. "Nothing from Grossman?"

"No."

"I wonder why he went to Santa Carla." Getting an ID from Lily on Ackerman's purse could have been accomplished by a less senior officer.

"Well how should I know?" Valerie said. "I'm just the clerk here." She left the door open and went back to her desk.

Probably Grossman had trampled on Valerie's already tender feelings, Rho thought. He could be abrupt, and he didn't understand what an institution she was, both here at the substation and throughout the town, where people were fond of saying, "You don't know? Ask Valerie Middleton. She knows everything."

Rho remained where she was, content to sit alone in the dimly lit room. From up front she could hear Wayne cursing; probably the old printer, which budgetary constraints prevented them from replacing, was out of ink. She tensed as his footsteps shambled down the hall. He stomped through the door, not seeing her as he headed for the cabinet where the cartridges were kept, then stopped short.

"What the hell're you doing in here, Swift? Why aren't you in Santa Carla with your buddy Grossman?"

"I wasn't asked along. And he's not my buddy."

"Looked like it this morning at Quinley's. Where've you been since then?"

"Interviewing a couple of witnesses about Ackerman. They weren't very helpful."

"Not like my sister, right?"

"Wayne, I'm sorry about Lily."

"Don't be. She deserves to pull some jail time. Give her a good scare, maybe knock some sense into her. What'd the techs turn up at Quinley's?"

"I don't know. I didn't stay around to see." The room seemed hot now and Rho felt claustrophobic. She wished he'd take his cartridge and get out.

Wayne appeared to have no intention of moving. He studied her with narrowed eyes for a moment. "It took all that time to conduct a couple of routine interviews?"

"Uh-huh."

"Or maybe they weren't so routine."

"What does that mean?"

"I heard Grossman talking to somebody on the phone when he got back from Quinley's. He said you were following up a lead on the canyon murders."

Dammit! There could be only one reason Grossman had talked about that in Wayne's hearing: He wanted to prompt Wayne to ask her about the interview with Cordova, in the hope he'd somehow implicate himself. Unfair to take advantage of a relationship that went back for more than a decade. And, thinking of fairness, didn't she owe it to Wayne to tell him what she knew? Allow him to prepare for the accusations that were sure to be leveled at him?

"Okay," she said, "I was talking with Gregory Cordova, down at Point Deception. It came out that he saw Claudia Blakeley meeting a man on the highway across from his property during the month before the murders. A man who took her to the ruins of Quinley's for extramarital sex."

Wayne's face paled and stilled. It was clear what she'd said was worse than he'd expected. A mixture of rage and hurt muddied his gaze. "You set out to gather evidence against me? *You*, Rho?"

"I'm sorry, but don't you see? Now we can clear this thing up." She put out a hand toward him, but he was already gone, rushing down the hall, across the office, out the door. By the time she reached the parking lot, his truck was laying rubber on the highway.

He was heading north, in the opposite direction from his home. Running, maybe, and it was all her fault.

Guy ended his phone conversation with Dun Harrison and went to stand at the window of his room, staring out over the roofs of the unfinished subdivision at the flat gray sea. Dun had reluctantly admitted to enticing him into the project. He had a buyer for the canyon property, he said, a well-known theatrical producer who wanted a private West Coast retreat and felt the place's notoriety would ensure that privacy. A man who wasn't squeamish about violent death and didn't believe in ghosts. But before the property passed from his hands Dun wanted one last chance at learning the truth of what happened there thirteen years before.

You couldn't blame him, and it was Guy's own fault he'd walked into the situation without knowing all the facts. His working methods dictated that. Still, he'd expressed enough annoyance at Dun's lack of straightforwardness that he'd extracted a promise from him.

His files were spread on the table in the semicircular

space formed by the turret window. He picked up the one containing the profiles of the victims and removed the photograph of Oriana being escorted to the plane at San Francisco International by her maternal grandmother. The child's face was a study in anguish as she looked behind her. Guy wanted to ask her what she'd been feeling at that moment, as well as if in the intervening years she'd remembered anything more about the murders. He'd made Dun promise to ask her if she'd consent to a telephone interview.

He set down the photograph and looked out the window again, feeling oddly hollow. He should have been elated at Dun's willingness to speak with Oriana. He should have felt good just being alive. Since he'd come to Signal Port he'd had a sense of an awakening, a return to his old self. But today he once again felt numb and disconnected.

"Why is that?" he asked, reaching for some connection, if only an imagined one.

Diana's voice didn't respond.

God, what if it continued to be silent? Then he'd be totally alone.

After numerous attempts to reach Wayne both by phone and radio, Rho finally called Grossman at the Investigations Bureau in Santa Carla and explained what had happened. "You deliberately let him overhear you talking about a lead in the canyon murders, didn't you?"

"Yes."

"You knew I'd feel obligated to tell him what we'd found out."

"Yes, again."

"Well, you got more than you bargained for, if he's really on the run. And I feel responsible."

"Maybe you should stop taking on the world's troubles, Swift. Concentrate on yourself for a change."

His words shocked her. She barely knew Ned Grossman, and it wasn't the place of a superior officer to give such personal advice. But he was right. She felt responsible for Wayne, her other colleagues, Valerie, her father, her fellow townspeople. Hell, she felt responsible for people whose names she barely recalled, people with whom she hadn't spoken in years!

Grossman said, "I'll put out a pickup order on Gilardi, and see you at the substation tomorrow at eight hundred hours."

As the dial tone buzzed in her ear, Rho found her gaze pulled into the chaotic pattern of the garment Valerie was knitting at her desk. Her thoughts had spun into a similar pattern, quite out of control. Suddenly she felt a need to anchor herself in the familiar. "Valerie, if anybody needs me, I'll be at Jack's."

Rhoda was coming down the steps of the substation as Guy crossed toward it. There was a tension in the set of her mouth and the way she moved. Something wrong, but, since she hadn't yet seen him, for once it wasn't his fault. He waved and she stopped, jiggling her keys.

"You on official business?" he asked.

"No. Were you looking for me?"

"Yes." He explained about his call to Dun Harrison. She seemed distracted while he spoke, and her reaction wasn't all he'd hoped for.

"Well, that's good news. If she agrees to talk with you."

He frowned. "I'll buy you a cup of coffee if you'll tell me what's wrong."

She hesitated. "I could use one, but I'll tell you what: Why don't we let my father give us a cup. I'm on my way to see him."

Curious about the man who had raised her, Guy followed in his car to the yacht harbor. It seemed like the loneliest place in the world today, and that wasn't just due to his mood. Many of the docks had collapsed and lay submerged in the oil-slicked water; a derelict fishing boat, its paint cracked and blistered, listed to one side on the murky bottom; sand had reclaimed much of the channel; trash dotted the jetty. The *Rhoda A,* no longer a handsome craft, was the marina's only functional tenant.

Rhoda came up beside him. "Pretty grim, huh?"

"In a way. Why does your father stay here?"

"There's no place else he wants to be."

Meaning he didn't care about his surroundings, and Guy wondered why.

Rhoda motioned to him and they began walking along the dock toward the CrisCraft.

A large man with razor nicks on his clean-shaven chin and broken veins on his nose was sitting on deck, an amber drink in hand. He pushed back his baseball cap and watched them approach, his apparent pleasure at seeing his daughter becoming tinged with wariness as he regarded Guy. "Come aboard, Deputy," he called. "Who's your friend?"

Rhoda stepped onto the boat with the natural ease of someone who had spent a good part of her life on the water. Guy followed clumsily. When Rhoda made the introductions, Jack Antolini's eyes glinted knowingly. "So you decided to take your old man's advice, did you?"

"For once."

Now what did that mean?

Jack led them below and offered them a choice of coffee or Irish whiskey. Rhoda opted for the former, and Guy, in the interest of manly fellowship, took the latter. As they sat down at the small table Jack motioned at a police scanner that was muttering on the galley counter. "I hear they're looking for your friend Wayne. He finally go too far?"

Rhoda's face grew troubled. "I don't know what to think, Dad." Guy listened with growing surprise as she explained about Wayne's sudden flight.

Jack shook his head. "Not right to put out a pickup order on him, Deputy."

"It was Ned Grossman who put it out. And before I reported to him, I did everything I could to raise Wayne on his personal radio, as well as called his house and anybody who might have seen him. If he's running, we can't politely ask him to come in and tell his side of the story." There was a testy note in Rhoda's voice that Guy hadn't heard before. Some friction between father and daughter.

Jack said, "I don't care what Wayne's involvement with those canyon people was, he's not a man who'd murder anybody, much less children."

"But this Chrystal Ackerman—"

"She may've been thrown off the cliff behind the old filling station, but that doesn't prove Wayne did it. He took the Blakeley woman there over thirteen years ago. That doesn't mean he's been back since."

Rhoda made a helpless gesture with both hands, then laced her fingers around her coffee mug. The tension in the small cabin was palpable now.

Guy said, "I think you're right, sir."

They both looked at him as if they'd forgotten he was there.

He cleared his throat and went on. "Wayne's a violent man, but his sister told me he only started acting out after the canyon killings. It's possible he really cared for Claudia Blakeley, and her death started a process of decline."

Jack glanced at Rhoda. "Well, he *did* lose those blood samples."

Now he was allying himself with her, as Guy had intended. "An honest mistake," he said.

"He let my girl take the blame."

"Covering his ass, and she let him."

"He might've known who did the killings and was trying to protect them."

"Might have."

Jack frowned, confused by Guy's shifting point of view. Rhoda stifled a grin. Guy was beginning to understand the dynamic between them, and while it amused him, he sympathized with both.

He said, "Rhoda mentioned you were in law enforcement all your working life. You must have some interesting stories."

Beside him Rhoda sighed, but the sound was full of relief.

At close to six when her father asked Guy to make a run to the supermarket for another fifth of Bushmills, Rhoda started to protest. But some unspoken agreement had been struck between the two men, and they ignored her. After Guy left she leaned on her elbows at the table, watching Jack tidy the galley and turn on the cabin lamps against the encroaching dusk.

"You've got that New York City journalist tamed good, honey," he said.

"He's far from tame, but at least I can keep an eye on him."

"Heard you took him to Vegas with you."

"Uh-huh."

"Ned Grossman know about that?"

"Not yet."

"Better not tell him."

"Why not?"

"Violation of procedure. Besides, Grossman's interested in you—and not just because you're a good deputy."

"What on earth would make you think that?"

"Not what—who. Valerie Middleton. She claims she can see it every time Grossman looks at you."

"When did she tell you that?"

"Last night, when I went by her house to try to cheer her up."

"You *what*?"

"Valerie had just lost her best woman friend. She needed some company."

The idea of her father calling on Valerie struck Rho as odd. Was that why he'd shaved and, she thought, raggedly trimmed his hair? "I didn't know the two of you were close."

"Valerie's the best friend I've got. How could you not know that? For over thirty years she took my phone messages and brought me coffee and held me together when things got to be too much."

Rho shook her head in amazement.

Jack frowned. "What, I can't have a woman friend? I was supposed to live like a monk after your mother took off?"

"But Valerie's husband—"

"He took off not much later. And things just happened."

She thought back to her childhood, remembering little things: the fudge and cookies Valerie would send home with Jack; how she was always there for her when he couldn't be; the weekends when she and Valerie's son, Joe, would be tended by a sitter while both parents were away from home. Easy to understand why such details had not added up when she was a child, but why hadn't she caught on later?

"Sometimes," she said, "I can't believe how little we know about the people we're closest to."

Jack sat down and took both her hands in his, bringing back memories of long, serious talks as he tried to be both father and mother to her. "Honey, since you discovered boys in seventh grade, you were too caught up in your own romantic life to notice mine. And you haven't been close to *anybody* for thirteen years now."

He was right. She hadn't. Tears welled up as she thought of all that lost time. Lost love. All that loneliness as she'd hidden within her carefully crafted emotional armor.

"Now don't cry. You hear me, Deputy?"

"Yeah, I hear you." She pulled her hands away,

grabbed a tissue from a box on the table, wiped her face, blew her nose.

"Everything's changing for you now," Jack said. "Changing for me, too. For the town. You can feel it."

"But is it changing for the better or for the worse?"

"In the long run, for the better, I think. How could it not? My pretty girl's got two men interested in her."

"Two? Who's the other one?"

"Good God, Deputy, use your eyes. It's written all over this Guy Newberry's face, even if he doesn't seem to know it yet."

When they left Jack Antolini's boat shortly after nine, Guy had to lean on Rhoda to keep from staggering. He and her father had gotten on like old pals, and even the huge deli sandwiches and potato salad that he'd brought back in defense against the fresh fifth of Irish hadn't counteracted the prodigious amount of booze he'd consumed.

"Nize man, y'r father," he said, and cursed himself for slurring his words.

"Thank you," she replied. "You need some fresh sea air. We'll take my truck and you can walk over for your car in the morning."

"Nize woman. You don' yell at me for drinking too much. Where're we goin'?"

"There's something you need to see if you're to understand this county."

Just what he needed at this juncture, a sightseeing tour. But anything was better than returning to his empty room, where Diana had ceased to speak to him. With some difficulty he climbed into the passenger's seat and fastened his belt securely. Even though she hadn't been drinking, this was a woman he could trust to drive like a maniac.

She took it at a reasonable speed on the access road and north on the highway to the town limits, then opened it up. Lights of the close-in houses flashed past, grew more sparse, and finally there were none at all. Rhoda kept her eyes on the road, her pleasure in driving evident. Guy hummed an aria from some opera—he couldn't remember which—and relaxed.

A sign for Deer Harbor appeared, and Rhoda braked, slowing for a wide place that contained nothing more than a propane company, garage, coin-operated laundry, and market. A few teenagers hung out under the market's lighted sign, smoking and passing around a bottle.

"Oughta arrest them," he mumbled.

"Why?"

"They're bad."

"They're exactly like I was at that age."

"I rest my case."

The truck slid neatly around a hairpin turn, its headlights illuminating a sign for Deer Harbor Campground. Guy closed his eyes and listened to the hum of the tires on the pavement as Rhoda sped up. He couldn't remember the last time he'd been pleasurably drunk. It had to've been before Diana—

Before. After.

He opened his eyes, trying to fight off the memories and sustain the good feeling. "Where are we?"

"Almost there."

"You're not a very informing woman. Not very."

"What's an 'informing woman'?" She sounded amused.

"One who tells me where the hell she's taking me."

"Have patience."

He watched the walls of what he assumed were large oceanfront estates slip past. "Money here," he said.

"Lots of it. Most are second-home people."

"And you locals don' like them."

"That depends. The ones we like want to be part of the community. They help our economy by shopping here and hiring local people for their yard work and repairs. The ones we don't like import everything from food to labor."

"If I had a second home here, I'd shop constantly and hire everybody in the whole damn county."

"If you had a second home here, I'd have to drive by constantly to keep tabs on what you were up to."

Odd note in her voice, even though the tone was light. What did it mean? He felt more sober now, and he looked analytically at her, but couldn't interpret it.

Rhoda braked abruptly and waited for the glaring lights of an oncoming car to pass, then turned left into a driveway flanked by stone pillars. Old stone pillars, judging from the cracks and coat of moss her headlights revealed. She drove slowly toward the sea, gravel crunching under the tires. In a cleared area surrounded by those strange plumed plants he'd seen at Point Deception she stopped and killed the engine.

"We're here," she said. "Let's take a walk."

He got out of the truck, shivering in the chill air. "These plants, what are they?"

"Pampas grass. It's worse than bamboo, takes over

everything." She began walking along a path made of railroad ties. "A few years ago the county funded a program to eradicate it, and for a while we thought it had worked, but now it's back full force."

"Pretty stuff. Why kill it?"

"Because it kills everything that gets in its way."

Guy thought of Cascada Canyon. And a faraway place called East Timor.

They continued along the path for some fifty yards, the sound of the sea ever louder. At its end a promontory jutted out over the water, surrounded by a low stone wall. Two figures stood there, shimmering white in the light of the full moon. Statues. Women in old-fashioned dress looking out to sea.

"What's this?"

"It's called *Women Who Wait*. A monument to those who died at sea."

"Who put it here?"

Rhoda walked between the statues, sliding an affectionate hand over each.

"This land belonged to Constance Giordani, the wife of a man who ran a fishing fleet out of Calvert's Landing in the late eighteen hundreds. He and his partner, her sister's husband, were drowned in a storm at sea. You see that light flashing on the point over there?"

He looked where she motioned and saw it reflected off a distant wall of fog.

Rhoda said, "That's the Cape Lookout Lighthouse. Was built in eighteen eighty. In nineteen twelve the lightkeeper died and a replacement couldn't be found, so Constance and her sister volunteered for the job and became, so far as I know, the only female lightkeepers in California. They kept the light until nineteen thirty-nine, when the Coast Guard took it over. Back then it had a crystal-and-brass Fresnel lens, which must've been a hell of a lot of work to maintain. Quite a tough job for two women. Now, of course, the light's unmanned and fully automated."

"What happened to the sisters after the Coast Guard took over?"

"They lived in their house on this property—we're standing on the old terrace—for the next thirty years. When Constance died, she willed the land and her remaining fortune to the county, with the stipulation that the house be torn down but the statues, which are modeled on her and her sister, remain in perpetuity."

Guy circled the figures, studying each. He'd expected their faces to show loss and grief, but he saw only strength. "The guidebooks don't mention this place."

"No. That's also in keeping with Constance Giordani's wishes. She wanted it to mainly be a private refuge for county residents. Some of us come here when we need . . . whatever it is we need. I've come here often during the past thirteen years."

Guy moved toward where she stood by the stone wall. Her face was very pale in the moonlight, her hair dark and sleek. "You brought *me* here. You must trust me not to write about it."

"Yes. And I brought you here because you need to know that this coastline is about more than violence."

Unconditional trust. How had he come to deserve this?

He was beside her now, and to cover his confusion he peered over the wall at the sea. Waves crashed at the base of the cliff, tearing at the land like monstrous jaws.

Somewhere he'd read that the rate of cliff retreat—erosion caused by wave action—was a foot per year. How long before this promontory and those statues of the brave women were gone? Sorrow washed over him with every swell of the surf.

"Guy?" Rhoda touched his sleeve. He turned toward her, and she put a hand to his cheek, guided his face down to hers, and kissed him. A real kiss, unlike the schoolboyish peck he'd given her the night before.

When she pulled away, her eyes searched his, glittering dark in the moonlight. Her hand remained on his cheek. She asked, "What is it that makes you so sad?"

He wanted to say he wasn't sad at all, but he couldn't give voice to the lie.

"At first I dismissed you as detached and arrogant, a sophisticated New Yorker viewing us with amusement and using us for his own purposes. But that's not so."

He shook his head, not trusting himself to speak.

"That's the real reason I brought you here. So you could tap into whatever this place has to offer. And I hoped you'd tell me . . ." She waited, eyes still on his.

At first his old self-protective mechanisms kicked in. There was no way he would allow another human being to witness his pain. Then he thought, She's already witnessed it. She needs to know where it comes from.

And I need to tell her.

The realization made him weak, both with relief and dread. He moved away from her and sat down on the retaining wall with his back to the relentlessly devouring sea. Unburdening himself to Rhoda would mean letting her into his life, and he knew all too well that a person who enters one's life can just as easily be lost. Of course, there was also a measure of loss in keeping someone at an arm's length. . . .

"I was married once," he began, "to a woman named Diana." Just speaking of her conjured up the image of her warm eyes and thick fall of chestnut hair. He could feel the softness of her skin, hear her low-timbred voice, smell her light perfume.

Rhoda sat down, leaving a respectful two feet between them, and waited. After a moment he went on. "We were happy. I suppose most people who've lost a spouse claim that, but in our case it's true. We shared both our lives and our work. But the work, that's where it went wrong. Maybe if we hadn't . . ."

He shook his head. For too long the thoughts of how it might have gone differently had tortured him. "Three years ago, Diana and I were on a two-week trip to East Timor. The former Portuguese colony that's resisted being absorbed into Indonesia for over twenty years." He heard his voice becoming flat and unemotional, even professorial. As Rhoda's had sounded when she'd taken him to the canyon. He was insulating himself too.

"I was gathering material for a book, and Diana was taking photographs. We were going to document the plight of eight hundred thousand people who were suffering extreme violations of their civil rights at the hands of the government in Djakarta. We thought we could make a difference." In his peripheral vision he saw Rhoda nod; she was also a person who wanted to believe she could make a difference.

"We were staying at a monastery outside of Dili, the capital city," he went on. "Guests of an old monk who was active in the struggle for independence and had offered to put us in touch with knowledgeable and forth-coming sources. The work went well, but the atmosphere was bad there. Government troops were everywhere. By day they caused a tension that was exacerbated by the heat. They were less noticeable by night, but still there was a feel of menace in the soft breeze.

"After a few days Diana and I realized we were being watched. By the beginning of the second week the old monk, who had acted as if he'd seen it all and feared nothing, became nervous. Diana wasn't a timid or fanci-ful woman, but she became infected by his fear. She begged me to leave early."

This was where the emotional terrain grew dangerous, where he could sink into a mire of self-loathing and -pity. He paused for a long moment before he added, "Four more days, I told her. Four more days to get the last few pieces of information I needed, and we'd be out of there. It was the worst mistake of my life."

He heard the sudden raw note in his voice and glanced at Rhoda. Neither her expression nor her body language acknowledged it. Allowing him his feelings without em-barrassment. He swallowed before he went on.

"The night before we were to fly home, the monastery was set on fire. The monk urged us to escape while we could, to the countryside where one of the sources I'd in-terviewed would shelter us. We hid in a shed on the man's property for a week, sleeping on the ground, refusing most of the food he tried to give us because we knew he needed it for his family. When he thought it was safe, we went back to Dili. The monastery was in ruins, the monk gone, presumably dead. And government soldiers were waiting for us."

Now he began speaking faster, rushing to get through this before he broke down. "The commander of the unit told us their orders were to escort us to the airport, but I doubted we'd ever arrive there. I could tell Diana did too. She was . . ." His voice broke and he shook his head. Raised his arms and pushed his hands palms-out in front of him, hoping to somehow relieve the pressure in his chest.

"She was worn out. Weak from lack of food and sleep. But she wasn't afraid, not like I was. She was angry. I saw her getting her camera ready. I should have stopped her, but instead I did nothing. As the soldiers approached us, she raised it for a last photograph. I heard the shutter click at the same time one of the soldiers shouldered his carbine and shot her in the head."

Rhoda moaned, a sound that told him she was living it with him.

"To this day," he said, "I can't sort out the sequence of events after that. Chaos and disbelief and pain, that's all. Then I was on a government transport plane, flying to Bangkok, where a State Department official met me."

"What did the government do about it?"

The fact that she'd spoken startled him. He looked into her eyes and saw the same kind of anger he'd seen in Diana's. Rhoda still believed in justice, and he feared someday the lack of it would break her.

"There was a cover-up, of course. The Indonesian government hadn't intended any harm to come to either of us; the soldier had acted on his own. They called it a dreadful, regrettable incident. And our government wasn't willing to offend an important Asian country of two hundred million people, so they accepted the official version and apology. They had Diana's body returned for burial in Massachusetts, where her family lives. And I had no strength to fight either government, so I retreated from the world. Where I've more or less been ever since."

"Less now."

". . . Maybe." His eyes were full of tears; he closed the lids against them, but they leaked out and slipped down his cheeks. He hadn't cried in three years, not since the night after Diana's funeral, shut away in the apartment that, without her, would never again be home. When Rhoda's hand touched his, a shuddering sob caught in his throat. He let it out and when he could speak again said shakily, "There's a footnote to the story."

"Oh?"

"Six months later I received a package postmarked Sydney, Australia, containing Diana's camera. Sent through one of those mailing services, no note or explanation, and the final roll of film still inside. It was a year before I could bring myself to take the roll to the processor, but when the prints came back I had my evidence. A shot of a young Indonesian soldier, his eyes hard with hatred, raising his carbine as his superior officer smiled in approval. That photo and its negative now live in my safe-deposit box, and if I ever find a way to use it, I will."

His tears were falling freely now, but he felt no need to stem them. He'd finally told it all, to someone who cared. Told it all, as he'd never have to tell it again.

Chrystal: Before

Friday, October 6
12:37 P.M.

Okay, there it is—Forrest Wynne's old Buick. All covered up with pine needles so you can't hardly tell what color it is. I remember him working on that car while Leo made music and smoked dope.

Jude said go around here to the right, walk six paces this way. Well, here I am.

Down on my knees now, scraping needles away. Thirteen years of 'em. Damp, and they smell moldy. There it is, though, just like she said—the manhole cover. Grab it, pull—

Shit! My nail! All torn and bloody.

Big deal, Chryssie. Buy yourself a manicure when you get home. You'll be able to afford one.

Okay. I got hold of it. Heavy. Pull up, push it over here and— Oh, yuck!

Oil and God knows what else, but down there's the leather pouch sealed in layers of Ziplocs.

Oh! It's like feeling around in a sewer. Where is it?

A stick, find a stick. There. Okay. Poke it in and—

Here it is! Lift up. Careful now.

Yes! You just grabbed hold of your future, Chryssie, even if it's all oily and disgusting—

Oh, Christ! What's that what's that?

Somebody yelling.

Hey, what're you doing there?

Hey!

Runnin', that's what I'm doing.

Runnin' for my fuckin' life. . . .

Thursday, October 12

To Rho, the group that assembled in the interrogation room for their 8 A.M. meeting seemed severely diminished, perhaps because up to now Wayne had played such a large role in her professional life. Ned Grossman, Denny Shepherd, and Harve Iverson would not feel the absence of their colleague as keenly; the two detectives had barely known him, and Iverson's tenure as commander was less than two years.

She sat at the table while the others got coffee, avoiding their eyes as her thoughts strayed to Guy Newberry. It wasn't the first time she'd been preoccupied with a man while waiting for a meeting to start, but never in quite this way.

Guy's story of his wife's tragic death and the grief he carried with him had touched her deeply and allowed her to open up to him about the full extent of the effect the canyon murders had had on her life. They'd connected on an intimate level, and she knew that if she'd given him any encouragement at all, they'd have ended up in bed together. But much as she was tempted, such a close to the evening didn't seem right. They were still too damaged and the emotional connection too new and frail to sustain the additional pressure that making love would surely bring. So she'd dropped him at the bed-and-breakfast and gone home to a cold, empty bed.

"Swift? Are you with us?"

She looked up, saw Grossman frowning at her. "Yes, sir," she said quickly.

"Good." He shuffled his papers, cleared his throat. "First of all, Deputy Gilardi was picked up in a bar in Eureka last night. He's returning from Humboldt County voluntarily, and I'll be interviewing him this afternoon. In light of your long-standing relationship, Swift, I'll want you to sit in."

She nodded, her spirits plummeting. What was Wayne feeling right now? Fear? Humiliation? Betrayal? Anger?

Try all of the above.

Grossman went on, "Chrystal Ackerman's purse was recovered yesterday morning, and I took it to Santa Carla for identification by Lily Gilardi. The lab processed it, found stains of a substance that also appeared on Ackerman's skin, tube top, and the passenger-side floor of the Mercedes. Motor oil, old and full of sludge, that didn't match what was in the car's crankcase. Any ideas on where it came from?"

Shepherd said, "The site of the old gas station, of course."

"I don't think so. There's no evidence the car was ever there."

He shrugged and jabbed the tip of his pencil into his scratch pad.

"Swift? Harve?" Grossman said.

Iverson shook his head.

Rho said, "No idea, sir."

"Okay, the contents of the purse were the usual items, except for a couple of sheets of paper with directions scribbled on them. They look to be directions to Cascada Canyon, which would support the presence of the hairs and the ankle bracelet Swift found." He passed around photocopies.

Rho skimmed them. "What's this at the bottom: 'stream, bridge, well, F.C. six paces'?"

"The location of Susan Wynne's money, of course," Grossman said.

"Did she get it?"

"If she did, it would provide a motive for her murder. Quarter of a mil is more than enough to kill for. Now, on to the evidence from Quinley's." He passed out glossy photographs. "Tire tracks. Two sets, not including the ones left by Alex Ngo's truck. Recent."

Rho compared the photos. The tread shown in one appeared new, while that in the other was nonexistent in the center, worn on the edges.

"The first is easy to identify," the detective said. "Firestone heavy truck series, the best they make. Very little wear. Driver pulled in as close to the cliff as possible, backed out, turned south on the highway."

"Nothing distinctive about them," Shepherd said.

"Look closer at the left rear imprint. You'll see a crescent-shaped nick in the tread. Once we have a suspect, that nick will help us nail him."

Grossman turned his attention to the next set of tracks. "This other vehicle pulled in behind the fence, turned, and exited north on the highway. That last photo shows footprints leading to the cliff that were probably made by workboots. Tire size indicates the vehicle was probably a light truck, maybe one of those foreign makes like Toyota. These're really distinctive."

Rho stared at the photograph. She was picturing an old light Ford pickup with impossibly worn tires. In her mind she heard her own voice saying, "You can't keep driving on those!" Heard the response, "The hell you say. They're good for another ten thousand miles."

Her father's voice. Her father's truck.

Guy rolled onto his back, acutely aware of his dry mouth and the pain above his right eyebrow. God, he'd really tied one on trying to keep up with Rhoda's father. Jack Antolini's system must process alcohol like most people's process water; the man had been coherent and steady when Rhoda and he left the boat.

The thought of Rhoda sent a stab of embarrassment through him, and he covered his eyes with his arm, trying to blot out the memories of the time they spent on the promontory. Impossible, though. Even his dreams had been filled with visions of her face in the moonlight. Her face, and those of the *Women Who Wait*.

Rhoda, asking, "What is it that makes you so sad?" Rhoda and the stone women, waiting for his answer.

He'd cried as he told her. No woman, not even Diana, had ever seen the adult Guy Newberry cry. But while Rhoda told him of over a decade of pain and loneliness, she hadn't shed a tear. Meaning she'd suffered far more than even he could imagine.

He lay still for a time, shielding his eyes from the light

that streamed through the windows. After a while his headache eased and thirst drove him to the bathroom. He gulped a glass of water there, then took another to the turret window and drank more slowly, surveying the scene outside.

A logging truck was pulled off on the shoulder opposite the inn, its driver checking a lopsided load. A kid on a skateboard performed expert turns on the cracked pavement of the subdivision. Offshore, fishing trawlers headed back to Calvert's Landing Pier with the morning's catch. Clouds hovered on the horizon.

Life as usual in Signal Port, but abnormal currents moved beneath its surface today, the thirteenth anniversary of the Cascada Canyon murders.

Abnormal currents beneath the surface of his life, too. Diana's voice was stilled. Forever, he suspected. He was alone.

As alone as Rhoda.

As alone as all the victims, in the end.

When she saw the *Rhoda A* buttoned up tight and Jack's truck gone, Rho felt a clenching in her gut. Easy, she warned herself, he's only gone to the store for his daily ration of Bushmills.

She stepped on board and immediately noted something different. A gallon can of boat paint and a brush sat in the shadow of the transom, and an orange heavy-duty extension cord snaked from below deck to a belt sander near the portside rail.

Not Irish, then. He'd gone to the hardware store for sandpaper.

Everything's changing for you. For me too . . . for the better, I think.

You were right, Dad. Night before last you shaved and trimmed your hair and paid a call on your longtime lady friend. This morning you started working on the boat. If only I didn't know about your truck having been at Quinley's—

She heard footsteps, turned and saw Guy walking along the access road to where they'd left his car the night before. He wore cords and a sweatshirt, and a baseball cap from under which the longish silver-gray hair at the nape of his neck curled.

He waved to her and called, "Jack okay?"

"More than okay. He's started working on the boat." She stepped onto the dock and walked toward him, feeling shy.

"Your father's got an iron constitution." He was pale under his tan, but otherwise looked no worse for the wear.

"You don't look half as bad as you ought to," she told him.

"Thanks a lot. My secret is a quart of water and a handful of vitamin Cs before bed, more water and Cs in the morning. You sleep well?"

"Yes. I was exhausted."

"No nightmares?"

"No. Why—?" And then she remembered what today was. "You know, I hadn't given a thought to it being the anniversary of the murders."

"Then you *have* come to terms with them."

"Guess so." They began moving toward their vehicles. "About last night—" she said.

"Last night I was—" he said simultaneously.

They both smiled wryly.

"Couple of emotional recluses, aren't we?" he commented. "Venture out, drop our baggage for each other to examine, then collect it and scurry back to our respective lairs."

"I don't want to do that anymore—retreat, I mean."

"Neither do I. We'll have to help each other stay out in the open." He took her hand. "So what's the news from the substation?"

She explained about Wayne, adding, "I hate the prospect of sitting across the table and interrogating him as if he were a criminal."

"You'll be just fine. Keep in mind that he may have a good explanation of why he ran."

She shrugged, unwilling to discuss it further. "There's something new from the lab on Ackerman."

Guy's eyes narrowed thoughtfully as she told him about the directions and the motor oil residue. "I think I know where it came from," he said. "Are you up to another trip to the canyon?"

Her pulse quickened. "Yes. Let's go."

"It's over here." Guy stepped off the driveway and walked toward the old car under the pines. "Unfortunately, I disturbed the evidence when I found it. The manhole cover was off, and, seeing what the contents were, I thought I should replace it."

He squatted down beside the makeshift oil sump, tugged off the cover, and motioned for Rhoda to have a look. She knelt beside him, thrusting her hand into the viscous liquid and feeling its consistency. Then she raised her fingers to her nose, sniffed and made a face.

She said, "There's a fair amount of oil splashed on the ground. And this stick is coated with it, as if someone used it to poke around in there. You notice that the other day?"

"I don't recall seeing it, but the light was bad. I took some photos, and they're supposed to be ready today. Maybe they'll show."

She stood and picked up a tree branch. After probing the sump with it, she propped it against the car's bumper. "Nothing in there but waste matter. Ackerman must've gotten the money."

"Then what happened to it?"

"When we find that out, we'll know who killed her." She took a tissue from her pocket and scrubbed her fingers. "I'm going to call in, get a photographer and technician here."

"I'll wait for you."

He watched as she walked away, admiring the trim lines of her small body and her strong, economical gait. Last night had put an awkwardness between them, but their earlier conversation had begun to bridge it.

Something moved in the tree above him. He looked up and saw a jay hopping about. Through the branches the sky was gray and gravid clouds blew across it from the west. Rain predicted, the first since he'd come here. He went back to the drive and walked along until he spotted the downed utility wire. One snip with insulated cutters and nine lives had been held hostage. One snip, and eight lives had ended.

Evil in the canyon, then and now.

*   *   *

"You've got one more day, Grossman, and then we're bringing in the FBI." Assistant Sheriff Pete Stedman's jowls were set and his small eyes glared out of their fleshy pockets. The department's second-in-command had made a special trip from Santa Carla to issue his ultimatum.

Rho glanced at Grossman and Shepherd to see how they were receiving it. The senior detective seemed relaxed, almost indifferent, and his fingers toyed idly with a pencil on the table in front of him. In contrast, Shepherd's face was red, his eyes stormy.

Grossman said, "We're very close to a break in the case."

"Where've I heard that before? You're down to, what? One deputy to assist now." His gesture toward Rho indicated he found her a poor one at best. "The other . . . Christ knows what went on there, and I think you're making a mistake allowing him to come in voluntarily. You got a woman dead, he's your only lead. And on top of that today's the anniversary of your other unsolved case, and now you tell me the Ackerman girl had a connection to those victims."

Rho expected Grossman to point out that he hadn't been with the department at the time of the canyon murders, but he said nothing.

Stedman added, "The former sheriff should have brought the feds in on that one a lot earlier than he did. We're not making the same mistake twice."

Grossman's expression remained neutral, but his fingers tensed on the pencil.

"One day," the assistant sheriff said. "Is that clear?"

The detective nodded, and Stedman heaved his considerable bulk from the chair. "Good."

Grossman watched him leave the interrogation room, moving only his eyes. Then he looked from Rho to Shepherd. "You heard the man."

"Shit!" Denny exclaimed. "Stedman's been sitting behind a desk for so long he's lost touch with what it's like in the field! Did he even read our latest reports? No. He's got his mind made up."

"He's afraid," Grossman said, "and if you had any sense, you would be too." He flopped a newspaper on the desk so they could see the front page.

The *San Francisco Chronicle*. NEW MURDER AWAKENS OLD FEARS ON SOLEDAD COAST.

"Shit," Shepherd said again.

"Yeah, it's hitting the fan for sure. By tonight the Sea Stacks'll be full of media people from all over. So let's get moving on this. You've got the list of people we've interviewed. We'll divide it up, interview each of them again. And again, if necessary."

Rho said, "That's not possible, in one day."

"Make it possible, Swift."

The sidewalks of Signal Port were deserted, except for some rowdy kids cutting school and a few adults that Guy instinctively recognized as journalists. He drove past houses with their curtains drawn and closed-up businesses. The pharmacy where he'd left his film to be developed was open, but there were no other customers. The man behind the counter located the packet and made change wordlessly.

In the parking lot a reporter and camerawoman from a

Sacramento TV station stopped him. What did he think of this new rash of murders? the man asked. He brushed by them with a curt "No comment" and went to the newspaper racks in front of the supermarket. The *San Francisco Chronicle*'s headline and photograph of the entrance to the canyon told him that Signal Port had once again been caught in the glare of publicity, and the citizens were barricading themselves against the sudden influx of media people.

At the Sea Stacks the parking lot was full of vehicles, and those who had been turned away had already found the B&B. Inside, a harried Kevin Jacoby was contending with a complaint from a writer for the *L.A. Times* whom Guy knew slightly and disliked heartily: He'd specifically asked for a king-size bed, but his room only had a queen. As Guy slunk up the stairs in order to avoid an encounter, Jacoby patiently explained that all the beds were queen-size.

Apparently Becca Campos hadn't come to work yet; Guy's room wasn't made up, and when he went to get a fresh towel from the linen closet he found it locked. The previously quiet Victorian echoed with noise. A woman in the opposite room was talking loudly on the phone, and Guy shut his door against her. The town had been taken over, and he resented it as much as if he were a long-term resident.

He unfolded the newspaper on the desk, skimmed the first few paragraphs of the story, then turned to the continuation inside. There was a full-page spread of all the victims, including Ackerman, and a final paragraph mentioned the Lindsay and Scurlock deaths as "strange coincidences." While the article was well enough researched, he sensed it had been hurriedly put together after the Santa Carla TV station had first aired news of the tragedies.

He refolded the paper, uncovering a message slip that had been left on the desk. Dunbar Harrison had called; Oriana was willing to talk with Guy at three o'clock, Pacific time. She would call him. He looked at the clock. Nearly three hours till then. He'd use the interval to bring his notes up to date, perhaps get a bite to eat, provided he could find a restaurant that was not swarming with press people.

The packet of photos caught his attention. He picked it up and tore it open. Removed the prints and shuffled through them.

They were blank, as if the film had passed through an X-ray machine.

"Rho, we've been over this before." Will Scurlock sat in his recliner chair, big hands dangling loose over its arms. His face was deeply lined and he looked as if he hadn't slept in days.

"I know, and I'm sorry to bother you. We're reinterviewing everybody we talked with."

"I don't think I can do this. Forty-eight hours ago I was making arrangements with the Neptune Society for my wife to be cremated. Burned up, like a hunk of dead wood. Her wishes. Me, I would've liked a nice casket for her, flowers, friends at the graveside. But Virge always said no, she didn't want a lot of fuss . . ."

After a moment he went on. "Yesterday I picked up the ashes in Santa Carla. That's them in the cheap brass box on the coffee table. Pick the least expensive, Virge said,

I'll only be in there a little while. I couldn't go against her. Tomorrow a buddy of mine's taking me up in his plane, and I'll scatter her at sea."

"Well, at least you're doing what she wanted. Will . . ." Rho hesitated. Virge's death wasn't the reason for her visit, but she wanted to clear up an issue that was bothering her. "Mimi Griggs told me about the life insurance policy on Virge."

"Policy? Oh, that. Mimi's idea. I was gonna cancel it, but when I told her, she gave me a sob story about needing the commission. I guess that makes me look bad, Virge dying like she did."

"That's not my concern at the moment. As I said, we only have today to close the Ackerman case, and I can't get it out of my head that Virge's death is connected with hers somehow."

"I told you what I know. We only saw her the one time."

"And that was around six on Friday evening?"

"I'm not sure. Maybe it was later. I brought Virge home, changed clothes, and drove back into town for a meeting at the hotel with Alan Lindsay."

"When was your meeting?"

"Seven thirty? Eight?" He shook his head.

"Don't you keep a calendar? Or a work diary showing the hours you put in?"

"Yeah, yeah I do. I'll get it." He stood up and shuffled off to the wing where he had his office.

Rho got up and moved to the front window. The sky had turned dark; the first storm of the season was predicted for this evening. Will's new Dodge Ram stood outside the garage, the passenger-side window rolled down.

She'd close it so the interior wouldn't be soaked in the expected downpour.

She approached the truck from the rear, noting a faint blue mark on the side of the right tire—a mark placed there by a meter maid in Santa Carla, the only city in Soledad County that had parking restrictions. The tire was new, but there was—

A nick. A distinctive crescent-shaped nick in the tread of a top-of-the line Firestone tire.

"I'd like to know what happened to this film," Guy said to the clerk at the pharmacy. He was a little man, bent and humpbacked, and his head thrust forward like a turtle's protruding from its shell. At the moment he looked as if he wished he could withdraw into it.

He said, "Maybe you overexposed it?"

"The entire roll?"

"It might've been bad film."

"I doubt that. It's high-quality film, and the photo supply store where I bought it is very conscientious about its stock."

"Well, I wouldn't know what happened."

"Who develops your film? Do you send it to a lab like Kodak, or is it done locally?"

"Locally. There's this freelancer here in town. Dave Moretti. Unless you specify Kodak, he's the one processes our orders."

Guy remembered Moretti from the canyon. He hadn't seemed to be the sort of amateur who would destroy an entire roll of film by accident.

*　　*　　*

Rho had squatted down and was examining the crescent shape on Will Scurlock's tire when he came up behind her.

"What's wrong?" he asked. "Do I have a puncture?"

She stood and faced him, trying to decide how to proceed. From this point forward Will should be considered a suspect in Chrystal Ackerman's murder, and she should read him his rights and take him to the substation for questioning. Recently California had seen a great increase in Miranda warning violations; the department had sent a memo urging deputies to exercise special caution. She didn't want to jeopardize the case when it eventually went to court, but on the other hand, Will was a friend, a neighbor. She'd known him her whole life.

"Not a puncture," she said. "A nick."

Will went closer, squinting at the tire. "Damn! That wasn't there last time I looked."

"When was that?"

"A week? Ten days? Whenever I last checked the pressure."

"You been driving on rough terrain since then?"

"Just up and down the highway to my job sites. Why're you so interested in it, anyway?"

Again she considered, and decided to go with her gut instinct. "We located the place where Ackerman's body went into the water—Quinley's old burger stand. There was a set of tire imprints. Firestone heavy-truck series. One of them had a nick that's an exact match with this."

Will's expression froze as he absorbed the information and its implications. "You think *I* killed that woman, Rho?"

"I'm sure you have some explanation."

"Well, I haven't. I don't know how an imprint of my tires could get there. The truck was in the garage all weekend. I only use it for business, use Virge's for personal stuff. Cleaner that way, in case the IRS starts looking at me. And I didn't even take it when I went to Alan Lindsay's house on Sunday, because Virge's Toyota was blocking the garage door."

"Have you been to the Quinley property recently?"

"I haven't been there since the burger stand closed down. Hell, nobody goes there except real estate agents and prospective buyers. And your father, of course."

A chill tickled her shoulder blades. "Jack goes there? Why?"

"To fish and take abalone, of course. That's one rich cove."

"But it's contaminated—"

"Has your dad ever stopped to think about health hazards? Not once in his life. The old buzzard drinks a fifth a day, eats everything they tell you not to, smokes cheap cigars. He'll probably outlive us all. He's been fishing that cove for years. In fact, I saw him pull out of there last Friday morning."

Friday morning. Not Friday night or Saturday. Shame washed over her for having entertained suspicions of her own father.

"You sure that's when you saw him?"

"Hell yes. Virge and I were heading up to Calvert's Landing for lunch and some heavy-duty shopping. Your dad recognized the Toyota and beeped." Will sighed heavily. "Such an ordinary thing, an ordinary trip. I never suspected that was the last lunch at Tai Haruru Virge and I would ever have."

*   *   *

The house where the photographer, Dave Moretti, had his studio was on a quiet side street at the northern end of town. At first Moretti was surprised but pleased to see Guy; he became silent and wary as Guy explained why he was there. Moretti's protruding front teeth nibbled nervously at his lower lip, and he cast anxious glances behind him as if he were afraid someone was listening.

"What exactly do you think was wrong with my film?" Guy asked.

"Defective, I suppose."

"I doubt that. It looked to me as if it had been exposed."

"A light leak in the camera, maybe."

"A leak would produce a spot on the image, not eradicate it."

"A large leak—"

"I would have noticed."

Moretti nibbled on his lip some more. "Since you're dissatisfied with my work, I'll be glad to refund the processing fee."

"I'd rather hear why you—an experienced photographer and processor—ruined my photographs."

"I didn't— Oh, hell, why not? It wasn't an official request."

"Someone asked you to destroy any film that came in for processing with my name on it?"

Nod.

"Someone connected with the sheriff's department?"

"Yeah."

"Let me guess: Deputy Wayne Gilardi."

"You got it. He told me you were gonna stir up trouble

that the town didn't need. Said if we all got together and discouraged you, you'd go back east where you belong."

"So you did this for the good of Signal Port."

"Hell, no. Wayne, he's somebody you don't want to get on the wrong side of." He paused. "And I didn't destroy the film."

"No?"

"Uh-uh. Those prints and negatives you got, they're not from your film. I got too much respect for other people's work to ruin it. So I used some film I had laying around here and kept yours in case you figured out what happened and complained. Now . . . tell you the truth, I'm kinda relieved."

"How long will it take you to develop and print my film?"

"Half hour, give or take."

"I'll wait."

Will Scurlock had decided he wanted to talk with his attorney before giving a more formal statement and promised to come to the substation at four that afternoon. After Rho left him she interviewed several more people on her portion of the witness list with little result, and now it was less than an hour before she and Ned Grossman were scheduled to meet with Wayne. A coil of anxiety wound tight in her stomach and she felt lightheaded. She'd eaten nothing all day, but the thought of food nauseated her.

When she entered the substation she found Valerie sitting idle at her desk, hands folded, staring down at its cluttered surface. Rho said to her, "I never did thank you for bringing Cody back the other night."

"I should thank *you* for leaving him here. He was a comfort to me." Valerie's hands twisted, one washing the other. "Jack phoned. He said he told you about us."

"Yes."

"I suppose you hate me for keeping it a secret all these years."

"*Hate* you? Never. You're good for him, and you've been like a mother to me. More of a mother than my own was, and now I know why. Probably it's just as well I didn't find out until I was ready to accept it. Besides, we're all entitled to our secrets."

Valerie smiled with relief and reached for a file in her inbox.

Rho went to her desk and began her report on her interview with Will Scurlock. His statement that he didn't know how the imprint of his truck tires came to be at Quinley's had rung true to her at the time, but now she feared she'd placed too much trust in him. How well did she really know Will? How well did she know any of her friends and neighbors?

The phone rang. Valerie spoke briefly with the caller, said, "Rhoda?" There was an urgent note in her voice that made Rho swivel away from the keyboard.

"That was Wayne. He's at home, cleaning up, and he wants you to come over there so the two of you can talk privately before he comes in."

"I can't do that. I'd be violating—"

"Rhoda, please, he sounded strange."

"How?"

"Like he'd been crying."

Wayne, cry? Never. Unless—

"Okay. I'm on my way."

*   *   *

Guy sat down at the desk in his room and shuffled through the prints Dave Moretti had made for him. The old car covered with pine needles. The oil sump with the stick glistening nearby. The Blakeley house. A few shots of the town taken along the highway. Images to refresh his memory when he wrote the book, back in New York a few months from now. Not particularly good photographs—he had little talent in that area—but serviceable enough for his purposes.

He set them down and thought of the long winter months he'd spend in Manhattan, hunched over the computer in his TriBeCa loft—a spacious and comfortable place he'd purchased after memories of Diana had driven him from their elegant co-op apartment in the East Sixties. Occasionally consulting photographs, maps, and notes jotted on index cards, but mainly working from his own memory and emotions, he'd create a living portrait of this town, its people, its tragedies. Every evening after he finished he'd relax in front of the gas-log fireplace, drink in hand, and—

Be lonely.

He'd been lonely most evenings since he'd lived in the loft, but now he found he couldn't face the prospect. The flickering flames that weren't a real fire no matter how artfully simulated. The single-malt scotch that warmed his body but not his soul. The muffled pulsing of a vibrant city that he kept at bay with well-insulated walls. The occasional but increasingly rare call from an old friend, fruitlessly pleading into the answering machine, "Pick up, Guy!"

He'd been lonely so long it had become a way of life that wouldn't change once he was safely home again.

Rho approached Wayne's house on Jasmine Street, anxiety making her heart hammer. His truck was in the driveway but silence hung over the half acre crowded with old sheds and an ancient rusted trailer. Pink plastic flamingos preened by the front walk.

When she rang the bell no one came. Oh God, she thought. She breathed deeply several times before she tried the doorknob. It turned and then she was inside and walking past the empty living room toward the den at the back of the house. Not bothering to call out, just walking silently past the framed needlepoint sayings Janie had hung there.

Today Is the First Day of the Rest of Your Life.

When Life Hands You a Lemon, Squeeze It and Make Lemonade.

If It's Not Broken, Don't Fix It.

Your Glass Isn't Half Empty—It's Half Full.

Upbeat sentiments for an abused wife. There to normalize her situation.

Nothing could normalize it now, though.

The door to the den was closed. Rho hesitated, nerving herself, then pushed it open.

Wayne was there in his faux-leather recliner chair. Dressed in his uniform for his final day on the job. Shoes shined. Fresh creases in his trousers. Badge polished.

And blood all over everything. Scattered fragments of bone and brain matter too.

Even though she'd expected this, Rho stood transfixed. Heard an animal-like moan, and realized it was hers.

"Jesus, Wayne, why? *Why*?"

She moved closer, flesh creeping, bile rising. Saw the gun whose kick had knocked itself from his dead hand. Saw the tape cassettes on the table beside him.

Two cassettes, neatly labeled. One for Janie and one for her.

Two forty. Still twenty minutes before Oriana Harrison—née Wynne—was due to call. Guy nibbled at the prepackaged sandwich he'd bought at the supermarket. Egg salad, probably yesterday's, and with his luck he'd get food poisoning. After another bite, he rewrapped it and tossed it into the wastebasket.

He switched on a couple of lamps against the gloom and went to the window. The sky had turned dark, and angry-looking clouds hovered offshore. There was a small TV on the bureau opposite the bed; he switched it on and surfed till he found the Weather Channel. Small-craft warnings. Possibility of dangerous wave action along the beaches. Heavy rain.

The room had grown chilly and there was no wood or kindling for the fireplace, let alone matches. Why had he earlier entertained negative thoughts about the gas log in his loft? It would amuse his friends back home to know he was freezing his ass off in sunny California!

Of course "sunny California" was a term descriptive only of the southern portion of the state, a place he'd found sociologically interesting but unappealing during the several months he'd lived there while consulting on film adaptations of his books. Northern California, at least the coastal area, was a land of unpredictable extremes. And, as he was finding out, unpredictable people—

A knock at the door. He shouted for the party to enter. Becca Campos, her arms full of sheets and towels.

"So you decided to come to work after all," he said testily.

She blinked at his sharp tone and wordlessly began stripping his rumpled bed.

After a moment her silence shamed him. "I'm sorry I snapped at you, Becca. I guess you were upset about the story in the San Francisco paper."

"Yeah. Seeing it all rehashed on the thirteenth anniversary . . . Well, it made me so nervous I just holed up at home."

"But you're here now. What changed that?"

She was tucking the sheet around the mattress, but she looked up and smiled shyly. "I'm getting outta Signal Port."

"Really. How'd this come about?"

"Well, my boyfriend came over. Clay. You met him. And when he saw how upset I was, he went, 'Honey, let's split tonight, drive to Reno and get married.' At first I couldn't say anything, I was so surprised. But when I realized he meant it, I couldn't turn him down."

"Congratulations, Becca. But I thought you said Clay was going back to his old life."

"That's right. And now I'll be going with him—as Mrs. Clay Lawrence." She finished making the bed and fluffed the pillows. "But don't you worry about being taken good care of, Mr. Newberry. I already got a girlfriend to take over here for me. Now I better get going. I

got a million things to do—pack and tell the landlord I'm
giving up the place; have the utilities turned off and close
out my checking and savings accounts. And I gotta get
my car serviced, because Clay's truck is dead, so we'll
just have to leave it. . . ."

In spite of her hurry, Becca prattled on and on, but Guy
barely responded. She was happy, and he didn't want to
spoil it for her. He feared Clay Lawrence would do that
soon enough. After he'd married her, run through her
money, driven her car into the ground, and left her.

Rho sat, her head bowed, numbed with grief, as she
and Ned Grossman listened to Wayne's final rambling
message to her.

It all started with Claudia. That surprise you,
Rho? That I could ever be serious about a woman?
Really love her? Well, I did. It started six months
before. May seventeen. She'd gone into Santa
Carla, was coming back late and had a flat down by
Quinley's. I stopped to help her. Had a bottle in the
truck, and we shared it. For a couple of years I'd
been taking women to this place I'd fixed up in the
back of the old burger stand, so that's where we
went. I thought she'd be like the rest of them.

But she wasn't. I'd never known anybody like
her before. She was smart, she had class, and she
said if we got out of this place we could make
something of ourselves. I was gonna leave Janie
and the kids; she was gonna leave Mitch and her
kid. But then on October eight she tells me she's decided to stick with her husband. They were leaving

the canyon because things had gotten too weird there. Going back to southern California. Her dad was sick and they could patch things up with him and start living like normal people.

As if her and me couldn't live like normal people. As if I wasn't normal.

You sure as hell know how mad I've been ever since then. I had something beautiful right there in my hands and all of a sudden it was gone. Really gone. *She* was gone. Forever. From then on, I've felt like I was drowning. Sink, push myself up, tread water for a while, sink, do the whole thing over again. And then that girl showed up. Jude and Leo Ackerman's daughter. I don't know why, but I suspected who she was as soon as I saw her body. Maybe something about her face. Anyway, there was her, and that asshole Newberry with his questions. And it all started weighing too heavy on me.

It's been too damn much and I'm too damn tired. I hate the man I am today. I've done terrible things. I've hurt my whole family. And you. I'm sorry I used you to cover up for losing those blood samples. Maybe if I hadn't you wouldn't've suffered so much after the murders. Or maybe you would've. I don't know.

I know I shouldn't be asking anything of you, but here's one last thing I want you to do. Go over all the old evidence and think about what those missing samples might've told us. I always felt they could've broken the case, but maybe that's just on account of guilt for being so careless. God knows I got my share of guilt—and then some. I wish I'd made Claudia tell me what kind of weirdness was going down in the canyon. She never liked to talk about her life there, but maybe if I'd insisted they wouldn't've got killed. Shoulda's and coulda's, huh? But please, Rho, go over the evidence again. Talk to Newberry. He's an asshole, but he's smart, and he might be able to help you put it together.

Funny. I'm doing this on the anniversary of the murders. Of Claudia's murder. Bad-luck thirteen.

Not funny, huh?

I'm sorry you're gonna be the one to walk in on this mess, but I don't want Janie or Cindy or Beth to find me. I know you can tough it out. I been watching you ever since that night in the canyon. You fell apart for a while there, but in the end you got through. Like I got through, in my own way. You're just gonna get through a lot better, for a lot longer. . . .

The rain started as Guy was waiting for Oriana Harrison's call, now nearly an hour late. He swiveled away from the desk when he heard the first drops and watched as it began sheeting down, turning the world to gray and obscuring his view of the sea. The forecast had said it would continue through tomorrow morning.

The phone shrilled. He caught up the receiver and spoke into it. Dun Harrison.

"I'm here with Oriana," he said. "She was delayed getting home. I'll put her on now."

The voice that hesitantly said his name was low-timbred, cultured, and adult. It surprised him, even though he knew Oriana was now nineteen, because in his focus on the murders he'd fixed her in his mind at age six.

He said, "Thanks for agreeing to talk with me. Your uncle has told you about the book I'm writing?"

"Yes." Pause. "Do you think you can find out what happened out there?"

"Maybe, with your help. How much do you remember about your life in Cascada Canyon?"

"For a long time I remembered very little. I was only six when I left California, and Nana—my grandmother—encouraged me to forget. But when I was in eleventh grade I had a breakdown and went into therapy for a couple of years. A lot of things came out."

"Do you mind talking about them?"

". . . Not if you think it will help you."

Go slowly, Guy warned himself. She's skittish and may bolt the conversation.

"Were they good or bad things?" he asked.

"Both."

"Let's talk about the good things first."

"Well, it was pretty there. We didn't have to go to school like other kids. My parents taught us a couple of hours a day, and otherwise we went to the beach or swam in a pond on the hill. Heath, Eric, Chryssie, and I had the run of the property; we made up all kinds of games. Heath and I had a great toy room. When the grown-ups had parties we stayed in the kid boxes and told ghost stories before we went to sleep."

"By 'kid boxes,' you mean those bunkhouses?"

"Yes. Uncle Bernhard built them for us."

Guy jotted Ulrick's name on a legal pad. Oriana's tone

had changed when she mentioned him. "He wasn't a real uncle, was he?"

"No, just a friend of my parents."

"Were you fond of him?"

"At first. It's complicated."

"Why?"

Silence. Guy waited it out.

"Excuse me for a minute, please." He heard her muffled voice speaking to someone in the background, and then a door closed. Asking her uncle to leave so she could talk in private.

"Mr. Newberry?" she said. "We may as well talk about the bad things now. I loved and trusted Bernhard Ulrick. All we kids did. And he paid back that trust by molesting me on at least three occasions. On one occasion, two weeks before the murders, he beat me and said that if I told my parents he'd kill me."

"Did you tell?"

"No. Heath did. He and Chryssie eavesdropped outside Bernhard's laboratory that day. He was acting seductive, trying to get me to tell him where the money was—a large amount of cash my mother had hidden somewhere on the property. Heath and Chryssie ran away, making noise. That angered Bernhard, and when I insisted I didn't know the hiding place, he beat me. He left marks, and I lied to my parents, told them I'd fallen."

"When did Heath tell them the truth?"

"A week later. He asked me if Bernhard had ever done anything bad to me, and I couldn't keep it a secret any longer. He went straight to our parents, and my father got in a fistfight with Bernhard and made him leave the canyon that same day."

Bernhard had left a week before the murders? How could that be?

Guy said, "He came back, though."

"Never."

"But he was killed along with the others."

"No he wasn't. I saw him afterwards."

"Where?"

"At the airport when I was boarding the plane to go home with Nana. I looked back and saw him standing in the crowd. He was wearing a hat and had grown a mustache, but he still had a bandage over the cut on his forehead from when he fought with my father. And his eyes: They were terrible. They looked at me like they did when he said not to tell or he'd kill me. I knew he was there to remind me of that. And I never did tell anyone about seeing him or what he'd done to me. Not until I told my therapist, and now you."

Rho pushed away from her desk, eyes burning. She'd gone over the old casefiles carefully, but nothing in them shed any light on Wayne's last request that she think about what the missing blood samples might have told them. More wishful thinking on his part than anything else, she supposed.

She put her feet up, closed her eyes. The image that appeared on her lids was of blood, bone, brain matter. Quickly she opened them and stared instead at the blackish window. Listened to the rain whacking down on the substation's flat roof. Two prisoners in the holding cell were yelling at each other; she wanted to go back and tell them to shut up, but couldn't summon the energy. Wayne would—

Wayne. Fresh pain stabbed at her. His oldest daughter, Cindy, had come home from her maid's job at a Westhaven motel just as the body was being removed, and gone into hysterics. Janie, when she arrived, was tearful but resigned. She probably realized she'd lost her husband long ago. God knew what was on the tape he'd made for her. . . .

Rho stood, closed the heavy casefile. Wayne was wrong; the answer wasn't in those missing samples, or anywhere else in the yellowing reports. Better to concentrate on the current case, although she had only this evening to do so. Tomorrow the FBI would arrive in town and take over. Tomorrow she'd feel as much of a failure as she had thirteen years ago.

Guy went over his notes on the conversation with Oriana for a second time, then picked up the photograph taken of her at the airport and studied the child's expression. What he'd earlier assumed to be anguish was actually fear. He'd missed its import, not being able to easily read children.

Of course, Oriana's insistence that she'd been looking at Bernhard Ulrick didn't prove a thing. To a severely traumatized six-year-old, many adults could resemble the one she feared. And as for repressed childhood memory, Guy had followed several cases where the phenomenon had been debunked. False memories could be created out of therapists' suggestions and adults' desire to believe.

Still . . .

He picked up the receiver and dialed Aaron Silber in New York.

*　　　*　　　*

The noise from the prisoners in the holding cell was grating on Rho's nerves. Again she thought about telling them to shut up, again she couldn't make the effort. After enduring it a few minutes more she decided to take her official vehicle home, go over the list of potential witnesses, select those who looked most promising, and later set out to talk with them.

When she arrived at her house on the ridge, she fed Cody, made herself coffee, and curled up on the sofa with the list and reports on the interviews. Even the portion assigned to her was daunting. As she scanned it, one name after another provoked memories: Nella Samson was her fourth-grade teacher; she'd had her first beer when Doug Scallini stole a six-pack from his parents' fridge; Harry Vincenzo had taken her to her first dance; she and Alice Worth had tried smoking behind Alice's father's barn and nearly set it on fire; old Mrs. York—my God, she was still alive!

Friends, neighbors. Many she hadn't stayed close to, but she knew their histories, what kind of people they were. And by and large the interviews with them revealed little. They'd seen Chrystal Ackerman and were sorry they hadn't stopped to help.

So what was happening here? A random killer roaming the coastline? If so, had he struck elsewhere?

She went to her computer, accessed the records for other coastal counties. No recent unsolved murders in Humboldt. None in west Mendocino, Sonoma, or Marin. San Francisco showed a shooting outside a bar near Ocean Beach that in no way fit the pattern. San Mateo and Santa Cruz were relatively crime free.

Someone on the Soledad Coast, then. A stranger lying

low in one of the area's many motels? Not likely. Given the current atmosphere, any suspicious stranger would have been reported.

"One of us," she said.

A familiar vehicle that passersby wouldn't have given a second thought to. A stop to pick up the girl at Point Deception after dark. The driver would have had a place to take her, an isolated place. He knew Cascada Canyon, Quinley's too. He could move freely, without attracting attention.

Chances were they hadn't interviewed him. But if he were clever he'd have come forward claiming to have seen his victim. She began scanning the list, looking for someone who fit the criteria, and halfway down a name stood out. She flipped through the file to Grossman's report of his interview with the man, read it. Innocuous as all the others, and yet . . .

She went to her computer, accessed her own report of an interview with him. Maybe. But maybe she only wanted to believe.

Allowing herself only a small degree of excitement, she began accessing other jurisdictions' records, searching as far back as two years. The name appeared on unsolved casefiles in Bellingham, Washington, and Lincoln County, Oregon. As she made inquiries of colleagues in both places her excitement grew until, upon finishing her final call, she pushed back from the desk, leaped to her feet, and shouted, "*Yes!*" A startled Cody jumped up and began barking.

All she had to do now was wait on a felony warrant from the Lincoln County Sheriff's Department. While detectives flew down from Oregon to question her man in conjunction with a thirteen-month-old murder, she'd extract from him a confession in the deaths of both Chrystal Ackerman and Virge Scurlock.

Guy stepped into the parlor of the inn and interrupted a tender scene between Kevin Jacoby and a short man whose left arm was in a cast. Rhoda had told him about the altercation between Jacoby and his partner, Brandon Fuller, but now it seemed they'd patched up their relationship.

Jacoby turned, flushed, but with a smile on his usually melancholy face. Guy said, "I'd like to ask a favor. May I use your fax machine?"

"Of course. It's on a side table in the office."

He nodded his thanks, went out and around the reception desk, closing the office door for privacy. After locating the machine, he dialed Aaron Silber's number. His assistant answered with the words, "Got it." Guy read the fax number to him, hung up, and waited, surprised to find his palms were damp. The line rang and paper began to curl from the machine. He restrained himself from looking at it till the machine gave its final beep.

At first he was disappointed. This photograph was of no one he knew. Then he told himself to take it slowly and look at individual features.

When he'd done that and assembled the face whole again, his fingers convulsed on the edge of the desk. That face was the answer to what had happened in Cascada Canyon thirteen years ago tonight.

Rho listened to the rain smacking down on her roof. From somewhere came a persistent dripping sound. One of the gutters she'd neglected to clean this year was overflowing.

The solutions to Chrystal Ackerman's and Virge Scurlock's murders were mostly there now. She needed to calm down, order her thoughts, work out a progression while she waited on the warrant. The detective she'd spoken with in Lincoln County had said he'd call her before it was faxed to the substation.

It would have been good to have someone to bounce her ideas off, but Grossman and Shepherd had been called into Santa Carla to confer with FBI agents, and when she'd earlier called the Investigations Bureau and asked to speak with one of them, she'd been told both were unavailable. Guy had not answered his phone at the inn.

"Okay," she told Cody, "I'll just have to do this by myself." He came over to her, nails clicking on the hardwood, and nosed her hand. She patted him absently.

A broken-down truck. Another borrowed for an aborted trip to Santa Carla. Aborted, because at Point Deception—

The doorbell rang. Cody snapped to attention. Rho went to the window and looked out, saw Guy standing on the porch, his hair wet and plastered to his scalp. She opened the door, said, "Guy, I'm glad to see you, but what brings you out on a night like this?"

"I have something to show you." He stepped into the house, dripping, and removed a curl of paper from inside his jacket and held it out to her.

It was a fax of a photograph. She stared at it in surprise. Even without the beard, skewed nose, and scar, she would have recognized the man by his deepset eyes. "Clay Lawrence. What're you doing with this?"

"That's not really Clay Lawrence."

"I know. I've been talking with the authorities in Washington State and Oregon. I'm reasonably certain this man is our killer. How did you get this picture?"

Guy moved past her, toward the fireplace. "In a minute. First tell me what the people up north told you."

"Okay. The real Clay Lawrence left Bellingham thirteen months ago on a two-week driving trip and was never heard from again. He was last seen in Depoe Bay, Oregon, in the company of a hitchhiker who looked enough like him to be his brother. His broken-down car turned up shortly afterwards in Brookings, and his remains were found in a shallow grave near Cape Perpetua, Lincoln County, just last week. They only got an ID on him three days ago. His neck had been broken." She waved the facsimile photo at Guy. "So what's his real identity?"

To her annoyance, Guy ignored the question. "Have you worked out a progression of events?"

"I was in the process of it when you arrived."

"So tell me."

He was opting for the methodical approach, and she'd do well to follow his lead. "Our man killed Lawrence, buried him, and stole his car. After it broke down, he hitched. When he was dropped off in Signal Port, he met Becca Campos and decided to stay on a while—he told me that himself. Will once said 'Clay' led a frugal, quiet life, mainly reading, meditating, and hiking on the ridge. The first Friday of every month he'd drive into Santa Carla to pick up supplies at Costco. But last Friday his truck was broken down—I saw it on Sunday, and it looked as if it hadn't run for quite some time. I think he asked Virge if he could borrow Will's truck for the trip." Now Rho felt a little breathless.

Guy sat down on the hearth, waiting for her to go on, and after a moment she did.

"Will thought the truck was in his garage all weekend. If he'd've known Virge loaned it to Clay, he'd've been furious. But Virge had a soft spot for their tenant, so she covered. On his way to Santa Carla, though, Clay spotted Ackerman at the turnout, picked her up, took her back to his cabin for sex. Something went wrong, and he killed her there, probably on Saturday, given her autopsy results. He couldn't keep the body at the cabin, because Virge had a habit of dropping in on him, so he stashed it where nobody ever goes—the canyon. Then, late at night when traffic was sparse, he retrieved it, drove it in Will's truck to Quinley's, where he put her into the sea. He never counted on having to kill Virge too."

Guy nodded. "I've always suspected that wasn't an accident. Why do you think he had to kill her?"

Rho began to pace, very excited now that she was able to put her theory into words. "Virge made a remark to one of the other patrons of the hotel bar on Sunday: 'Don't ever try to do someone a favor. You might end up owing more than you can handle.' Doesn't make a lot of sense until you consider that she was drinking, slurring her words. I think she meant to say 'knowing.'"

"Knowing who killed Ackerman?"

"Right. On Friday she did Clay a favor by loaning him the truck. She probably told him to have it back by a certain time on Saturday, in case Will wanted to use it for a business appointment he had scheduled on Sunday. If Clay was late bringing it back, she'd have gone to his cabin to check on him. And she might've seen Ackerman."

"So why didn't she report it when she found out the girl had been murdered?"

"Probably because she didn't want to believe Clay was responsible. That was Virge: She always thought the best of people she liked, wanted to give them the benefit of the doubt. She was making a decision in the bar, to confront Clay and give him a chance to explain. And sometime on Sunday afternoon or evening she slipped out of the house and went to his cabin."

Guy nodded. "It works for me so far. Did he kill Virge at the cabin? Persuade her he had nothing to do with the girl's death and then agree to accompany her to the canyon, as she'd asked him to before?"

"I'd say he killed her at the cabin, then took her body there, as he had Ackerman's. Only this time he decided to stage an accident. Remember, there was only one set of footprints leading to the ledge, large ones made by Virge's shoes. Virge had big feet; Clay could've put on her shoes, carried her there, and thrown her over."

"The prints were deep, consistent with someone carrying a heavy load."

"Right. Afterwards, Clay probably took a roundabout way down to the body, replaced the shoes, and made his way home across the stream on bare feet."

"Okay," Guy said, "that works for me too. Most of it does, except for a couple of details. Clay didn't settle here because he met Becca Campos. He didn't spend all his time reading, meditating, and hiking. And he didn't pick up Ackerman on a whim."

"Oh?" She realized she was about to hear something important, and sat down on the hearth beside him.

He said, "Clay came here deliberately, although probably coincidentally, at the time the guards were taken off the canyon. He spent a good deal of his time in a methodical search for Susan Wynne's hidden money. And he went after Ackerman because he saw her find it."

"But that would mean he knew—"

"Yes. The man in that photograph"—he motioned at the fax she still clutched—"is no stranger to Cascada Canyon. It was taken about a year before he first came there."

"For God's sake, Guy, who is he?"

"Bernhard Ulrick."

Guy watched as Rhoda's lips parted in astonishment. "But . . . Ulrick died with the others."

"No, he didn't." He explained about his conversation with Oriana Harrison. "After I talked with her, I considered the physical evidence: The body in the drug lab was so badly shot up that it was unidentifiable, and the blood samples had disappeared. Did your department try to make an identification from fingerprints or dental records?"

"Yes. But Ulrick's prints weren't on file anyplace. And his teeth, well, there weren't enough of them intact. We had to assume the body was his. If you're right . . . who do you think died in the lab?"

"It's always been taken for granted that there was more than one killer, right?"

"Right."

"Suppose Ulrick lured his accomplice up the canyon on some pretext after the others were dead, and blew him away."

Rhoda nodded slowly. "One of his drug dealing associates, then. We'll probably never know his identity, unless Ulrick talks."

"I think I know who the accomplice was."

She blinked. "How could you?"

"Think about the things we felt in the canyon, Rhoda. We were so busy tapping into the victims' feelings that we ignored the killers' state of mind. But there *is* another strong emotion you feel there: anger. Ulrick was angry because the families had thrown him out when they learned he'd molested Oriana. Thrown him out before he could find the money. And the week before that, someone else left the canyon suddenly: Devon Wynne's boyfriend. What if they threw him out too?"

"Why?"

"The biographical sketch of Devon that I have says she was addicted to abusive relationships. If this boyfriend beat her up while they were living with Forrest and Susan . . ."

"Yes, of course. If they threw him out, he would have been angry enough to join forces with Ulrick. Of course, Susan's money was the real inducement. They planned to coerce her into telling where it was hidden."

"Only Susan wouldn't tell them. She knew she was going to die anyway, and she was buying time for her children. Ulrick probably never expected to wait all these years before he could look for it. But I wonder why he didn't find it, in a methodical year-long search."

Guy shrugged. "He didn't know or had forgotten about the oil sump. Ackerman knew where the money was from her mother, but before she dug it up, it was buried under thirteen years' worth of pine needles."

Rhoda's small face grew still and thoughtful. After a moment she glanced at her watch. "God, I wish Lincoln County would call about that warrant. I want Ulrick in custody tonight."

A memory stirred in the back of Guy's mind. As it moved to the forefront, alarm brought him to his feet. "Forget the warrant. Better go after Ulrick right away." He explained about Becca's plans to travel with him to Reno that night.

Rhoda went quickly to the phone, dialed, and asked for Detective Grossman. "Try Detective Shepherd, then," she said after a pause. "What? . . . Okay, thanks anyway." She broke the connection, dialed again. "They're on their way back here with the FBI agents who've been brought in," she said to Guy. "I can't waste time tracking them down."

He listened as she called Central Dispatch and asked for backup to meet her at the cabin on the Scurlock property. When she hung up she told him, "Central says there's a slide on the highway up near Deer Harbor. People have been hurt and every available unit is on the scene, except for one down at Westhaven. Its ETA at the cabin is forty minutes, but I'm going on ahead—"

"I'm going with you."

"No you're not."

"Don't waste time arguing with me."

She scowled, then grabbed her bag and jacket and headed for the door. "Come on, if you must."

* * *

As she got into the cruiser, Rho keyed the mike and let Central know she was proceeding. Guy hadn't shut his door when she gunned the powerful vehicle down her driveway.

She said, "When we get to the cabin, I want you to stay in the car and keep low, in case he's armed."

"But—"

She didn't need civilian interference now! "This is my *job,* Guy. I can handle it."

". . . Okay. Your call."

She sped south through town, past a TV crew filming in front of the hotel. The media frenzy that had begun earlier was at full strength. Once they were into forestland, the dripping trees compounded the rain. It was coming down so hard now that the wipers couldn't clear it fast enough. Mud oozed across the road from the eastern upslope; on one patch she braked too sharply, skidded, and had to fight to bring the car out of it. Guy had momentarily closed his eyes—maybe praying for the first time in his life.

She tromped on the accelerator as they neared the entrance to the canyon, urging more speed from the cruiser on the straightaway. The tires started to slide on the blind curve above Point Deception, but she corrected and held them to the road. She leaned forward, trying to see the centerline. As they came up on the Scurlock driveway, a pair of headlights appeared.

"Car coming out," Guy said. "Looks like Becca's Honda."

"Turning north. Our good luck. He'll have to stop at the slide." She reached for the mike to ask that Ulrick be detained there, told Guy, "Get down! He'll know this isn't a routine patrol if he sees two heads. We never patrol in pairs."

She'd slowed the cruiser to a normal speed, and the Honda passed it as she was calling in, traveling at a crawl. She peered over at it but couldn't identify its driver. When it was out of view, she made a U-turn and followed. The Honda continued to creep, then veered across the centerline.

"What—?" she said.

It was pulling into the turnout. Going to Point Deception, where it all had started.

Guy hunched over, smelling a medley of odors from the floor mat, none of which he cared for. He felt the heavy vehicle leave the pavement and brake abruptly, sliding him forward so his head connected with the dashboard.

"What's going on?" he asked through his pain.

"They're at Point Deception. Somebody's getting out of the driver's seat . . . walking toward the fence."

"Who?"

"Ulrick, I think."

Guy straightened as Rhoda released the shotgun from its brace. She asked, "You know how to use a handgun, don't you?"

"Yes."

"Good." She pulled a gun from her bag and thrust it into his hand, grip first. A .357 revolver. "Take this. Becca may be in the car. If so, I want you to get her out of there. She won't be armed—she has a horror of guns—

but she may resist you or try to warn Ulrick. Use force if necessary, but bring her back here and see she stays put."

"And where'll you be?"

"Going after Ulrick."

He hesitated. Her job, she could handle it.

"Follow me," she said, opening her door.

Order not necessary, he thought. I'd follow you anywhere.

Rain lashed Rho as she stepped out of the cruiser into a deep puddle. When she started across the highway she had to lean into gale-force wind. Guy was right behind her.

They ran across the pavement to a stand of pines at the south end of the turnout. Becca's old Honda was nose-in toward the fence, its headlights off, motor running. On the bluff a faint beam of light bobbed about; Ulrick had a flashlight. Rho noted its location, then stared intently at the car.

"I can't tell if Becca's in there or not," she said.

"Me either."

"He may have left her as a lookout." She motioned to Guy. "This way."

Gregory Cordova's fence was strung with barbed wire here. Rho held it apart so Guy could slip through, then followed. She felt her jacket snag, wrenched at it, tore it free. "I'll go first," she said, moving her feet tentatively till she found a deer track. She inched along on slick, flattened grass, then back upslope to where the fence continued around the turnout.

"Okay," she said, "from here on you're on your own. If you crouch down and follow the fence she won't see you. At the far side where the No Camping sign is, you'll be in her blind spot."

He hesitated. She was afraid he'd try to stop her from going after Ulrick alone, but he simply said, "Be safe." Then he was gone, ducking down behind the split rails.

Rho waited a moment, conjuring up an image of the terrain. She and her father had crossed Point Deception many times to fish in Lantern Cove. Later she'd come here for high school beer busts and to neck in the grass with boyfriends. She knew this bluff as well as anyone— certainly better than Ulrick.

Lily Gilardi had told her about encountering Chrystal Ackerman as she emerged from a clump of pampas grass. Chrystal was acting "freaky," as if she had been doing something wrong. That must be where she'd hidden the money, and where Ulrick was going. He'd managed to extract its location from Ackerman, but Rho didn't want to consider what methods he'd used.

Okay, the thickest stand of the insidious plants had always been dead center on the bluff. That bought her time, because from where Ulrick had crossed the fence the fishermen's path would take him due north. In the dark and the rain it would be a while before he realized he'd gone out of his way and decided to double back.

She found the deer track again and started down the slope. She'd lost sight of the bobbing flashlight beam; when she reached a good vantage point she stopped and scanned the bluff. There it was, nearly at the northwest cliff edge. The rain was letting up, although the wind was still brisk. Now she could hear the crash of waves in the cove. She began moving along the track again, slipped, and went down on one knee.

Dammit, that bastard Ulrick had waited thirteen years for the money, and he had to choose a night like this to claim it! Of course, he hadn't chosen, not exactly. He'd probably planned to stay in town till his lease ran out, to avoid suspicion. But the influx of media people had changed that plan. Ulrick was no fool. He had to know that sooner or later someone might dig up a more recent photograph of him and he'd be recognized. He needed to retrieve the money and get out tonight.

She crept along the track, toward where the pampas grass grew thickest. Ulrick's light had vanished. Cradling the shotgun, she paused every few yards to search for it. Nothing moved but the pale fronds, frantic in the wind. She could hear nothing over its howl and the roar of the surf.

Guy. How was he doing? Had he gotten Becca safely to the cruiser?

Sound from below? She peered through drizzle.

Nothing.

Sound from above!

She whirled, shouldering the shotgun.

No one.

God, she was letting the storm and Ulrick's unseen presence spook her!

She drew deep, calming breaths. Reminded herself that this was *her* territory, *her* advantage.

When she was fully in control, she went on.

When Guy crept up in the blind spot of Becca's car, he saw the front seat was empty. He checked the backseat, the trunk, then shut off the ignition and pocketed the keys. As added insurance, he raised the hood and disconnected every cable and wire he could find.

He crouched behind the vehicle, staring at the fence and clutching Rhoda's .357—a weapon which he, a stringent advocate of gun control, could use and use well because his father had insisted no son of his be less than a perfect marksman—and felt profoundly useless.

Her job, yes. She could handle it, yes. But he couldn't handle the danger to her. Couldn't handle the fear of losing her. He had to do something.

He pushed away from the car and ran across the turnout. Stepped over the fence and moved downslope, feet angled on the slippery ground, digging for purchase. The rain suddenly smacked down again, so heavily that he couldn't see a foot ahead. After a ways something sodden and hairy touched his face. He slapped at it. One of those damned fronds.

From what Lily had said, he figured the Ackerman girl must have buried the money in a clump of pampas grass. He was close to it, close to Rhoda. Close to Ulrick, too . . .

He stood still, listening. Heard nothing. Peered around. Saw only darkness. Closed his eyes and willed his ears to tune in to a frequency humans seldom employed.

Rhoda, he thought, where are you?

Snapping sound. To the right. He slewed about. Brought up the .357.

No one.

What if the cocksucker had grabbed her? Overpowered her? Right now he might be—

No. She could handle him. He had to believe that.

Another sound. Similar to the last. Origin uncertain.

He made a three-sixty sweep with the gun. Saw nothing.

I feel like a kid, he thought. A scared kid lost in the dark with a popgun. It's been years since I fired on anything, and never on a living person, but if he's got Rhoda . . .

Yeah, I'd fire. Dead accurate. In a heartbeat. I couldn't save my wife, but I *can* help here.

He began creeping through the sodden fronds.

Another sound. Pause. Another. Where—?

Something hit him. Hard. A tall, slender body, ramming him full force, knocking him onto his back. The air went out of his lungs, but he held onto the gun with all his strength.

He tried to yell, but what came out was a grunt. Then his attacker was on him, hands gripping his throat. He couldn't move the gun, which was pinned between their struggling bodies.

The hands tightened, choking him.

In reflex he pulled the trigger.

The man's body jerked convulsively. The hands relaxed on his throat. Then they were gone and the weight lifted away from him. He raised his head, struggled to rise. Bernhard Ulrick was scrabbling upslope on all fours. Guy rolled onto his stomach, gripped the gun with both hands, and fired after him. The shot went wild, but Ulrick reversed direction and began limping toward the sea.

"Stop right there, Ulrick!" Rhoda's voice, from not far above. "Sheriff's department. You're under arrest."

Ulrick seemed to hesitate, as if surprised to hear his rightful name, then kept going.

A shotgun blasted.

Ulrick staggered and went down. Dead hit.

Guy buried his face in the mud and sobbed with relief.

It seemed like a long time but couldn't have been more than a few minutes before Rhoda's hand touched the back of his wet head. The hand was unsteady, the voice more so, when she said, "Fucked up again, Newberry."

She got him into a sitting position, cradled his body against hers. He pressed close, wished he could stop crying, and after a while realized she was crying too.

"Hey." He raised his head and touched her cheek. "Hey, don't."

"I almost lost it," she said. "I've never had to kill anybody before."

"One thing my father taught me—"

"I know. The first thing *my* father taught me about guns: They've got only one purpose. If you have to shoot, shoot to kill." She drew a deep, fluttering breath. "And that's what I did. I blew the bastard's head off."

Sunday, October 15

R ho was sitting on her front porch in a patch of morning sunlight when Guy came to say good-bye. She watched as he walked toward her, his silvery hair gleaming, and thought of the first time she'd seen him. Even in her agitation about nearly running him down, she'd thought him a handsome man. Now she knew there was much more to him than good looks.

He smiled as he sat down beside her. "You seem rested. Still no nightmares?"

"Nope. That's all over now. What time does your plane leave San Francisco?"

"Six this evening."

They sat quietly for a moment. Cody came out of the underbrush, trailing twigs and leaves as usual. He nosed Guy's hand and Rho smiled when she saw him hesitate before rubbing his ears.

You probably could get fond of the dog, she thought, then put the notion aside.

She said, "Grossman and Shepherd are leaving today

too. Ned's going to put my name up for promotion to detective. They need somebody to direct investigations in the coastal area."

"Congratulations! You've earned it."

"I don't know about that, but the pay increase would help keep old Cody in dog food." Still, she felt a warm glow of pride.

"I take it Grossman's given up on searching for the money?"

"Now that he's had Ulrick's cabin and its surroundings torn apart, he has. Becca couldn't tell him anything; she had no idea the money existed, much less that Ulrick had been searching for it."

Guy grimaced. "Thank God she was still at home packing when he went to retrieve it. She's having a hard enough time dealing with who and what her boyfriend was, without having been there when he died."

"She's having a hard time, but Kevin Jacoby and Brandon Fuller are giving her lots of TLC. She'll be okay."

"You know, I still don't understand why Grossman didn't catch on about why Ulrick went to Point Deception that night."

She smiled slyly. "Well, I sort of let him think Ulrick skidded into the turnout and fled as I was giving chase."

"You what—? Why?"

"If I'd've told, the department would've dug up the bluff looking for the money. And then we'd've had the media back, with all the attendant problems. That money's caused enough tragedy and grief."

"I agree. The Harrisons don't need it, and if you asked them, they'd probably say they don't want it. Let it lie."

A strong, crisp wind rustled through the trees. To Rho's amusement, both Cody and Guy keened the air.

He said, "You know, a man could get a lot of writing done on the Soledad Coast."

She cautioned herself against rising to the bait, said lightly, "He could."

"Especially if his local deputy—pardon me, detective—were driving by to check up on him."

"Especially."

"If I had a second home here, I'd buy and hire locally."

"I'd see to it that you did."

He smiled at her, fine lines around his eyes crinkling. "Well, it's a thought."

"And a good one."

"I'll hold on to it." He stood, pulled her to her feet. "Got to go now." He leaned toward her, touched his lips to hers. At first the kiss was light, casual; then they both moved closer, and it deepened. When they finally parted, she had to lean on the porch pillar to steady herself.

"It *is* a thought," he said softly, and moved toward his car.

She remained where she was, shading her eyes from the sunglare as she watched him drive away.

"He'll be back," she told Cody. "No question about that."

Guy didn't get his erratic emotions under control until he reached Point Deception. A few more seconds in Rhoda's arms and he would've been a goner. As it was . . .

He stopped the car just off the pavement and stepped out. The day was clear and brilliantly blue, with not a trace of fog on the horizon. Even the skeletal trees couldn't detract from its loveliness, and the bright green secondary growth beneath them gave promise. The plumes of pampas grass danced in the wind. Except for the crime-scene tape that fluttered along the fenceline, you'd never have guessed what violence had taken place here.

After a few minutes he got back in the car and continued south, traveling at high speed, taking pleasure in maneuvering the curves. Thinking of New York, his loft, the great book he'd write there. The true-life adventures of Guy Newberry were sure to make the best-seller lists—

You damn fool man.

"So you're back. Why'd you call me that?"

Because you're as much of a horse's ass as ever, and you're leaving the best thing that's happened to you since me.

"Who said I'm leaving forever?"

Aren't you?

"I most certainly am not."

Good. You need that woman. And you don't need me any longer.

Softly he whispered, "Good-bye, Diana."

June 19, 2002

The county-owned bulldozer rumbles across Point Deception on another foray in the ongoing struggle to eradicate the tenacious pampas grass. Belching fumes into the previously clean air, it tears away at the land and sends moles scurrying from their burrows. The operator scowls at a particularly large and stubborn clump, then scoops it up. The machine lumbers toward the cliff and dumps its load into Lantern Cove.

A leather pouch encased in layers of plastic bags balances precariously on top of the heap. Then the strong offshore wind topples the pile, and the pouch falls into the lapping waves. Come high tide, larger waves will bear it south and bury it at sea.

MARCIA MULLER has written many novels and short stories. Her novel *Wolf in the Shadows* won the Anthony Boucher Award. The recipient of the Private Eye Writers of America's Lifetime Achievement Award, she lives in northern California with her husband, mystery writer Bill Pronzini.

More
Marcia Muller!

Please turn this page
for an excerpt
from

Dead Midnight

available wherever books
are sold.

MONDAY, APRIL 16

Glenn Solomon, San Francisco's most prominent criminal-defense attorney, and I were braving traffic—angling from Momo's restaurant where we'd just had lunch toward the city's handsome new baseball stadium. Pacific Bell Park struck me as a perfect combination of the old and new: red brick, with the form and intimate atmosphere of early urban ballparks, yet comfortable and equipped with every modern amenity. And, most important in this car-infested city, easily accessible by public transportation.

"You been to a game there yet?" Glenn asked me.

"Of course I've been to a game. You let me use your season tickets last June."

"Ah, yes. Hottest temperatures for that day in the city's history. You and your friends in the sun right behind third base. You greased up with SPF 30, poured bottled water on your heads till it boiled, and left after the third inning. And to make matters worse, that game was the first time the Giants played well in the new park. You'll never stop reminding me, will you?"

"Not till I get another crack at those great seats."

"Mmm." Glenn nodded noncommittally, his mind already having strayed from baseball.

Like the ballpark, Glenn Solomon was a perfect blend of old and new San Francisco. Over an unhurried lunch, his cell phone turned off, he'd wined and dined me without a word about business. As waiters hovered, eager to please a cornerstone of the local legal establishment, he'd flattered me by asking about Hy, about the home we'd recently built on our Mendocino Coast property, about some recent startling developments in my personal life. But now his focus had shifted into high gear, and soon he would trot out all his persuasive skills in order to interest me in taking on a job that I gathered, from his reticence so far, was one I'd surely want to turn down.

But he wasn't ready yet, and I walked along the Embarcadero beside him, content to enjoy the view of Treasure Island and the sailboats on the Bay. When we reached Miranda's, my favorite waterfront diner, and he still hadn't spoken, I frowned and glanced at him. Glenn was a big man, silver-haired, rotund in a prosperous fashion, with a clean-shaven chin that looked strange to me because he'd worn a full beard the whole time I'd known him. In spite of his bulk he handled himself gracefully, and he cut an imposing figure, attracting many glances as we strolled along.

Glenn was known as a genial fellow among his golf and tennis partners; a kind and generous employer to his staff; a respected litigator among his fellow bar association members; a bulwark of strength to both clients and friends in need. And to his wife of twenty years, Bette Silver, he was a pussycat with a lion's roar. But Glenn could also be devious and sly. His quick mind, sharp tongue, and caustic wit demolished those who opposed him; his attack mode both in and out of the courtroom was formidable. I'd stood up to some tough characters in my years as an investigator, but I'd long ago decided I would never want to get on the wrong side of Glenn Solomon.

He noticed me studying him and touched my elbow. "Let's sit a while."

There was a bench in front of Miranda's, flanked by planter boxes where tulips and daffodils bloomed. The flowers were evidence of the gentle side of the cafe's owner, an often brusque former longshoreman nick-named Carmen Miranda from his days off-loading banana boats at China Basin. Glenn and I sat there, but only after he—with great ceremony—dusted it off with his crisp white handkerchief.

We were facing the waterfront boulevard, as wide as the average city lot, with a median strip where stately palms grew and vintage streetcars rattled along. A red one passed, its bell clanging. Directly opposite us was the condominium complex where my nephew and operative, Mick Savage, lived with another of my staff, Charlotte Keim. They were built with white stucco, incorporating a great deal of glass block and chrome, and to either side of it were other complexes, with shops, delis, and restaurants on the street level—all evidence of the revitalization of our waterfront.

In 1989 this area was at the bottom of a steeply descending curve. Years before most of the shipping industry had fled to Oakland or other West Coast ports; factories and warehouses stood abandoned; many piers were vacant, run-down, and rat-infested; the torching of buildings for insurance money was not uncommon. Then, on October 17, the tectonic plates along the Loma Prieta Fault shifted, the earth heaved, and one of the ugliest structures in the city, the Embarcadero Freeway, crumbled. When its ruins were razed, bay vistas that hadn't been seen for over thirty years were revealed, and we all realized that San Francisco could have a beautiful waterfront.

Now, with the redevelopment still continuing, the heart of the city has gradually moved from such traditional places as the financial district and Union Square to the water's edge, where it pumps lifeblood into long-moribund areas. New buildings rise, and old structures are being converted to offices or live-work lofts. Technology-related firms have relocated to the South of

Market, and close on their heels have followed the trendy restaurants, clubs, and boutiques that their owners and employees require. Even the crash of the hot tech market hasn't put too much of a damper on the vibrant ambience of South Beach, SoMa, and Mission Bay, and the future looks bright there. Of course, all change comes with its price, and in San Francisco's case, it has been costly.

As if he knew what I was thinking, Glenn said, "too much, too fast."

"The changes in the city? Yes."

"I don't mind most of them. The Mission Bay complex, for instance, that's exciting: six thousand more badly needed apartments, the new UCSF campus, all the open space. It's good development. No, it's the divisiveness that bothers me. The haves versus the have-nots. The old people who can't afford to remain in the neighborhoods where they were born. Young families and working-class people who can't afford the rents. The black community shrinking. It changes the face of the city, makes it a playground for rich people. What's the average rent on a two-bedroom apartment in a decent neighborhood these days?"

"I'm not sure. I paid well under a hundred thousand for my house, but last year a smaller one down the street sold for five hundred to a couple from Silicon Valley—and it was advertised as a fixer-upper. Office rents're coming down since the dot-com companies started failing; I've been watching them in case the Port Commission doesn't renew my agency's lease on the pier next year. But they were astronomical to begin with."

Glenn waved to a man in blue Spandex who was jogging by. "One of my young associates," he said. "Top talent out of Columbia. I had to pony up 125,000 to get him. All these baby nouveaux throwing money around as if it were confetti. If the dot-com fire hadn't fizzled, we'd be ass deep in them by now." He sighed. "Don't misunderstand me, my friend. I don't begrudge those who've earned it. And I like the new vitality in the city, even if we do have the worst political machine west of Chicago. But I wish . . ."

"You wish the bucks were spread around more evenly. Or that the haves exercised some old-fashioned concern and charity."

"Exactly. This isn't an abstract conversation, you know. It's leading up to the reason I asked to meet with you today."

At last he was getting around to the matter at hand. I glanced at him, expecting to see the crafty expression—what he called his "wolf look"—that always accompanied his efforts to enlist my aid in a near-impossible case. But instead I saw only deep melancholy.

He said, "I am about to ask a very personal favor of you."

* * *

The matter he wanted me to investigate, Glenn explained, was atypical for his practice. A civil case, which he almost never took on. A wrongful-death suit against an on-line magazine called *InSite*.

InSite's market niche was chronicling the new and the hip in the Bay area: whatever restaurant the hordes were about to flock to; hot artists, authors, and celebrities; trendy products and fashions. In short, a *W* of the local wired set. I myself had visited their site a few times: to check out good shops for unusual Christmas presents; to read an interview with Mick's father, Ricky Savage, whom they'd described as a "country-and-western icon"; to see what subjects my reporter friend, J.D. Smith, was currently delving into. The writing was lively and informative; the content changed frequently. *InSite* and a handful of other quality on-line publications such as *Salon* had survived the recent economic downturn.

I asked Glenn, "What's the personal angle?"

"The suing family are people I count among my closest friends: The *InSite* employee who died was my godson."

"And how was the company at fault?" Working at a magazine didn't sound like particularly hazardous duty.

"Have you heard of *karoshi*?"

I shook my head.

"The word is Japanese. Literally it means to die of overwork. A common phenomenon in that country—

responsible, they estimate, for between one thousand and ten thousand deaths per year."

"What kind of deaths? Heart attacks? Strokes? Pure exhaustion?"

"All of those, and more. Until recently the majority of such deaths seldom resulted in litigation, but last year the family of one victim successfully sued a large Tokyo advertising agency. My clients, who are of Japanese descent, knew of the case and decided to see if the same could be accomplished in the U.S. courts."

"And you need my agency to document that the employer was liable for your godson's death."

"Yes. And I want you, Sharon, not one of your operatives."

"Of course." The concept was intriguing. Why had Glenn felt he needed to ply me with expensive food and wine in order to interest me? I pulled my minicassette recorder from my bag, and said, "I'll need some particulars now, so I can open a file. And I'll need copies of your files on the case as well. What's the family's name?"

"Nagasawa."

"That sounds familiar."

"You've probably seen the name in the paper. They're patrons of the arts and supporters of a number of local charities. I went to college with Daniel Nagasawa, who is an eye surgeon and owns one of those clinics that do corrective laser treatment. His wife Margaret has a small press that publishes quality children's books. They have—had—three sons. Harry, the oldest, is twenty-nine and a resident in cardiac surgery at U.C. Medical Center. Roger, my godson, was twenty-six when he died, the middle child. Eddie's twenty and still down at Stanford, studying a combination of physics and computer science, top of his class."

"From their given names, I judge the family has been in this country a while."

"Four generations. Daniel's grandfather came over from Osaka to work on a truck farm in the Central Valley, and ended up owning his own farm near Fresno. He left his son a going concern that earned enough to put Daniel through college and medical school. The Nagasawas are worth many millions now."

"Okay, what about Roger? What was he like?"

Glenn's face grew more melancholy. "An underachiever in a family of overachievers. Had a degree in journalism from the University of Michigan—the only one of the boys who ever lived far from home. Personally, I think he chose Michigan in order to escape the family pressures. After graduation, he drifted from one reporting job to another, moving west with each change. A year and a half ago he returned to San Francisco, and a friend recommended him for a staff position at *InSite*. Roger saw it as an opportunity to excel, eventually exercise promised stock options, and measure up to the rest of the family."

"He told you that?"

"Yes. We were close. But apparently not as close as I thought."

"What does that mean?"

Glenn ignored the question. "The atmosphere at *Insite* was brutal. Sixteen-, twenty-hour days, seven days a week, and no comp time. Low pay, and their promises of stock options went unfulfilled. The editor and publisher, Max Engstrom, is an egomaniac who delights in abusing and humiliating his subordinates. Stupid stuff, reminiscent of hazing in college fraternities, but it cuts to the core when a person's sleep-deprived and unsure as to whether he'll have a job the next day. And particularly hard to take for a sensitive young man who's desperate to win his family's love and approval."

"So what happened? Did Roger die because the hazing went too far?"

Glenn's mouth twitched and his eyes grew liquid. "You could say that. Two months ago, on Valentine's Day, Roger committed suicide. Stopped his car on the Bay Bridge, climbed over the railing, and jumped. Beforehand he mailed a letter to his parents in which he apologized for being a failure."

I'm sorry.

Joey's note. God, the parallels were so obvious! A man who drifted from job to job. An underachiever in a family of overachievers.

A man who killed himself.

Suddenly I felt light-headed. I touched my fingers to

my forehead. It was damp, and the too-heavy lunch I'd eaten now lay like a brick in my stomach.

"Sharon?" Glenn said.

I pressed the stop button on my recorder. "I'm okay," I said after a moment. "But I can't take this case. There's no way I can take it."

And there was no way I was going to discuss Joey's suicide with Glenn. Too much of my private life had been the subject of conversations over the past six months. Bad enough that I was repeatedly forced to explain—as I just had at lunch—that when the man whom I'd thought to be my father died in September, I'd discovered that I had a birth father living on the Flathead Indian Reservation in Montana. That while I had a family in California, I also had a birth mother, a half sister, and a half brother in Boise, Idaho.

No, I couldn't take this case, but I'd find some way of explaining why that didn't involve Joey. Or so I told myself until Glenn spoke again.

"I know about your brother," he said. "Hank told me."

Hank Zahn, my closest male friend since college, had betrayed a confidence.

"The subject came up because of Roger," Glenn added.

"And you, like a typical lawyer, saw a way to capitalize on it."

"That's not fair."

"No, what's not fair is you asking me to do this. Why

would you want me to take on a case that would continually remind me—"

"Perhaps you need to be reminded, and to deal with it."

"What're you saying? That you're offering me the job for its therapeutic value?"

Glenn stood, put both hands on my shoulders, and looked into my eyes. "Yes, for its therapeutic value—for you, me, and the Nagasawas."

"Sorry, the answer is no."

He studied me for a moment longer, then straightened, smiling faintly. "I'll have copies of my files messengered over to you by close of business."

"So that's how it is. You understand why I've got to tell Glenn I can't take the case."

Curled up on my sofa, a cat draped across the back with its paws dangling onto my head, another purring on my feet, I was sipping a glass of wine and talking on the phone with my birth father, Elwood Farmer. Elwood was one of the few people I knew whom I could find wide-awake and eager for conversation at 11:30 P.M.— the hour I'd finished reading Glenn's files on Roger Nagasawa's death.

"I understand why you *think* you can't take it," he said.

I could picture him seated in his padded rocker in front of the woodstove in his small log house in Montana.

He'd be wearing a plaid wool shirt and jeans, his gray hair unkempt and touching his shoulders, a cigarette clamped in the corner of his mouth, its smoke making him squint. We'd taken to talking every couple of weeks, feeling our way toward a comfortable father-daughter relationship. Unfortunately, the conversations were not always amicable, because I harbored a resentment toward him for having suspected my existence my whole life but making no effort to find me, and he was plainly bewildered at how to be a parent to a forty-one-year-old stranger.

"What?" I said. "You think I *should* accept a job that's going to make me dwell on Joey's suicide?"

"I didn't say that."

"Well, *do* you?"

"What I think isn't important."

"Come on, Elwood. Be a father for once. Give me some advice."

"I'm only learning to be a father. And I don't believe in imposing my opinion upon another person."

"I just want to know what you think."

". . . I think the answer is already within you."

"Oh, for God's sake! If you're going to get mystical, or whatever you call this, I'm going to hang up."

"Good. Hang up and call me back when you've assembled your thoughts."

*   *   *

Assemble my thoughts, my ass! He pulled that crap on me when we first met, but it isn't going to work this time.

Who is this man to me, anyway? Somebody who donated his sperm to my birth mother, that's all. End of his connection to both Saskia and me. Later, when she was in worse trouble than the pregnancy, he didn't return her phone call because he was preoccupied with the woman he eventually married.

Why should I care what he thinks?

Assemble my thoughts. Hah!

"I'm sorry I hung up on you."

"I know you are."

"I've assembled my thoughts."

"Yes."

"And I know what you mean by the answer already being within me. I can't refuse this case, because I'm a truth-seeker. If working on this Nagasawa investigation can help me to understand why Joey killed himself . . . Well, it's something I have to do."

"Not so difficult to figure out, was it?"